## Enid Blyton

Enid Blyton, who died in 1968, is one of the most successful children's authors of all time. She wrote over seven hundred books, which have been translated into more than forty languages and have sold more than 400 million copies around the world. Enid Blyton's stories of magic, adventure and friendship continue to enchant children the world over. Enid Blyton's beloved works include The Famous Five, Malory Towers, The Faraway Tree and the Adventure series.

*All eight titles in the Adventure series are also available individually from Macmillan Children's Books*

1. THE ISLAND OF ADVENTURE
2. THE CASTLE OF ADVENTURE
3. THE VALLEY OF ADVENTURE
4. THE SEA OF ADVENTURE
5. THE MOUNTAIN OF ADVENTURE
6. THE SHIP OF ADVENTURE
7. THE CIRCUS OF ADVENTURE
8. THE RIVER OF ADVENTURE

# The Valley of Adventure

# The Sea of Adventure

## Enid Blyton

MACMILLAN CHILDREN'S BOOKS

*The Valley of Adventure*
First published 1947 by Macmillan and Co Ltd
Revised edition published 1988 by Pan Books Ltd
*The Sea of Adventure*
First published 1948 by Macmillan and Co Ltd
Revised edition published 1988 by Pan Books Ltd

This double edition published 2002 by Macmillan Children's Books
a division of Macmillan Publishers Limited
20 New Wharf Road, London N1 9RR
Basingstoke and Oxford
Associated companies throughout the world
www.panmacmillan.com

ISBN 978-0-330-39836-7

11 13 15 17 19 18 16 14 12

A CIP catalogue record for this book is available from the British Library.

Printed and bound in the UK by
CPI Mackays, Chatham ME5 8TD

# The Valley of Adventure

# Contents

1  Up in Bill's aeroplane                        9
2  Bill gets his way                            15
3  A grave mistake                              21
4  Wherever can we be?                          27
5  A little exploring                           33
6  What are the two men up to?                  41
7  A wonderful find                             46
8  Kiki talks too much                          53
9  New plans                                    59
10 A fine hiding-place                          65
11 The cave of echoes                           71
12 Behind the waterfall                         78
13 Safe in the cave                             84
14 The poor prisoner                            90
15 A disappointment for the men                 96
16 Rescue of the prisoner                      103
17 A treasure map                              109
18 Now for Windy Pass!                         115
19 A great disappintment – and a plan          122
20 Signposts to the treasure                   128
21 The strange caves                           134
22 The treasure at last!                       140
23 The guardians of the treasure               146
24 Juan finds the caves                        153
25 Philip's astonishing plan                   159
26 The getaway                                 165
27 A discovery – and a fine idea               171
28 The day after the storm                     178
29 A very strange journey                      184
30 Bill gets busy                              190
31 An exciting finish                          197

# 1

# Up in Bill's aeroplane

Kiki the parrot was annoyed. She had been left all alone for a day, and she talked angrily to herself.

'What a pity, what a pity, what a pity, poor, poor Polly! Ding-dong bell, Polly's down the well, good morning, good morning!'

Mrs Mannering put her head in at the door of the room where Kiki was sitting.

'Kiki, don't be so absurd! Talking away to yourself all day like that! The children will soon be back.'

'Ding-dong bell,' said Kiki mournfully, and made a cracking noise with her beak.

'I suppose you miss Jack,' said Mrs Mannering, coming into the room and shutting the door carefully behind her. 'He won't be long now, Kiki. You'll hear him and the others any minute. Now be a good bird and don't make any more noise.'

Kiki opened her beak, swelled up her throat and gave her famous imitation of an express train screeching on entering a tunnel. Mrs Mannering put her hands to her ears.

'Naughty Kiki, naughty! How many times have we told you not to do that?'

'How many times have I told you to shut the door, shut the door, shut the door,' answered back Kiki, and ruffled up her feathers so cheekily that Mrs Mannering gave her a tap on her beak.

'Funny old bird,' she said. 'Ah, listen – that sounds like the children coming back. They've been up in an aeroplane, Kiki! Fancy that! That's why you had to be left alone all day!'

'Jack, Jack, Jack!' screamed Kiki, hearing the voice of her owner. Four children burst into the room, their faces red with excitement.

'Hallo, all of you!' said Mrs Mannering. 'How did you like it? Was it fun being so high up in the air?'

'Oh, *Mother!* It was the greatest fun in the world!'

'Aunt Allie, I shall buy an aeroplane of my own as soon as ever I'm grown up.'

'Mother, you ought to have come. Bill piloted the plane and he was *marvellous.*'

'I wasn't airsick, Aunt Allie, though Bill gave me a paper bag to be sick in.'

Mrs Mannering laughed. All the four spoke at once, and she had hard work to make out what they said. Kiki gave a loving screech and flew to Jack's shoulder.

The four children sank into chairs and prepared to relate their day's adventure. There were Philip and Dinah, Mrs Mannering's children, dark-eyed, dark-haired just as she was, and both with tufts of hair that insisted on sticking up in front. Both Dinah and Philip were called Tufty at school. Then there were the other two, Jack and Lucy-Ann, brother and sister, who had no mother and father, and lived with 'Aunt Allie,' as they called Mrs Mannering. All four were like one family.

Jack and Lucy-Ann Trent were very alike. They both had red hair and green eyes, and were so covered with freckles that it was quite impossible to find a bit of pink skin on their faces, arms or legs. It was not surprising that Jack was so often called Freckles.

Kiki the parrot belonged to him. He had had her for years, an amusing and talkative parrot, with a gift for repeating anything she heard, and for imitating any noise, from a sewing machine to an express train. She adored Jack and was miserable when she was not with him.

Jack had a passion for birds, and Philip had a great liking

for animals of all kinds. He was wonderfully good with them, and they obeyed him and loved him in a marvellous manner. He always had some kind of unusual pet about him, which caused quarrels between him and his sister Dinah, who was scared of most animals and of nearly all insects. But now all four were thinking of nothing whatever but their glorious flight in their friend Bill's new aeroplane.

Bill Smugs was their firm friend. He and they had had hair-raising adventures together. In one adventure they had gone down old copper mines to track clever forgers. In another they had happened on a nest of dangerous spies. As Bill Smugs said, those children simply '*fell* into adventures.'

Now Bill had actually been presented with a fine aeroplane, to help him in his work. The children had been wild with excitement when he had written to tell them this at school.

'I bet he'll take us up for a flight,' said Jack. 'I just bet he will.'

'We'll make him,' said Philip. But they didn't need to make him, for he was quite willing to show off his aeroplane to them, and to demonstrate how well he could fly it after only a short training.

'Mother, we went far higher than the clouds,' said Dinah. 'I looked down on them and they didn't look like clouds a bit. They looked like a great big snow field. It gave me quite a funny feeling.'

'I had a parachute strapped to me in case I fell, and Bill showed me the ripcord I had to pull in case of danger,' said Lucy-Ann, the youngest, her eyes shining. 'But there wasn't any danger.'

'We flew right over our old home, Craggy-Tops,' said Philip. 'It was so strange, looking down on top of it. And we flew over here too, Mother, and our house looked like a toy one.'

'Aunt Allie, Bill says it's frightfully exciting flying at

night, and seeing the little pinpricks of lights shining up from the dark countryside,' said Jack. 'We begged and begged him to take us on a night flight, but he said he would have to ask *you*. You will say we can go, won't you? Golly! I can't imagine what the boys at school will say when I tell them about going up in a private plane, day and night.'

'Day and night,' repeated Kiki. 'Ding-dong bell.'

'She's got ding-dong bell on the brain,' said Jack. 'There's a small child next door who keeps reciting nursery rhymes, and Kiki listens and picks up bits of them. Yesterday she kept moaning about "three blind mice," today it's "ding-dong bell." Don't know what it will be tomorrow.'

'Humpy dumpy,' said Kiki obligingly.

'Humpty, dumpty,' corrected Jack. 'Not humpy dumpy.'

'Humpy dumpy bumpy,' said Kiki solemnly, and scratched her head with a claw. 'Humpy, dumpy . . . '

'All right, all right,' said Jack. 'Aunt Allie, *can* we go up at night with Bill? He's coming to ask you tomorrow, so do say yes.'

'I suppose I shall have to,' said Mrs Mannering with a laugh. 'You and Bill! So long as you don't go headlong into another awful adventure.'

'Adventures aren't awful,' said Philip. 'They are simply lovely!'

'Not to the people who aren't in them,' said Mrs Mannering. 'I feel quite ill sometimes when I think of the adventures you children have had. No more, please.'

'All right. We won't get into any more these summer holidays,' said Lucy-Ann, giving her aunt a hug. 'We won't worry you. I don't want any more adventures anyhow. I've had enough.'

'Well, if we *do* have another, we'll leave you out of it, Lucy-Ann.' said Dinah scornfully.

'No, we won't,' said Philip, giving Dinah a poke in the

back. 'We can't do without Lucy-Ann.'

'Now, don't quarrel, you two,' said Mrs Mannering, foreseeing one of their everlasting squabbles boiling up. 'You're tired now, all of you, after such a lot of excitement. Go and do something quiet till supper time.'

'Sing for your supper,' put in Kiki. The children laughed.

'You're an idiot, Kiki,' said Jack affectionately. 'Did you miss us today? Well, I was scared you might fly out of the aeroplane in fright, if we took you. But I expect you'd have been quite a sensible old bird, wouldn't you, and sat on my shoulder all the time?'

Kiki pecked lovingly at Jack's ear, and made a crooning noise. She sat as close to him as she could. The children began to talk about their exciting day.

'Wasn't it lovely going to the aerodrome and getting in on our passes, and walking up to Bill just as if we were grown-ups?' said Philip. 'And golly, wasn't Bill's aeroplane fine?'

'I didn't think it would be so big,' said Lucy-Ann. 'You know, it was funny – I sort of held my breath when we started off, thinking I'd get a funny feeling when we left the ground, like I do in a lift – and I never even knew when the wheels left the runway and we were in the air! I got quite a shock when I looked down and saw we were over the housetops.'

'It seemed awfully easy to fly a plane,' said Jack. 'Easier than driving a car. I wish Bill would let me have a shot.'

'Well, he won't,' said Philip. 'I say, wasn't it odd when we got into the air pocket and the plane suddenly dropped down without warning? My tummy sort of went up into my throat.'

The others laughed. 'Mine did too,' said Lucy-Ann. 'I'm glad I wasn't sick. It was a waste of that nice strong paper bag, but I'm glad I felt all right.'

'We went hundreds of miles, I should think,' said Jack. 'I

felt a bit funny when we were over the sea. It looked so enormous and so flat. I shouldn't like to fall out over that! What a splash!'

'I bet mother will say we can go on a night flight with Bill,' said Dinah. 'I could see in her face that she was going to say yes. If only we could! Bill said we could fly to his old home, land at dawn, and spend the rest of the night with him, sleeping all we liked in his two spare rooms – we needn't get up till twelve if we didn't want to. Fancy flying all night and going to bed at dawn!'

'Then we'd fly back in the afternoon, I suppose,' said Jack. 'Gosh, I'm glad we've got Bill for a friend. I do think he's an exciting sort of person. It's thrilling, too, to know that he's always on some sort of secret job, and never says a word about it – always snooping out some deadly secret. I wonder if he's on any job now?'

'You bet he is!' said Philip. 'That's why he's got this aeroplane. May have to take off at any moment after spies or somebody. Hope I'm with him when he does.'

'Well, you won't be,' said Dinah. 'Bill would never run us into danger.'

'I shouldn't mind if he did,' said Philip. 'Hallo, there's the gong for supper! I'm jolly hungry.'

'That's nothing new,' said Dinah. 'Come on – let's go and see what there is. Smells like bacon and eggs.'

They went to their supper. They were all hungry, and finished up the eggs and bacon and plum cake in no time. Kiki helped herself to the plum cake too, till Mrs Mannering protested.

'Jack! *Will* you stop Kiki picking all the raisins out of that cake? Look at the mess she's making! There won't be any cake left soon. Smack her on her beak.'

'Naughty Kiki!' said Jack, and tapped her on her beak. 'Don't eat it all.'

'How many times have I told . . . ' began Kiki, but Jack

was too tired to talk to her.

'Don't argue,' he said. 'I'm so sleepy I'll have to go to bed.'

Everyone felt the same – so off they went, and were soon asleep and dreaming of flying aeroplanes over the clouds, somersaulting and looping the loop in a most amazing but perfectly safe manner.

# 2

# Bill gets his way

Bill came along to lunch the next day. He had a ruddy face, twinkling eyes and a rather bald head with plenty of hair at each side. The children rushed to meet him. Mrs Mannering smiled at him.

'You gave the children a wonderful time yesterday,' she said. 'And now I hear that you want to take them on a night flight. I can't think why you want to bother yourself with a pack of children like these.'

'Ah – you never know when they're going to embark on some wonderful adventure,' said Bill Smugs, grinning round at them. 'I don't want to be left out of it, you know. Besides, I feel sorry for you, Mrs Mannering, having to put up with them for eight or nine weeks these summer holidays – I thought it would be a kind deed if I took them off your hands for a while.'

'Well, what do you want them to do?' asked Mrs Mannering. 'Just go for a night flight, spend the night at your old home and come back the next day?'

'That was the first idea I had,' said Bill. 'But now I hear I'm due to have three or four days off – and I thought maybe you could spare the children for longer. We could fly to my old home, and then stay there and mess about a bit. There are heaps of wild birds for Jack to see, and I've no doubt that Philip will find plenty of even wilder animals. The girls will enjoy the change too.'

'Oh! It *does* sound good!' cried Jack, and the others agreed. Mrs Mannering listened and thought for a moment.

'Yes – I don't see why they shouldn't go with you, Bill. I know you'll look after them all right and see that they don't get mixed up in any awful adventure again.'

'I can promise you that,' said Bill. 'There are no adventures to be found anywhere near my old home. It's a most peaceful, quiet place. Nothing doing at all.'

'Well, if you promise not to rush into danger or trouble, you can go,' said Mrs Mannering to the delighted children. 'When do you want them, Bill?'

'Tomorrow, if possible,' said Bill. 'The job I am on seems to be hanging fire at the moment, so I might as well take my few days now.'

'What's the job, Bill? Do, do tell us!' begged Lucy-Ann. Bill laughed.

'I couldn't possibly tell,' he said. 'All my work is secret, you know that. I'll tell you all about the job when it's over and done with, though. You'll find it jolly interesting.'

'We'll have to pack suitcases, won't we?' said Dinah. 'If we're going to stay a few days, I mean. We may want a change of clothes – and macks.'

'Yes, bring jerseys and shorts to mess about in,' said Bill, 'and macks too, because it always seems to rain at my home. And, Mrs Mannering, could you spare a few rugs, as I may not have quite enough blankets for so many visitors?'

'Of course,' said Mrs Mannering. 'I'll look some out for you.'

'I'll bring my lovely camera,' said Jack. 'There'll be room for odds and ends like that in the plane, won't there, Bill?'

'Plenty,' said Bill. 'Bring your field glasses too, because

you may want to have a squint at the different birds in the hills around.'

'Oh, it *will* be exciting!' said Jack, his eyes shining at the thought. 'I can't wait till tomorrow. Let's go today!'

'The plane's not ready,' said Bill. 'Got to have something done to her today. Anyway, my leave doesn't start till tomorrow. You get everything packed and ready, and come to the aerodrome tomorrow night. Be there at eleven o'clock sharp. I'll order a car to call for you and take you there.'

'What a time to start on a journey!' said Mrs Mannering. 'I don't know that I *al*together like it.'

'You can't change your mind now, you can't!' cried the children.

'No, I won't,' said Mrs Mannering. 'But somehow I don't feel very easy in my mind about it all. Oh, children, you won't go and do anything dangerous, will you?'

'There's nothing dangerous for them to do,' said Bill. 'I'll look after them all right. Anyone doing anything dangerous will be sent back to you, Mrs Mannering.'

The children laughed. Then Jack's face fell. 'I say – what about Kiki? She won't like me being away for some days. Can I take her with me? What about the plane – will she be all right in it?'

'You'd better put her into a basket or something,' said Bill. 'She might get scared at the noise and fly off. She'll be all right in a basket on your knee. We can't leave her behind.'

'Right,' said Jack pleased. 'Do you hear that, Kiki old bird? You're to travel in a basket – and mind you behave yourself!'

'Wipe your feet,' said Kiki, 'put the kettle on, kettle on! Poor, poor Polly!'

'Idiot!' said Jack, and scratched her poll. 'All I hope is that you don't try to imitate the noise an aeroplane makes. Your express train screech is bad enough.'

They all had a pleasant lunch and then Bill departed. The

17

children went upstairs to put together their things. Dinah put a whole packet of chocolate into her case, in case there were no shops at Bill's home. Jack stuffed a packet of biscuits into his case. He often woke up at night and liked a biscuit to nibble then.

'Better take plenty of films with you Jack, if you're thinking of photographing birds,' said Philip. 'I bet there won't be anywhere to buy them where Bill lives. It's somewhere buried right down in the country.'

Mrs Mannering came up to see what they were packing. It was a cold August, with rather a lot of rain, and the children would need a fair amount of warm things. They had put in pullovers and jerseys and macks and sou'westers. She added rubber boots too, thinking that shoes would not be of much use if they walked over wet fields.

'I've found you some rugs,' she said. 'You can each take one. They are old, but very thick and warm, and as good as two blankets. If Bill hasn't enough blankets for you it won't matter at all – the rugs will give you plenty of warmth. Don't forget to bring them back, now!'

Jack got his camera ready. He looked out his rolls of films. He debated whether or not to take one of his bird books with him, and then decided not to, because his suitcase was already very heavy.

'Everything's done now, Aunt Allie,' said Lucy-Ann, sitting on her suitcase to make it shut. 'I wish tomorrow would hurry up and come. Fancy flying in the dark in Bill's plane! I never in my life thought I would do that. I hope it's a long long way to Bill's home.'

'It is,' said Mrs Mannering. 'Now let me see – I'd better pack you sandwiches and cake to take with you for the journey, because you are sure to be hungry if you stay up all night. I'll do those tomorrow. Have you found a basket for Kiki, Jack? And what about taking some food for her?

There's a new packet of sunflower seeds come today. Put it into your suitcase.'

Jack found a good basket for Kiki, with a lid that closed down. He put it on the table. Kiki flew over to it at once in curiosity. She hopped inside and looked out comically.

'Clever bird,' said Jack. 'You know it's your travelling basket, don't you?'

'God save the Queen!' said Kiki, and began to rub her curved beak up and down the edge of the basket.

'Don't do that, said Jack. 'You'll break it. Stop it, Kiki!'

Kiki climbed out and flew to Jack's shoulder. She rubbed her beak against his hair.

'Ding-dong bell,' she murmured. 'Polly's in the well. Ding-dong bell.'

'Polly's in the basket, you mean,' said Lucy-Ann. 'Kiki, you're going in an aeroplane. Think of that!'

The day went slowly – far too slowly for the children. The next day was even slower. By the time that tea time came the children felt that night would never never come.

But when supper time came they felt more cheerful. The car was coming at a quarter past ten to take them to the aerodrome. Then into the plane they would get with Bill and off they would go into the darkness. Somehow it seemed far more thrilling to fly through the dark night than through the sunshiny day.

Ten o'clock struck. The suitcases and rugs were taken down to the hall. Jack's camera was there too, and a large packet of sandwiches and cakes. Jack wore his field glasses on a strap over his shoulder. Kiki's basket was in the hall also, but Kiki was still free. She was not going into the basket till the last moment.

'Here's the car!' cried Philip, his sharp ears hearing the engine purring up to the door. 'Come along! Goodbye, Mother! Look after yourself well till we come back!'

'Goodbye, Aunt Allie,' said Jack, giving her a hug. 'We'll send you a postcard. Hi, Kiki, come on – it's time you got into your basket.'

Kiki made a bit of a fuss going in. She was excited because of the excitement of the four children. It took quite a time to get her into the basket and shut the lid down. She began to shout at the top of her voice.

'Poor Polly, poor Polly, down the well, down the well, up the hill, in the corner!'

'She's mixing up Ding-dong bell and Jack and Jill and Jack Horner,' said Lucy-Ann with a giggle. 'Be quiet, Kiki! You ought to be glad you're coming with us, even if you have to travel in a shut basket!'

All the goodbyes were said. 'I don't like letting you go, somehow,' said Mrs Mannering. 'It's silly of me – but I don't. I've got an uncomfortable feeling – as if you're going off into another dreadful adventure.'

'We promise not to,' said Philip earnestly. 'Don't you worry, Mother. We'll be all right, and you'll see us turning up, like bad pennies, in a few days' time. Anyway, Bill's on the phone and you can always ring him.'

The taxi revved up its engine. It moved off down the drive, with Mrs Mannering left standing at the door, waving. The children waved back, excited. They were really off.

'Now for the aerodrome!' said Philip, pleased. 'I thought tonight would never come. What's the time? Oh, we're early. Good. Got the passes, Jack?'

'Dinah's got them in her bag,' said Jack. Dinah fished them out. They were passes that would take them into the aerodrome, and up to Bill himself.

It was a good way to the aerodrome. The night was very dark. Clouds covered the sky, and a few drops of rain spattered the windscreen.

'Here's the aerodrome at last!' cried Jack, seeing the lights through the window. 'Look at the flare-path – all lit up. Isn't it fine? Don't the aeroplanes look enormous in the shadows at each side? Here, Dinah – where are the passes? We've got to show them now.'

The passes were shown to the man at the entrance to the aerodrome and the children went in.

'I'll set you down here and you can speak to your friend,' said the taxi man. 'Then I'll run on to his aeroplane and dump the luggage beside it for you. So long!'

'Now we'll find Bill,' said Philip as the car drove off. 'There he is, look! Hi, Bill, we're here!'

# 3

# A grave mistake

Bill was talking to three or four men very earnestly. He waved to the children, a tall, burly shadow in the night.

'Hallo, kids! I'm busy for a few minutes. You cut along to the aeroplane and wait for me. Stow your cases in at the back where mine is. I'll be about ten minutes or so.'

'Right, Bill,' said Jack, and the four of them moved off to where the taxi man had put their cases, beside an aeroplane not very far away.

It was dark where the aeroplane stood, but the children could see enough to pick up their cases. They climbed up the ladder and into the cabin.

The inside of the plane was in darkness. The children had no idea how to put the lights on. They felt their way to the back of the plane and put down their things. They threw their rugs there too. Jack put Kiki's basket down carefully Kiki had been most indignant all the way.

'Humpy dumpy bumpy,' she said. 'Pop goes the weasel!'

There was a large crate in the middle of the plane. The

children wondered what was in it. Was it empty or full? It must be something Bill was taking back with him.

'It's blocking up all the inside,' said Jack. 'We can't sit down properly with that thing there. Let's squat down on our rugs at the back. We'll be quite comfortable there. Perhaps Bill will shift the crate a bit when he comes, and tell us where he wants us to sit.'

So they sat down patiently on their rugs and waited. The noise of the plane's engines went on and on, and it was impossible to hear anything else, though once Jack thought he could hear somebody shouting.

He went to the door and looked out. But all was darkness and Bill was nowhere to be seen. What a time he was!

He went back to his place, yawning. Lucy-Ann was half asleep. 'I wish Bill would come,' said Philip. 'I shall go to sleep if he doesn't.'

Then a lot of things happened very quickly indeed. Over and above the sound of the engine came the sound of shots – gunshots. That made the children sit up in a hurry.

Then another shot sounded – and then there came the noise of someone clambering hurriedly up the steps into the plane, and a man flung himself down in the control seat. Another followed, panting, hardly to be seen in the darkness. The children sat as if they were frozen. What in the world was happening? Was one of the men Bill? Who was the other – and what was the hurry? The first man took the controls of the plane, and to the children's amazement it began to taxi forwards. They were off! But why hadn't Bill spoken to them? Why hadn't he at least looked round to see that they were safely inside?

'Keep quiet,' said Jack to the others. 'If Bill doesn't want to speak to us, there's a reason. Maybe he doesn't want the other fellow to know we're here. Keep quiet.'

The plane rose into the air, its propellers making a great whirring noise. It headed swiftly into the wind.

The men shouted to one another, but the children could not make out what they were saying because the noise of the engine was so loud. They sat quiet and still, hidden from view by the big crate standing in the middle of the plane.

Bill said nothing to them at all. He didn't call out to know if they were there. He didn't send his companion along to see if they were all right. He simply took no notice of them at all. It was very queer and Lucy-Ann didn't like it a bit.

One of the men fiddled about and found a switch. He pulled it down and a light shone out just by the men, but the rest of the plane was still in darkness. Philip peeped round the crate, meaning to catch Bill's eye if he could.

Almost at once he came back to the others, and sat down very quietly. He said nothing.

'What's up?' asked Jack, sensing the Philip was worried.

'You go and look round that crate,' said Philip. 'Have a good look at the two men.'

Jack went and peered round. He came back feeling puzzled and scared. 'Neither of those men is Bill,' he said 'Golly – it's funny!'

'What do you mean?' said Lucy-Ann in alarm. 'One must be Bill. Why, this is Bill's aeroplane!'

'Yes, but *is* it?' said Dinah suddenly. 'Look where the light catches those seats, Lucy-Ann – they are red – and the ones in Bill's plane were green. I remember them quite well.'

'So they were,' said Jack, remembering too. 'Golly! We're in the wrong plane!'

There was a long silence. Nobody knew what to think about it. They were in the wrong plane – not Bill's at all! Two strange men sat at the controls – men who would probably be extremely angry when they found their un-expected passengers. Neither Jack nor Philip liked the look of the men in the least. They had really only seen the backs of their heads, and the side face of the man when he had turned to shout to his companion – but neither of the boys had felt drawn to the two men.

'They've got such thick necks,' thought Jack. 'Oh, gosh this is awful! And there were those shots, too – were they anything to do with these men? They clambered into the plane in a frightful hurry and set off at once. I do believe we've stumbled into an adventure again.'

Philip spoke cautiously to the others. It was no good whispering, because whispers couldn't possibly be heard. So Philip had to speak loudly, and trust that he would not be heard by the men in front.

'What are we going to do? We *have* got into the wrong plane! That's the fault of that stupid taxi-man, putting down our things by the wrong aeroplane. It was so dark that we ourselves couldn't possibly tell which plane was which.'

Lucy-Ann sat close to Jack, frightened. It wasn't very nice to be high up in the air, lost in the darkness, in the wrong aeroplane with men that none of them had seen before.

'What *can* we do?' wondered Jack. 'We really are in a mess. Honestly, those two men won't half be mad when they see us!'

'They might tip us out,' said Lucy-Ann in alarm. 'And we haven't got parachutes on. Jack, don't let them know we're here.'

'They'll have to know sooner or later,' said Dinah. 'What idiots we are – getting into the wrong plane! I never thought of that.'

There was a silence again, with everyone thinking very hard.

'Shall we just stay here at the back of the plane on our rugs, and hope we shan't be noticed?' said Philip. 'Then, when we arrive somewhere maybe we can slip out of the plane and look for help.'

'Yes – that's the best idea,' said Jack. 'We are well hidden here, unless the men come round to the back for something. Maybe they will arrive at their destination, get out without

24

seeing us, and then we can slip out ourselves and ask for help to get back home.'

'I did want to stay with Bill,' said Lucy-Ann, almost in tears. 'Whatever will he be thinking?'

'Goodness knows!' said Jack gloomily. 'He'll be hunting all over the aerodrome for us. You know, I believe that must have been Bill I heard shouting, when I went to the door to see. He must have gone to his own plane, found we weren't there and yelled for us. Dash! If only I'd guessed that!'

'Well, it's too late now,' said Philip. 'I hope Mother won't be worried. Oh dear – she'll think we've fallen headlong into another adventure. And we promised not to.'

The aeroplane roared on through the dark night. The children had no idea whether they were flying north, south, east or west. Then Jack remembered his pocket compass and took it out.

'We're flying east,' he said. 'I wonder where we're going to. I don't somehow feel as if I'm in a plane at all, as I can't look out and see the ground far below.'

The others felt the same. Lucy-Ann lay down on the rugs and yawned. 'I'm going to sleep,' she said. 'I shall only feel frightened and worried if I keep awake.'

'It's a good idea of yours,' said Philip, and he stretched himself out on the rugs too. 'We shall be sure to wake up if we arrive anywhere.'

'Anyone want a sandwich or bit of cake?' asked Dinah, remembering the picnic packet. But nobody did. The shock of finding themselves in the wrong aeroplane had taken away their appetites completely.

Soon all of them but Jack were asleep. He lay awake, thinking hard. Had Bill been mixed up in the shooting they had heard? Were these two men anything to do with the job Bill had been working on – the 'secret' job? It might be just possible that Jack and the others might find out something that would help Bill. It was important not to let the two men know that they had some hidden passengers in their plane.

Kiki gave an exasperated screech in her basket. Jack jumped. He had forgotten Kiki. He tapped the basket and spoke in as low a voice as he could, hoping that Kiki would hear him.

'Shut up, Kiki! Don't make a noise, whatever you do. It's very important to be quiet. You hear me, Kiki? You must be quiet, be quiet, be quiet.'

'Be quiet,' repeated Kiki, from inside the basket. 'Shhhhhhhhh!'

Jack couldn't help smiling. 'Yes,' he said, putting his face close to the basket. 'Shhhhhhhh!'

Kiki was quiet after that. She was a mischievous, noisy bird, but she would always be quiet if Jack wanted her to be. So she sat inside her basket, trying to tuck her head under her wing and go to sleep. But the loud sound of the plane's engine upset her. She had never heard such a noise before. She longed to imitate it, but fortunately she didn't try just then.

After a bit the two men changed places and the second one took over the controls. The first one yawned and stretched. He got up and Jack's heart almost stopped beating in fright. Was he going to come to the back of the plane? He wondered whether or not to wake the others.

But the man did not come to the back. He stood up for a few minutes as if to stretch his legs. then lighted a pipe. Blue smoke drifted to the back of the cabin. Jack was most relieved to see the man sit down again.

The boy soon grew sleepy too. He lay down close to the others, quite glad of his coat, for it was very cold. Soon he was asleep. Only Kiki kept awake, cracking her beak now and again, puzzled and wondering what this strange night adventure meant.

The plane flew on in darkness, passing over towns and villages, fields, rivers and woods. It passed over the sea to where the lights of ships shone dimly. Lights of the towns twinkled up, and here and there the flare path of an aerodrome shone up to the sky. But the plane did not fly down. It swept over them all, heading east, to the dawn.

Then, just before dawn, it began to circle round more slowly. It dropped as it circled, and once banked so steeply that the children almost rolled over. It awoke them and they sat up, wondering where they were. They remembered at once and looked at one another with wide eyes.

'We're going to land. Where shall we find we are? Look out for a quick escape as soon as we get the chance,' they whispered to one another. 'Down we go – we're landing!'

# 4

## Wherever can we be?

The aeroplane landed with a slight bump that shook the children and made them gasp. Then it ran along a little way on its huge wheels, and stopped. They had arrived.

But where? Dawn had come, and light came in at the windows, but it was not full morning yet. One of the men switched off the throbbing engines. At once a great quiet and peace came into the cabin. How marvellous not to have that enormous noise flooding into their ears any more! The children were glad.

They heard the men's voices. 'We've made good time – and a good landing too. You brought her in well, Juan.'

'We've not got much time to spare,' said Juan. 'Come on – let's get out and stretch our legs. We'll go to the hut and have a meal.'

To the children's enormous delight the men clambered out of the plane and disappeared. They hadn't even gone round to the back of the crate and seen the children! Maybe they could escape and get help at once. Anyway they would be able to send word to Bill and Mrs Mannering telling them not to worry.

'Come on,' said Jack, getting up cautiously. 'Let's squint out of the window and see where we are. On an aerodrome, I hope. We'll probably see a mechanic or two, and ask them to direct us to someone in authority.'

They all crowded to the nearest window. But what a shock when they looked out!

They were not on an aerodrome at all. They were on a broad flat piece of grassland in a valley – and that valley seemed to be surrounded on all sides by towering mountains.

'Gosh!' said Jack. 'Where are we? Back of beyond, I should think.'

'We're in a valley,' said Philip. 'With mountains all round – awfully beautiful – but awfully lonely! How can we get help here? There won't be a plane to take us back, that's certain.'

There wasn't a house or any kind of building to be seen. The view from the other side of the plane was exactly the same – mountains on every side. They seemed to be at the bottom of them, in a green valley. It was very strange. Why should the men come there?

'What are we going to do?' asked Dinah. 'Do we get out – or stay in – or what?'

'Well – I don't know what you think, Philip,' said Jack, 'but I don't like any of this. I don't like those men, I don't like the way they flew off in the middle of the night after what sounded like a lot of shooting – and I don't like this lonely valley either. But all the same I think it would be a good idea if we got out and snooped round a bit. There must be people somewhere about – shepherds, perhaps – somebody like that.'

'What country are we in?' asked Lucy-Ann. 'Shall we be

able to speak their language?'

'I don't suppose so for a minute,' said Philip. 'But we'll just have to try and make ourselves understood.'

'I wonder what those men have come here for,' said Dinah thoughtfully. 'It seems a funny lonely place to come to. I don't think they are up to any good. I think it would be just as well to get out now, whilst we can, and hide, and then see if we can't find someone to help us. We can report everything to Bill when we get back.'

'That's the best idea,' said Jack at once. 'I'll be glad to be in the open air again. This plane's jolly stuffy.'

They looked cautiously out of every window to see if they could spot the two men. But there was no sign of them at all.

'Better get going,' said Jack. 'What about our suitcases – and rugs – and Kiki?'

'Don't leave them here,' said Philip. 'We don't want the men to guess we've been passengers in their plane. Take them with us.'

So the four of them left the plane and handed down their cases and rugs to one another. Kiki uttered a few words of annoyance at being lifted about like luggage, but only in a very low voice.

Soon all the children were standing outside the plane, wondering which way to go. Jack suddenly nudged Philip and made him jump.

'Look! Look over there!'

They all looked and saw a thin spire of blue smoke rising into the air.

'The men have made a fire down there, I should think,' said Jack in a low voice. 'Better not go in that direction. We'll take this path here – if it *is* a path.'

The little procession wound round some big rocks, and came to where a stream burbled down the hillside. It gushed out not far off as a spring, and became a little stream almost at once.

'We could drink from that,' said Philip. 'I'm thirsty. But

I'm not hungry yet. Funny!'

'Well, we're all a bit tired and worried and puzzled,' said Jack. 'Let's get some water into our hands and lap it up. I'm thirsty too.'

The water was cold and crystal clear. It was delicious. All the children felt better for a drink. Dinah dipped her hanky into the stream and wiped her face. She felt much fresher then, and Lucy-Ann did the same.

'The thing is to find a good hiding place for ourselves and these cases,' said Jack. 'I'm afraid if those two men start wandering about they may come across us. Where *can* we go?'

'Let's go straight on,' said Dinah. 'Up the hill here. If we keep up a little we shall be able to see the plane down in the valley and keep our sense of direction a bit. Keep among those trees.'

'That's a good idea,' said Philip, and they made their way slowly towards the trees. They felt safer among them. The men could not spot them there. On the other hand, they found that they could no longer see the plane.

'We can always spot it by climbing up a tree,' said Jack. 'I say – look there – is that a house?'

Set in a clearing was what looked like a house. But when the children got near they found that it was almost burnt out – just a blackened ruin, empty and deserted.

'What a pity,' said Philip. 'We could easily have asked help from the people who lived there. I wonder how the house got burnt.'

They went on a little higher, through a copse of silver birch trees. They saw another building a little higher up – but to their astonishment and dismay that too was a blackened, scorched ruin. There was no sign of life anywhere about it.

'Two burnt houses – and nobody to be found anywhere,'

said Jack. 'Very curious. What's been happening in this valley?'

Higher up still they could see yet another house – would that be burnt out too? They laboured up to it, and gazed on it in despair.

'Quite burnt out,' said Dinah. 'What an awful thing! What's happened to the people who lived here? There must have been war here, or something. I do wonder where we are.'

'Look – that cowshed, or whatever it is, isn't very much burnt out,' said Jack. 'Let's go over and see if the roof is still on. If it is, we could put our things there.'

They made their way to the broken-down cowshed. It seemed as if the flames had got hold of one half of it but had left the other half. The roof was almost off, but at the back was a sheltered place, with stalls where cows had once been put.

'This is all right,' said Jack, making his way into the last stall of all. 'The roof here will keep out the rain if it comes – and there are some jolly big clouds about. We can put our things here.'

'The floor's dirty,' said Lucy-Ann, turning up her nose in disgust.

'Well, we may perhaps be able to find a broom or something to get it clean – and we'll spread it with grass or bracken for a carpet,' said Dinah. 'Then, if we spread out our rugs on it, we could even sleep here. We may not be able to find anyone to help us today. We could spend the night here.'

They put their cases in the corner and draped the rugs over them. Kiki was put down on top in her basket. She gave a squawk of protest.

'Do you think it would be safe to let her out?' said Jack. 'She'll sit on my shoulder for hours now, I'm sure, if I tell her to. She must be so uncomfortable cooped up in that box.'

'Yes — let her out,' said Philip. 'If she does fly off for a bit and the men see her they won't know what she is or who she belongs to. She'll give them a fright if she begins to talk.'

Kiki was set free. She was overjoyed. She clambered out of the basket and flew to Jack's shoulder. She nibbled his ear fondly.

'Where's your handkerchief?' she said. 'How many times have I told you to . . .'

'All right, Kiki, all right,' said Jack. 'Not so loud, there's a good old thing.'

'Shhhhhhhhhh!' said Kiki at the top of her voice. Then she said no more, but just sat and cracked her beak.

'Well — what are our plans?' said Philip, sitting on his suitcase. 'Shall we go exploring a bit further and see if we can find anyone to help us? Or shall we keep an eye on those men and see if we can find out why they've come here? Or shall we just stay here and hide?'

'I think we'd better go exploring,' said Jack. 'The most important thing really is to find help. We simply must get back home at once if we can. Aunt Allie and Bill will be worried to death about us.'

'This is such a lovely valley,' said Dinah, looking out of the tumbledown cowshed. 'I can't think why it isn't packed with houses and cattle and sheep. But I can't see a soul. I can't even see any smoke anywhere — except for that bit over there, where the men are. It's very mysterious. Why are all those houses burnt, and why isn't there anyone here?'

'Well, we've only seen just a bit of the valley and hillside,' said Philip. 'We may go round a corner and come on a whole village. Aren't those mountains enormous?'

'Yes. They make a ring all round this valley,' said Lucy-Ann. 'I wonder where the way out it. Mountains always have passes through them, don't they?'

'Yes,' said Jack. 'But I shouldn't care to go looking for one if I didn't know the way. See that mountain over there? It's got a white tip. I bet that's snow. It shows how high it must be.'

It certainly was a beautiful valley, and the mountains that guarded it were magnificent. But it had a deserted lonely air about it, and even the few birds that flew by every now and again seemed silent and cautious.

'There's something mysterious here,' said Jack. 'You know – I believe – yes, I really do believe – we're in for another adventure.'

'Rubbish!' said Philip. 'We shall find a farm near by, get help, have a message sent somewhere, find a car road, go to the nearest town by car, and from there to an aerodrome. And I bet you we'll be home by tomorrow.'

'I bet we won't,' said Jack. Lucy-Ann looked alarmed.

'But what about meals?' she said. 'We've only got Aunt Allie's picnic packet – and few biscuits and some chocolate. We'll starve if we don't get home quickly. There's nothing to eat here.'

Nobody had thought of that. It was a nuisance. An adventure was one thing – but an adventure without anything to eat was quite another thing. That wouldn't do at all.

'I don't think we'll make this an adventure after all,' said Jack. But an adventure it was – and they were only at the beginning of it, too.

# 5

# A little exploring

The four children went to the broken-down door and gazed out at the towering mountains around them. They seemed to hem the valley in and make it a green prison. None of the children had seen such high mountains before. Clouds hung about halfway up two or three of them, and their tops showed now and again as the clouds shifted and parted.

'It's a very lonely kind of place,' said Jack. 'I bet there's all kinds of strange birds here – but I've only seen one or two so far. It's funny that those men should have known where to land in this valley – that smooth strip of grass makes a splendid landing ground. It looks as if they've been here before. But why should they come *here*? There doesn't seem anything to come for at all – no hotel, not even a cottage that isn't burnt, as far as we can see.'

'Oh, there may be,' said Philip. 'Hey, look at that little lizard! I've never seen one like that before. What a pretty little fellow!'

The lizard ran close by Philip's feet. The boy bent down quietly and his left hand caught the tiny creature by the neck. If he had caught it by the tail it would probably have snapped off, and the lizard would have run away without it.

'Oh, put it down, Philip, do!' said Dinah. 'Horrid creature!'

'It isn't,' said Philip. 'Look at its dear little feet with fingers on. Do look, Dinah.'

Dinah gave a squeal and pushed Philip away. Lucy-Ann and Jack looked at the tiny lizard with interest.

'It's like a very, very small dragon,' said Jack. 'Open your hand and see if it will stay with you, Philip.'

'Of course it will!' said Philip, who always seemed to exercise a strange spell over any creature he picked up. He opened his hand and let the lizard lie on his open palm. It made no attempt to escape at all.

'See? It wants to stay with me,' said Philip. 'And so it shall. What's your name, little thing? Lizzie? Well, of course, I might have known that.'

Lucy-Ann giggled, forgetting her worries for a moment.

What a lovely name for a lizard! Lizzie. Just like Philip to think of that.

'I'll see if I can catch a few flies for you, Lizzie,' said Philip, and went to a sunny patch where flies were buzzing. He caught one and held it in finger and thumb over the lizard's head. In a trice the fly was gone, and the lizard blinked with pleasure.

'Now I suppose you'll let the lizard live in your pocket or somewhere about you for ages,' said Dinah in disgust. 'I shan't go near you. If you haven't got a mouse down your neck you've got a toad in your pocket or a baby hedgehog crawling about you, or a few beetles. I think you're an awful boy.'

'Don't let's squabble now,' said Jack. 'We've bigger things to bother about than lizards.'

The lizard popped into Philip's sleeve. Kiki had been watching it with her head on one side. She was not fond of Philip's pets, and was often jealous of them.

'Pop goes the lizard,' she said, making one of her unexpected apt remarks. The others roared with laughter. Kiki was pleased. She swayed herself from side to side and cracked her beak.

'Shhhhhhhhhh!' she said.

'Oh, Kiki, I'm glad we brought you,' said Jack. 'Now, everybody, what are our next plans?'

'Well, we simply must do a bit of exploring and see if there is anyone living in this valley,' said Philip. 'If there is, we're all right. If there isn't – well, it's just too bad. We'll have to stay here till we're rescued.'

'Rescued! And how do you think anyone is going to rescue us if they haven't the foggiest idea where we are?' demanded Dinah. 'Don't be silly, Philip.'

'Well, do you propose to live here in this valley for the rest of your life, then?' said Philip. 'Oh, here's Lizzie again – coming out of my other sleeve. Lizzie, you're a jolly good explorer, I must say. I wish you could tell us the way out of this valley.'

Dinah went as far from Philip as she could. She simply could not bear his pets. It was a pity, because they were really amusing and friendly.

'You know, we'll have to be careful we don't get lost,' said Lucy-Ann anxiously. 'This valley and these mountainsides are so enormous. We must keep together always.'

'Yes, we must,' agreed Jack. 'And we must always be able to get back to this shed, too, because our things are here. At least we shall have shelter here, and our rugs to lie on. If only we had plenty to eat! Those biscuits and chocolate won't last long.'

'Your compass will come in jolly useful, Jack,' said Philip, remembering it. 'Look here – what about setting off now, and doing some more exploring, making this shed a kind of headquarters to come back to?'

'Yes, we will,' said Dinah. 'But let's cover up the suitcases and things with something in case those men come here and see them.'

'They won't,' said Philip. 'What could they possibly want to come snooping round an old burnt cowshed for? We can leave the things here all night.'

They went out of the shed. The sun was just over the mountaintops now, shining into the valley. The children saw the spire of smoke rising straight up from the fire the men must have made.

'So long as we keep away from that direction, we should be all right,' said Jack. 'Come on – let's take this path. It really looks as if it was once a proper path from this place to somewhere else. We'd better notch the trees here and there as we go, to make sure we find our way back.'

Lucy-Ann liked the idea of that. It reminded her of pioneers and trackers and their ways. Jack and Philip each took out his knife. They made a cut on every fifth tree until they came out of the little wood and found themselves on a flower-strewn, grassy hillside.

'It's lovely, isn't it?' said Lucy-Ann, looking round at the carpet of flowers. 'I've never seen such bright colours. Look at that blue flower, Jack – it's bluer than the sky itself. And oh, look at this tiny pink flower – masses of it!'

'Shall we be seen out on this bare place?' asked Dinah suddenly. Jack and Philip looked downwards into the valley. They had been climbing up, and were now on the mountainside.

'There's the plane!' said Jack. 'And look out – isn't that one of the men walking over to it? Lie down flat, all of you!'

They all promptly lay down flat. Jack had his field glasses on and he put them to his eyes. He could now see clearly that the man was the one called Juan. He had a dead white face, black, thick, curly hair and a small black moustache. His neck was thick and his body was thick too. He disappeared into the plane.

'He's got into the plane. Wonder if he's going off?' said Jack. 'Will he leave the other man behind? He hasn't started up the engines yet.'

After a minute or two the man came out again, carrying something, though Jack could not see what it was. He walked off in the direction of the smoke. There was a thicket of trees near by and he disappeared into this.

'He just went into the plane to get something,' said Jack. 'Now he's gone again. I think perhaps we'd better go another way, because if we can see *him* he could certainly see *us*, if he looked up. See that gully over there? We'll go that way. We shall be well hidden there.'

They made their way to the gully, which was a regular suntrap. There had obviously been a way up there at some time or other. The children followed it, climbing higher. They came to a ledge that ran dangerously round part of the mountainside. Jack went first.

It wasn't as dangerous as it looked. 'I think it's all right,' he called. 'It's wider than it appears. Come on. I'm sure it leads to somewhere.'

They made their way round the ledge, and came to where the hillside gave them a marvellous view down into the valley and all around.

It was completely deserted. Not a cow or sheep or goat to be seen. A little higher up was a black, charred building that had clearly been a very large farm-house. Only the blackened beams were left, and part of the stone walls. Everything else had fallen to the ground and lay in a miserable ugly ruin.

'Another ruin!' said Jack, in awe. 'What *has* been happening in this beautiful valley? I simply can't understand it. Why should houses be burnt like this? I'm beginning to think there isn't a soul here besides ourselves and those two men.'

'I think you're right,' said Philip. 'There's no smoke to be seen anywhere, and not a single domestic animal, not even a dog. But what I can't make out is why no one has come here from the surrounding valleys to rebuild the houses and graze their cattle on this marvellous grass.'

'Perhaps there's something bad about this valley,' said Lucy-Ann with a shiver. 'I don't like the feel of it very much.'

They sat down in the sun, which was now climbing high. They suddenly felt terribly hungry. Dinah unexpectedly produced biscuits and chocolate from a bag she carried.

'I guessed we'd all be hungry soon,' she said. 'So I brought half the biscuits and choc we had with us.'

'Jolly good idea,' said Philip, pleased. 'Hey, Lizzie, come out and have a crumb!'

Dinah at once went a good distance away. Lizzie came out from Philip's open collar and ran down his front. It was plain that she meant to stay with Philip.

'Lizzie's down the well,' remarked Kiki, pecking a piece of chocolate from Jack's fingers.

'Kiki! Give that back!' cried Jack. 'Where are your manners?'

'Down the well, down the well,' said Kiki, who seemed to have got the well on her brain.

They were all thirsty after the chocolate and biscuits. 'I wish we could find something to drink – nice cool clear water like we found in the spring,' said Jack.

'Down the well,' said Kiki.

'All right. You find us a well of water,' said Jack.

'Would it be safe to have a snooze?' asked Dinah, suddenly feeling very sleepy. 'It's nice here in the sun.'

'Well – only just a little one,' said Philip. 'I should think we're safe enough here. Those men wouldn't come up as far as this.'

'You know – I think I can hear water somewhere,' said Lucy-Ann as she lay flat on her back, the sun shining on her freckled face. 'Not very near. Listen, all of you.'

They listened. Certainly they could hear something that was not the wind blowing round. What could it be? It didn't sound like the gurgling of a spring.

'We'll go and see,' said Jack. 'You stay here, girls, if you like. Philip and I will go.'

'Oh, no,' said Lucy-Ann at once. 'I'd rather come with you. You might lose us.'

So all four went off together in the direction of the curious noise. They climbed higher, and came to a rocky, stony part which was steep and hard to climb. But the noise was now much louder.

'Once we round the next corner, we'll see what it is,' said Jack. 'Come on!'

They climbed a little higher and then the path led abruptly round a crag of rock. It widened out a little the other side, and all four children stood gazing in awe at what was making the noise they had heard. It was a waterfall – but what a big one! It fell from a great height, almost sheerly down the mountainside, and cascaded far below them, fine spray rising high in the air. It wetted their faces as they stood there, and yet they were quite a good way from the mass of water.

'What a wonderful sight!' said Philip, awed. 'I've never seen such a big waterfall in my life. What a noise it makes. I almost have to shout. Isn't it grand?'

Far below the waterfall resolved itself into a winding river that curved round the foot of the mountain. The children could not see where it went to. The tumbling water shone and sparkled as it fell, and here and there rainbows shimmered. Lucy-Ann thought she had never seen a lovelier sight.

She licked the spray off her face. It formed into little drops and ran down to her mouth. 'I'm drinking the spray,' she said. 'Oh, look! – there's a puddle in that rock, made of the continually falling spray. Do you think it would be all right to drink it?'

It was very clear and sparkling. Jack tasted it. 'Yes, it's fine,' he said. 'Have some.'

They watched the waterfall for some time. Kiki was simply thrilled with it. For some reason or other it filled her with mad delight. She flew near to it, getting splashed with the drops, squawking loudly.

'It's a magnificent sight!' said Dinah, gazing at the roaring waterfall. 'I could watch it all day.'

'We'll come again tomorrow,' said Jack. 'But I really think we ought to be getting back now to that cowshed. Come on – it's plain there's nobody to help us just here.'

# 6

# What are the two men up to?

Lucy-Ann was half afraid they might lose their way going back. But the boys had taken good note of everything. It was when they got to the wood that difficulty might have arisen, but here the notched trees soon set them right.

They saw that the plane was still down in the valley. So the men were somewhere about. It would be as well to be careful, and Jack told Kiki to be quiet. The waterfall seemed to have gone to her head, and she had been very noisy coming back, singing and squawking loudly.

'There's our shed,' said Lucy-Ann thankfully. It felt quite like home, coming back to it from that enormous mountain-side, 'I hope all our things are safe.'

They went inside. Yes, their things were there, exactly as they had left them. Good!

The sun was now sliding down the sky. It was about tea-time. The children wondered whether to finish the rest of their chocolate and biscuits.

'Better not,' said Jack. 'We'll have them before we go to sleep tonight if we're terribly hungry. Oh – wait a minute – what about the stuff Aunt Allie packed for us? Haven't we still got that? We haven't eaten it?'

'No, of course we haven't,' said Dinah. 'I was saving it up. We've got so little that I thought we'd better not start on that picnic packet yet.'

'But all the sandwiches will be stale,' objected Philip, who was feeling very empty indeed. 'What's the good of that? We might as well eat them whilst they're eatable.'

'Well – we could eat the sandwiches, and leave the cake and the chocolate and biscuits for tomorrow,' said Dinah.

'But first let's get this place ready for us to sleep in tonight. It's filthy.'

'I don't want to sleep here,' said Lucy-Ann. 'I don't like it. Why can't we sleep outside? We've got our macks to lie on, and four rugs – and we can unpack some of our clothes and have them for pillows.'

'But it might pour with rain,' said Dinah.

'I could perhaps rig up some sort of roof,' said Jack, looking round at the ruined shed. 'There's some old posts here – and there's a piece of corrugated iron. If Philip gave me a hand, I could rig up the iron sheet on the old posts.'

The two boys tried to do this, but the sheets of iron was not held safely enough. The girls were terrified it might blow off on to them as they slept.

'If only we could find a cave!' said Lucy-Ann.

'Well, we can't,' said Jack, rather cross that all his efforts with the posts and the iron were of no use. 'Anyway, I don't think it's going to rain. Look at the clear sky. If it does pour, we'll have to get into the stall at the end of the cowshed, that's all.'

Their work with the posts had made them hungrier than ever. Dinah undid the picnic packet and took out sandwiches and huge slices of cake. They ate the sandwiches in silence, enjoying every bite immensely.

'Wonder what those men are doing,' said Jack at last. 'I can't see any smoke rising now. Shall I slip down towards the plane, keeping well hidden, and see if I can see them?'

'Yes,' said Philip. 'You're sure you know your way there and back? Don't get lost for goodness' sake!'

'If I do, I'll get Kiki to do her express engine screech,' said Jack with a grin. 'Then you'll know where we are all right.'

'Look in that plane if you get a chance, and see if you can spot any food there,' called Dinah. Jack went off with Kiki on his shoulder. Lucy-Ann didn't at all like him going off alone. She wished she could have gone with him, but she knew he wouldn't have let her.

'Let's get our beds ready,' said Dinah, who always liked to be doing something. 'Come on, you two – help to unpack the cases and get out something for pillows – and our macks to lie on.'

Whilst Jack was gone the other three were very busy. Soon they had a cosy-looking bed spread on the grass under a big birch tree. First there were the four macks, to keep the damp out. Then there was one big thick rug for softness. There were four piles of woollies for pillows, and finally the other three rugs for coverings.

'That looks very good,' said Dinah approvingly. 'Pull that rug a little over this way, Lucy-Ann. That's right. Philip, you're to sleep right on the outside. I won't have the lizard crawling over me in the night.'

'Lizzie won't hurt you,' said Philip, taking the lizard out of one of his sleeves. 'Will you, Lizzie? Stroke her, Dinah – she's sweet.'

'*Don't*, Philip!' said Dinah with a squeal, as Philip brought the lizard near to her on his outstretched hand. 'I'll box your ears if you dare to let that lizard touch me!'

'Oh, don't tease her, Tufty,' begged Lucy-Ann. 'Let *me* have Lizzie for a bit. I love her.'

But Lizzie would not go to Lucy-Ann, much to her annoyance. She ran up Philip's sleeve and disappeared. Little bumps appearing here and there in his jersey showed where she was.

Dinah looked up at the sky. It was quite clear. The sun had almost gone, and soon the first stars would prick through the sky. She felt tired and irritable.

So did the others. Their short night and the shock they had had were beginning to make themselves felt. Lucy-Ann felt that at any moment a violent quarrel might spring up between Dinah and Philip.

So she took Dinah off to the spring with her, and they

43

washed in the cold clear water, and drank. They sat there a little while, enjoying the beauty of the valley and the mountains around.

'They seem to be crowding in on us,' said Lucy-Ann. 'Coming closer.'

'How you do imagine things!' said Dinah. 'Come on – let's get back. Jack should be here soon and I want to hear what he's got to say.'

They went back. Philip had laid himself down on the coats and rugs, and was yawning. 'I was just coming to look for you girls,' he said. 'What a time you've been! Jack isn't back yet. I hope he's all right.'

Lucy-Ann felt scared. She adored her brother. She went to stand on a rock, so that she might see when he came. She turned to the others as soon as she got there.

'He's coming!' she called. 'And Kiki's on his shoulder.' She jumped down from the rock and rushed to meet Jack. He grinned at her, and Kiki flew off his shoulder to perch on Lucy-Ann's.

'I was beginning to get worried, Jack,' said Lucy-Ann. 'Did anything happen? Did you see the two men? What were they doing?'

They came up to Dinah and Philip. 'My word, what a fine bed!' said Jack, and he sank down on it. 'This is something like! I'm jolly tired.'

'What happened, Jack?' asked Philip. 'Anything?'

'Not much,' said Jack. 'I got as near to the plane as I could, but I didn't dare to go right up in case I was seen, because, as you know, it's right out in the open. I couldn't see or hear anything of the men at all.'

'Was Kiki good?' asked Lucy-Ann anxiously. 'I kept on thinking she might screech or something and draw attention to you.'

'She was as good as gold,' said Jack, scratching Kiki's poll. 'Weren't you, Kiki? Well, I thought the next thing to do would be to try and find where the men were – where that smoke came from. So, keeping as much to the bushes and trees as I could, I made my way towards the smoke. They must have lighted their fire again, because the smoke rose up quite black and thick.'

'Did you see the men?' asked Dinah.

'I heard their voices first,' said Jack. 'Then I thought it would be a good idea to climb a tree and use my field glasses. So up I shinned and came to the top of a nice little tree. Not far below me, near a tumbledown hut, were the two men, cooking something over a fire they had made.'

'Gracious!' said Lucy-Ann. 'Weren't you scared of being seen?'

'No. The tree hid me all right,' said Jack. 'And I hadn't made a scrap of noise. I got my field glasses and looked through them. The men were studying some kind of map.'

'Whatever for?' said Dinah wonderingly. 'I should think they know this part of the world pretty well or they wouldn't have been able to land so easily.'

'Well, they've come here for *some* reason, haven't they?' said Jack. 'Goodness knows what – but certainly for some definite reason. They must be looking for something or someone – and the map will probably show them what they want to know. I heard one say, "This way – and then up here," as if they were planning some sort of expedition.'

'We could follow them,' said Dinah at once. 'Then we'd know.'

'No, thanks,' said Jack. 'I'm not going mountain climbing behind those men. They look jolly tough. What I say is – let them get off on their expedition – and we'll be able to explore that hut of theirs – and the plane too. We may find something to tell us who they are and what they're after.'

'Yes. Let's do that,' said Lucy-Ann sleepily. 'Perhaps they'll go tomorrow. I hope they do. Jack can watch them with his field glasses – and when they're safely gone we can do a good old snoop round.'

'There's really nothing more to tell,' said Jack with a yawn. 'I couldn't hear any more. The men rolled up the map and talked in low voices. So I shinned down the tree and came back. And here I am.'

'Let's snuggle down and go to sleep,' said Lucy-Ann. 'I simply can't keep my eyes open. We're safe here, aren't we?'

'Perfectly, I should think,' said Jack, lying down contentedly. 'Anyway, Kiki will give us warning if anyone comes near. Good night.'

'Good night,' said the others. Philip added a few words.

'Dinah, don't yell if a spider runs over you, or a rat or a hedgehog. There are sure to be plenty out here.'

Dinah gave a squeal and covered her head up at once. Then there was silence. They were all fast asleep.

# 7

---

# A wonderful find

Soon the stars filled the sky. An owl hooted, and the wind whispered something in the trees overhead. But the four children did not see the stars nor hear the owl and the wind. They were tired out. They slept solidly, and though Dinah was almost smothered with the rug over her head, she did not wake or move.

Kiki slept too, her head under her wing. She was perched on a branch of the birch tree just over Jack's head. She awoke when she heard the owl, and hooted back softly. Then she put her head back under her wing and slept again.

When dawn came the children were still asleep. Kiki awoke before they did. She stretched out first one wing and then the other. She erected the feathers on her head and shook them. Then she scratched her neck thoughtfully and gazed down at Philip.

Lizzie the lizard was also awake and was running over the rug that covered Philip. She came to where Philip's feet stuck out and disappeared under the rug there. Kiki's sharp eyes watched the little moving bump she made under the rug as she made her way all the way up Philip's body and appeared by his neck.

'Wipe your feet,' said Kiki suddenly to the lizard. 'How many times, how many times have I told you to wipe your feet?'

Lizzie was startled. She leapt from Philip's neck on to Jack and stood half hidden in his hair, looking up into the trees, though she could focus nothing there. Kiki, annoyed at seeing Lizzie daring to tread on her beloved master, gave an exasperated squawk and flew down to peck the lizard, who promptly disappeared under the rug again.

Kiki landed heavily on Jack's middle and gave a vicious peck where the rug covered Philip's right leg, for she could see the moving bump there that meant the lizard was running downwards. Both Jack and Philip awoke with a start.

They stared up into the trees, amazed to see green leaves waving above them. Then they turned their heads and saw one another. In a flash they remembered everything.

'Couldn't think where I was,' said Jack, and sat up. 'Oh, Kiki, it's you on my middle, is it? Do get off. Here, have some sunflower seeds and keep quiet, or you'll wake the girls.'

He put his hand in his pocket and took out some of the flat seeds that Kiki loved. She flew up to the bough above, cracking two in her beak.

The boys began to talk quietly, so as not to disturb the girls, who were still sleeping peacefully.

'Gosh, I feel better now,' said Jack, stretching out his arms. 'I was so tired last night I could have cried. What about you, Philip?'

'I'm all right too,' said Philip, and he yawned hugely. 'But sleepy still. Well, we haven't got to get up for breakfast. We shan't hear any gong sounding here. Let's have another snooze.'

But Jack was now too wide awake to snooze. He slipped out from under the rug and went to wash himself at the spring. He gazed downwards and saw the spire of smoke rising up just as it had yesterday.

'Those fellows are up and about,' he said to himself. 'Must be getting late in the morning, I suppose. The sun's fairly high. Blow! I forgot to wind up my watch last night.'

Soon the girls woke up and were amazed to find they had slept soundly all the night through and had apparently not even stirred. Dinah looked to see where Lizzie was.

'It's all right,' said Philip amiably. 'She's down one of my socks. I like the feel of her tiny fingers on my leg.'

'Ugh! You're awful!' said Dinah. 'Well, I'm going to wash. Then we'll have breakfast – only cake and biscuits, I'm afraid.'

Unfortunately they were all so hungry that they devoured the cake, the biscuits and the rest of the chocolate too. Now there was no food left at all.

'We'll just *have* to do something about it – about the food question, I mean,' said Dinah. 'Even if it means eating your lizard, Philip.'

'She wouldn't make more than a mouthful, would you Liz?' said Philip. 'Hallo – what's that?'

'That' was the sound of voices. Hurriedly the four children got up, and, dragging their rugs, macks and other clothes with them, they ran quickly to the cowshed. They dumped the things into the last stall and crouched there, panting.

'Have we left anything at all out there?' whispered Jack.

'Don't think so,' whispered back Philip. 'The grass is a bit flattened, that's all. Let's hope they won't notice it.'

There was a crack in the side of the old cowshed and Jack put his eye to it. They had only just got away in time. The men were coming slowly up towards the birch trees, talking. They came to where the children had slept the night before.

The men walked right past the spot, then one of them stopped and looked back with a puzzled expression. He gazed at the place where the children had slept. What he said they couldn't hear, but he pointed to the flattened grass. Both men then walked back and looked earnestly down at it.

'What's done that?' asked the man called Juan.

'Funny,' said the other man. He had a large pink face with full lips, and his eyes looked small in comparison. 'Some animal, perhaps?'

'Why – that's big enough for an elephant or two to lie on!' said Juan. 'Shall we have a look round?'

The other man looked at his watch. 'No. Not now,' he said. 'When we come back, perhaps. We've got a lot to do today. Come on. It can't be anything really.'

They went on again and were soon lost to sight among the trees. 'I'm going to get up a tree with my field glasses and follow them with them as they go,' said Jack to the others. 'We must make certain they really are gone before we show ourselves.'

He went cautiously out of the shed and ran quickly to a tall tree. He was up it in a trice, for he was an excellent climber. He sat at the top, balanced on a swaying branch, his legs wound tightly round it. He put his glasses to his eyes.

As soon as the men came out on to the grassy, flowery part of the hillside he saw them. They did not take the same direction as the children had taken the day before, but kept on the flowery part for a long time. Jack could see them easily with his glasses. Then they took out a map or paper and stood there looking at it between them.

'Not sure of their way,' thought the boy. 'Ah – now they're off again.'

The men began to climb steeply and Jack watched them as long as he could see them. Then they rounded a great crag of rock and disappeared from sight. He slid down the tree.

'Gracious! We thought you'd gone to sleep in the tree,' said Dinah impatiently. 'I'm tired of waiting in this filthy shed. Have the men gone?'

'Yes. They're far away now,' said Jack. 'It's quite safe to come out and have a look round. They didn't go the way we did. I watched them climbing very steeply up the mountain-side. Come on – let's get off whilst we can.'

'We could go and have a look inside the aeroplane now,' said Dinah. So they all hurried down to the valley, and came to where the big aeroplane stood on its enormous wheels. The four children climbed up the steps into the cockpit.

'The big crate's gone,' said Jack at once. 'I wonder how they got it out. It must have been empty or they could never have managed it between them. Look – there's where we hid the other night!'

Philip and Jack hunted all round the plane for food or information. But there was no food at all, and not a scrap of paper that would give them any idea as to who the men were or why they had come there.

They all climbed out again. 'Blow!' said Jack. 'We're no better off now! Not even a bar of chocolate. We shall starve!'

'If we could explore that hut you saw the men by last night, I bet we'd find plenty of food,' said Dinah. 'Don't you remember the men saying, "Let's go to the hut and have a meal"? Well, they couldn't have a meal without food, could they? – so the food must be there.'

This was a distinctly cheering idea. Jack led the way to where he had seen the men sitting by the campfire the night before. The fire was almost out, though it was still smouldering a little.

The hut lay near by. It was tumbledown, but not burnt as had been all the other buildings they had seen. Rough repairs had been done to it. The one window looked strong, and was hardly big enough for anyone to get in or out, if he had wanted to. The door was also a strong one. It was shut.

'Locked, of course,' said Jack, giving it a tug. '*And* they've taken the key. Who did they imagine was going to come along and take anything? They don't know a thing about *us*.'

'Let's look in at the window,' said Lucy-Ann. 'We could see inside easily.'

Jack hoisted Philip up. The boy looked inside, finding it difficult at first to make out anything, because the interior of the shed was dark. The only light came in from the small window.

'Ah – now I can see better,' said Philip. 'There are a couple of mattresses – and rugs – and a table and some chairs – and a stove of some kind. And gosh – just look at *that*!'

'What?' cried everyone impatiently. Lucy-Ann jumped up and down, trying to see in at the window too.

'*Stacks* of food!' said Philip. 'Tins and tins of it! And pots and jars of stuff! Golly, they make my mouth water.'

Jack could bear Philip's weight no longer. He set him down with a jerk.

'Hoist *me* up, now,' he said, and Philip gave him a hoist. Jack's eyes nearly fell out of his head when he saw the food, neatly piled on shelves that ran along one side of the hut.

'It's a kind of storehouse, or resthouse,' he said, jumping down from Philip's back. 'My word, if we could only get some! Why did those men take the key? Distrustful creatures!'

'Can we get in at the window?' asked Philip, and he looked eagerly up at it. 'No, we can't. Not even Lucy-Ann could get in there. Besides, it can't be opened. It's just a pane of glass set into the window frame, with no catch or fastener to open it. We'd have to smash it – and that would give away the fact that somebody was here.'

The children wandered gloomily round the shed. Then they set off to see if there was anything else to be found near by. But there wasn't.

'I suppose we'd better get back to our own shed and remove our things, and hide them somewhere else in case those men do have a look round when they come back,' said Jack. 'How I hate leaving all that food in this shed! I'm starving.'

'So am I,' said Lucy-Ann. 'I could almost eat Kiki's sun-flower seeds.'

'Well, have some,' said Jack, holding out a handful. 'They're not poisonous.'

'No, thanks,' said Lucy-Ann. 'I'm not as starving as all that.'

Philip went up to the door of the shed and glared at it. 'I'd like to knock you down,' he said. 'Standing there between ourselves and a good square meal. Take that!'

To the great amusement of the others he aimed a hearty kick at the door, and then another.

It flew open. The children gasped in surprise, and stared. 'It wasn't locked, after all!' cried Jack, 'just shut. What idiots we were to think it was locked! Come on – now for a feast!'

# 8

## Kiki talks too much

They all crowded into the dimly lighted shed. They gazed joyfully at the piles of things on the shelves.

'Biscuits! Tongue! Pineapple! Sardines! Milk! Gosh, there's everything here!' cried Jack. 'What shall we start on?'

'Wait a bit. Don't let's disarrange the shelf so much that the men will know someone has been here,' said Philip. 'Better take tins from the back, not the front. And we won't eat the fruit and other stuff here – we'll take it away with us.'

'I think,' said Jack slowly – 'I really do think it would be a good idea to take away as much of this as we can carry, in case we are stuck in this valley for some time. We may as well face the fact that we are completely lost, and cut off from the world we know, and may not be rescued for ages.'

The others looked solemn, and Lucy-Ann looked scared as well.

'You're right, Freckles,' said Philip. 'We'll help ourselves to as much as we can carry. Look, here's a pile of old sacks. What about filling a couple of them with the tins and carrying them off between us? We could take dozens of the tins then.'

'Good idea,' said Jack. 'Here's a sack for you and Dinah to fill, and here's one for me and Lucy-Ann.'

Philip stood on one of the chairs and reached his hand behind the front row of tins on the shelf. He threw down tin after tin, and the others put them into the two sacks. What a store there was in that hut!

Soon the sacks were full and almost too heavy to carry. It was nice to think of all that food waiting to be eaten. Jack found a tin-opener, too, and put it in his pocket.

'Before we go, let's have a look and see if we can find any papers or documents that will tell us something about these mysterious airmen,' said Philip. But although they hunted in every corner, and even under the pile of sacks, they could find nothing.

'I wonder what they did with that crate they had in the plane,' said Jack. 'We haven't found that anywhere. I'd like to have a squint at that too.'

The crate was not in the shed. So the children wandered out and had another good look round. And, in a copse of young trees and bushes, with a tarpaulin over them, they found about six of the wooden crates.

'Funny,' said Jack, pulling away the tarpaulin. 'Look – lots of them – all empty! What are they going to put into them?'

'Goodness knows!' said Philip. 'Who would bring empty crates to this deserted valley, hoping to find something to fill them? Only madmen!'

'Oh – you don't really think those men are mad, do you?' said Lucy-Ann in alarm. 'What shall we do if they are?'

'Keep out of their way, that's all,' said Philip. 'Come on. Did we shut that door? Yes, we did. Now, heave-ho, Dinah, catch hold of your end of the sack and we'll go back to our shed.'

Stumbling under the weight of the clanking sacks, the four children made their way slowly back to the shed they had hidden their things in. Jack dumped his sack, and then ran to climb the tree he had climbed before, in order to sweep the countryside with his field glasses, and see if the men were by any chance returning yet. But there was no sign of them.

'All clear at the moment,' said Jack, going back to the others. 'Now for a meal – the finest we've ever had because we've never been so hungry before.'

They chose a tin of biscuits and opened it. They took out about forty biscuits, feeling perfectly certain that they could manage at least ten each. They opened a tin of tongue, which Jack carved very neatly with his penknife. Then they opened a tin of pineapple chunks and a tin of milk.

'What a meal!' said Jack, sitting down contentedly on the sun-warmed ground. 'Well – here goes!'

Never did food taste so completely delicious. 'Mmm-mm-mmm,' murmured Lucy-Ann, meaning, 'This is simply gorgeous.' Kiki imitated her at once.

'Mmm-mm-mm! Mmm-mm-mm!'

No word was spoken except when Dinah saw Kiki delving too deeply into the tin of pineapple.

'Jack! Do stop Kiki! She'll eat it all!'

Kiki retired to a branch of the tree above, a large chunk of pineapple in her claw. 'Mmm-mm-mm!' she kept saying. 'Mmm-mm-mm!'

Dinah went to the spring and rinsed out the empty tin of milk. Then she filled it with clear cold water and came back. She emptied the cold water into the pineapple juice left at the bottom of the tin and shook it up. Then she offered everyone a pineapple drink to end the meal.

'Gosh! I do feel better now,' said Jack, and he undid his belt to let it out two or three holes. 'Thank goodness you lost your temper and kicked that door, Philip. We were so sure that it was locked, and the key taken.'

'Silly of us,' said Philip, lying down and shutting his eyes. 'What are we going to do with the empty tins?'

'*You're* obviously going to do nothing,' said Dinah. 'I'll push them down a rabbit hole. The rabbits can lick them out.'

She picked up a tin and gave a scream. She dropped it, and Lizzie the lizard ran out in a hurry. She had been sniffing in delight at the crumbs of tongue left there. The tiny creature ran to Philip, and disappeared down his neck.

'Don't tickle, Lizzie,' murmured Philip sleepily.

'I'd better keep a watch out in case the men come back,' said Jack, and he climbed his tree again. Lucy-Ann and Dinah stuffed the empty tins down a large rabbit hole.

Kiki looked down the hole at the tins in surprise, then walked solemnly down and began to tug at one of the tins.

'No, Kiki, don't!' said Lucy-Ann. 'Jack, take Kiki with you up the tree.'

Jack whistled. Kiki flew to him at once and perched on his shoulder as he climbed his tree, moving from side to side when a bough threatened to knock her off.

'We'd better bring out all our cases and things, ready to hide them somewhere better than in the cowshed,' said Dinah. 'If those men do look round here when they come back, they'll see them in the cowstall, as sure an anything!'

So the two girls lugged everything out, Dinah grumbling because Philip lay apparently asleep and would not stir himself to help them. Jack came down the tree.

'No sign of them yet,' he said. 'Now the thing is – where can we hide these things really well?'

'Down the well,' suggested Kiki, hearing the word 'well.'

'Shut up, Kiki,' said Jack. He looked all round but could think of nowhere. Then an idea struck him.

'I'll tell you where would be a jolly good place,' he said.

'Where?' asked the girls.

'Well – see that big tree there? – the one with thick spreading branches – we could get up there and pull up our things quite easily, and hide them in the leafy branches. No one would think of looking up there, either for us or our belongings.'

The girls gazed at the thickly-leafed tree. It was a horse-chestnut tree, dark and full of glossy leaves. Just the place.

'But how can we get the suitcases up?' asked Dinah. 'They're not terribly big – but they're quite heavy.'

Jack undid a rope from round his waist. He nearly always

had one there. 'Here you are!' he said. 'I can climb up the tree and let down this rope. You can slip it through the handle of one of the suitcases and knot it. Then I'll give a jolly good heave – and up it'll come!'

'Let's wake Philip, then,' said Dinah, who didn't see why her brother shouldn't join in the labour of heaving things up a tree. She went over and shook him. He awoke with a jump.

'Come and help us, you lazy thing,' said Dinah. 'Jack's found a marvellous hiding place for us all.'

Philip joined the others and agreed that it was indeed a fine place. He said he would go up with Jack and pull up the cases.

Kiki was most interested in all the proceedings. When Jack hung the rope down the tree, she flew to it and gave it such a tug with her beak that it was pulled from Jack's hand and fell to the ground.

'Kiki! What did you do that for, you bad bird?' called Jack. 'Now I've got to climb all the way down and up again! Idiot!'

Kiki went off into one of her neverending cackles of laughter. She waited her chance and once again pulled the rope from poor Jack's hand.

Jack called her sternly. She came, cracking her beak, not quite liking Jack's stern voice. He tapped her very sharply on the beak.

'Bad Kiki! Naughty Kiki! Go away! I don't want you. No, GO AWAY!'

Kiki flew off, squawking dismally. Jack was not very often cross with her, but she knew he was this time. She retired inside the dark cowshed, and sat high up on a blackened beam, swaying herself to and fro.

'Poor Kiki! Poor, poor Kiki!' she groaned. 'Pop goes Kiki!'

Jack and Philip soon hauled everything up and stowed it safely away in the forks of the big spreading branches. Then

Jack shinned up a bit higher and put his glasses to his eyes. What he saw made him call urgently to the girls.

'The men are coming! Quick, get up! Have you left anything behind? Have a look and see!'

The girls took a quick look round. They could see nothing. Lucy-Ann climbed the tree quickly, with Dinah just behind her. They settled themselves on broad branches and peered down. They could see nothing at all, for the leaves were far too thick. Well, if they couldn't see down, certainly nobody could see up. So that was all right.

Soon they could hear voices. The men were coming near. The children sat as quiet as mice in the tree. Lucy-Ann felt a terrible longing to cough and she put her hand over her mouth.

Down below, the men were making a good search of the old cowshed. They found nothing, of course, for everything had been removed by the children. Then they wandered out again and looked at the flattened grass. It puzzled them very much.

'I'll just have one more look in that shed,' said the man called Juan. He disappeared into the shed once more. Kiki, who was still up on the blackened beam, sulking, was annoyed to see him again.

'Wipe your feet,' she said severely. 'And how many times have I told you to shut the door?'

The man jumped violently and peered all round. Kiki was huddled in a corner up in the roof and he could not see her. He looked in all the other corners of the room, hardly believing his ears. He called to his companion.

'Look here,' he said, 'somebody just now told me to wipe my feet and shut the door.'

'You're mad,' said the other man. 'You can't be feeling well.'

'Pussy down the well,' announced Kiki. 'Well, well, well! Use your handkerchief.'

The men clutched one another. Kiki's voice was so unexpected in that dark shed.

'Let's be quiet and listen,' said Juan. Kiki heard the words 'be quiet.'

'Shhhhhhhhhshhhhhhh!' she said at the top of her voice. That was too much for the men. They fled out into the open air.

# 9

# New plans

Kiki was glad to see the two men go. 'Shut the door!' she shouted after them. 'Shut the door!'

The men ran off, and only stopped when they were well away from the shed. Juan mopped his forehead.

'What do you make of *that*?' he said. 'A voice – and nothing else!'

The other man was rapidly recovering.

'Where there's a voice there's a body,' he said. 'There's somebody here – somebody playing tricks on us. I thought when I saw that flattened piece this morning that we were not alone here. Who's here? Do you think anybody's got wind of the treasure?'

The four children, hidden well in the leaves of the tree, just above the heads of the two men, pricked up their ears at once. Treasure! Oho! So that was what the men were after in this lonely, deserted valley. Treasure!

'How could anyone know what we know?' said Juan scornfully. 'Don't get nerves just because you heard a voice, Pepi. Why, maybe it was just a parrot.'

Pepi laughed loudly. It was his turn to be scornful now. 'A parrot! What will you say next, Juan?' he said with a sneer.

'Have you ever known parrots to live here before? And talking ones, too? If that's a parrot, I'll eat my hat and yours as well!'

The listening children grinned at one another. Lucy-Ann thought she would like to see Pepi, whoever he was, eating his hat. He would have to eat Juan's too, for Kiki was most certainly a parrot.

'It's somebody hiding about here,' said Pepi. 'Though how they got here goodness knows. Juan, maybe there is a cellar beneath that cowshed. We will go and find out if anyone is hiding there. He will be very – very – sorry for himself.'

The children didn't like the tone of his voice at all. Lucy-Ann shivered. What horrid men!

They went cautiously to the cowshed. Juan stood at the broken down doorway. He called loudly:

'Come out of the cellar, whoever you are! We give you this one chance!'

No one came out, of course. For one thing there was no one to come out, and for another there was no cellar to come from. Juan held a revolver in his hand. Kiki, rather alarmed at the shouting voice, said nothing at all, which was for-tunate for her.

The silence was too much for Juan. He took aim at where he supposed a cellar might be and a shot rang out. BANG!

Kiki almost tumbled off the beam in fright and the four children nearly fell out of their tree. Jack just clutched Lucy-Ann in time and held her tightly.

BANG! Another shot. The children imagined that Juan must be firing blindly, merely to frighten the person he thought he had heard talking. What a pity Kiki had been in the shed, sulking. Jack felt most alarmed. He was afraid she might have been shot.

The men came out again. They stood looking about for

some moments and then walked near to the chestnut tree, talking.

'No one there now. Must have slipped off. I tell you, Pepi, there has been someone here – maybe spying on us!'

'Well, he surely wouldn't give himself away by telling us to wipe our feet and shut the door,' said Pepi scornfully.

'We'll come back tomorrow and search this place completely,' said Juan. 'I'm certain there's somebody here. Talking English, too! What does it mean? I feel very alarmed about it. We didn't want anyone to get wind of our mission.'

'Certainly we must search this place well,' said Pepi. 'We must find out who is the owner of that voice. No doubt about that. I'd start a good hunt now, but it's getting dark and I'm hungry. Come on – let's get back.'

To the children's huge relief the men disappeared. Jack, who by climbing to the very top of the tree could see the aeroplane, waited till he could see the two men passing by it on their way to their own hut.

Then he called down to the others, 'All clear now. They're by the plane. My word – what a shock I had when those shots went off! Lucy-Ann nearly fell off her branch.'

'Lizzie shot out of my pocket and disappeared,' said Philip. 'I say, I hope Kiki's all right Jack. She must have been scared out of her life when the shots rang out in that little shed.'

Kiki was sitting petrified on the beam when the children went into the cowshed. She crouched down, trembling. Jack called to her softly.

'It's all right, Kiki. Come on down. I'm here to fetch you.'

Kiki flew down at once and landed on Jack's shoulder. She made a great fuss of him. 'Mmm-mm-mm!' she kept saying. 'Mmm-mm-mm!'

It was dark in the shed. The children didn't like it. Lucy-Ann kept feeling there might be someone hiding in the

61

corners. 'Let's go out,' she said. 'What are we going to do tonight? Is it safe to sleep where we did last night?'

'No. We'd better take our rugs and things somewhere else,' said Jack. 'There's a patch of bushes higher up where we'd be sheltered from the wind and hidden from view too. We could take them there.'

'I say – do you know what we left in the shed?' said Philip suddenly. 'We left our sacks of tina. Look, there they are in that corner.'

'What a mercy the men didn't notice they were full of something!' said Jack. 'Still, I'm not surprised they took no notice of them really. They just look like heaps of rubbish. We'll drag them up to the bushes, though. Our store of food is too precious to be left behind.'

They dragged the sacks to the patch of bushes and left them there. Then they debated what to do about the things up the tree.

'Let's just bring down the rugs and our macks,' said Jack. 'The clothes we used for pillows are wrapped in the rugs. We could leave the suitcases up there. We don't want to drag them about with us.'

It was now getting so dark that it was quite difficult to get the rugs and macks down, but they managed it somehow. Then they made their way again to the bushes. Dinah and Lucy-Ann spread out the 'bed,' as they called it.

'It won't be so warm here,' said Dinah. 'The wind creeps round rather. Where are we going to hide tomorrow? Those men will look behind these bushes, that's certain.'

'Do you remember that waterful?' asked Philip. 'There seemed to be a nice lot of rocks and hiding places down towards the foot. I believe we could climb down there and find quite a good place.'

'Yes, let's,' said Lucy-Ann. 'I'd like to see that waterfall again.'

They all lay down on the rug. They pressed close together,

for it was certainly cold. Dinah took a pullover from her 'pillow' and put it on.

Suddenly she gave a scream, making the others jump. 'Oh! Oh! There's something running over me! It must be a rat!'

'Well, it isn't,' came Philip's delighted voice. 'It's Lizzie! She's found me. Good old Lizzie!'

So it was. How the little lizard had discovered where Philip was nobody could imagine. It was part of the spell that Philip always seemed to exercise on wild creatures.

'Don't worry, Dinah,' said Philip. 'Lizzie is safe in my pocket now. Poor thing, I bet she felt dizzy falling down the tree.'

'Dizzy Lizzie,' said Kiki at once, delighted with the two words. 'Dizzy Lizzie.'

Everyone laughed. Kiki was really funny at times. 'Doesn't she love to put words together that have the same sounds?' said Lucy-Ann. 'Do you remember last hols she kept saying 'Fusty-musty-dusty' till we nearly screamed at her?'

'Fusty-musty-dusty, dizzy Lizzie,' said Kiki at once, and screeched.

'Don't,' said Jack. 'You're only showing off now, Kiki. Go to sleep. And if you dig your claws into my tummy like you did this morning, I'll smack you.'

'God save the Queen,' said Kiki devoutly, and said no more.

The children talked for a little while longer. Then the girls and Philip fell asleep. Jack lay on his back, with Kiki on one of his ankles. He looked up at the stars. What was the good of promising Aunt Allie they wouldn't have any more adventures? The very night they had promised her, they had whizzed off in a strange aeroplane to an unknown valley, where, apparently, some sort of 'treasure' was hidden. Most extraordinary. Most – extra— And then Jack was asleep too, and the stars shone down on the four children, moving across the sky till dawn slid into the east and put out all the stars one by one.

Philip awoke early. He had meant to, for he did not know how early the men might start hunting for the owner of the 'voice.' He awoke the others and would not listen to their protests.

'No, you've really got to wake up, Dinah,' he said. 'We must start early today. Go on – wake up! – or I'll put Dizzy Lizzie down your neck.'

That woke poor Dinah up properly. She sat up and tried to slap Philip, but he dodged away. She hit Kiki instead. The parrot gave a surprised and aggrieved squawk.

'Oh, *sorry*, Kiki,' said Dinah. 'Sorry. I didn't mean that for you. Poor, poor Kiki!'

'What a pity, what a pity!' said Kiki flying off in case Dinah sent out any more slaps.

'We'll have a quick breakfast,' said Jack. 'Sardines, biscuits and milk, I think. I saw a tin of sardines at the top of one of our sacks. Yes, here it is.'

They saw smoke rising up from where the two men were, and knew that they too were up. So they finished their breakfast quickly, and Dinah once more pushed the tins down a convenient rabbit hole. Then they ruffled up the grass on which they had been lying, so that it didn't look quite so flat.

'I think we'd better find a good hiding place for most of these tins,' said Philip, 'and take just a few of them with us to last us for today. We can't possibly lug these heavy sacks along all the way.'

'Couldn't we drop them into the middle of these bushes?' said Dinah. 'They're awfully thick. Nobody would guess they were there. We could slip back and fetch any we wanted.'

So the sacks were dropped into the middle of the bushes,

and certainly no one could see them unless they actually crawled into the very middle. Then the children gathered up their rugs, macks and odd clothes and set off. The boys carried the tins, and Jack had his camera and his glasses as well. So they were heavily laden and could not go very fast.

They took the same way that they had taken before. When they came to the grassy, flower-strewn hillside they sat down for a rest. After all, the men would hardly be following them! They would be hunting all round and about the cowshed.

Suddenly, from far off, Jack caught sight of a brilliant, twinkling flash. He lay down flat at once, telling the others to do the same. 'There's someone using field-glasses down there,' he said. 'We may not be seen if we lie flat. I just caught the flash of the sun on the eye-lenses. Dash! I forgot the men might sweep the mountainside with glasses. They'll be after us if they've seen us.'

'Let's crawl to that rock and get behind it,' said Philip. 'Come on. Once we're behind there we can get on and find the waterfall.'

# 10

## A fine hiding-place

When they were behind the rock the children felt sure they could not be seen, and they breathed more easily. Philip looked round and about. The gully they had been in before lay a little to the left. They could reach it without being seen from below.

'Come on,' said Philip, choosing a path that put rocks or bushes between them and the valley below. 'This way.'

Up the hot gully went the children, and came to the ledge

that ran round a steep bit of the mountain. They made their way round and once more saw the wonderful view they had seen before. Above them stood the ruined, burnt-out farm-house. Lucy-Ann carefully didn't look at it. It gave her such a miserable feeling to see the blackened beams and fallen walls.

They stood and listened for the sound of the waterfall. It came softly to their ears, a continous, musical sound, like a far-off orchestra playing a simple tune.

'What a lovely noise!' said Dinah. 'Philip, shall we climb down or up now? If you want to go to the foot of the waterfall and hide somewhere among the rocks there, we ought to climb down, oughtn't we? Last time we climbed up – over that rocky, stony bit.'

The boys stood and considered. 'It would perhaps be best if we went down this time,' said Jack at last. 'Those rocks just above the waterfall may be slippery to climb down on, for they will be wet with the spray. We don't want to slip, and we're carrying so many things that we haven't free hands to use.'

So they chose a way that led downwards. Philip went first, finding the safest path he could; not that there was a real path, of course, for there was not. As they came near to the waterfall, spray blew around them, and left a fine wet mist on their hair. They were hot with climbing and the spray was deliciously cool.

They rounded a corner, and saw the whole of the cas-cading water at once. What a sight! Lucy-Ann drew a quick breath of awe and delight, and stood staring.

'What a thunderous noise!' shouted Jack, trying to make his voice heard. 'It makes me feel all excited.'

'It does me too,' agreed Dinah. 'As if I want to do a jig or a hornpipe or something. And it makes me want to shout and yell.'

'Well, let's!' said Jack, and he began to caper and shout as if he was mad. The others did the same, except Lucy-Ann. It was almost as if they were trying to outshout and outdance the tumbling, roaring water.

They soon stopped, quite exhausted. They were on a flat rock which was wet with the flying spray. They were not nearly at the foot of the water after all, but about a quarter of the way up the fall. The noise filled their ears, and sometimes the force of the spray made them gasp. It was somehow very exciting.

'Well,' said Jack at last, when they had gazed their fill at the waterfall, 'let's think about a good hiding place. I must say I don't think those men would dream of coming here to look for us.'

They all looked about for a cave or mass of rocks in or behind which they could hide. Lucy-Ann looked a little doubtful.

'I don't know if I can bear to hear this terrific noise going on in my ears all the time,' she called to Jack. 'It makes me feel a bit dizzy.'

'Dizzy Lizzie,' remarked Kiki at once. She too had been excited by the waterfall and had shouted with the others.

'Well, you'll have to put up with the noise,' said Jack. 'You'll soon get used to it.'

Lucy-Ann looked worried. She was quite sure she wouldn't get used to that thundering going on all the time. She would never, never be able to sleep through it.

The children wandered about by the waterfall, not going too near it because of the thick spray around it. They couldn't seem to find any good place to hide in at all. All the rocks there seemed to be wet, and there seemed to be no comfortable spot in which to put their things.

'Our rugs would be soaked in no time with the fine mist that hangs about the fall,' said Dinah. 'And we can't possibly lie on wet rugs. I don't believe this is such a good idea after all.'

Jack was climbing a little higher. He came to where a giant fern grew. It hung down like a great green curtain and was lovely to see. Jack wondered whether they could hide behind it.

He pushed aside the hanging green fronds and gave a shout at once. The others didn't hear it because of the noise of the water.

'Golly!' said Jack to himself. 'There's a cave behind this hanging fern – and it will be quite dry because the fern screens it from the spray. It's like a great thick curtain! Hey, you others!'

But again nobody heard him. Jack couldn't wait for them to pay attention to him. He went through the hanging fronds and found himself in a dim dry cave, with a fairly low roof, and moss growing on the floor. He felt it. It was dry. Probably when the fern died down in the autumn, the spray flew into the cave and the moss then grew damp and flourished well. But now it was like a soft, dry green bed.

'This is just – exactly – the place for us,' said Jack, delighted. 'Absolutely marvellous! Nobody could possibly see us here because the fern hangs down over the entrance, and it was only quite by accident I found it. It would be a most exciting place for us.'

There was a ledge running round one side of it, like a bench. 'We could put all our things there – tins and so on,' said Jack to himself. 'And when we've put our macks down on this moss we'll have a most lovely bed. I really *must* tell the others.'

It was quite time that he showed himself, for the others had now missed him and were yelling at the tops of their voices for him.

'Jack! JA-CK! Where are you? JACK!'

Jack heard their voices as he pushed aside the fern-fronds and looked out, just his head showing. Dinah and Kiki suddenly caught sight of his face peering out of the fern some way above them. Kiki gave a squawk of surprise and flew up at once. Dinah jumped.

'Look!' she yelled to Philip and Lucy-Ann. 'Look where Jack is — hiding behind that giant fern!'

Jack put his hands to his mouth and yelled at the top of his voice, trying to drown the noise of the waterfall. 'Come on up here! I've found something marvellous!'

The others climbed up eagerly. Jack held aside the green fronds for them. 'Won't you come into my parlour!' he said politely. 'So pleased to see you all.'

They passed through the green curtain into the cave behind. They called out in delighted surprise.

'What a lovely place! Nobody could ever find us here!'

'There's a soft green carpet on the floor! It's moss!'

'The roar of the fall isn't nearly so loud here! We can hear ourselves speak!'

'Glad you like it,' said Jack modestly. 'I found it quite by accident. It's perfect, isn't it?'

It was. Lucy-Ann was relieved that the thunder of the waterfall was lessened here, in the cave. Dinah was thrilled with the softness of the moss. Philip was pleased by the real safety of such a hiding place. Nobody would ever find it except by chance.

'Let's go and fetch our things from the rock where we left them,' said Dinah, who always liked all her belongings set out neatly together. 'There is plenty of room for them here. I shall put our tins of food on that rocky ledge.'

'We can only *just* stand upright,' said Philip. He went to where the green fronds hung down over the entrance, making the cave rather dark. He parted the fronds and at once a ray of sunshine fell into the cave, lighting it up well.

'We could tie back some of the fern so that we get the sun in the cave,' said Philip. 'We've got a jolly good view of the waterfall from here – and we can see everything around well, so that if anyone comes we shall spot them at once. It's fine.'

'I shan't mind living here a bit for a little while,' said Lucy-Ann happily. 'I feel safe here.'

'You may have to live here a *long* while,' said Philip. 'Well – I can think of worse places.'

'Those men would never find us here,' said Jack. 'Never!'

He tied back some of the fronds, and the children sat down on the floor for a little while, enjoying the sunshine that now poured in. The moss was like a cushion to sit on.

After a bit they all climbed down to where they had left their rugs and tins and other things. They carried them up to their new home. Dinah arranged the loose things on the rocky ledge. They looked nice there.

'We shall have a lovely soft bed tonight,' she said. 'We ought to sleep jolly well in here. It's not musty or stuffy.'

'Fusty-musty-dusty,' said Kiki at once, remembering the three words she had learnt in the last holidays. 'Fusty-musty-dusty, fusty . . .'

'Oh, don't begin that again, Kiki,' said Jack. 'We got tired of that long ago.'

Kiki flew to his shoulder, and looked out of the strange little cave. There was really a wonderful view outside – first of all, the cascading waterfall, with rainbows caught in it here and there; then beyond it the steep mountainside, and far beyond that, lower down, the green valley which stretched to the foot of steep mountains on the opposite side, towering up one behind the other.

It was about time for a meal again. All the children seemed to get hungry at the same time, and they glanced at the tins on the shelf or ledge. Jack felt for his tin-opener.

'You mind you don't lose it,' said Philip. 'That's our most precious possession at the moment, Jack – your tin-opener.'

'Don't worry. I shan't lose it,' said Jack, and began to

open a tin. Kiki watched with her head on one side. She liked these tins. They had most exciting things inside, she considered.

Soon they were sitting eating hungrily, looking out of the cave entrance to the sparkling waterfall not far off. It was nice to sit there munching away, with that lovely view outside, the soft moss beneath them, and the warm sun on their bare legs.

'We do seem to have some adventures,' said Jack. 'It's most peculiar the way we can't seem to keep out of them. I do hope Bill and Aunt Allie aren't worrying too much about us. If only we could get word to them!'

'We can't,' said Philip. 'We're stuck here all alone, with no means of getting into touch with anyone as far as I can see – except those two men. I'm blessed if I know what to do. Thank goodness we've got plenty of food.'

'We'd better go back to that bush where we dumped the rest ot the tins and fetch them along here as soon as we can,' said Jack. 'What we've brought won't last us more than today. Will you two girls be all right if Philip and I go along and get what we can? We shan't be able to bring them all at one go. We must make several journeys.'

'Yes, we shall be quite all right here,' said Dinah, giving Kiki the last bit of salmon out of her tin. 'You set off this afternoon. You can leave Kiki here to guard us.'

# 11

## The cave of echoes

It was very early in the afternoon. The boys knew they would have plenty of time to go to the bush where their tins were hidden and fetch them to the cave. Perhaps between them they could carry one sack.

'We'd better go now,' said Jack. 'We'll have to keep a sharp lookout for those men, because they were going to have a jolly good look round, and we don't want them to spot us. Now, you're sure you girls will be all right?'

'Quite,' said Dinah lazily. She felt glad she was not going to go all the way back to the bush and then drag a heavy sack to the cave. She lay back on the moss. It was so very very soft, and springy too.

Jack slung his field glasses round him. They might be useful in trying to spot any men from far off. He and Philip slid through the green fronds of fern. Jack called back to the girls, raising his voice high.

'If you *should* happen to spot anyone near here, remember to untie the string that ties back these ferns *at once*, see?' he said. 'Then they will swing back and the cave will be completely hidden. Lucy-Ann, see that Kiki doesn't follow us.'

Lucy-Ann had Kiki on her shoulder, where Jack had just put here. She put her hand round the bird's ankles and held her. Kiki knew then that she was not supposed to go with Jack and Philip and she gave a dismal squawk.

'What a pity, what a pity!' she said gloomily, and raised up her crest fiercely. But Lucy-Ann would not let her go. She held her until Jack and Philip were out of sight. Then she lowered her hand and Kiki flew off her shoulder and out of the cave. She perched on a rock looking for Jack.

'Down the well,' she said grumpily. 'Blackbirds down the well.'

'No, blackbirds in a pie,' said Lucy. 'What a bird you are for getting things mixed up, Kiki!'

'Poor Kiki!' said Kiki, and cracked her beak loudly. 'Poor Kiki!'

She flew back into the cave. Dinah was fast asleep, stretched out on the green moss, her mouth open. Kiki flew over and put her head on one side, looking at Dinah's open mouth. Then she plucked up a bit of moss with her curved beak.

'Kiki! Don't you dare to put that into Dinah's mouth!' cried Lucy-Ann, knowing Kiki's mischievous ways. 'You're a bad bird!'

'Wipe your feet,' said Kiki crossly, and flew to the back of the cave. Lucy-Ann turned over on her tummy and watched her. She didn't trust Kiki in this mood.

The sun poured into the cave. It felt breathless in there. Lucy-Ann thought it would be a good idea to untie the fronds and let them swing together, to keep out the sun. So she pulled the bit of string that Jack had shown her and at once the ferny curtain descended, and the cave was lost in a dim green twilight, rather exciting to be in.

Dinah didn't wake. Lucy-Ann lay on her tummy again, thinking of all that had happened. The noise of the waterfall came in, rather muffled now, for the curtain of fronds was very thick.

'Kiki,' said Lucy-Ann. 'Kiki, where are you?'

There was no answer from Kiki. Lucy-Ann tried to make out where the parrot was. She must be sulking because Philip and Jack hadn't taken her with them. Silly old Kiki!

'Kiki! Come over here!' said Lucy-Ann. 'Come and talk to me. I'll teach you "Three little kittens have lost their mittens".'

Still there was no answer from Kiki, not even a squawk. Lucy-Ann wondered why. Even if Kiki sulked she would usually talk back if anyone spoke to her.

She peered towards the back of the cave. No Kiki there. She looked at the ledge on which their goods were neatly arranged. No Kiki there.

Well, where was she then? She hadn't flown out between the fern-fronds, that was certain. She must be *somewhere* in the cave!

On the rocky ledge was a torch. Lucy-Ann felt for it and took it into her hand. She switched it on and flashed it round the cave. Kiki was nowhere to be seen. She was not even perched up anywhere in the low roof of the cave. How very mysterious!

Lucy-Ann now felt quite alarmed. She awoke Dinah, who sat up, rubbing her eyes, cross to be awakened.

'What's the matter?' she said. 'I was having such a lovely snooze.'

'I can't find Kiki,' said Lucy-Ann. 'I've looked everywhere.'

'Don't be silly. She's gone out of the cave after Jack, I expect,' said Dinah, even crosser. She lay down again and yawned. Lucy-Ann shook her.

'You're not to go to sleep again, Dinah. I tell you, Kiki was here a little while ago – at the back of the cave – and now she's gone. Absolutely vanished.'

'Well, let her – she'll come back all right,' said Dinah. 'Leave me alone, Lucy-Ann.'

She shut her eyes. Lucy-Ann didn't like to say any more. Dinah could be so fierce when she was cross. The little girl sighed and wished the boys were back. What *had* happened to Kiki?

She got up and walked across the moss to the back of the cave. The rock was folded in on itself there, and there was a space behind one of the folds. Lucy-Ann looked cautiously into the dark space, expecting to see Kiki hiding there, ready to cry 'Bo' at her, as she sometimes most annoyingly did.

But Kiki wasn't there. Lucy-Ann flashed her torch up and down the little hidden corner, and suddenly her torch came to a stop, focused on one place.

'Why – there's a hole there!' said Lucy-Ann in surprise. 'That's where Kiki must have gone!'

She clambered up to the hole, which was about shoulder-high. It was just big enough for her to squeeze through. She expected to drop down into another cave the other side, but she didn't. The hole went upwards slightly, a round, narrow tunnel. Lucy-Ann felt sure Kiki must have disappeared into this cold, dark little tunnel.

'Kiki!' she yelled, and flashed her torch in front of her. 'Where are you, idiot? Come back!'

No sound from Kiki. Lucy-Ann squeezed herself right into the round tunnel, wondering how long it was. It was almost as round as a pipe. Maybe water had forced its way through at one time, but now it was quite dry. Lucy-Ann could not hear any sound of the waterfall once she was in the tunnel, though she listened hard. It was very quiet there.

'KIKI!' she yelled. 'KIKI!'

Dinah heard the yell in her dreams and awoke with a jump. She sat up crossly again. But this time Lucy-Ann was not in the cave with her. Now it was Dinah's turn to feel scared. She remembered that Lucy-Ann said that Kiki had suddenly disappeared. Now it seemed as if Lucy-Ann had too. The fronds of fern were hanging over the entrance, Lucy-Ann would not have pushed out through them without telling Dinah she was going out.

Dinah examined the cave well. No Lucy-Ann. Oh, goodness, now what had happened to her and Kiki?

She heard another yell, sounding rather muffled and distant. She went to the back of the cave and discovered the hidden space. She fetched another torch from the ledge and shone it up and down. She stared in amazement when she saw two shoes sticking out of a round hole about as high as her shoulder.

She tugged at Lucy-Ann's ankles and yelled at her. 'Lucy-Ann! What *do* you think you're doing? What's up that hole?'

Lucy-Ann yelled back. 'I don't know, Dinah. I found it by accident. I think Kiki must have gone up it. Shall I go up and see if I can find her? You come too.'

'All right,' called Dinah. 'Go on up.'

Lucy-Ann wriggled further up the narrow pipe-like tunnel. It suddenly widened out, and by the light of her torch she saw below her another cave – but a vast one this time.

She managed to get out of the hole, and had a look round at the cave. It was more like an underground hall. Its roof was very high indeed. From somewhere in its dim vastness came a mournful voice.

'What a pity, what a pity!'

'Kiki! So you are here!' cried Lucy-Ann, and then listened in astonishment to the echo that sounded immediately. 'Here, here, here, are here, and here!' cried the echoes, repeating themselves in a weird and strange manner.

'Hurry up, Dinah!' called Lucy-Ann, not liking the echoes at all.

'Up, Dinah, Dinah, Dinah!' called the echoes at once. Kiki flew over to Lucy-Ann, frightened. So many voices! Whatever could they all be?

'Poor Kiki!' said the parrot, in a fright. 'Poor Kiki!'

'Kiki, Kiki, Kiki!' called the echoes. The parrot shivered and gazed all round, trying to see who called her. She suddenly gave a loud and defiant squawk.

At once a score of squawks sounded all round, as if the cave was filled with hundred of parrots. Kiki was simply astounded. *Could* there be so many birds there that she couldn't see?

Dinah crawled out of the hole and stood by Lucy-Ann. 'What an enormous place!' she said.

'Place!' shouted the echoes.

'Everything we say is repeated,' said Lucy-Ann. 'It's weird.'

'Weird, it's weird,' said the echoes.

'Well, let's whisper, then,' said Dinah, whispering herself. The cave was at once filled with mysterious whispers, which scared the girls even more than the repeated shouts they had heard. They clutched one another. Then Dinah recovered herself.

'It's only the echoes,' she said. 'You often get them in enormous caves like this. I wonder if anyone has ever been here before.'

'Never, I should think,' said Lucy-Ann, flashing her torch all round. 'Fancy! We may be treading in a place that no one else has ever trodden in before!'

'Let's explore the cave a bit,' said Dinah. 'Not that there seems much to see, but we might as well do something whilst we're waiting for the boys.'

So they walked slowly round the great dark cave, their footsteps repeated a hundred times by the echoes. Once, when Dinah sneezed, the girls were really frightened by the enormous explosive noises that came from all round them. The echoes certainly enjoyed themselves then.

'Oh, don't sneeze again, Dinah,' begged Lucy-Ann. 'It's really awful to hear the echoes sneezing. Worse than hearing them squawk like Kiki.'

They had gone almost all the way round the cave when they came to a passage leading out of it – a high, narrow passage, between two walls of rocks.

'Look at that!' said Dinah, surprised. 'A passage! Do you suppose it leads anywhere?'

'It might,' said Lucy-Ann and her eyes gleamed. 'Don't forget, Dinah, that those men are after treasure. We don't know what kind – but it's just possible it might be hidden somewhere in these mountains.'

'Let's follow the passage, then,' said Dinah. 'Kiki! Come along. We don't want to leave you behind.'

Kiki flew to her shoulder. In silence the two girls entered the narrow, rocky passage, their torches gleaming in front of them. What were they going to find?

# 12

# Behind the waterfall

The passage was a very winding one. It led a little downwards, and the floor was very uneven to the feet. The girls
tripped and stumbled very often. Once the roof came down
so low that they had to crawl under it. But it grew high again
almost at once.

After a while they heard a noise. They couldn't imagine
what it was. It was a deep and continous roar that never
stopped even for a second.

'What's that?' said Dinah. 'Are we getting into the heart
of the mountain, do you think, Lucy-Ann? That's not the
roar of a mighty fire, is it? What can it be? What is there that
could make that noise in the middle of a mountain?'

'I don't know,' said Lucy-Ann, and immediately wanted
to go back. A fire in the heart of a mountain, a fire that
roared like that? She didn't in the least want to see it. She felt
hot and breathless at the thought.

But Dinah wasn't going back now that they had come so
far.

'What, go back before we've found out where this passage
goes to?' she said. 'Of course not! The boys would laugh like
anything when we told them. We don't often get the chance
of discovering something before they do. Why, we might
even happen on the treasure, whatever it is, Lucy-Ann.'

Lucy-Ann felt that she didn't care at all about the
treasure. All she wanted was to get back to the safety of the
cave with the green fern curtains.

'Well, you go back, then,' said Dinah unkindly. 'I'm going
on!'

It was more frightening to think of going back to the cave

of echoes by herself than to go on with Dinah. So poor Lucy-Ann chose unwillingly to go on. With that peculiar, muffled roar in her ears she pressed on down the winding passage, keeping close to Dinah. The roar became louder.

And then the girls knew what it was. It was the waterfall, of course! How stupid of them not to think of that! But it sounded so different there in the mountain.

'We're *not* going into the heart of the mountain after all,' said Dinah. 'We're coming out somewhere near the water-fall. I wonder where.'

They got a tremendous surprise when they did see day-light. The passage suddenly took one last turn and took them into subdued daylight, that flickered and shone round them in a curious way. A draught of cold air met them, and something wetted their hair.

'Lucy-Ann! We've come out on to a flat ledge just *behind* the waterfall!' cried Dinah in astonishment. 'Look, there's the great mass of falling water just in front of us! – oh, the colours in it! Can you hear me? The water is making such a noise.'

Overwhelmed by surprise and by the noise, Lucy-Ann stood and stared. The water made a great rushing curtain between them and the open air. It poured down, shining and exultant, never stopping. The power behind it awed the two girls. They felt very small and feeble when they watched the great volume of water pouring down a few feet in front of them.

It was amazing to be able to stand on a ledge just behind the waterfall and yet not to be affected by it in any way except to feel the fine spray misting the air. The ledge was very wide, and ran the whole width of the fall. There was a rock about a foot high at one end of the ledge, and the girls sat down on it to watch the amazing sight in front of them.

'What will the boys say?' wondered Dinah. 'Let's stay here till we see them coming back. If we sit on this rock, just at the edge of the waterfall, we can wave to them. They will be so astonished to see us here. There's no way of getting to the ledge from above or below, only from behind, from the passage we found.'

'Yes. We'll surprise the boys,' said Lucy-Ann, no longer frightened. 'Look, we can see our cave up there! — at least, we can see the giant fern whose fronds are hiding it. We shall easily be able to see the boys when they come back.'

Kiki was very quiet indeed. She had been surprised to come out behind the great wall of water. She sat on a ledge and watched it, blinking every now and again.

'I hope she won't be silly enough to try and fly through the waterfall,' said Lucy-Ann anxiously. 'She would be taken down with it and dashed to pieces. I know she would.'

'She won't do anything silly,' said Dinah. 'She's wise enough to know what would happen if she tried something like that. She may fly out round the edge of the waterfall, though. Still, there shouldn't be much danger for her in that.'

The girls sat there for a long time, feeling that they would never get tired of watching the turbulence of the waterfall. After a long time Lucy-Ann gave a cry and caught Dinah's arm.

'Look — is that the boys coming? Yes, it is. They've got a sack between them. Good! Now we shall have plenty of food.'

They watched the two boys labouring up the rocks that led to the cave. It was no good waving to them yet. Then suddenly Dinah stiffened with horror.

'What's the matter?' said Lucy-Ann in alarm, seeing Dinah's face.

'Look — someone is following the boys!' said Dinah. 'See — it's one of the men! And there's the other one too! Oh, my goodness, I don't believe either Philip or Jack knows it! They'll watch where they go and our hiding place will be found! JACK! PHILIP! OH, JACK, LOOK OUT!'

She went to the very edge of the waterfall, and, holding on to a fern growing there, she leaned out beyond it, yelling and waving, quite forgetting that the men could see and hear her as well as the boys.

But alas, Jack and Philip, engrossed in the task of getting the heavy sack up the rocks, neither saw nor heard Dinah – but the men suddenly caught sight of her and stared in the utmost astonishment. They could not make out if she was girl, boy, or woman, for the edges of the waterfall continually moved and shifted. All they could make out was that there was definitely someone dancing about and waving behind the great fall.

'Look!' said one man to the other. 'Just look at that! See – behind the water! That's where they're hiding. My word, what a place! How do they get there?'

The men stared open-mouthed at the waterfall, their eyes searching for a way up to it that would lead to the ledge where the excited figure stood waving.

Meantime, Jack and Philip, quite unaware of the following men, or of Dinah either, had reached the curtain of fern. Philip pushed the ferns aside, and Jack hauled the sack up through them, panting painfully, for it was heavy.

At last the sack lay on the floor of moss. The boys flung themselves down, their hearts thumping with the labour of climbing up steeply to the cave, dragging such a heavy sack. At first they did not even notice that the girls were not there.

Not far off, some way below, stood the two men, completely bewildered. In watching Dinah behind the waterfall, they had just missed seeing Jack and Philip creep through the ferns into their cave. So when they turned from gazing at the waterfall, they found that the boys they had so warily followed had utterly disappeared.

'Where have they gone?' demanded Juan. 'They were on that rock there when we saw them last.'

'Yes. Then I caught sight of that person waving down there, and took my eyes off them for a minute – and now they've gone,' growled Pepi. 'Well, there's no doubt where they've gone. They've taken some path that leads to that waterfall. They hide behind it – and a clever place it is, too. Who would think of anyone hiding just behind a great curtain of water like that? Well, we know where to find them. We'll make our way to the water and climb up to that ledge. We'll soon hunt the rats out.'

They began to climb down, hoping to find a way that would lead them to the ledge behind the waterfall. It was difficult and dangerous going, on the slippery rocks.

In the cave the boys soon recovered. They sat up, and looked around for the girls.

'Hallo – where are Lucy-Ann and Dinah?' said Jack in astonishment. 'They promised to stay here till we got back. Surely to goodness they haven't gone wandering about anywhere? They'll get lost, sure as anything!'

They were not in the cave. That was absolutely certain. The boys did not see the hole in the fold of rock at the back. They were extremely puzzled. Jack parted the ferns and looked out.

To his enormous astonishment he at once saw the two men clambering about on rocks near the waterfall. His eyes nearly dropped out of his head.

'Look there!' he said to Philip, closing the fronds a little, fearful of being seen. 'Those two men! Golly, they might have seen us getting in here! How did they get here? We saw them safely by the plane, on our way to the bush!'

Dinah had now disappeared from behind the waterfall. She could not make up her mind whether or not the men had seen the boys climbing in through the fern to their cave. In any case, she thought she ought to warn them of the men's appearance. She felt sure that neither Jack nor Philip knew they were there.

'Come on, Lucy-Ann,' she said urgently. 'We must get back to the boys. Oh, goodness, look at those men! I believe they are going to try and get over here now. They must have spotted me waving. Do come quickly, Lucy-Ann.'·

Shivering with excitement, Lucy-Ann followed Dinah along the dark, winding passage that led back to the cave of echoes. Dinah went as quickly as she could, flashing her torch in front of her. Both girls forgot all about Kiki. The parrot was left sitting alone behind the waterfall, spray misting her feathers, watched the clambering men with interested eyes. She had not heard the girls going off.

Dinah and Lucy-Ann came out into the cave of echoes at last. Dinah stopped and considered. 'Now, where exactly was that hole we came through?' she said.

'Came through, through, through,' called the echoes mockingly.

'Oh be *quiet*!' cried Dinah to the echoes.

'QUIET, QUIET, QUIET!' yelled back the irritating voices. Dinah flashed her torch here and there, and by a very lucky chance she found the hole. In a trice she was in it, crawling along, with Lucy-Ann close behind her. Lucy-Ann had an awful feeling that somebody was going to clutch her feet from behind and she almost bumped into Dinah's shoes in her efforts to scramble down the hole as quickly as possible.

Jack and Philip were peeping through the ferns watching the men, when the girls dropped out of the hole at the back of the cave, came round the fold of rock and flung themselves on the boys. They almost jumped out of their skin.

Philip hit out, thinking that enemies were upon them. Dinah got a stinging blow on the ear, and yelled. She immediately hit out at Philip and the two rolled on the floor.

'Don't, oh, don't!' wailed Lucy-Ann, almost in tears. 'Philip, Jack, it's us! It's us!'

Philip shook off Dinah and sat up. Jack stared in amazement. 'But where did you come from?' he demanded. 'Golly, you gave us an awful scare, I can tell you, jumping out like that! Where have you been?'

'There's a hole back there we went into,' explained Dinah, giving Philip an angry look. 'I say, do you two boys know that those men were following you? They were not very far behind you. We were scared stiff they would see you climbing in here.'

'Were they *following* us!' said Jack. 'Golly, I didn't know that. Peep out between these fronds, you girls, and see them hunting for us down there.'

# 13

## Safe in the cave

They all peeped out between the fern fronds, Lucy-Ann holding her breath. Yes, there were the two men, clambering about dangerously near the waterfall.

'But what are they doing down *there*?' said Jack in wonder. 'Why look for us there? They must have know we didn't go that way, if they were following us.'

'Well, they must have seen me waving to you from behind the waterfall,' said Dinah. 'They must think that's where our hiding place is.'

'Waving to us from behind the waterfall?' said Philip in the utmost amazement. 'What are you talking about, Dinah? You must be bats.'

'Well, I'm not,' said Dinah. 'That's where Lucy-Ann and I were when you came up the slope there to climb into the cave. We were standing behind the waterfall, and I tried my hardest to attract your attention and tell you that those two men were following you.'

'But – how in the world did you get *behind* the waterfall?'

asked Jack. 'It was an idiotic thing to do. Fancy climbing up those slippery rocks, and getting behind the water! You might have been . . . '

'We didn't go that way, silly,' said Dinah. 'We went another way.' And she told Jack and Philip all about the hole at the back of the cave that led down into the cave of echoes, and the passage that came out behind the roaring waterfall. The boys listened in the greatest amazement.

'Gosh! How extraordinary!' said Jack. 'Well, I suppose the men just caught sight of you down there, Dinah, and took their eyes off me and Philip for a minute, and lost us. We must have climbed into this cave through the fern just as they were watching you. What a good thing!'

'That's why they're messing about down there on those wet rocks,' said Philip, grinning. 'They think that that is our hiding place, behind the fall, and they want to get there and find us. They don't guess that isn't the right way. I can't for the life of me see how they can possibly get behind the water from any of those rocks in front. If they're not jolly careful, they'll get swept off by the water – and down they'll go like lightning.'

Lucy-Ann shuddered. 'I don't want to see them do that,' she said, and wouldn't peep out of the ferns any more.

But Dinah and the boys watched in glee. They felt safe up there in their fern-hidden cave, and it was fun to watch the two men slipping about on the rocks near the water, getting angrier and angrier.

Kiki was still behind the waterfall, watching them with interest. Suddenly she gave one of her dreadful cackles of laughter, and the men heard it even through the roar of the water. They looked at one another, startled.

'Hear that?' said Juan. 'Somebody yelling their heads off, laughing at us. Wait till I get them, that's all. They must be just behind the sheet of water. How *do* they get there?'

It was impossible to get behind the waterfall from above

85

or below. Quite impossible. The men realised this after they had fallen many times, and once almost slipped off a wet rock into the cascading water itself. They sat down on a ledge a good way from the water and mopped their heads. They were hot and angry, and their clothes were soaked.

They were puzzled, too. Where had those boys come from? Was there a whole camp of people somewhere? Were they hiding in the mountains? No, that could not be so, for they would have seen them roving the countryside in search of food. There could only be a few people. They must have sent out the boys to seek for food.

The children watched in delight. There was something very enjoyable in seeing their enemies at a loss, in being able to see their every action and yet not be seen themselves. Even Lucy-Ann had another peep now that she knew they were no longer slipping about the waterfall.

'We'd better go,' said Juan. 'If that's their hiding place they can keep it. We'd better get somebody else here to help us. We could put him to guard this place. If he sat here, he could see if anyone came up to get behind the water. Come on, I'm fed up with this.'

They stood up. Jack watched them through the fern-fronds. Were they going back to their hut, or to the plane, perhaps? Then, seeing that they were going to pass rather near to the cave, the boy hastily closed the fronds and pushed the others back.

'Keep quiet,' he said. 'They may come fairly near.'

They came extremely near. They took a way that led them right past the cave itself. The children sat as still as stone, hearing the men scrambling along outside. Suddenly the fern swayed and shook, and Lucy-Ann's hand flew up to her mouth to stifle a scream.

'They're coming in, they've found us,' she thought, and her heart almost stopped beating. The fern rustled again, and then there was quiet. The footsteps passed, and the children heard the voices of the two men saying something they could not catch.

'Have they gone?' wondered Dinah, and looking at Jack, she raised her eyebrows. He nodded. 'Yes – they were gone – but what a terrible fright everyone had had when they grasped hold of the fern to help them along! Little did Juan and Pepi dream that four silent children sat within two feet of them then.

Jack parted the fern again. There was no sign of the men. He felt sure they must have gone back, but he did not dare to go out and spy. 'Better lie low for a bit,' he said. 'We'll have a meal. I'll creep out and spy around later on. Where's Kiki?'

Nobody knew. Then Dinah remembered she had been with them behind the waterfall. They had gone back without her in their anxiety to warn the boys about the two men. She must still be there.

'Blow! We'd better go and fetch her,' said Jack. 'I don't really feel like moving just now, either – I'm really tired with dragging that heavy sack along so far.'

A voice spoke outside the cave . . . a gloomy, dismal, reproachful voice.

'Poor Kiki! All alone! What a pity, what a Kiki, poor pity!'

The children laughed, and Jack parted the fronds cautiously, in case by any chance the men were still anywhere about. Kiki clambered through, looking very sorry for herself. She flew to Jack's shoulder and nibbled his ear gently.

'All aboard!' she said more cheerfully, and cracked her beak. Dinah ruffled up the feathers on her head.

'Kiki must have flown out from behind the waterfall and come straight here,' she said. 'Clever Kiki! clever old bird!'

'God save the Queen,' said Kiki. 'Wipe your feet!'

Jack's tin-opener came out again, and a choice of tins and jars was made. There was a small tin of biscuits still to be finished, and the children chose some pressed meat to go with them, and a large tin of juicy apricots. Jack opened the fronds just a little to let in enough daylight to see by. Once again they thoroughly enjoyed their meal, and Kiki got into trouble for taking more than her fair share of apricots.

The children waited some time before they dared to creep out of the cave. When the sun was well down, Jack clambered out between the fronds, and had a good look round. There was no sign of the men at all. Jack found a high place from which, if he sat there, he could see for a good way in any direction.

'We'll take it in turns to keep watch,' he said. 'You can come in half an hour, Philip.'

They had a fine time clambering all about. They found some wild raspberries, and ate great quantities of them. They were delicious. Kiki ate them too, murmuring 'Mmmmmmmmmm' all the time.

Each of them took turn at keeping watch, but there was nothing to see. The sun went down behind behind the mountains, and twilight came. They all went back to the cave.

'It will be lovely to sleep here tonight,' said Lucy-Ann, pleased. 'This moss is so nice and soft. Like velvet.'

She stroked it. It *felt* like velvet too. She helped Dinah to put down macks and a rug to lie on, and made pillows of pullovers and jerseys.

'A drink of apricot juice and a few biscuits for everyone,' said Dinah, as they all sat down on the 'bed.' She handed out the biscuits. Jack parted the fern-fronds and tied them firmly back.

'Must have a little air in the cave,' he said. 'It will get jolly stuffy with four of us here.'

'Five,' said Dinah. 'Don't forget Kiki.'

'Six,' said Philip, producing the lizard. 'Don't forget dizzy Lizzie.'

'Oh, I really hoped you'd lost her,' said Dinah crossly. 'I haven't seen her all day.'

They finished their biscuits and lay down. It was quite dark now outside. Their 'bed' felt warm and soft. They all snuggled down, making nice cosy places for themselves.

'I should really enjoy all this, if only I knew that Mother wasn't worrying about us,' said Philip, pulling the rug over him. 'I haven't any idea at all where we are, but it's a very beautiful place. Doesn't that waterfall sound lovely, singing in the night?'

'It's singing jolly loudly,' said Jack, yawning. 'But I don't think it will keep *me* awake. Oh, Kiki, do move off my middle. I can't imagine why you will keep perching there at night. Go on one of my feet.'

'Wipe your feet,' ordered Kiki, and flew to Jack's right foot. She put her head under her wing.

'Tomorrow Philip and I must go to that cave of echoes you told us about and stand behind the waterfall,' said Jack. 'Fancy you girls having a little adventure like that all on your own!'

'*Little* adventure!' said Lucy-Ann. 'Why, it was a jolly big one – especially when we suddenly saw that we were just behind the waterfall!'

Dinah was very much afraid that Lizzie would run over her during the night, and lay awake some time expecting the feel of her tiny feet. But Lizzie was curled up in Philip's armpit, tickling him dreadfully when she moved.

Lucy-Ann was asleep almost at once, and soon the others were too. The waterfall roared all through the night without ceasing. The wind sprang up and moved the big fronds of the fern. A fox or some other creature came sniffing up to the cave entrance, was alarmed at the smell of humans there and fled away silently.

Nobody stirred, except Philip when the lizard woke up, felt cramped, and made her way to another nice warm spot, this time behind his ear. He awoke for a second, felt Lizzie moving, and then shut his eyes immediately again, pleased with the feel of the tiny feet.

Towards morning a throbbing sound awoke all four children. It penetrated into the cave, sounding even louder than the waterfall. Jack sat up at once, surprised. What could that be?

The noise grew louder and louder, it seemed as if it was coming right down on their heads. Whatever *could* it be?

Rr-rr-rr-rr-rr-rrRRRRRRRRRRRRRRRRRR!

'It's a plane!' cried Jack. 'A plane! Come to rescue us. Out of the cave, quick!'

They all tumbled out of the cave and looked for the plane. One was climbing into the air, a large shape against the sky. It had evidently come very near the side of the mountain, and had awakened them by its noise.

'A plane to rescue us?' said Philip scornfully. 'Not likely! That's the plane we came here in – the men's plane, idiot!'

# 14

## The poor prisoner

Sure enough, it was the men's plane. The children all recognised it quite well as they watched it vanishing into the distance. It flew towards the west.

'Wonder if it's going back to Bill's aerodrome?' said Jack. 'Wonder if Bill knows what those men are up to?'

'We don't know very much ourselves, except that they are after some sort of treasure,' said Philip. 'But, honestly, what treasure they think they can find here in this place beats me.'

'Beats me too,' said Jack. 'Well – there they go! Do you

suppose they'll come back?'

'Sure to,' said Philip. 'They won't give up as easily as that. Maybe they've gone to report that there are other people here now — for all they know, after the treasure too! And they might bring back more men to smell us out.'

'Oh,' said Lucy-Ann in alarm. 'I don't want to be smelt out.'

'Do you think *both* men have gone?' asked Philip.

'I should think so,' said Jack. 'But we can go and have a jolly good look round and see. If one man is left, he'll be somewhere near that shed of theirs. He won't know how many of us there are here — he may think there are men with us, you know, and not dare to move about too much by himself.'

But when the children left the cave later in the morning and went to 'have a squint,' as Jack said, they could find no sign of either Juan or Pepi. There was no fire. It had been stamped out. And this time the shed was well and truly locked, and the key taken. No amount of shaking or kicking would open the door.

'Well, if we'd known the men were going to fly off, we might have asked them for a lift,' said Jack with a grin. 'I wonder when they'll come back — if they do come back, that is.'

'Not till it's daylight tomorrow, I should think,' said Philip. 'I expect they'll take off at night again. Let's go and have another squint at those crates.'

But there was really nothing to see. They were empty as before, and the tarpaulin was over them. The children played about for some hours, and had a meal under a tree. They went to get a tin or two from the rest of the store still hidden in the bush. Jack opened them.

After the meal Philip suggested that they should go back to the waterfall and the girls should take them to the cave of echoes, and down the passage that led behind the water. So off they went, first hiding all trace of having been near the men's shed.

But when they got back to their cave, Jack gave a most annoyed exclamation and began to feel in all his pockets.

'What's the matter?' said Lucy-Ann.

'Well, do you know what I've done? I've gone and left the tin-opener behind,' said Jack. 'Think of that! What an idiotic thing to do! I thought we might want another tin opened, so I put it down at the roots of that tree we had our picnic under – and I must have left it there. I haven't got it, anyway.'

'Oh, *Jack*! But we can't have a meal without opening a tin,' said Philip, seeing awful visions of a hungry night. 'Gosh – you *are* an ass!'

'Yes, I know,' said Jack gloomily. 'Well, there's only one thing to be done. I must go back and get it. You explore the cave of echoes with the girls, Philip, and I'll take Kiki and go back for the opener. Serves me right.'

'I'll come with you, Jack,' said Lucy-Ann, sorry for her brother.

'No, you've had a jolly long walk already,' said Jack. 'You go with the others. Anyway, I'll be quicker by myself. I'll just have a sitdown before I start back. I can always explore the cave another time.'

He sat down on the moss. The others sat with him, sorry for him, knowing how annoyed he must feel with himself. But it would be still more annoying to have to go without meals. The opener must certainly be fetched.

After about half an hour Jack felt able to start back again. He said a cheery goodbye to the others, and left, scrambling quickly down the rocks. They knew he would not lose his way. They all felt they knew it quite well by this time.

Jack had Kiki on his shoulder, and they talked together all the way. Kiki was simply delighted to have Jack all to herself. He was nearly always with the others. They talked complete nonsense and both of them thoroughly enjoyed it.

Jack arrived at last at the tree under which they had had their lunch. He looked for the opener, half fearful in case it had been removed by somebody. But it was still there, lying where he had left it. He picked it up and put it into his pocket.

'Three cheers,' he said.

'Three blind mice,' said Kiki. 'Handy spandy, humpy dumpy.'

'I agree with you,' said Jack. 'Well, we'll get back, I think. Twilight will soon be coming and I don't fancy going back in the dark. Off we go, Kiki, up the hill.'

'Jack and Jill,' agreed Kiki.

'Jack and Kiki, you mean,' grinned Jack, turning to go. Then he stood still suddenly and listened. Away in the distance he could hear a sound he knew – a familiar, throbbing sound. Rr-rr-rr-rr-rr!

'Gosh, Kiki! – are those fellows coming back so soon?' said Jack, staring into the western sky, which was still faintly gold. 'Yes – that's a plane all right. But is it theirs?'

The plane came nearer, growing larger and larger. An idea came into Jack's mind. He ran to where the men's shed was, and climbed quickly up into a tree not far from where they had their camp-fire. He spoke sternly to Kiki.

'Now, quiet, Kiki. Not a word. Do you understand? Shhhhhhh!'

'What a pity, what a pity!' said Kiki in a curious hoarse whisper, and then was silent, pressing against Jack's neck as she sat on his shoulder.

The plane roared nearer. It circled lower and lower. It dropped to the long smooth strip that made such an excellent runway. It bounced along on its high wheels and then came to a stop. Jack could not see the plane from where he was.

But he was counting on the men coming to the shed or to their fire, and he was right. They soon arrived, and Jack peered out through the leaves, nearly overbalancing in his efforts to see properly, for twilight was almost there.

This time there were four men. Jack looked very hard. He could see that one man was evidently a prisoner. He had his hands tied behind him. How strange!

He shambled along, his head bent, going from side to side a little as if he was dizzy. Now and again one of the others would give him a shove to keep him straight. They came straight to the campfire.

Juan set to work to light it. Pepi went off to the shed to get some tins. He took a key from his pocket and unlocked the door. He came out carrying tins of soup and meat.

The prisoner sat down on the grass, his head bent. It was obvious that he was not feeling well – or was he merely afraid? Jack couldn't tell. The fourth man, who was a kind of guard for the prisoner, as far as Jack could make out, sat by the fire saying nothing, watching Juan and Pepi.

At first they talked in low voices and Jack could not hear their words. They drank hot soup, and then carved up a tongue from a glass jar. They ate bread with it which they had brought from the plane. The prisoner looked up and saw them eating, but the three men did not offer him anything. He said something in a low voice. Juan laughed.

He spoke to the guard. 'Tell him he won't get anything to eat or drink till he tells us what we want to know,' he said.

The guard repeated this in some language that Jack could not make out. The prisoner said something and the guard struck him on the cheek. Jack watched in horror. Fancy hitting a man when his hands were tied! What cowards!

The man tried to dodge. He bent his head again and sat dismally there.

'He says you've got the map, what else do you want?' said the guard.

'We can't read the map,' said Juan. 'It's all messed up. If he can't explain it to us, he'll have to show us the way tomorrow.'

The guard translated this to the prisoner. He shook his head. 'He says he is too weak to walk so far,' said the guard.

'We'll drag him all right,' said Pepi, and took another piece of tongue, making himself a thick sandwich. 'Tell him he's to take us tomorrow. If he won't, he gets nothing to eat or drink. He'll soon come round when he's half starved.'

They finished their meal. Then Juan yawned. 'Me for bed,' he said. 'There's a chair for you, Luis, in the hut. The floor's good enough for the prisoner.'

The man begged to have his hands untied, but they would not allow him to. Jack felt very sorry for him. They stamped out the fire and went to the hut. Jack imagined Pepi and Juan on the mattress, and Luis in the only comfortable chair. The poor prisoner would have to lie on the cold, hard floor, with his hands still tied behind him.

Jack waited till he thought the coast was clear, then he slipped quietly down the tree. Kiki had been as good as gold all the time. Not even a whisper had come from her beak. Jack tiptoed to the hut. He peeped cautiously in at the window. A candle burned in the hut, and by its flickering light he could make out the four men. The prisoner was trying to make himself comfortable on the floor.

It was almost dark. Jack hoped he would be able to get back to the cave all right. He slipped his hand into his pocket and was relieved to find a small torch there. That was good!

He was very clever in the dark, for he had eyes like a cat. Once or twice he stopped, unable to think which way to go – but Kiki always knew. She simply flew a little way in front and called to him, or whistled.

'Good old Kiki!' said Jack. 'I couldn't have found my way without you, that's certain.'

The others were very worried about him. When darkness

95

fell and still no Jack had arrived, Lucy-Ann wanted to go and look for him.

'I'm sure he's lost, I'm certain of it,' she said, almost in tears.

'Yes, and *we'd* all get lost too, if we went out on the mountainside in this darkness,' said Philip. 'I expect he hunted about for that opener, saw that twilight was coming, and decided not to risk coming back in the dark. He'll be back tomorrow morning early, for certain.'

It was too dark to do anything. Dinah had made the 'bed' and they lay down on it, Lucy-Ann very worried. She was sure something had happened to Jack.

Then there came a scrambling noise up near the cave, and the fern was parted and pushed aside. All the children sat up, their hearts beating. Was it Jack – or had their hiding place been discovered?

'Hallo, there!' came Jack's familiar voice. 'Where's everybody?'

He switched on his torch and saw three delighted faces. Lucy-Ann almost fell on him.

'Jack! We thought you were lost. What *have* you been doing? And we're so hungry, too. Have you brought the tin-opener?'

'Yes, I've brought that – and plenty of news as well!' said Jack. 'What about a meal whilst I tell you all about it?'

# 15

# A disappointment for the men

Tins were opened once more, and Kiki gave a delighted chortle at the sight of her favourite pineapple. Lucy-Ann pressed close to Jack.

'What happened to you? I can't wait to hear. Tell me quickly.'

'Let me have a bite first,' said Jack irritatingly, knowing quite well that all the others were longing to hear his news. But as he was longing just as much to tell it as they were to hear it, he soon began his story.

'So the plane's back!' exclaimed Philip, as Jack began to tell everything. 'Both men back too?'

Jack told of the four men. Lucy-Ann was distressed to hear about the poor prisoner.

'I'm beginning to see daylight,' said Philip at last. 'Some-where in this valley is hidden treasure – maybe stuff belonging to the people whose houses have been burnt. Those two men heard about it, and somehow managed to get a map that showed them the hiding place. But they can't find it by that map, so they've got hold of somebody who knows the way.'

'That's it,' said Jack. 'He's foreign. Maybe he once belonged to this valley, and even hid the things himself. They've captured him and mean to make him show them the hiding-place. They're not giving him anything to eat or drink till he shows them what they want to know.'

'Brutes!' said Dinah, and the others agreed with her.

'Do you think he *will* show them?' asked Lucy-Ann.

'I hope he will for his own sake,' said Jack. 'And I'll tell you what I propose. I propose that somehow or other one or more of us follow them, and see where this hiding place is. The men can't possibly take everything away at once. We might be able to get help, and save the rest of the stuff being stolen by the men. It can't belong to them.'

'What do you think the stuff can be?' asked Lucy-Ann, visions of gold bars and beautiful jewels floating in her mind.

'Can't tell you,' said Jack. 'I think we're somewhere in the depths of Europe, where war has been, and as you know, plenty of treasure of all kinds was hidden in odd places by many, many people, good and bad. My guess is that it's something of that kind these men are after. They speak English, but they're not English. Perhaps from South America? Goodness knows.'

The others sat silent, thinking over what Jack had said. They thought he was probably right. But Lucy-Ann didn't at all like the idea of following the men. Suppose they discovered that they were being followed, and captured them?

'It might be best if Philip and I did the stalking tomorrow,' said Jack. 'I don't think you girls should be mixed up in it.'

This made Dinah angry, though Lucy-Ann was secretly relieved.

'You're not going to keep all the excitement to yourselves,' said Dinah. 'I'm coming too.'

'No, you're not,' said Jack. He switched on his torch and shone it at Dinah's face. 'I thought you'd be glaring,' he said. 'Cheer up, Dinah. After all, you and Lucy-Ann had an adventure yesterday, when you found the cave of echoes and the passage that leads to the waterfall. Give us boys a chance.'

'Well, it's all very well,' grumbled Dinah, but she did not press the point any more, much to Lucy-Ann's relief.

'Where's Lizzie?' asked Dinah, not liking to settle down till she was quite sure of the lizard's whereabouts.

'Don't know,' said Philip annoyingly. 'She might be anywhere. Under your pillow, perhaps.'

'She's here,' said Jack. 'Kiki's one side of my neck and Lizzie's the other, keeping me nice and warm.'

'What a pity!' said Kiki, and cackled loudly.

'*Don't!*' said everybody at once. Nobody liked Kiki's awful cackle. She put her head under her wing, offended.

All the children lay down. They were sleepy. 'Our fourth night in this valley,' said Philip. 'The valley of adventure. I wonder what will happen next.'

Soon they were all asleep. Lizzie ran across Lucy-Ann and cuddled down by Dinah, who would certainly have objected strongly if she had known. But she didn't know. So she slept peacefully.

Everyone felt cheerful the next morning.

'Really,' said Dinah, reaching down some tins from the ledge, 'I'm beginning to feel I've made this cave my home half my life. It's extraordinary how soon we get used to anything new.'

'How are we going to find out when those men are starting, and what way they go?' said Philip.

'Well, if you remember, the two of them came in this direction, not the other, when they set out with the map before,' said Jack. 'I think if we go to that big black rock we always pass on the way here, we may spot them. Then we can follow easily enough.'

So when they had finished their meal they set off cautiously to the big black rock. They crouched behind it, and Jack kept peering out to see if there was anything to be seen.

After about an hour he gave a low exclamation. 'Hallo! Here they come – all four – prisoner still with his hands tied, stumbling along, poor thing.'

The four men passed some distance away. The children saw them well. They recognised the two men they knew, and Jack told them the fourth man was called Luis. The prisoner's name he didn't know. It was plain that the poor man was giddy for lack of food and drink.

'Now, you girls stay here, see?' said Jack. 'At any rate, till we are well out of sight. Then go back to the waterfall, and keep somewhere about there. Don't get lost! Take Kiki, Lucy-Ann. We don't want her with us.'

Lucy-Ann took Kiki and held her ankles. Kiki gave such an angry squawk that the children looked uneasily after the four men to see if by any chance they had heard. But they hadn't.

Jack and Philip made ready to set off. 'I've got my field glasses,' said Jack. 'I can keep the men well in sight, while following quite a long way behind, so that they won't spot us. Cheerio!'

The boys went off cautiously, keeping to every bit of cover they could. They could still see the men far away in the distance. 'Do we need to mark the way we're going?' asked Philip. 'Or shall we be able to find the way back, do you think?'

Better mark things where we can,' said Jack. 'You never know. Mark rocks with white chalk. Here's a bit. And trees we will notch.'

They went on, climbing upwards a good way behind the four men. Soon they came to a very steep place, difficult to keep their footing on, because the surface was so loose that they slid down continually.

'I hope they've undone that poor prisoner's hands, panted Jack. 'I'd hate to do climbing like this and have my hands bound so that I couldn't save myself when I slipped.'

When they came to the end of the rough piece, the men were nowhere to be seen. 'Blow!' said Jack. 'That bit held us up too long. Now we've lost them!'

He put his field glasses to his eyes and swept the mountainside. Some way to the east and above them he suddenly saw four small figures. 'There they are!' he said. 'It's all right. I can see them. That way, Tufty.'

On they went again, going more quickly now because the way was easier. They picked wild raspberries as they went, and once stopped for a drink at a little clear spring of water that gushed from under a rock.

They did not lose sight of the men again except for a moment or two. The men did not turn round, or use field glasses at all. Plainly they did not expect anyone to follow them.

Now the boys came to a very desolate part of the mountainside. Big boulders had rolled down. Trees had been torn in half. Great ruts had been torn out of the earth and rock, and although the grass was growing everywhere to hide the scars, it was clear that some catastrophe had happened here.

'An avalanche, I should think,' said Jack. 'I guess a terrific fall of snow happened here – bringing down with it boulders and rocks of all sizes – knocking down trees and scoring those ruts. Last winter, I should think.'

'Where are the men?' said Philip. 'I can't see them now. They went round the ledge.'

'Yes. We'll have to be careful how we go round,' said Jack. 'We might easily be seen coming round there. There's not much cover in this devastated bit.'

So they went very cautiously round the ledge – and it was a good thing they did, for almost at once they heard voices and saw the four men.

Jack pressed Philip back. Just above the ledge was a bush. The boys climbed up to it, pressed against it, and parted the leaves so that they might see through. They found that they were looking down into a rocky gully.

Here, too, there had evidently been a great fall of rocks. In front of one heap stood the prisoner. His hands were now untied. He was pointing to the heap of rocks, and saying something in his rather dull, low voice. The guard translated, and Jack strained his ears to hear what he had to say.

'He says the entrance was here,' the guard said. The four men stared at the fall of rock.

'Exactly where?' said Juan impatiently, and glared at the prisoner. He pointed again, mumbling something.

'He says he didn't know there had been a fall or rock here,' said the guard. 'He says the entrance seems to be blocked up. But if you try to lift away some of these rocks, maybe you could find enough room to go in.'

Juan flew into a temper, but whether with the prisoner or the annoying fall of rocks it was difficult to say. He fell upon the boulders and began to drag at them feverishly, shouting to Luis and Pepi to help. The prisoner at first did nothing but sat down miserably on a rock. Juan shouted at him too, and he dragged himself up to help, though he was too weak to do anything in the way of lifting.

He pulled at a rock, staggered and fell. The others let him lie where he fell, and went on dragging at the great stones, panting and wiping the sweat from their foreheads.

The two boys watched them. It looked impossible, from where they were, to unblock any cave entrance there. 'Why,' whispered Jack to Philip, 'hundreds of stones must have fallen there! They'll never, never be able to shift them like that!'

Evidently the men thought so too, after a while, for they gave up pulling the boulders about and sat down to rest. The guard pointed to the fallen prisoner and spoke.

'What about him? How are we going to take him back?'

'Oh, give him some food and a drink,' growled Juan. 'He'll be all right, then.'

'We'd better go now,' whispered Philip. 'They'll be starting back soon. Come on. How disappointing that we haven't discovered anything, though! I did hope we might see something of the treasure.'

'If it's hidden behind that wall of fallen stone it'll need powerful machinery to get it out,' said Jack. 'Nobody could move those bigger stones by hand. Come on, quickly.'

They set out on their way back, going as quickly as they could, glad that they had marked rocks and trees or they might have missed their way here and there.

The girls welcomed them, and poured questions on them. But the boys shook their heads most disappointingly.

'The treasure cave is blocked up,' said Jack. 'I only hope the men don't give up and leave this valley altogether. We'll be properly stranded then.'

# 16

## Rescue of the prisoner

Some while after Jack and Philip had got back to the cave, Lucy-Ann, who was looking out between the fern fronds, gave a cry. 'I say, there's a man down there! – look, by the waterfall! Two men – no, three!'

Jack pulled the string which tied back the fronds and let them swing together to hide the cave. Then, parting the fronds carefully, he looked through.

'I might have guessed they would come back this way, to have another hunt for us here,' he said. 'Blow them! One – two – three of them. Where's the prisoner?'

'Fallen by the way, I should think, poor fellow,' said Philip, peering out too. 'He looked terribly feeble.'

The children watched the three men eagerly to see what they meant to do. It was soon clear. Luis and Juan were to go back to their hut, but Pepi was to be left to keep watch on the waterfall, to see who went in and out, and to try and discover the way that was used. The children could not hear what was said, but it was all plain enough.

Luis and Juan departed. Where the prisoner was nobody could guess. Pepi sat down on a rock that overlooked the waterfall, just about the level of the ledge where the girls had stood the day before.

'Blow!' said Jack. 'How can we get in and out without being seen? It's true he's got his back to us, but he might turn round at any time.'

Lucy-Ann began to worry about the prisoner. 'Suppose he has fallen down on the way, and the men have left him there,' she said. 'He'd die, wouldn't he?'

'I suppose so,' said Jack, feeling anxious too.

'But Jack, we can't leave him to die,' said Lucy-Ann, her eyes big with horror. 'You know we can't. I shan't rest till I know what's happened to him.'

'I feel rather like that too,' said Jack, and the others nodded. 'There was something awful about the hopeless way he sat. I'm sure he was ill.'

'But how can we find out what's happened to him, whilst that fellow down there is guarding this place?' said Philip gloomily.

Everyone fell silent. It was a puzzler. Then Lucy-Ann brightened up. 'I know,' she said. 'There's one certain way of making sure Pepi doesn't see anyone creeping out of this cave.'

'What?' said Jack.

'Well, if one or two of us got behind the waterfall and capered about a bit to attract the man's attention, he would be all eyes for them, and wouldn't notice anyone creeping out of this cave,' said Lucy-Ann.

'There's something in that,' said Jack, and Philip nodded. 'Yes, quite a good idea. Well, there's no time like the present. Shall we give a performance for dear Pepi now? You two girls could go and caper about, if you like – you are quite safe when you're behind the waterfall, because nobody can possibly get at you there, unless they go that same way as you do. And Pepi certainly doesn't know that way. Whilst you are attracting his attention, Philip and I will go off and see if we can see any sign of the prisoner.'

'Well, wait here till you see us behind the water,' said Dinah and she got up. She and Lucy-Ann disappeared up the hole at the back of the cave. The boys waited patiently for them to appear behind the waterfall.

After some while Philip clutched Jack's arm. 'There they are! Good old Lucy-Ann, good old Dinah! They're having a fine old game down there. What are they waving? Oh, they've taken off their red pullovers and they're waving them like mad – doing a kind of dance.'

Pepi caught sight of them at once. He stared in surprise, and then stood up. He yelled and shouted and waved. The girls took no notice at all, but went on capering. Pepi began to try all kinds of ways to get to the waterfall.

'Now's our chance,' said Jack. 'Come on. His eyes will be glued on Lucy-Ann and Dinah for ages.'

They crept quickly out of the cave, swinging the fronds closely together behind them. They climbed up the rocks there and soon took cover so that they could not be seen. When the girls saw that they were safely out of the cave and could no longer be seen, they left the waterfall ledge and went back into the passage that led to the cave of echoes. They had done their bit.

The boys made their way cautiously over the rocks, keeping a good lookout for the others. When they were quite a long way from Pepi, they stopped to take counsel.

'Now – should we go back to that blocked up cave where apparently the treasure is, and see if we can find the prisoner fallen by the way – or shall we scout a bit in the other direction – back to the men's hut, to see if by any chance they've taken him there?'

'Better go to the men's hut,' said Philip, thinking. 'I don't think it's *very* likely they've left him to die by the wayside. They might still want to get something out of him.'

So they made their way back to the men's hut. How well they knew the way now! They saw the smoke of the fire long before they came near, and by that they knew the men were back.

There was no sign to be seen of the two men or of the prisoner. Cautiously the boys peered through the trees near the hut. The door of the hut was shut and presumably locked. Were the men inside?

'Hark, isn't that the sound of the plane's engine running?' asked Philip suddenly. 'Yes, it is. Are those fellows going off again?'

They went to a place from which they could see the plane well by means of Jack's field glasses. The men were not going off – merely doing something to their plane. There was no sign of the prisoner being with them.

'Stay here, Philip, with my field glasses and keep an eye on the plane and the men,' said Jack, pushing his glasses into Philip's hand. 'Come and tell me at once if they stop their work there and go towards the hut. I'm going to peep in at the hut window and see if the prisoner is there. I'm worried about him.'

'Right,' said Philip, and put the field-glasses to his eyes. Jack sped off. He soon came to the hut. He tried the door. Yes, it was locked all right. He crept round to the window and peeped in.

The prisoner was there. He was sitting in the chair, the picture of misery, his face in his hands. As Jack looked, he heard him groan deeply, and it was such a dreadful noise that the boy's heart was wrung.

'If only I could get him out!' he thought. 'No use breaking the window. It's too small even for me to get in, and certainly that fellow couldn't squeeze out. What can I do? I can't break down the door. It's jolly strong!'

He went all round the hut two or three times, but there was absolutely no way of getting in. He stood and stared at the door, hating it. Horrid strong thing!

And then he saw an unbelievable sight. There was a nail at one side of the door, and on it hung – a key! A large key! A key that surely must fit the door. Otherwise why should it be there? It must have been put there so that any of the men could go in and out at any time without waiting for the one who had the key.

With trembling fingers Jack took the key from the nail.

He put it into the lock of the door. He turned it. It was stiff—but it turned all right.

The door swung open and Jack went in. The prisoner, hearing the door open, looked up. He stared in surprise at Jack. The boy grinned at him.

'I've come to set you free,' he said. 'Like to come with me?'

The man did not seem to understand. He frowned a little and stared even harder at Jack.

'Spik slow,' he said. Jack repeated what he had said. Then the boy tapped himself on the chest and said, 'I am your friend. Friend! Understand?'

The man evidently did understand that. A slow smile broke over his face. It was a nice face — a kindly, sad, trustable face, Jack thought. The boy held out his hand.

'Come with me,' he said.

The man shook his head. He pointed to his feet. They were bound tightly with rope, which the man obviously had not had the strength to untie. Jack whipped out his pocket-knife in a trice. He sawed through the thick strands and they fell apart. The man stood up unsteadily, looking as if he was about to fall. Jack steadied him, thinking that he would never be able to walk all the way to their cave. He seemed even weaker than before.

'Come on,' said the boy ugently. 'We haven't much time to lose.'

Jack put the cut pieces of rope into his pocket. He led the man to the door, put him outside, and then carefully locked the door again, hanging the key on its nail. He grinned at the prisoner.

'Bit of a surprise for Juan and Luis to find you've apparently walked through a locked door,' said the boy. 'I'd like to be here when they unlock the door and find you gone.'

Jack took the man's arm and piloted him away into the cover of the nearby trees. The man walked very unsteadily.

He gave a groan every now and again as if it hurt him to walk. Jack felt more and more certain that he would never be able to get to the cave.

He wondered what to do. Perhaps he could park the man in the old cowshed he and the others had found the first day they had arrived? He could put him in the last cowstall, and then fetch him the next day, when he was a little more recovered. That would be the best thing.

'You stay here a minute,' said the boy, thinking he had better run to Philip, tell him what had happened, and get him to keep guard till he got the man safely installed in the shed.

Philip was intensely surprised to hear what Jack had to tell him. He nodded and agreed to stay on guard till Jack came for him.

'The men seem to be overhauling the plane,' he said. 'Looks as if they'll be busy for some time.'

Jack helped the stumbling prisoner over to the cowshed. It took a long time to get there, because the man went so slowly.

Once there, he sank down in the stall and panted painfully. He was certainly an ill man. But there was no doctor for him – only Jack's gentleness, for which he seemed to be very grateful.

'You stay here till tomorrow, when I will fetch you to a safer hiding place,' said Jack, speaking very slowly indeed. 'I will leave you water to drink and food to eat.'

The boy meant to open a tin or two from the store still hidden in the bush. He could easily get them and leave them beside the man.

'The man tapped his chest. 'Otto Engler,' he said, and repeated it two or three times. Jack nodded, and pointed to his own chest.

'Jack Trent,' he said. 'Me Jack – you Otto.'

'Friend,' said the man. 'You – English?'

'Me English,' said Jack gravely. 'You?'

'Austrian,' said the man, pronouncing it in a curious way. 'Friend. Good friend. Why you here?'

Jack tried to explain how it was he and the others had come, but it was too complicated for the man to understand and he shook his head.

'Not understand,' he said. Then he leaned forward to Jack and spoke in a low voice.

'You know of treesure?'

'Treesure? Oh, you mean treasure,' said Jack, 'Not much. You know – of treasure?'

'I know all,' said the man. 'All! I draw you map – where treesure is. You good boy. I trust you.'

# 17

## A treasure map

Jack's first feeling on hearing this was one of tremendous excitement. Then his face fell. He knew where the treasure was. Behind that fall of rock. What use was that? Nobody could get at it there.

'I know where treasure is,' said Jack, trying to speak slowly and simply. 'I saw you show the men this morning – but the rocks had fallen together, and they could not get into the treasure-cave behind.'

The man gave a short laugh. He seemed to understand. 'They are fools,' he said. 'Big fools. There is no treesure there.'

Jack stared at him. 'Do you mean to say – you fooled them?' he said. 'You knew that fall of rocks was there – and you took them to it, and pretended that the entrance to the treasure was all blocked up? Isn't the treasure behind those rocks after all?'

The man was frowning hard in his attempt to follow all that Jack was saying. He shook his head.

'No treesure thère,' he said. 'I fool Juan and Pepi. Ah, ah, how they hurt their hands when they pull – so – at the rocks!'

Jack couldn't help grinning. What a fine trick to play! Well, then – where *was* the 'treesure'?

'I draw you map,' said Otto. 'And I tell you way out of valley too. By the Windy Pass. You will go that way, you and your friends, and you will take the map to a good friend of mine. It is time now to find the hidden treasure.'

'But why can't you come with us?' said Jack. 'Surely you could show us the way, Otto – the pass – and come to your good friend?'

'I am very ill man,' said Otto. 'If I do not get doctor and – how you say it? – middisin . . . '

'Yes, medicine,' said Jack.

' . . . middisin soon, I die,' said Otto. 'I have bad heart, very very bad. I get pain very bad. I not walk far now. So you take treesure map, you good boy, and you take pass out of valley, and go to Julius, my good friend. Then all will be well.'

'All right,' said Jack. 'I'm very sorry about you, Otto. Wish I could do something. I'll do my best to get to Julius quickly and bring back help to you. Do you think you might be able to walk to our hiding place tomorrow, and hide there whilst we go?'

'Pardon?' said Otto. 'You talk too quick, I not understand.'

Jack spoke more slowly. Otto nodded. He understood the second time.

'You leave me here today, and tomorrow perhaps I be

strong enough to go with you to your place,' he said. 'We will see. If not, you must go through the pass and find Julius. I draw you map now, and I draw you also the way to the pass. Windy Pass. It is very, very narrow, but not difficult to, to . . .'

'To travel through?' said Jack. Otto nodded. He found a pencil and a notebook and began to draw. Jack watched him with interest. The waterfall appeared in the map. So did an oddly shaped rock. A bent tree came into the map, and a spring of water. Little arrows were drawn showing in what direction to go. It was really rather exciting.

Otto folded up the map. He gave it to Jack. 'Julius will know,' he said. 'He will read the map. Once he lived in the big farmhouse not far from here. But our enemies burnt it down, and all the other farms too, and took our cows and our horses, our pigs and everything we had. Many they killed, and only few of us escaped.'

'Now tell me the way to the pass,' said Jack.

Otto once more drew a map. The waterfall appeared in it. Jack put his finger on it.

'I know this water,' he said, speaking slowly so that Otto would understand. 'Our hiding place is near. Very near.'

'So!' said Otto, pleased. 'The way to the pass is above the waterfall. You must climb to where it flows out of a hole in the mountainside. There – I have drawn you the way.'

'How shall we find Julius?' asked Jack.

On the other side of the pass is a village, half burnt,' said Otto. 'You will ask anyone you meet to tell you where Julius is. They will know. Ah, Julius worked against the enemy all the time. Everyone knows Julius. He should be a great man now among his people – but times are strange and maybe he is no longer great, now that we have peace. But still, everyone knows Julius, and he will know what to do when you give him the treesure map. I will also write him a letter.'

Otto scribbled a short note, and gave that also to Jack. It

was addressed to Julius Muller.

'Now you must leave me,' said Otto. 'You must go back to your friends. If I am better tomorrow I will come with you. But my heart is bad today, so bad. Always it pains me here.' He pressed his hand over his heart.

'Well, goodbye, and thank you,' said Jack, getting up. 'I do hope you will be safe here. There is meat for you, and tinned fruit, all ready opened. Well – so long till tomorrow.'

The man smiled a tired smile, sank back against the wall of the cowshed and closed his eyes. He was completely exhausted. Jack felt very sorry for him. He must get help as soon as he could, if Otto was not better by tomorrow. He and others would get out of the valley by the pass and go and find Julius at once, whoever he was. If he was a friend of Otto's, he might be able to get a doctor immediately.

Feeling much more cheerful about things, Jack went out of the cowshed. Golly, what would the others say when they knew he had the map of where the treasure-cave was to be found – and directions as to how to get out of the valley!

Philip came running up, out of breath. 'The men have just left the plane and are walking towards their hut,' he said. 'Come on, we'd better go. Is the prisoner safely in the shed?'

'Yes. Hope the men don't go there looking for him,' said Jack. 'Come on – let's get back to the girls. We shall have been away from them for ages.'

'We must look out for Pepi on the way back,' said Philip, as they set off. 'He may have got tired of watching the waterfall and the girls capering about, and have decided to cut back to the others.'

'I say – do you know what *I've* got?' said Jack, unable to keep the news to himself for a moment longer.

'What?' asked Philip.

'A map showing where the treasure is!' said Jack.

'But we know where it is,' said Philip. 'Behind that fall of rocks we saw this morning.'

'Well, it isn't!' said Jack triumphantly. 'The prisoner – his name's Otto – he fooled them properly. He pretended the treasure was in a cave behind the fall of rocks – he knew the rocks had fallen, but he thought he could pretend he didn't know about them, and say the treasure was blocked by the landslide there. See?'

'Golly, and all the time the treasure was somewhere else!' said Philip. 'That was good work. Have you really got a map of the whereabouts of the treasure, Jack? And did you find out exactly what the treasure is?'

'No, I forgot to ask him that,' said Jack. 'But I found out an awful lot. I've got directions to find the pass that leads out of this valley – and a note to a man called Julius – and I know how these houses and things got burnt and why. Otto says if he's strong enough tomorrow he'll take us to the pass himself – but he gave me the maps in case he wasn't able to come with us. They're quite clear.'

This was really exciting news. Philip felt overjoyed. It looked as if they would be able to escape from the valley at last – and get help – and perhaps be in at the discovery of the treasure.

'Look out! – I believe I saw something moving over there,' whispered Jack suddenly, and the two boys crouched behind a bush. It was a good thing they did, for Pepi emerged from a thicket of trees and walked rapidly towards them. But it was obvious that he hadn't seen them.

Without a glance at their bush he strode on. 'I bet he's hungry and wants a meal,' grinned Jack. 'Good thing I spotted him. We'd have bumped right into him in two seconds. Well, that's good – we can hurry on now without being afraid of being seen. Gosh, I'm hungry!'

They both were. It was ages since they had had anything to eat. Thoughts of tinned salmon, sardines, tongue, apricots, peaches and pears floated before the mind's eye of both boys. They hurried as much as they could.

113

They were thankful when they pushed aside the fern-fronds and saw the girls sitting in the cave behind. Dinah had got a fine meal ready and waiting.

'Good old Dinah!' cried Jack. 'I could almost give you a hug!'

Dinah grinned. 'Pepi's gone,' she said. 'Did you meet him?'

'Almost collided with him,' said Philip. 'Gosh, I could eat a whole tin of salmon by myself. How have things been with you and Lucy-Ann, Dinah? All right?'

'Very dull,' said Dinah. 'Nothing doing at all, except a few capers now and again behind the waterfall to keep Pepi interested. You should have seen his efforts to find the way up. Once Lucy-Ann and I really thought he had been swept away by the water. He slipped and fell, and disappeared for about twenty minutes. We were quite relieved when we saw him again.'

'What about you boys?' said Lucy-Ann. 'You look cheerful. Got good news? What about that poor prisoner?'

With their mouths full the boys told of all they had done that day. The girls listened eagerly. When Jack fished the maps out of his pocket they fell on them with delight.

'A treasure map!' cried Lucy-Ann. 'I always wanted to see a real one. Oh, here's our waterfall, look! Surely the treasure isn't anywhere near it?'

'When are we going to find the treasure?' asked Dinah, her eyes shining.

'We're not going to,' said Jack, and her face fell at once. He explained why. 'We've got to get out of this valley, and find this fellow Julius. Apparently he will see to the unearthing of the treasure, whatever it is. Sorry to disappoint you, girls – but honestly, I do really think we ought to get out as quickly as we can, and let Aunt Allie and Bill know where we are. We should waste a lot of time looking for the treasure, and I think that now we've been told where to look for the pass out of the valley we ought to take it, and get help for ourselves and for poor old Otto too. He's a very ill man.'

It was clear that Jack was right. Dinah heaved a sigh of regret. 'I would so very much have liked to go and find that treasure,' she said. 'But never mind – perhaps this Julius man, whoever he is, will let us join the treasure-hunt with him. We might stay for that!'

It was now almost dark. The boys were tired out. They lay down on the 'bed' which Dinah had already made, feeling very sleepy. But the girls wanted to talk, and so did Kiki. They had had a very dull day. They chattered away, Kiki joining in, but the boys could hardly find the energy to answer.

'Kiki's been in and out of the cave of echoes today, yelling and squawking for all she was worth,' said Lucy-Ann. 'She's not afraid of the echoes any more. 'You should have heard the echoes when she did her express train screech!'

'Jolly glad I didn't,' said Jack sleepily. 'Shut up, now, everyone. Get to sleep, because we've got an exciting day before us tomorrow, fetching Otto – and going to find the pass – and looking for Julius.'

'It looks as if this adventure is about to come to an end,' said Lucy-Ann.

But she was quite wrong. It wasn't anywhere *near* its end.

# 18

# Now for Windy Pass!

Next morning the children peeped cautiously through the fern-fronds to see if by any chance Pepi was on guard again. But there was no sign of him.

'I do wonder what Juan and Luis thought when they got

back to their hut, unlocked it – and found the prisoner flown,' said Jack with a grin. 'They'll be astonished to find he went through a locked door.'

'Oh, they'll guess one of us rescued him,' said Dinah 'Won't they be wild? I do hope they don't find him in that cowshed. He might tell tales of us.'

'He wouldn't,' said Jack at once. 'He's got a nice trustable face – rather like Bill's but not so strong.'

'I wish Bill would suddenly arrive here,' said Lucy-Ann with a sigh. 'I do really. I know we have managed things awfully well, but somehow when Bill comes along I feel really safe.'

'Well, you're safe enough now, aren't you?' demanded Jack. 'Didn't I find you a jolly good hiding place?'

'Yes, fine,' said Lucy-Ann. 'Oh, look, Philip – Kiki's after Lizzie!'

Lizzie had appeared down Philip's leg, and Kiki, who happened to be sitting near, had given a delighted squawk and pecked at her – but the lizard was a little too quick. She ran into Philip's shoe.

'Stop it, Kiki!' said Philip. 'Well – now we'd better get busy.'

'Busy, dizzy Lizzie,' said Kiki at once, and the children laughed.

'Really, Kiki's awfully clever at putting the same-sounding words together,' said Lucy-Ann. 'Busy, dizzy Lizzie – I'd never have thought of that. Clever Kiki!'

Kiki squawked and raised her crest high. She rocked herself from side to side, as she often did when she felt pleased with herself.

'Vain bird! Conceited bird!' said Jack, and scratched her poll. 'You leave Lizzie alone. She's about the most harmless pet Philip's ever had.'

'Well, she's better than those awful rats and mice and spiders and beetles and hedgehogs he's had running about him,' said Dinah with a shudder. 'I really quite like Lizzie, compared with them.'

'*Gracious*!' said Lucy-Ann, astonished. 'You *are* improving, Dinah!'

Lizzie and Kiki both joined in the breakfast the children had, though Kiki kept a sharp eye to see that Lizzie didn't take anything *she* wanted. When they had all finished they made their plans for the day.

'We'll fetch Otto first,' said Jack. 'Philip and I, I mean. No need for us all to go. Perhaps you two could pack up a few tins for us all to take with us when we go to look for the pass through the mountains. We shall want a meal on the way.'

'Right,' said Dinah. 'I hope you'll find Otto better. Then when you bring him here, we'll have a snack before we set out. Then over the pass we'll go, and find Julius – and somehow manage to send off a message to Mother and Bill. Maybe Bill will fly over in his plane . . . '

'And join the treasure hunt and let us help,' said Lucy-Ann. 'What a nice plan!'

It did seem a very nice one indeed. The boys set off, leaving Kiki behind with the girls. They went quickly over the mountain slope, keeping a good lookout, however, for Pepi and the others.

But they saw nobody. They made their way carefully to the cowshed. Jack left Philip on guard near by to give warning if anyone came near. Then he tiptoed to the shed and peeped in. There was no sound in there at all.

He could not see the last cowstall from where he stood. He walked softly in, stepping over the fallen rubble. He spoke softly.

'Otto! I'm back! Are you better?'

There was no reply. Jack wondered if the man was asleep. He made his way to the last stall.

It was empty. Otto was not there. Jack glanced round quickly. What could have happened?

The boy saw that the opened tins of meat and fruit that he had left for Otto were untouched. Otto had not eaten anything left for him. Why?

'Blow! Those men must have come looking for him when they found that he was gone from the hut,' thought Jack. 'And they found him here. Gosh! — what have they done with him? We'd better look out for ourselves, in case the men are on the watch for us. They'll know someone must have set Otto free, even if he has held his tongue about me.'

He went back to Philip. 'Otto's gone,' he said. 'Dare we have a squint at the hut? We might find out something then — what they've done with Otto, for instance.'

'Let's shin up that big tree we've climbed before,' said Philip. 'The one that we can see the plane from. If we saw all the men round about the plane, we'd know it was safe to go to the hut; but I don't feel inclined to run into danger if we think the men are by the hut. They might be watching for us to come again. If we're captured, the girls wouldn't know what to do.'

'All right. I'll climb the tree,' said Jack, and up he went, with Philip close behind him. He put his field glasses to his eyes to focus them on the plane — and then he gave a loud exclamation.

'Gosh! The plane's gone again! It isn't there!'

'No — it isn't,' said Philip in surprise. 'Well — *I* never heard it go this time, did you, Jack?'

'Well, I did think I heard a throbbing noise last night when I was half asleep,' said Jack. 'Yes, now I come to think of it, it must have been the plane I heard. Well, we've probably frightened the men away. They got the wind up when they knew other people were here — in a hiding place they couldn't find — people who rescued their prisoner.'

'Yes — and when they found they couldn't get at the treasure because a rock-fall had apparently blocked the entrance to it, I suppose they thought it wasn't much use staying,' said Philip. 'So they've gone. Thank goodness! Now we can go back to the girls, and shoot off to the pass quickly. To tell you the truth, I was a bit worried about taking Otto with us, because from what you said it didn't sound as if we'd be able to go very fast with him. And if he'd had a heart attack by the way we wouldn't have known what to do.'

'I wonder where they've taken him to,' said Jack. 'Let's hope that now they find they can't get any more out of him they've taken him back to where he belongs, and will get a doctor to him.'

They climbed down the tree, and set off back to the girls as fast as they could. Now for the pass.

The girls were most surprised to see the two boys back so soon – but they were even more surprised to see they were alone.

'Where's Otto?' asked Dinah.

'Down the well,' said Kiki. Nobody took any notice of her and she screeched.

Jack explained. 'The plane's gone – and Otto's gone – so I suppose they've all gone off, disgusted at not being able to get at the treasure. Good riddance to them!'

'Hear! hear!' said Dinah, very much relieved to know that their enemies were safely out of the way. 'Well, what are we going to do now?'

'Go and look for the pass,' said Jack. 'I've got the map Otto drew. What a mercy he gave it to me! We'd never find the pass by ourselves without a map, I'm sure of that. I mean, the pass out of these mountains might be anywhere. Apparently there *is* only one pass, and that's this one – the Windy Pass. Come on, let's go. Packed up a few tins, Dinah?'

'Yes,' said Dinah. 'Now, where do we go from here? Up or down?'

'Up,' said Philip, poring over the map that Jack took from

119

his pocket. 'Up – to where the waterfall begins – here, look. Then we go along a rocky ledge – see, Otto's drawn it – then we come to a thick wood, look – and then up a steep bit to another ledge. Then we come to a proper road – the pass road that I suppose all the people of the valley used when they wanted to leave this district and visit another. Once we're on that road I shall feel better.'

'So shall I,' said Dinah fervently. 'It will be nice to see a *road*. We might even see somebody walking on it.'

'Shouldn't think so, as we haven't seen anyone in this valley at all except ourselves and the men,' said Jack. 'It strikes me as a bit queer, I must say, to think that although there's a perfectly good pass in and out of this lovely valley, it appears to be quite deserted. I wonder why.'

'Oh, I expect there's a good reason,' said Dinah. 'Come on, do let's go. The first part will be easy, because we've only got to keep near the waterfall.'

But it wasn't quite so easy as she thought, for the mountain cliff was exceedingly steep there, and the children had to do a lot of stiff climbing. Still, they managed it, for their legs were well used to walking and climbing by now.

The waterfall roared by them all the way. It made a terrific noise as it fell, and Lucy-Ann thought how nice it would be when they reached the top and didn't have to listen to quite such a colossal din.

After some time they came to where the waterfall began. It gushed out of a great hole in the mountainside and fell sheerly down, tumbling against huge rocks on the way. It was really a marvellous sight to see.

'Goodness, it does give me a funny feeling to see that great mass of water coming out of the mountain,' said Lucy-Ann, sitting down. 'It's so *sudden*, somehow.'

'I suppose when the snows melt, and the rain pours down, there is a terrific amount of water soaking down into the mountaintop,' said Jack. 'And it all collects and has to get out somehow. This is one way it gets out – through this hole – making a tremendous waterfall.'

'Where do we go now?' asked Dinah, who was very impatient to get out of the valley.

'We go up on that rocky ledge,' said Jack. 'Golly, it looks a bit narrow – it runs right over the waterfall! Lucy-Ann, don't you dare look down, in case you feel giddy.'

'I don't much feel as if I want to walk along there,' said poor Lucy-Ann.

'I'll help you,' said Jack. 'You'll be all right as long as you don't look down.'

They went along the rocky ledge quite safely, Lucy-Ann holding tightly to Jack's hand. Kiki flew above their heads, squawking encouragement.

'See how they run, see how they run!' she called, having apparently remembered the second line of 'Three Blind Mice.'

Lucy-Ann gave a giggle. 'We're not exactly running, Kiki,' she said. 'Oh, thank goodness the ledge has come to an end. Now we go through that wood, don't we?'

Jack looked at his map. 'Yes – apparently we go straight through. Where's my compass? I'll set it so that we walk in a straight line in the direction Otto has put on his map.'

They entered the wood. It was a pine wood, rather dark and silent. Nothing grew under the tall pine-trees. The wind blew them and they made a loud whispering noise, which upset Kiki.

'Sh!' she called. 'Shhhhhhhhhh!'

'Here's the end of the wood!' called Jack. 'Now for another steep bit to another ledge – and we'll look down on the road. Come on, everybody!'

# 19

## A great disappointment
## – and a plan

It certainly was a stiff climb again, up the steep, rather stony
slope to the ledge they could see some way above. Lucy-Ann
almost cried because her feet kept slipping so.

'I take one step up, and slip two steps back,' she wailed.

'Well, hang on to me, then,' said Philip, and gave her a tug
up each time she took a step.

They all wanted a rest when they came to the next ledge,
and to their delight they saw a patch of wild raspberries
growing there. They could sit down in the canes and feast as
they rested. Lovely! Kiki liked the raspberries very much
indeed, and ate so many that Jack called to her.

'Kiki! You'll go pop!'

'Pop goes the weasel,' answered Kiki, and helped herself
to a few dozen more raspberries.

Soon they all felt they could go on again. They were very
high up now, and could see even more mountains towering
behind the ones they knew. It was a most magnificent sight.

'I feel very small and lost somehow, with all those great
mountains sitting there,' said Lucy-Ann, and the others felt
the same. 'Come on – let's go round the ledge now. We shall
soon see the road. Thank goodness this ledge isn't narrow.
It's almost wide enough to take a car.'

It was not so easy walking round the ledge as Lucy-Ann
thought, however, for there had been a fall of rocks there,
further along, and there was a good deal of scrambling
about to be done. They were thankful when they had got
over the rock-fall and come to smoother ground again.

The ledge rounded a bend in the mountainside, and then,
quite suddenly, the children saw the road below them. Yes,

it was really a road! They stood and looked at it in delight.

'I never thought I should be so pleased to see a road again,' said Dinah. 'The road out of the valley! The road to Somewhere at last!'

'Look,' said Lucy-Ann, 'it winds up from quite a long way down. We can't see where it goes to from here, because it's hidden round the bend.'

'You can see the pass, the Windy Pass, from here, though,' said Jack, pointing. 'See where this mountain and the next almost touch? That's where the pass must be – fairly high up and awfully narrow. I bet we'll have to go through it in single file.'

'No, we won't,' said Philip scornfully. 'It's bound to be wide enough to take a cart. It only looks narrow because we're far off.'

'Come on, let's get down to the road,' said Dinah, and began to climb down to it. They were about twenty feet above it.

'I say, isn't it overgrown with grass and weeds!' said Jack, astonished. 'That shows how little it has been used lately. Strange, isn't it? You'd think the people would put their only road out of the valley into some sort of order.'

'It's jolly peculiar, *I* think,' said Philip. 'Come on – we can at least see it's a road, even if it is overgrown with weeds.'

They walked along the road for some way. It wound upwards always, following long curves in and out on the slopes of the mountain. At last the children could clearly see where the Windy Pass must be, a narrow passage between the two mountains, theirs and the next.

It was cold so high up and the wind was very strong. If the children had not been warm with climbing they would have shivered. As it was, they were all as warm as toast.

'Now – round this next corner – and I bet we shall see the pass!' cried Jack. 'Then hurrah for the way out of this mysterious valley!'

They rounded the corner. Yes – there lay the pass – or what must once have been the pass. But it was a pass no longer.

Something had happened. The narrow way between the great mountains was blocked high with great rocks and black boulders. It was impassable.

At first the four children didn't quite take it in. They stood and stared in wonder.

'What's happened there?' said Jack at last. 'It looks like an earthquake or something. Did you ever see such a terrible mess?'

'Great holes have been blown in the rocky walls on either side of the pass,' said Philip. 'Look, even high up there are holes like craters.'

They stared in silence, and then Jack turned to the others. 'Do you know what I think has happened?' he said. 'Well, when enemies were here, fighting, they bombed the pass – and blocked it. All that devastation has been caused by bombs – I'm sure it has.'

'Yes, I think you're right, Jack,' said Philip. 'It's just what it looks like. Aeroplanes must have flown just over the pass, and dropped scores of bombs on the narrow road there. It's absolutely impassable.'

'Do you mean – we can't get out?' asked Lucy-Ann in a trembling voice. Philip nodded.

'Afraid so,' he said. 'Nobody could get over that steep, high, dangerous wall of blown up rocks. This explains why people haven't come along to live in this valley yet. I suppose most of those living here were killed, and the rest escaped over the pass. Then it was blown up and nobody could come back. Those men in the plane, Juan and the rest, must have got wind of some treasure hidden in the valley, and thought they would try to enter the place by plane. About the only way to enter it, too.'

Lucy-Ann sat down and cried. 'I'm so disappointed,' she

wailed. 'I thought we were going to escape from this horrid, lonely valley, I really did. But now we're still prisoners here – and n-n-n-nobody can come in to rescue us!'

The others sat down by Lucy-Ann, feeling rather desperate too. They stared hopelessly at the blocked pass. What a terrible blow! Just as they had so hoped they would be able to escape, and get to Julius, and tell him about the treasure.

'Let's have something to eat,' suggested Dinah. 'We'll feel better then. No wonder we feel a bit dumpy now.'

'Humpy dumpy,' said Kiki at once. That made them laugh.

'Idiot!' said Philip. '*You* don't care about a blocked up pass, do you, Kiki? You could fly over. It's a pity we can't tie a message to your leg and send you over to Julius for help.'

'Oooh – couldn't we do that?' said Lucy-Ann at once.

'No, silly! For one thing, Kiki would probably tear the message off her leg,' said Jack, 'and for another she'd never know who to go and look for. She's a clever bird, but not as clever as that.'

They felt a lot better after their meal. They ate it with their backs to the blocked pass. Nobody could bear to look at it.

'I suppose we'll have to go back to our cave,' said Dinah at last. 'Doesn't seem anything else to do really.'

'No, I suppose there isn't,' said Jack rather gloomily. 'What a sell, isn't it?'

They had a good long rest. The sun was very fierce, but the wind was so strong that they were never too hot. In fact Lucy-Ann went to a rock that sheltered her from the wind, because she felt too cool.

They started back after their rest. They were not nearly so cheerful and talkative as when they had set out that morning. The thought of having to stay in the lonely valley, after having such high hopes of escaping, was very damping to all of them.

Lucy-Ann looked so miserable that Jack tried to think of something to cheer her up. He thought of something really startling.

'Cheer up, Lucy-Ann,' he said. 'Maybe we'll find the treasure now, to make up for our disappointment.'

Lucy-Ann stopped and stared at him, thrilled. '*Really*?' she said. 'Oh, *Jack* – yes, let's look for the treasure ourselves now!'

Everyone stopped and thought about it for a few exciting moments. 'Well, why not?' said Philip. 'We can't get word about it to Julius, because we can't get over the pass. Those men have gone, and Otto is gone too. There's only us left. We might as well hunt for the treasure. It would be something exciting to do, to pass away the time.'

'How simply gorgeous!' cried Dinah. 'Just what I've always wanted to do – hunt for treasure. When shall we start? Tomorrow?'

'I say – suppose we really found it!' said Philip, looking thrilled. 'Should we get a share of it, I wonder?'

'What a good thing Otto gave you the map, Freckles!' said Dinah to Jack. She always called him Freckles when she felt in a very good humour. 'Let's have a look at it.'

Jack took it out of his pocket. He unfolded the sheet of paper and spread it out. Otto had marked it with compass directions, just as he had marked the map showing the way to the pass.

'See the things he has drawn or printed,' said Jack. 'See this funny shaped rock – it's shaped like a man in a cloak, with a ball-like head. If we saw that rock, we'd know it was a signpost to the treasure.'

'And what's this – a bent tree?' asked Dinah. 'Yes, but how are we to know where to look for them? We can't go wandering all over the mountainside looking for queer-shaped rocks and bent trees and things.'

'Of course not,' said Jack. 'We'd have to begin properly,

from the beginning – and the beginning is the waterfall we know. Otto drew a path from where the cowshed is to the waterfall, see – well, we can start right *at* the waterfall without bothering about the path. Then, from the top of the fall we must look for that bent tree, and walk to there. Then from the bent tree we look for this – let's see, what did he say that was? – oh yes, it's a stretch of smooth black rock – well, when we get there, we look next for a spring of water – and from there we look out for that funny shaped rock. Then somewhere about there is the treasure.'

'Golly!' said Lucy-Ann, her eyes nearly popping out of her head. 'Let's get back to the waterfall and start straight away. Come on!'

Jack folded up the map and looked round at the three excited faces. He grinned. 'The treasure won't be much use to us, cooped up in this valley as we are,' he said. 'But it will be something really thrilling to do.'

They set off once again, their minds busy with treasure-hunting. If only they could find what those men had been looking for and had not found! What would Bill say? He would wish to goodness he had been with them. He always said they fell into adventure after adventure.

When they got back to the waterfall, the sun had gone in, and huge black clouds hung over their mountain. Enormous drops of rain began to fall. The children gazed in disappointment at the lowering sky.

'Blow! said Philip. 'There's going to be a rain storm, I should think. No good going off treasure hunting in this. Better get into the cave before we get soaked. Here comes the rain properly!'

They only just got into their cosy cave in time. Then the rain pelted down in torrents, and added its voice to the roar of the waterfall.

'Rain all you like!' called Jack. 'But do be sunny to-morrow – we're going treasure hunting!'

# 20

## Signposts to the treasure

They slept very soundly indeed that night, for they were tired out. The rain fell all night long, but towards dawn the clouds cleared away, and the sky, when the sun rose, was a clear pale blue. Lucy-Ann liked it very much when she parted the soaking fern fronds and looked out.

'Everything's newly-washed and clean, even the sky,' she said. 'Lovely! Just look!'

'Just the day for a treasure hunt,' said Jack. 'I hope this sun will dry the grass quickly, or we shall get our feet soaked.'

'Good thing we brought so many tins out of the men's hut,' said Dinah, reaching down two or three. 'Are there still some in that bush where we first hid them, Jack?'

'Plenty,' said Jack. 'I took one or two to open for Otto the day before yesterday, but there are heaps left. We can go and get them some time.'

They tied back the fern fronds and ate their breakfast sitting at the front of the cave, looking out on the far mountains, backed by the sky, which was now turning a deeper blue.

'Well, shall we set off?' said Jack, when they had finished. 'Kiki, take your head out of that tin. You know it's completely empty.'

'Poor Kiki!' said Kiki. 'What a pity!'

They all scrambled out of the cave. Things were certainly drying fast in the hot summer sun. 'Look, those rocks are steaming!' said Lucy-Ann in surprise, pointing to some nearby rocks. So they were. They looked most peculiar with the steam rising up.

'Better take some food with us,' said Jack. 'Got some, Dinah?'

'Of course,' said Dinah. 'We can't come all the way back here for food.'

'We've got to get to where the waterfall begins, just as we did yesterday,' said Jack. 'Follow me, all of you. I know the way.'

They soon stood at the top of the waterfall, and once more watched the great gush of water surge out from the heart of the mountain. It seemed twice as big and turbulent as the day before.

'Well, I suppose the underground water has been swelled up because of last night's rain,' said Philip. 'And so the waterfall is bigger and stronger.'

'Yes, that's the reason,' said Jack, raising his voice to a shout because of the noise of the water. 'Kiki, stop screeching in my ear.'

The waterfall excited Kiki, and she made a terrible noise that morning. Jack would not have her on his shoulder after a while, because of her screeches. She flew off in a huff.

'Now, what about that bent tree?' said Dinah, remembering. By this time they were standing a little way above the beginning of the waterfall. 'I can't see any bent tree at all!'

'Oh, golly – don't say there isn't a bent tree!' groaned Jack, looking this way and that, all round and about and above his head. 'Gosh, there doesn't seem to be one, does there?'

There didn't. What few trees they could see were perfectly straight. Then Lucy-Ann gave a cry and pointed downwards. 'There it is, isn't it? – just below us, on the other side of the waterfall. Look!'

They all went to stand by Lucy-Ann, and looked. She was right. On the other side of the fall, some way below them, was a curiously bent tree. It was a birch tree, and why it should have grown so bent over was a puzzle. The wind was no stronger there than anywhere else. Anyway, it was decidedly bent and that was all that mattered.

They crossed above the beginning of the waterfall, clambering over the rocks, and then scrambled down on the other side of the fall. They reached the bent tree at last.

'First signpost,' said Jack.

'No second,' said Dinah. 'The waterfall is really the first.'

'Well, second then,' said Jack. 'Now for the third – a big stretch of flat black rock – a wall of it, I should think.'

They all looked in every direction for a stretch of black rock. This time it was Jack's keen eyes that spotted it. It was some way off, and looked difficult to reach, for it meant climbing along the steep face of the mountainside, which just there was very cliff-like.

Still, it had to be done, so they set off. It was easier after the first stretch, for there were all kinds of plants and bushes firmly rooted in the sloping cliff, and these could be used as handholds or footholds. Jack helped Lucy-Ann along, but Dinah scorned Philip's help, especially as she knew he had the lizard somewhere about him.

It took them at least half an hour of stiff scrambling and climbing to reach the wall of black rock, though actually, in distance, it was not so very far. They stood by the rock, panting.

'Funny shiny black rock,' said Jack, running his fingers over the smooth surface. 'Wonder what it is.'

'Oh, never mind,' said Dinah, impatient to get on. 'What's our next signpost? This is the third.'

'A spring of water,' said Philip. 'Isn't that right, Jack – or shall we look at the map?'

'No – I know it by heart,' said Jack. 'A spring of water is next. Not that I can see one at all – though I wish I could because I could do with a drink after that hot scramble. My hands are filthy, and so are my knees.'

'Yes, we could all do with a jolly good wash now,' said

Philip. 'A good old rub and a scrub.'

'Rubbenascrub,' said Kiki, and went off into one of her dreadful cackles.

'Stop it, Kiki,' said Jack. 'I'll give *you* a rubbenascrub in a minute.'

There was no spring of water to be seen. Lucy-Ann began to look very disappointed.

'Cheer up!' said Jack. 'We may not be able to *see* the spring from this wall of rock – but we can surely find it if it's anywhere near.'

'Let's listen,' suggested Dinah.

So they stood perfectly still and listened. 'Shhhhhh!' said Kiki annoyingly.

Jack smacked her on the beak. She gave a dismal squawk and sat silent. And, in the silence of the peaceful mountain-side, the children heard the tinkle-tinkle of water – a merry, gurgling noise, cheerful and friendly.

'I can hear it!' cried Lucy-Ann in delight. 'It comes from somewhere over there.'

She leapt across to a little thicket of trees, and there, hidden deep in the flower-strewn grass, bubbled a clear spring, trickling down the hillside, a tiny stream of crystal cold water.

'It starts just up there, look,' said Jack, and pointed to a big bush. The spring bubbled out from below the bush. 'Fourth signpost!'

'Now for the fifth – and last!' said Lucy-Ann excited. 'Oooh – do you honestly think we are getting near to the treasure? It's really not *very* far from our waterfall cave. I thought I could hear the faint, distant roar of the fall when I stood listening for the gurgling of the spring.'

'I thought I could too,' said Dinah. 'Now, what do we look for next?'

'The oddly shaped rock,' said Jack. 'You know – like a man in a long cloak, with a round head at the top.'

'Easy!' said Philip triumphantly, and pointed upwards. 'There it is – quite clear against the sky!'

They all looked up. Philip was right. There stood the curious-shaped rock, easy to see against the sky.

'Come on!' said Jack excitedly. 'Up we go! Come along, treasure hunters!'

They climbed up to where the odd-shaped rock stood. Other rocks lay about, but this one was much taller, and, because of its height and shape, it stood out among the others.

'Our last signpost!' said Jack. 'And now – where's the treasure?'

Ah, yes – where was the treasure? Lucy-Ann looked about the hillside as if she half expected it to be strewn there. The others began to search for a cave opening. But nobody could find anything.

'Why didn't you ask Otto exactly where to find the treasure, after coming to the last signpost?' complained Dinah, tired and disappointed, coming over to Jack.

'Well, I didn't know *we* were going to look for it, silly, did I?' said Jack. 'I thought Julius Muller was going to take charge of the treasure hunt. No doubt if he got as far as this he'd know where the treasure was all right.'

'Well, it's most awfully disappointing to come all this way, and read the map so well, and then not find a thing,' said Dinah, who was cross and tired. 'I'm fed up. I shan't hunt any more. You can all go on looking if you like, but I'm going to have a rest.'

She flung herself down, and lay flat, looking upwards at the steep mountainside above her. It was ridged with flat slabs of rock, sticking out here and there like ledges. Dinah examined them lazily with her eyes. Then she sat up suddenly.

'Hi!' she called to the others. 'Look up there!'

They came over to her and looked up. 'See those big

ledges of rock sticking out all the way up the cliff-side?' she said. 'Like shelves. Well, look halfway up – see one that sticks out rather far? Look underneath it. Is that a hole there?'

'It does look rather like a hole,' said Jack. 'Maybe a fox-hole, though. Still, it's the only sizeable hole hereabouts, so we'd better explore. I'll go up. Coming, Tufty?'

'Rather,' said Philip. 'It doesn't look difficult. Aren't you two girls coming too?'

Dinah forgot that she was fed up, and she joined in the climb to the hole under the ledge of rock. When they got there they found that it was a very big hole indeed. It could not possibly be seen from above, for the shelf of rock stuck right out over it and hid it. It could only be seen from one place below, at a certain angle – and that was the place where Dinah had flung herself down some time back.

'Bit of luck you happened to spot it, Dinah,' said Jack. 'We might have hunted all day and never found it. I wonder if this is the entrance to the *real* treasure-cave.'

They peered down. The hole yawned below them, dark and appearing rather vast. 'Where's my torch?' said Jack, and, taking it from his pocket, he switched it on.

The children gazed down into the hole. It seemed nothing but a hole. No treasure was there. But, as Jack swung his torch a little further down, Dinah thought she caught sight of a passage further back.

'I believe,' she said, almost falling into the hole in her excitement, 'I do believe it goes right back, into a passage.'

Kiki flew off Jack's shoulder and disappeared into the hole. A mournful voice floated up to them.

'What's down there, Kiki?' called Jack.

'Three blind mice,' answered Kiki, solemnly and untruthfully. 'Three blind mice. Pop!'

'You're a fibber,' said Jack. 'Anyway – down we go to find the . . . '

'Three blind mice,' said Kiki, and went off into an imitation of Lucy-Ann's giggle.

# 21

## The strange caves

Jack went down the hole first. He lowered himself right in, and only had to drop about a foot to the ground below.

'Lucy-Ann, you come next,' he said, and helped her down. Then came the others, excited and eager. Had they really found the treasure cave?

'It simply must be the hiding place for the treasure!' said Jack. 'There isn't another hole or cave anywhere. Now, let me flash my torch round a bit.'

At the back of the hole, as Dinah had thought, there was a passage – quite a wide one, and fairly high. A very tall man could have walked down it with ease.

'Come on!' said Jack, his voice shaking with excitement. 'We're getting warm!'

They followed him down the passage, Kiki sitting on his shoulder. Lucy-Ann held on to his sleeve, half fearful of what they might find.

The passage was wide and high all the way along, but wound about a little. It went downwards, and kept more or less in the same direction, for all its windings – that is, towards the heart of the mountain.

Suddenly the passage came to an abrupt end. Jack paused, and gasped. In front of him was a most extraordinary sight.

His torch shone brightly on to an unending mass of brilliant columns, hanging from the high roof of a cave. Whatever could they be?

Lucy-Ann clutched his arm and gasped too. She stared at

the shining white things. She saw that other white columns were growing up from the floor of the cave too. Some had met the hanging ones, and had joined, so that it seemed as if the cave roof was being supported by pillars.

'Jack! What is it? Is it the treasure?' whispered Lucy-Ann.

'It's icicles, isn't it?' said Dinah in an awed tone. 'I've never seen anything so beautiful in my life! Look at them hanging down – so still and white and lovely!'

'No – they're not icicles,' said Jack. 'They are stalactites – at least, the hanging ones are. They're not made of ice, either – but of limestone, I think. My word – what a sight!'

The children stood quite still and gazed their fill at the silent, beautiful cave. Its roof was as high as a cathedral, and the graceful stalactites hung down from it in dozens, gleaming in the light of Jack's torch.

'The ones growing up from the floor are stalagmites, I think,' said Jack. 'Aren't they, Philip? Do you know anything about them? I've never in my life seen anything like this before!'

'Yes – they're stalagmites,' said Philip. 'I remember seeing pictures of them. Stalactites and stalagmites. Gosh, what a sight!'

Kiki tried to say the two words and couldn't. Even she seemed to be awed by the amazing and unexpected discovery.

'Oh, look!' said Lucy-Ann suddenly, and pointed to what looked like an old, old shawl carved in ivory. 'Look – this has grown here too – it's just like a shawl – even to the pattern in it! And look at that sort of gate over there – all carved too! Surely somebody made them – surely they didn't just grow!'

'Well – they *formed*,' said Jack, trying to explain. 'You know – just as the crystals in a snowflake form. They don't grow because they're not alive – they *form*.'

Lucy-Ann couldn't quite understand. Secretly she

thought that all the marvellous hanging pillars had grown, and then got frozen in their beauty.

I thought this must be the treasure!' she said, half laughing.

'I'm not surprised,' said Jack. 'It's too beautiful for words. Fancy finding a cave like this! It's like an enormous underground cathedral – it just wants an organ to begin playing a grand and magnificent hymn.'

'There's a kind of path down the middle,' said Dinah. 'I don't know if it's just a natural path, Jack, or whether it has been made by man. Do you see what I mean?'

'Yes,' said Jack, flashing his torch along it. 'Bit of both, I think. Well – shall we go on? There's no treasure here.'

They went along the middle of the great silent hall, surrounded on all sides by the hanging icicle-like pillars. Lucy-Ann pointed out many that had joined with columns growing from the ground.

'The drops of water from the stalactites must have dripped to the ground, and made stalagmites form there, growing up to meet the column above,' said Philip. 'They must have taken ages and ages to form – hundreds of years. I say – no wonder this cave feels awfully old to us. I feel as if there is no Time here at all – no years, or days of the week or hours – just nothing.'

Lucy-Ann didn't like that very much. It gave her a strange feeling of being only a dream, and not real. She took hold of Jack's arm and was glad to feel its nice, solid warmth.

They walked slowly to the end of the enormous cave. A great archway stood there, and that too was set with stalactites, which, however, did not hang far down. The children could walk under them with ease.

'This archway is quite like a tunnel,' said Philip. His voice sounded big and hollow there and made them all jump. Kiki gave a mournful cough, which was magnified to a hollow, giant cough that startled everyone very much.

They came to another cave. The roof of this was not so high as the one before, and only small, icicle-like stalactites hung from it.

'Do those stalactites shine in the dark?' asked Dinah suddenly. 'I thought I saw something glowing in the corner over there.'

Jack switched off his torch – and immediately the children gasped. For up in the roof and over the walls there glowed thousands of tiny stars. They were green and blue, and shone and flickered in a most enchanting manner.

'Gracious! What are they?' whispered Dinah, amazed. 'Are they alive?'

The boys didn't know. They watched the shimmering flickering stars, that seemed to go in and out like elfin lights. 'Might be a kind of glowworm,' said Jack. 'Aren't they lovely?'

He put on his torch again and the roof shone brightly in the yellow-white light. The stars disappeared.

'Oh, do put your torch out!' begged Lucy-Ann. 'I want to watch those stars a bit longer. I never saw anything so fascinating in my life! They shine like phosphorescence – all blue and green and green and blue; look how they flicker off and on. Oh, I wish I could take a hundred back with me and put them on my bedroom ceiling at home!'

The others laughed, but they too thought that the shining, flickering stars were most entrancing to watch. Jack did not put on his torch again until each had gazed his fill.

'That's two simply wonderful caves,' said Lucy-Ann with a sigh. 'What will the next one be? I really do feel as if we'd discovered Aladdin's Cave, or something like that!'

A long passage, leading downwards, led out of the cave of stars, as Lucy-Ann named it.

'We found a cave of echoes, a cave of stalactites and a cave of stars,' she said. 'I like this part of our adventure. Now I'd like to find a cave of treasure.'

The tunnel they were in was wide and high like the first passage they had entered. Jack's torch suddenly shone brightly on something on the floor. He stopped.

'Look at that!' he said. 'What is it?'

Dinah bent to pick it up. 'It's a brooch,' she said. 'A brooch without its pin. The pin's gone. It must have broken and the brooch fell off whoever was wearing it. Isn't it perfectly lovely?'

It certainly was. It was a large gold brooch, about three inches wide, set with brilliant red stones, as red as blood.

'Are they rubies?' said Dinah in awe. 'Look how they glow! Oh, Jack, do you think this is a bit of the treasure?'

'Probably,' said Jack, and at once excitement caught hold of the children again, and their hearts began to beat fast. A ruby brooch, set in carved gold! What would the other treasure be? Wonderful visions arose in the children's minds and they stumbled on their way eagerly, their eyes searching the ground for any other gleaming jewel.

'If we could find a cave of jewels,' said Lucy-Ann. 'Oooooh – all gleaming like stars and suns! That's what I would love.'

'We might find something like that,' said Dinah. 'If we do, I shall deck myself from head to foot with them and pretend I'm a princess.'

The passage went on and on, still leading downwards, but, when Jack looked at his compass, he saw that he was no longer going into the heart of the mountain, but in the opposite direction. He hoped they wouldn't suddenly come out into the daylight without finding the cave of treasure.

Suddenly they came to steps that led downwards. They were carved out of the solid rock, steep, wide steps that curved as the passage curved.

'Almost a spiral stairway,' said Jack. 'Where are we coming to now?'

There were about twenty of the steps. Then came an enormous door, made of some kind of stout wood, set with iron studs. The children stood and stared at it.

A door! What was behind it? Was it locked and bolted? Who had put it there, and why? Was it to shut in the treasure cave and guard it?

There was no handle to turn. There was not even a lock to be seen. There were great bolts, but these were not shot into place.

'How can you open a door without a handle?' said Jack in despair. He pushed at the door, but it remained quite firm.

'Kick it, like we did the door of the hut,' said Philip, and Jack kicked it hard. But the door did not open.

They stared at it in despair. To come so far and then to be stopped by a door! It was too bad. Jack shone his torch all over the door, from top to bottom.

Lucy-Ann's sharp eyes noticed something. 'See that iron stud?' she said, pointing. 'It's much brighter than the others. I wonder why.'

Jack shone his torch on it, and saw that it was slightly bigger than the others – and also, as Lucy-Ann said, it was brighter, as if it had had some handling.

He pressed it. Nothing happened. He banged on it with a stone. No result at all.

'Let *me* try,' said Philip, and pushed Jack aside. 'Shine your torch on it closely. That's right.'

Philip took hold of the iron stud and shook it. It seemed to give a little. He shook it again. Nothing happened. Then he thought of twisting it.

It twisted round very easily indeed. There was a loud click – and the door swung slowly open. Jack switched off his torch, afraid that anyone in the cave might see them – though if anyone had been there surely they would have heard the bangs and kicks at the door.

The door now stood wide open. A dim light shone beyond, showing another cave. Lucy-Ann clutched Jack's arm in fright.

'It's full of people,' she whispered. 'Look!'

# 22

# The treasure at last!

The four children stared breathlessly through the open door. They saw something that made them feel very creepy.

In the dim light figures stood about all over the place. Their eyes gleamed queerly, and their teeth shone in the darkness. Their arms and necks flashed and glittered with jewels.

The children clutched one another in fright. Who were these strange, silent folk, standing about with gleaming eyes, covered with jewels?

The people in the cave did not move. They did not speak a word either. Not one of them was sitting. All were standing. They stood there, some turned towards the frightened children, some turned away. Why didn't they speak? Why didn't they point to the children and say, 'Look — who's there?'

Lucy-Ann began to shiver. 'Let's go back. I don't like them. They're not alive. Only their eyes are.'

Kiki suddenly gave a squawk, left Jack's shoulder, and flew to the shoulder of one of the nearby figures, a woman dressed in clothes that glowed richly in the half-light of the cave.

Still the woman did not move. How strange! The children suddenly felt much better when they saw that Kiki did not seem in the least afraid of the queer company.

'Polly put the kettle on,' said Kiki, and pecked at the hair of the woman he was sitting on.

The children held their breath again. What would the woman do to Kiki – enchant her with her strange eyes, cast a spell on her and turn her into stone? Perhaps all these people had been turned into stone?

'Let's go back,' said Lucy-Ann urgently. 'I don't like this cave. I don't like these people, or their horrid gleaming eyes.'

Jack suddenly jumped down the step that was below the great open door. He marched boldly into the silent cave. Lucy-Ann squealed and tried to catch his sleeve.

Jack walked right up to the woman on whose shoulder Kiki sat. He peered closely at her. He looked into her wide open glittering eyes. He touched her hair. Then he turned to the horrified children.

'What do you think? She's a statue – all dressed up beautifully – with real hair – and jewels for eyes! What do you think of that?'

The others could not believe it – but they were very thankful to hear Jack's words, and to see him wandering among the crowd of still figures, apparently quite un-harmed.

Philip and Dinah stepped down into the cave of figures too, but Lucy-Ann still did not quite dare to. She watched the others looking at the strange, beautiful statues, and tried to make herself join them.

At last she screwed up her courage to step down into the cave. She looked fearfully at the woman on whose shoulder Kiki had flown. Yes – Jack was right. She was nothing but a beautiful statue, with a finely-moulded face and a cloud of dark hair. She had magnificent jewels for eyes, and her glittering teeth were exquisite jewels too. Round her neck were golden chains, set with precious stones, and her waxen fingers gleamed with rings. Round her waist was the most beautiful belt that Lucy-Ann had ever seen, carved and set

141

with shining red and blue stones.

There were dozens of these statues in the cave, some of men and some of women. Some of them carried small babies in their arms, fat, smiling babies dressed in the most exquisite clothes, set with thousands of tiny pearls.

It was the babies that gave Jack the clue to what the statues were.

'Do you know what they are?' he said. 'They are statues taken from churches somewhere in this country. This one represents Mary, the mother of Jesus – and the little baby is meant to be Jesus Himself. That's why they are adorned with such lovely jewels. People have spent heaps of money on them to make them beautiful.'

'Oh yes – and some of them are carried in processions at church festivals,' said Dinah, remembering how her mother had once described such a festival to her. 'Well, fancy – statues taken from churches! Whatever for?'

'Stolen, I should think,' said Jack. 'Stolen by people who took advantage of the troubled war-times, and hid them here – meaning to collect them when they had a chance.'

'They must be worth a lot of money,' said Philip, fingering the magnificent jewels. 'Gosh, I did get a terrible fright when I first saw them! I honestly thought they were real people.'

'So did I,' said Lucy-Ann, who had now recovered. 'I couldn't bear them to stand so still and silent. I nearly screamed with fright!'

'We were idiots not to guess they were statues,' said Dinah. 'I say – where does the light come from that lights these statues? It's only a faint sort of light, but it's enough to see them by quite well.'

Jack looked all round. 'It must be a sort of phosphorescent glow from the walls and roof of the cave,' he said. 'It's rather a greenish light, isn't it?'

'I say – there's another archway here!' called Philip, from

beyond the statues. 'Come and see. I believe there's another cave beyond.'

They all went to see. Through the archway was yet another cave, lighted with the same dim, greenish glow. In it were stacked great square, oblong or round, flat things. There were no statues at all. The children went to see what the flat things were.

'Pictures!' said Jack, as he tried to swing one to face him. 'Enormous ones! Where did they come from? Churches too, do you think?'

'Oh – picture galleries very likely,' said Philip. 'Maybe they are famous and quite priceless pictures – very old, too. Look at that one – it looks terribly old-fashioned. My word – these things may be worth a fortune – heaps of fortunes! I remember reading not so long ago about pictures that were worth two or three million pounds!'

'I didn't know there was so much money in the world,' said Lucy-Ann, startled. She gazed in awe at the dusty, dim old pictures, tracing their great carved frames with her finger.

'Some of the pictures have been taken out of their frames to bring them here,' said Jack, pulling at a roll of thick canvas. 'Look, this one must have been cut from its frame and rolled up so as to be taken away easily.'

There were about fifty rolls of canvas besides the framed pictures. Jack shone his torch on to many of the pictures, but none of the children thought the subjects interesting. So many were portraits of rather fat and stern-looking men. Others were scenes from the Bible, or from old legends.

'Well, this really is a find!' said Jack. 'I bet if those men could have found these, they would have made a simply enormous fortune selling them.'

'Of course – they were after all these,' said Philip. 'And that's what those crates were for. To pack them in. They

143

meant to crate them carefully and fly them away little by little. What a brain wave on their part!'

'And Otto fooled them!' said Jack. 'Took them to a rock-fall and said the treasure cave was behind it – so they meekly gave up and flew off. What idiots!'

'And *we* found everything!' rejoiced Lucy-Ann. 'Oh, I wish we could tell Bill!'

'Are there any more caves?' wondered Jack, and walked over to the end of the second cave. 'Yes! Here's another archway and another cave. Books here! And old documents! Come and look!'

'Old books are sometimes as precious and as rare as old pictures,' said Philip, gazing round at the piles of enormous, heavily-bound books. 'I say – look at this one! It's a bible, but in a foreign language. Isn't it enormous? Look at the old printing!'

'These really *are* caves of treasure,' said Jack. 'Treasure from churches, libraries and picture galleries. I suppose the war-lords must have hidden them away, meaning to get them when peace came and make a lot of money out of their loot. How awful to steal things like this, though!'

'There's a little cave here, just off this book-cave,' called Dinah, who was exploring by herself. 'There is a big chest here. Oh, and another – and another! What's in them, I wonder?'

Jack came over to her and lifted up the heavy lid of one chest. He stared down in surprise at the glittering coins piled together in the chest.

'Gold!' he said. 'The gold coinage of some country, I can't tell which. I've never seen gold coins like these before. My goodness, there's a fortune in that box too – and in that chest, and that one! Fortunes everywhere!'

'It's like a dream,' said Lucy-Ann, and she sat down on one of the chests. 'It really is. A cave of gleaming icicles, or stalags— whatever you call them! A cave of stars! A cave of glittering, jewelled statues! A cave of pictures, and a cave of old books! And now a cave of gold! I can't believe it.'

It did seem extraordinary. They all sat down on the oak chests and rested. The dim greenish light still shone everywhere, a kind of pale glow that did not seem to come from anywhere in particular, and yet was everywhere.

It was very quiet there. The children could hear themselves breathing, and a cough from Jack sounded startlingly loud.

Then another sound came through the stillness – a sound so completely unexpected and surprising that nobody could believe their ears!

'Cluck! Cluck-luck-luck!'

'Whatever's that?' said Lucy-Ann at last. 'It sounded like a hen clucking.'

'Must have been old Kiki,' said Jack, looking around for her. But she was just near by, sitting on another chest, humped up, looking rather dismal. She had had enough of caves. The children stared at her. Could it have been Kiki?

They listened to see if she would make the same noise again. But she didn't stir. And then the noise came once more, quite clearly, from another direction altogether.

'Cluck-luck-lurrrrrrk! Cluck-luck-lurrrrk!'

'It *is* a hen!' said Jack, jumping up. 'Making an egg-laying noise. But – a hen – in these caves! It's impossible!'

All the children were now on their feet. Dinah pointed to some steps at the back of the little cave of gold. 'That's where the noise comes from,' she said.

'I'll go up first and see if it really *is* a hen,' said Jack. 'I can't believe it.'

He went cautiously up the steps, and at the same time the clucking began again. Kiki woke up and heard it in astonishment. She immediately began to cluck too, which evidently astonished the hidden clucker, who got very excited and let off a perfect volley of clucks.

Jack came to the top of the steps. There was another door there, but not a very stout one. It was ajar. He pushed it open a little more, very slowly, so that he might see in without attracting attention, though he did not expect to see anything but a hen.

What he saw transfixed him with astonishment. Philip dug his fingers into his back.

'Go on, Jack – what's up?'

Jack turned round to the others. 'I say,' he said in a half whisper, 'it's awfully odd – but there's a little cell-like room up here – furnished – table and chairs and a lighted lamp! And – there's a meal on the table!'

'Come down quickly, then,' whispered Dinah. 'We don't want to bump into anyone. It must be someone who's guarding the treasure till the others come to get it. Come down!'

But it was too late. A curious, quavering voice came from the cell-like room into which Jack had peeped. A few strange words reached them – but they couldn't understand a single one. *Now* what was going to happen?

# 23

# The guardians of the treasure

The children stood absolutely still, holding their breath. Who was there, in that little room at the top of the steps? The voice came again, repeating the words that the children could not understand.

Then to the top of the little flight of steps came a brown hen! It stood there, its head on one side, peering down at the children. 'Cluck!' it said, in a friendly kind of voice. 'Cluck-luck!'

'Cluck!' said Kiki at once.

Lucy-Ann clutched Dinah. 'Was it the hen talking before?' she whispered in amazement.

It wasn't, of course. The quavering voice came again, and to the children's surprise it sounded really frightened.

Nobody came to where Jack stood almost at the top of the steps. The boy screwed up his courage and marched into the little room.

At the other end of it, under a small archway or rock, stood an old, old man. Behind him was a woman, just as old, but more bent. They stared at Jack in amazement, and then, turning to one another, they poured out a stream of hurried words that the children could not understand at all.

Lucy-Ann wondered what Jack was doing up in the little room. Somebody ought to be with him. She went up the steps and joined Jack. The two old people stared at the red-haired freckled child, so like Jack.

Then the old woman made a crooning noise, pushed past her husband and went over to Lucy-Ann. She put her arms round her and kissed her. Then she patted her hair. Lucy-Ann was surprised and not very pleased. Who was this funny old woman who suddenly seemed so affectionate?

She called to the others. 'Dinah! Philip! Come along up! It's two old people here with their hen!'

Soon all four children were in the little underground room. As soon as the old man heard them talking, he joined in eagerly, speaking English in a strange, clipped way.

'Ah, ah! You are English children! That is goot, very goot. Once, long time ago, I was in your so beautiful country. I was in a big London hotel.'

'Thank goodness he speaks English,' said Philip. 'I say – what are they doing here, with the treasure? Are they in league with the other men?'

'Have to find out,' said Jack. 'They seem quite harmless, anyhow. But there may be others.' He turned to the old man.

The old woman was still making a fuss of Lucy-Ann. Evidently they had not set eyes on children for a long time.

'Who else is here besides you?' demanded Jack.

'Just me and Elsa, my old wife, and our hen Martha,' answered the old man. 'We guard all those things in the caves, till the day when they go back to their right homes. May that day come soon!'

'I don't believe the poor old things know that the war was over long ago,' said Jack to the others, in a low voice. 'I wonder who left them here to guard these things.' He turned to the old man again. 'Who told you to guard these things?' he asked.

'Julius Muller,' said the old man promptly. 'Ah, what a great man! How he worked against the enemy, even when they were shooting and bombing and burning in our valley! It was he who discovered that the enemy was using our mountain caves to hide away these treasures – treasures stolen from our churches and many other places.'

'Just what we thought,' said Philip, intensely interested. 'Go on – tell us more.'

'Then the people fled from our valley,' said the old man. 'Many were killed. The valley was empty, all save me and Elsa, my old wife. We hid with our hens and our pig, and no one found us. Then one day Julius Muller found us and ordered us to come here, by a way he knew, and guard the treasure – not for the enemy, no – but for him and the people! He said that one day the enemy would be defeated and would flee away – and then he and the others would come back to find the treasure – but he has not come.'

'He can't,' said Jack. 'The pass is blocked. No one can get in or out of this valley now – except by aeroplane. The war has been over a long time. But bad people are after the treasure – people who have heard it is hidden here, and have come to steal it.'

The old fellow looked scared and bewildered, as if he only

half understood what Jack was telling him. The children thought that he must have lived so long underground that his mind could not take in much news from the outer world. To him, his wife, the treasure, and perhaps his hen, were the only things that mattered.

'Do you live here, in this room?' asked Lucy-Ann. 'Where do you get your food from? Does your hen like living underground?'

'There are great stores of food here,' said the old man. 'There is even corn for Martha, the hen. When we first came here, we had six hens and our pig. But the pig died. And one by one the hens died. Only Martha is left. She does not lay many eggs now. Perhaps one in fourteen days.'

'Cluck,' said Martha in a proud voice. She was evidently proud of her one egg a fortnight.

Kiki repeated the cluck and then went off into a series of quacks. The hen looked surprised and alarmed. So did the two old people.

'Shut up, Kiki,' said Jack. 'You're showing off.'

'What is that bird?' asked the old man. 'Is it a – how do you call it? – a parrot?'

'Yes,' said Jack. 'She's mine. Always goes with me everywhere. But I say – don't you want to know how *we* came here?'

'Ah, yes, of course!' said the old man. 'It is all so surprising, you understand – and my wits are dull now – I cannot take in many things at once. You must tell me about yourselves, please. Wife, what about some food for these children?'

Elsa did not understand and the old man repeated what he said in her own language. She nodded and smiled a kind toothless smile. Taking Lucy-Ann by the hand, she went over to where tins and jars stood on a rocky ledge.

'She's very keen on Lucy-Ann,' said Philip. 'She can't fuss over her enough.'

The old man heard and understood. 'We had a little granddaughter,' he said. 'So like this little girl, with red hair and a sweet face. She lived with us. And one day the enemy came and took her away and we never saw her again. So now my wife sees her little lost one in your sister. You must excuse her, for maybe she really thinks her small Greta has come back.'

'Poor old things!' said Dinah. 'What an awful life they must have led – lost under this mountain, guarding a treasure for Julius Muller, waiting for him for ages, not knowing what had happened outside in the world! If we hadn't come, they might never have come out again!'

To the children's delight, Elsa got them a really fine meal. She would not let poor Lucy-Ann leave her side, though, so the little girl had to trot everywhere with her. Jack told the old man a little of their own story, though it was plain that the old fellow did not really follow it all. His wits were dull, as he said, and he could not really understand all this sudden news from a world he had almost forgotten.

Kiki enjoyed herself enormously. Martha, the hen, was obviously used to keeping the old couple company and pecked about under the table, brushing against everyone's legs. Kiki climbed down to join her, and kept up an interested, if one-sided conversation with her.

'How many times have I told you to wipe your feet?' she asked Martha. 'Blow your nose. Put the kettle on.'

'Cluck,' answered Martha politely.

'Humpy dumpy,' went on Kiki, evidently anxious to teach Martha a few nursery rhymes now. 'See how they run! Quack, quack, quack, quack!'

The hen looked surprised, ruffled up her feathers and stared at Kiki. 'Cluck, luck, luck,' she said, and pecked up a few crumbs.

Lucy-Ann and the others giggled at this conversation. Then Lizzie also thought she would join the company, as there was plenty of food going. She ran down Philip's sleeve and appeared on the table, much to the old woman's alarm.

'Meet dizzy Lizzie,' said Philip politely.

'I say – they must think we're queer visitors!' said Dinah, keeping a watchful eye on Lizzie in case she came any nearer. 'Walking in like this – with a parrot and a lizard – and staying to dinner!'

'I don't think they are bothering much,' said Philip. 'Just enjoying the change. It must be nice to have company after being alone so long.'

When they had finished the meal, the old woman spoke to her husband. He turned to the children.

'My wife says, are you tired? Would you like a rest? We have a beautiful place to rest in, when we want to enjoy the sun.'

This surprised the children very much. The sun! How did these old people ever see the sun – unless they went through all the cave and passages to the hole that gave on to the mountainside?

'Where do you go to rest then?' asked Jack.

'Come,' said the old man, and led him out of the little cell-like room. Elsa took Lucy-Ann by the hand. They all followed the old man. He went along a broad passage, hollowed out of the rock.

'I should think most of these tunnels were hollowed out by underground rivers at some time or other,' said Jack. 'Then they took a different course, and the tunnels dried up, and became these passages, linking all the caves together.'

The passage twisted a little and then quite suddenly came into daylight. The children found themselves on a flat ledge of rock, hung about by ferns and other plants, full in the sun. How simply delicious!

'Another way into the treasure caves,' said Dinah. But she was wrong. Nobody could possibly enter the caves by way of the ledge. The ledge of rock jutted over a great precipice that fell sheer down many hundreds of feet. No one, not even a goat, could climb up or down to it. It was, as the old man said, a fine, sunny resting place – but that was all.

Martha pecked about on the ledge of rock, though what she could find there the children couldn't imagine. Kiki sat near by and watched her. She had formed a firm friendship with Martha. The children rather liked Martha themselves. She was such a nice, plump little thing, friendly and natural, and as much of a pet to the old couple as Kiki was to them.

They all lay down in the sun. It was delicious to feel its warm rays after being so long underground. As they lay there they heard something rumbling in the distance.

'The waterfall,' said Lucy-Ann. 'Fancy – we must be fairly near it, if we can hear it!'

They lay there sleepily. The old fellow sat on a rock near by, smoking a pipe. He seemed very contented. Elsa had disappeared.

'Isn't it strange to think we've found the treasure – and can't do anything about it at all!' said Dinah. 'We're stuck here. No way of getting word to anyone. And never will have, as far as I can see, till the pass into the valley is unblocked – and that may not be for ages!'

'Oh dear – don't say such gloomy things,' begged Lucy-Ann. 'Anyway, the men are gone. That's one good thing. I felt awfully afraid when they were in the valley too. Thank goodness they've gone!'

She spoke too soon. There came a familiar throbbing noise – and the children sat up at once.

'The plane's back! Blow! Those men will be about again now – and maybe they've even got the real truth out of Otto – where the treasure *really* is!' said Jack. 'We shall have to be jolly careful now.'

# 24

## Juan finds the caves

The children held a council of war. What would be the best thing to do? Suppose the men did know the way into the treasure caves now, and came to them? They would begin to take away the treasure, that was certain.

'And we can't stop them,' said Philip. 'They are jolly tough men. They wouldn't let a pack of children and two old people prevent them from taking what they wanted. I can't think why they've come back unless it is to search for the treasure again and find it this time.'

Everyone agreed with Jack. 'If only we could escape and get news to Bill,' sighed Philip. 'But there simply isn't a way.'

The plane had not come into sight – they had only heard the sound of its engines. The old man did not seem to have heard anything at all. The children decided not to tell him, in case he got into a panic.

'What do you think it would be best for us to do?' said Philip. 'Stay here with the old couple and see if the men do come and take anything away? We can hide somewhere quite easily. Or go back to our own fern cave beyond the waterfall? I always felt safe there. And we've got plenty of food there too.'

'There's plenty here,' said Dinah. 'Let's stay here. After all, if the men do come, we can hide in that stalactite cave – there are plenty of hiding places there, behind those frozen columns. They won't see us. One of us could always be on guard there, to see who comes in or out.'

'Perhaps you're right,' said Jack. 'We must just wait and see what happens. Once the men really do find the treasure caves, there will be a lot coming and going – taking the treasure to the plane – taking off with it in the air – coming back again to fetch more – and so on.'

'Shouldn't be surprised if they bring more planes here, as soon as they've discovered exactly where the treasure is,' said Philip. 'It would be a slow business taking one or two crates at a time.'

'Lucy-Ann is asleep,' said Dinah. 'I think I'll snooze too. It's so lovely here in the sun. Those men won't be along yet, so nobody needs to be on guard in the caves.'

'It would be almost better to be on guard at the entrance,' said Philip thoughtfully. 'Then we could spot anyone in plenty of time.'

'Yes, that's a much better idea,' said Jack, settling down to snooze too. 'I'm sure the men won't be along today. The sun's going down. They'll wait till tomorrow.'

That night the children spent in the old couple's 'bed-room.' It was a smallish cave leading off from their 'sitting room,' where the children had had their meal. In the 'bed-room' was a pile of rugs, spotlessly clean, and the old people insisted on giving up this room to the children.

'We can sleep in chairs,' said the old man. 'That will be no hardship.'

The old woman covered Lucy-Ann up carefully and even kissed her goodnight. 'She really thinks I'm Greta, her lost grandchild,' said Lucy-Ann. 'I just can't stop her making a fuss of me, because I'm so sorry for her.'

In the morning, after another good meal, Jack said he was going to take first watch at the entrance to the passage that led to the caves. Philip was to take second watch, two hours later.

The boy settled himself down on the edge of the hole, under the big slab of rock that stuck out from the hillside. It was a fine sunny morning. The others thought they would go and examine some of the statues in the statue cave, and the old man said he would tell them their histories, and where they had come from.

Jack sat there, gazing out down the hillside. He could see a long way. He could see scores of high mountains around, one behind the other. The pine forests on them looked like short grass. He put his field glasses to his eye to watch the birds around.

It was a disappointing district for wild birds. There seemed to be very few. Jack swung his glasses from side to side of the hill, examining everything.

And then he suddenly got a tremendous shock. He had trained his glasses on to a bush, behind which he thought he had seen a quick movement. He had wondered if some bird or animal was hiding there.

He saw no bird. Instead, he saw the head and shoulder of Juan – and Juan was gazing steadily up at him through a pair of field glasses, just as Jack was gazing down at him through field glasses too!

Jack was simply petrified. He stared down through his glasses, and Juan stared up, each seeing the other quite clearly. So Juan had come once more to seek the treasure! Had he come to that cliff-side by chance – or had he got the same map from Otto that Jack had had?

'I've given the show away properly now,' thought Jack angrily. 'I've only got to pop into this hole and he'll know where the entrance is at once. But if I wander away on the hillside, he'll be after me. What a fix I'm in!'

Juan did not take his eyes off Jack. He knelt there by the bush, his field glasses fixed on the boy, watching his every movement.

'He can't possibly see the hole that I'm sitting on the edge of,' thought Jack. 'I think perhaps it would be best if I left this place and began to climb up the hillside. If I do, and Juan follows, he may miss the hole altogether.'

He was about to do this, when Philip leapt up beside him.

'My turn now, Freckles,' said Philip. 'Hallo, what are you looking at?'

'Pity you came just then,' said Jack. 'There is Juan down there, Philip — and he's got his glasses trained on to me — and on you too now! I was just about to crawl up the hillside to make him chase me, and perhaps miss this hole, when you came. Now he'll know there's a cave here and he'll be up in no time.'

'Golly!' said Philip, alarmed. 'We'd better warn the others at once then.'

'Yes, it's the only thing to do now,' said Jack, and he jumped back into the hole. 'Come on. It won't take Juan long to be up here. Blow! Why didn't I think he might be about already?'

They made their way quickly along the passage and through the many caves. They came to the little cell-like room and found the others there. Jack hurriedly told them what had happened.

'We must hide,' he said. But the old couple did not seem to take this in. They would not hide.

'We have nothing to be afraid of,' said the old man in a dignified manner. 'They will not hurt us.'

'You have plenty to be afraid of,' said Jack desperately. 'Do come and hide!'

But they wouldn't. Jack could not waste any more time in arguing, because he wanted to get the girls to safety. He hurried them off.

'In the cave of stalactites?' asked Dinah. Jack nodded. But when he came to the cave of silent statues, he paused. Wouldn't this be a better place? Suppose they all stood at the back, in the dim shadows, and posed like statues? Would anyone notice them? It was worth trying.

'Take shawls off some of the figures,' said the boy. 'Wrap them round you. Stand quite still right at the back there.'

It didn't take long to drape themselves and stand right at the back. 'Do you remember that game called statues that we used to play?' whispered Lucy-Ann. 'You had to stand quite still, or you were caught. I feel like that now.'

'Well, be sure you stand still or you *will* be caught,' said Jack. 'Sh! Isn't that somebody?'

'Shhhhh!' said Kiki at once. Jack smacked her on her beak.

'Be quiet! Do you want to give us away, silly bird?'

Kiki opened her beak to squawk and then thought better of it. She flew off somewhere and disappeared. Jack was quite glad to see her go, for he didn't want her chattering and attracting attention to them.

A noise came from the tunnel beyond. Somebody was already there. It must be Juan.

'He's already gone through the cave of stalactites and the cave of stars,' whispered Philip. 'Now he's in the tunnel leading here. He'll be at the door in a minute. Pity we didn't shut it. He might not have guessed how to twist that iron stud to get it open.'

The door was almost closed, but not shut. As the children watched it, in the dim greenish glow of the cave, they saw it slowly pushed open. Then the gleaming barrel of a revolver came round it. Juan was evidently taking no chances.

Lucy-Ann gulped. Oh dear! She hoped the gun wouldn't go off. She didn't like guns at all.

The door was opened wide and Juan stood there, revolver in hand. He gasped when he saw the silent figures standing about, their curious eyes gleaming.

'Put your hands up!' said Juan sharply, to the statues. The statues did nothing of the sort. Juan's hand trembled. The children guessed he was feeling panicky as they had felt when they too had first seen the strange silent company.

'Wipe your feet!' ordered a sharp voice, and the children jumped violently. It was Kiki. She was sitting just above

Juan, on a ledge of rock.

'Who's there?' shouted Juan. 'I tell you I'll shoot if anyone moves.'

The statues didn't move – not even the four live ones.

'Who's there?' called Juan again.

'Three blind mice,' answered Kiki, and went off into a terrible cackle of laughter. It was almost too much for Juan. He backed a little, and tried to see which of the statues was talking.

'Pop goes the weasel!' said Kiki, and then began to cluck like Martha. Juan's hand trembled again. But he advanced a little, going down the step into the cave. Then he saw, as the children had seen, that the figures were only bejewelled statues, and he laughed loudly.

'Fool!' he said to himself.

'Fool!' repeated Kiki, and Juan swung round at once.

'Who's there? One of you children, I suppose. Wait till I get you!'

Kiki began to mew like a cat. The man looked for this unexpected cat, then decided it was one of the children again, playing a trick on him. Kiki flew silently to the next cave and began to talk to herself there.

'One, two, button my shoe, see how they run!'

The man took one more glance at the company of statues and went into the next cave. The children heaved a sigh of relief. But they dared not move yet.

It seemed a very long time till the man came back. With him came the two old people, evidently very frightened Juan shouted at them in their own language, and the children could not understand a word.

Then, without another glance at the statues, Juan went through the stout oaken door and shut it. The bang echoed loudly through the cave and made everyone jump.

Then they heard another sound which made their hearts

sink. It was the noise of strong bolts being shot home on the other side of the door.

Crash! Crash, crash! All three bolts were shot firmly into place. Now the door could not possibly be opened from the inside.

'Did you hear that?' groaned Jack. 'We're prisoners now. If only we'd hidden in the cave of stalactites or the cave of stars, we'd have been all right. We could have got out of the hole. Now we can't. We'll have to stay here till the men set us free – if they ever do.'

# 25

## Philip's astonishing plan

The old couple looked panic-stricken when four of the statues apparently talked and came alive. But when the children took off their borrowed draperies and carefully gave them back to the right statues again, the old couple saw who they were.

Elsa came running to Lucy-Ann and fondled her. The old man stood trembling.

'What did he say to you?' demanded Jack.

'He said he was going to make us prisoners here, and that he was bringing others back with him to remove all our treasure,' said the old man. Tears suddenly poured down his cheeks. 'He is a bad man. Have I guarded these beautiful things all this time to let them fall into the hands of a man so bad?'

'It's sickening,' said Jack. 'We simply can't do a thing! We shall just have to stand by and watch those rogues take away everything, pack them into crates and fly off with them!'

'Let's go out to that sunny ledge,' said Dinah. 'I can't bear this gloom any more. I shall feel better when we are out there. Let's ask the old man if his wife would bring a picnic meal out there, Jack. You and Philip can help her to bring it. I can't think properly down here in the dark, with all those statues trying to listen.'

'All right,' said Jack, seeing that Dinah was on the point of tears. 'You go off with Lucy-Ann and Kiki. We'll soon come. You'll feel better in the sunshine.'

'Wasn't Kiki clever to lead the man away from us?' said Lucy-Ann. 'He *was* scared when she suddenly spoke to him. So should I have been! I should have thought it was one of the statues speaking.'

She and Dinah made their way to the sunny ledge. Dinah threw herself down there thankfully.

'I don't like this adventure any more, Dinah, do you?' asked Lucy-Ann. 'It's not so bad if there's something we can *do* – but we seem to be helpless here.'

'I like to make adventures go the way I want them to,' said Dinah rather sulkily. 'I don't like them to make me do things I don't like. Don't talk to me, Lucy-Ann. I shall snap at you. I feel cross.'

'It's only because of the strain we went through whilst we were pretending to be statues,' said Lucy-Ann.

'Don't sound so grown-up,' snapped Dinah. 'It's not that I just feel bad tempered because I want to get out of this valley and I can't.'

Lucy-Ann said nothing more. She settled down in the sun, waiting for the picnic that Jack and Philip would soon be bringing out with Elsa. Kiki sat murmuring to herself near by. Martha the hen arrived and began pecking about companionably. Kiki talked to her, and she clucked back.

Dinah forgot her bad temper when the others came out with a picnic meal. They had a good feast and then discussed all the morning's happening once more. In the middle of the discussion they heard the sound of the plane again, and this time saw it rising high into the sky.

'Why, they're off again!' said Jack in surprise. 'Why?'

'Probably to get other men along to help in removing everything, now they really do know where the treasure is,' said Philip. 'And as you suggested, Jack – they might even bring more planes.'

It was hateful feeling that they were complete prisoners. Jack and Philip went desperately to the bolted door once and tried to move it – but it was hopeless of course. The bolts were old but still very strong.

There was nothing to do, and they felt bored. They went to examine the statues more closely and to look at the old pictures and the musty old books.

The statues were loaded with magnificent jewels. Some of the figures were really beautifully made and dressed, but others were crude and garish. Each one, however, was adorned with jewels, though the children were not able to tell if all the gleaming brooches, dazzling earrings and necklaces, glittering bracelets, belts and rings were really valuable or not. Probably some were, and others were only semi-precious.

'I expect the men will strip the statues of their jewellery, and take only that, leaving the figures behind,' said Jack. 'They will crate the pictures and books.'

'Why couldn't we strip the jewels off and hide them away somewhere so that the men wouldn't get them?' suddenly said Dinah. 'I don't see why wicked men like that should have them.'

'Good idea!' said Jack. 'Come on – we'll take the jewellery now and hide it somewhere!'

But as soon as they began to remove it, the old couple flew at them in horror.

'Not do that! Ah, bad boy!' cried the old man, removing a brooch from Jack's hand.

161

'We only want to hide the things from those men,' protested Jack. 'They'll be back and steal these things soon.'

'They belong to these,' said the old man, waving his hand towards the statues. 'They must not be removed by anyone. It is against the law of the Church.'

The children did not try again. It was plain that Elsa and the old man would fly into a rage if they attempted to. They seemed to think that it was a very wicked and unholy act to take away any of the adornments belonging to the figures.

The long day passed at last. Nobody slept very well that night. They were worried about what was going to happen. It was horrid to feel they were at the mercy of rogues like Juan.

They were all out on the sunny ledge the next morning, early, having breakfast there. They had no meals in the caves now if they could help it.

'Listen,' said Dinah suddenly. 'I can hear the plane coming back.'

They all listened, the old couple too. The noise grew louder. It became very loud indeed. Then Jack leapt to his feet.

'It's not just one plane! It's many! Look, there's one! – circling down – and another over there! – and here comes another! Gracious! Juan's got quite a fleet of planes!'

There were four altogether. Evidently Juan meant to do the job properly. The children pictured the planes landing one by one on the long wide strip of grass at the bottom of the valley.

'Now we can expect things to happen,' said Jack. 'The whole of the treasure will be gone soon.'

'What a shame!' said Dinah. 'And we can't do a thing to stop it!'

'If *only* we could get word to Bill!' said Jack desperately. 'But there's no way out of the valley except in one of those planes.'

Philip stared at Jack a moment. Then he said something so

exciting that the others could hardly believe their ears.

'Yes – that's the only way out. And I'm going to take it.'

There was silence. Then Jack spoke, astonished.

'Whatever do you mean? You can't fly a plane.'

'Of course not. But I can *hide* in one!' said Philip. 'Didn't we hide, all of us, in a plane, coming here? Well, why shouldn't I hide in one *leaving* here? I bet I could hide unseen – and slip out when I had a chance, and get word to Bill about everything.'

'Philip! It's a *grand* idea!' said Jack. 'But I'll go, not you.'

'You jolly well won't!' said Philip. 'It's *my* idea! Nobody else is going to pinch such a gorgeous idea. I'm going, see?'

'I don't want either of you to go,' said Lucy-Ann. 'You might be seen. Something awful might happen to you. Don't leave us.'

'Jack will be with you,' said Philip. 'And the old couple. You'll be all right. I tell you, it's the only way to get help – to fly off in one of the planes, when the men go on their next trip. They'll have to come back two or three times to take all these things – and, if only I can get word to Bill, he can catch the men actually doing the stealing!'

'It sounds too good to be true,' said Dinah. 'I don't believe you can do it. Anyway – how are you even going to get to the plane? You know we're bolted in. Nobody can get out.'

'I shall watch my chance and slip out through that door when the men are going to and fro,' said Philip, enjoying his planning. 'Then I shall hide in the cave of stalactites and go up the passage to the hole as soon as I can. Then I'll get along back to the planes, and choose one to hop into. I don't reckon they will have left anyone on guard there, as they think we're all well and truly imprisoned.'

'It sounds easy, but it won't be,' said Jack. 'Better let me do it, Tufty.'

'Think again!' said Philip. 'This is my own pet adventure, see?'

'You might even be able to squeeze into a crate,' said

Dinah thoughtfully. 'Nobody would think of looking into a packed crate.'

'Good idea!' said Philip. 'In fact, jolly good!'

'Well, we can expect quite a horde of men here today,' said Jack. 'It will surprise the poor old couple. They will be in a dreadful state when they see their well-guarded treasure going.'

'Philip, we won't pretend that we are any of the statues today when the men come,' said Dinah. 'Only you. The men are sure to have a hunt round for us if they can't find us today, so we'd better all be found, except you. You can be a statue again, and wait your chance to rush out of the door.'

'Yes. I think I will,' said Philip. 'It may not work, but it's the only thing to do. Now – when will those men be along? It will take them about an hour and half to get here. It's half an hour since we saw the planes. I mustn't leave it to the last minute to put myself in place.'

'Better go now,' said Lucy-Ann, who was on pins and needles about the whole thing. 'We'll come with you and see that you're in a good place and really look like a statue.'

They all went down the passage, and made their way through the various caves to the one in which the statues stood. Martha the hen came too. She had attached herself to Jack now, and followed him wherever he went. She had laid an egg that morning, and the old woman had made Lucy-Ann have it for breakfast.

'Look! – there's a half-hidden ledge here not far from the door,' said Dinah eagerly. 'If you stood there you would hardly be seen, it's so dark there. And you would be near the door to creep out if you got a chance.'

'Yes, that does seem the best place,' said Philip. 'It really does. Now what about a shawl or something to drape over my head? I don't want my short hair to give me away.'

They found a very big shawl and draped it carefully round him. He went to stand on the little ledge, and everyone agreed that it was a splendid place.

'You can hardly be seen,' said Jack. 'Well, good luck, Tufty. We'll go now, and we shan't hide. We shall let the men see us and hope they'll think there's nobody else in the caves at all. If you can't escape we shall know, because you'll still be about tonight.'

'Goodbye,' said Philip, looking exactly like a statue. 'Don't worry about me. I'll be off and away soon, and I'll get word to Bill and Mother. We'll soon rescue you, don't you worry!'

# 26

# The getaway

In about an hour's time Philip heard the sound of footsteps and then the bolts of the door were shot back. Juan's revolver appeared round the opening door again. But this time there was no Kiki to talk to him – nobody to be seen or heard except the silent company of statues.

Juan came down into the cave. Other men followed him. Philip watched them through a fold of the shawl. He hoped they wouldn't start stripping the jewels off the statues at once, or they might discover him.

The men exclaimed in wonder at the statues. They had powerful torches with them which they switched on at once. Philip was not prepared for that. He shrank back into his corner, glad of the draping shawl.

The men were a rough-looking lot, and they called out to one another in surprise as they saw the gleaming jewels on the necks and arms of the statues. Some of them grabbed brooches and necklaces at once. Juan gave a sharp order and the men replaced them sulkily.

Philip counted the men. There was eight. Otto was not among them, but that was not surprising. Juan, Pepi and Luis were there. There were two men for each aeroplane, apparently.

Juan led the way to the next cave, through the tunnel. Their footsteps echoed hollowly as they passed through. Philip wondered if they would all go on to the next cave – and the next. If so, he could slip out of the open door straightaway, and make his way down the hillside at once.

He listened. He could hear the men's voices from the next cave, where the pictures were. Then footsteps again, farther away. Then only a faint murmur of voices.

'They've gone to the cave of books – and then they'll go to the cave where the gold is,' thought Philip. 'I've plenty of time to get through the door and away.'

He dropped his shawl on the floor and went quietly to the door. He was through it in a trice. Up the winding steps he went, off to the cave of stars – then to the cave of gleaming stalactites. He began to feel safer. He didn't think there would be anyone on guard outside the hole, but he meant to be careful there.

There was nobody on guard. The hillside was empty. Philip climbed out of the hole and began to make his way downwards. Soon he was well on his way, keeping a sharp look-out the whole time just in case all the men had not gone down into the caves.

He was tired and hungry by the time he reached the men's hut. Thank goodness the door was open and there was nobody about! The boy got himself a good meal. He found a box containing bars of chocolate, and slipped some of the bars into his pocket, in case he had to go some time without food.

Then he went along to the planes. There they were, four of them, looking quite big as he walked beside them. Which should he get into?

He climbed up into the cabin of each and looked inside. In the last one there was a big heap of coats and rugs. It seemed the best plane to get into. He could pile the things over him and hide himself that way. He didn't at the moment see any chance of squeezing himself into a crate, as Dinah had suggested. Anyway, the crates were not in the plane, they were under the tarpaulins, where they had always been.

Having decided exactly what he was going to do, he had plenty of time left on his hands. He knew that the men would not be back for some time. They would be carrying heavy, awkward loads and would go far more slowly than he had gone.

He amused himself by snooping around. He went into the hut and found a coat hanging up there. He ran his hands through the pockets, thinking that any information he could get hold of might be useful to Bill, when he got to him.

There was a notebook in one of the pockets. Philip flipped over the pages. He could make nothing of it. It contained sentences in some kind of code, and plenty of numbers. Perhaps Bill could make head or tail of it. He couldn't!

He went to the cowshed. There was nothing to be seen there but the still-open tins of fruit, swarming with flies. Philip stared at them. 'Oh yes – they are what Jack left for Otto,' he thought. 'Ugh, look at the flies!'

He took a stick, dug a hole and buried the evil-smelling tins and their contents. Then he strolled off again and came to the tree where they had all once hidden. He squinted up and saw something. 'Golly, what's that?'

Then he remembered. 'Of course – we left our suitcases up there. I'd forgotten all about them. Fancy them still being there!'

He debated whether to get them down and hide them. 'No,' he thought, 'they might be found, and then the men might start looking for me. I'll leave them there.'

He kept a good look out for the returning men as the

afternoon wore on. He helped himself to some biscuits and a tin of peaches about five o' clock. Still no sign of the men.

But about ten minutes later he saw them far away in the distance. He was by the planes, waiting, ready to jump into the one he had chosen as soon as he saw the men coming.

He counted the men quickly. Yes – eight – so they were all back. He climbed up the steps and leapt into the cabin. He went to the pile of rugs and coats and got underneath, pulling them over him so that not even the toe of his shoe showed.

'Good thing it's a hot day,' he thought. 'The men certainly won't want their coats or macks.'

He heard the voices of the men. Evidently they were pleased with their successful day. Then there was a silence. They had passed the planes, and were on their way to the hut. 'Probably get themselves a meal, and then pack up the things they have brought from the treasure caves,' thought Philip. He yawned. He felt sleepy now that he was lying down.

Soon he was asleep, and he slept so soundly that he did not even stir when, some hours later, two men entered his plane. But he did wake when the propellers swung round as the engines suddenly roared out! He nearly gave himself away by sitting up in a fright.

Then he remembered where he was, and lay perfectly still, wondering if it was nighttime. He could see nothing under the pile of coats, of course. It might have been midnight or noon for all he knew.

One by one the planes took off. Philip's plane went last of all. He felt it leave the ground like a bird and then he was away in the air.

'They haven't seen me! They don't guess they've got me on board!' thought Philip, delighted. 'It was easy after all. Hurrah!'

He fell asleep again, and the planes roared on through the

night. Where were they going? To a secret landing-place? To an ordinary aerodrome?

The other children, who were sleeping that night out on the ledge, heard the roar of the planes as they left. It was such a hot night that they had felt stifled indoors and had begged the old couple to let them take the rugs out on the ledge.

'You will not walk in your sleep?' the old man had said. 'You might walk off the ledge!'

'Not one of us walks in our sleep,' said Jack. 'We'll be all right.'

Elsa, the old woman, had not wanted Lucy-Ann to sleep out on the ledge at all, and had almost cried when Lucy-Ann had insisted. Kiki and Martha were both there too. But the lizard wasn't. She was with Philip, sharing his adventure.

The children had had a horrid day. The men had found both them and the old couple in the 'sitting room' and had shouted at them and questioned them, and frightened them very much. The old man had told them that he had been living in the caves for a long time, guarding the treasure, and the men had jumped to the conclusion that the children also had been living there with them.

'Good thing they didn't ask us how we got to this valley,' said Jack afterwards. 'They just took it for granted that we and the old people came here together ages ago.'

The old man and woman had rushed to the rescue of their beloved statues when the men had begun to strip off the jewellery. The men had struck the poor old things and shouted at them. The old man had taken his weeping, trembling wife away, and the children had done their best to comfort them.

They had not gone near the men again, but had gone to sit on the sunny ledge, and wondered if Philip had managed to escape. 'I'm sure he did,' said Lucy-Ann. 'All the men kept together, and Philip could easily have slipped out of the cave of statues when they came to question us.'

The men had gone at last, taking with them a haul of jewels, one very precious figure, some pictures and a few old papers. Two of them carried a box of the gold between them. The children pictured their difficulties, hauling it up and down the mountainside.

The men had bolted the door behind them again, and once more the little company were prisoners. How they wondered what was happening to Philip! Had he managed to hide in one of the aeroplanes? Would he slip into a crate? When would the planes go off?

They knew that the planes had gone when they awoke in the night to hear the throb of the engines. They all sat up and listened. Kiki gave a squawk and pecked Martha to wake her.

'There go the planes,' said Jack. 'I bet Philip's in one. Now we shall soon be rescued. What a shock for Bill when he hears all about us! Do you think Bill will fly over in his aeroplane too?'

'I hope so,' said Lucy-Ann fervently. 'I'm longing to see Bill again. I sometimes feel as if we'll be in this valley all our lives.'

'Don't be silly,' said Dinah. 'Oh, Kiki, leave Martha alone. Whatever are you doing to her to make her cluck like that?'

'Shhhh!' said Kiki cheekily.

'Don't talk back to me!' said Dinah, lying down again. 'Well, I'm glad we heard those planes. Good luck to you, Philip, wherever you are!'

'Good luck!' called the others, and Kiki echoed the words too. 'Good luck!'

'Cluck-luck-luck!' said Martha the hen, sounding exactly as if she was joining in with the good wishes as well!

# 27

# A discovery – and a fine idea

The next day the men were all back again in the four planes. They soon arrived once more at the treasure caves, going through the old books and papers, unrolling the dozens of canvases and looking at the pictures. They had gone to find the children and the old couple and had shouted at them again.

They had found out that somebody had helped himself to food from the hut, and they could not make it out. Hadn't they imprisoned all the children and the old people in the caves?

The children, of course, guessed at once that it was Philip who had helped himself to the food. But they were not going to say so. So Jack put on a bewildered air and replied quite stupidly, and Dinah did the same. Lucy-Ann sobbed and the men soon gave up questioning her.

As for the old couple, they knew nothing, of course. They did not even appear to have missed Philip. The men gave up their questioning after a while, and returned to their work.

Elsa was sad to see Lucy-Ann sobbing. She took her by the hand and led her into the 'bedroom.' She took down a picture she had put on a ledge there, and showed Lucy-Ann a space behind. Lucy-Ann stared at it.

'What is it?' she said. Then she called to Jack. 'Jack! Come here, and bring the old man. The old woman doesn't understand what I say.'

They came, and when Jack saw the yawning space behind the picture, he turned to the old man.

'What's that? A hidey-hole?'

'Oh, it is only a hole in the wall,' said the old fellow. 'My wife did not like it, so she covered it with a picture.'

The old woman poured out a torrent of words to him. He turned to Jack. 'My wife is sad because your little sister is frightened by those men. She says she can hide in this hole and they will not find her.'

'Let me see what it's like,' said Jack, and climbed into it. It was more than a hole. It was a tiny, round dark tunnel that had once been a waterway. Where could it lead to – if it led anywhere?

'It's a little tunnel!' Jack called back. 'Rather like the one that led out of our fern cave into the cave of echoes. I'll see if it goes anywhere.'

He crawled on for some way, and then it suddenly dipped down so steeply that he could have slid down it if it had not been so narrow. It ended in a hole that seemed to open out in the roof of a much bigger passage. Jack flashed his torch down. Yes, that really *was* a passage down there! He crawled back to the girls.

'Come behind me,' he said. 'I may have found a way of escape. We'll have to use a rope though.'

They crawled in single file till they came to the hole that dropped into the wide passage. Jack undid the rope he always carried round his waist. He tied it to a rock and let it drop down into the passage, then down he went.

The girls followed. Jack flashed his torch up and down the passage. 'Which way shall we go?' he said.

'I can hear a funny noise,' said Lucy-Ann. 'It's the water-fall, I do believe!'

They went down the passage towards the noise – and to their intense surprise and delight they came out on to the ledge behind the waterfall, the one on which Lucy-Ann and Dinah had capered about to hold their attention of Pepi some days before.

'I *say*! It's the waterfall ledge – and that is the passage that leads back to the cave of echoes!' said Jack. 'Would you believe it? We can get back to our old fern-cave and we shan't be prisoners in the treasure caves any more. Let's go and fetch the old couple too.'

He went back down the passage, swarmed up the rope, wriggled back up the little tunnel and came out into the sitting room. He told the old man where the passage led to. 'Come too,' he said. 'We will take you to a safe place.'

The old man laughed sadly. 'We cannot do as you do and crawl and climb,' he said. 'It is impossible. You go, and we will put back the picture over the hole and no one will guess.'

Jack went back to the girls, Kiki with him. 'Pity we couldn't take Martha too,' he said. 'I got quite fond of her. But the old people would miss her. They simply won't come with us. I think they're right, too – they'd never be able to swarm along that little tunnel, and swing down that rope – nor would they ever be able to get down into the fern cave. Come on! I'm longing to get back to our own cave. Ha ha – we've escaped after all! Won't those men be wild!'

'I hope they won't hurt those two old people,' said Lucy-Ann anxiously. 'She was such a dear, gentle old woman.'

They went down the winding passage and came to the cave of echoes, where Kiki annoyed them by squawking and screeching all the time, bringing back echoes of hundreds of magnified squawks and screeches that almost deafened them.

They got through the little drainpipe-like tunnel that led to the back of the fern cave, and dropped thankfully down to the rugs still spread out there.

'Home again,' said Jack, and laughed. 'Funny to think we feel this is home – but I really do.'

They settled down for a rest. 'Those men must have gone off somewhere in their planes last night, unloaded their goods and taken off again almost at once to get back so quickly,' said Dinah thoughtfully. 'I really hardly expected to see them in the caves today. I didn't hear the planes come back, did you?'

'No – but the wind has changed, so maybe the sound didn't blow in our direction,' said Jack. 'It's not so sunny now – looks like rain again. The wind's jolly strong.'

'We shall have to keep a look out for Bill and Philip if they come,' said Dinah. 'Philip won't know we're here, will he?'

'Do you girls mind if I go this evening and just have a snoop round about the men's hut?' asked Jack. 'You know – in case by any chance old Tufty didn't get away but got caught and is a prisoner.'

'Golly! I didn't even *think* of that!' said Lucy-Ann in horror. 'Oh, Jack, surely you don't think he got caught, do you?'

'Not for a minute,' said Jack cheerfully. 'But it would be just as well to make sure. I'd better go now whilst the men are busy in the caves. By the way, were all eight of them there, do you know?'

'I *think* so,' said Dinah, frowning. 'But I really couldn't be certain. Do you remember, Lucy-Ann?'

'No. I didn't look at them,' said Lucy-Ann. 'Horrid things!'

'I expect they were all there,' said Jack. 'Brr-r-r-r – the wind's cold today. I'll put on an extra jersey. So long, girls, I'll be back in a short time!'

Off he went, following the familiar way back to the men's hut. He did not think that Philip would have been caught, but still, he must make sure. He scouted cautiously about. The hut door was shut. He went up to it and peeped in at the window. No Philip there. Good!

'Better just pop up to the cowshed,' thought Jack. 'They might have got him tied up there.' So off he went. No – it was empty – good!

There was a sudden rush of wind such as often sweeps through a mountainside valley. A torrent of rain came down and the boy ran for a tree. It was the tree in which they had once all hidden, a good big thick one, that would keep the rain off. He crouched there whilst the wind whipped round him.

There was such a noise of wind that the boy did not hear footsteps coming behind the tree. He did not see the burly figure of Pepi there, staring in surprise at the crouched boy.

In a trice Pepi was round the tree and had got hold of Jack's shoulders. The boy gave a howl of fright. Pepi gripped him tightly.

'Let me go!' yelled Jack. 'You brute, let me go! You're twisting my shoulder!'

Pepi took up a stick and grinned. 'A little of this will do you good,' he said. 'You boys are a lot of trouble to us. Where are the others? You will tell me or I will beat you black and blue.'

'Let me go!' yelled Jack, and kicked hard at Pepi's ankles. The man gave a yelp of pain and hit Jack on the back with the heavy stick. Jack kicked him again.

What would have happened to poor Jack is easy to guess – if something hadn't happened to Pepi first! The wind howled round and shook the tree violently. Something fell from the tree and hit the raging man full on the shoulder. He dropped down at once, shouting, clutching at his shoulder. Jack sped off into the wind. He turned and looked back. Pepi was trying to get up, groaning. The wind howled again, and the big tree spat out something else that hit Pepi on the head. He fell back and did not move.

'Golly!' said Jack, staring. 'It's two of our suitcases that we left up the tree! They just blew down at the right moment. I hope they haven't killed him.'

He went back cautiously to the still man. No, he wasn't killed – just completely knocked out. Jack saw his chance at once. He took his rope and roped the man's hands firmly together, and then his feet. Then he tied him to the tree.

'Now you won't be able to come after me, my dear Pepi,' said Jack, taking a quick look up the tree in case the remaining two suitcases should come down. 'I suppose the others left you here on guard today, as they knew somebody had been at the food. Well, you won't be much use as a guard for the rest of the day, but never mind. The tree will shelter you from the storm.'

Suddenly such an extraordinary idea struck Jack that he stood perfectly still and gasped. Then he struck his hands together and yelled out loudly:

'I must do it, I must, I must! But have I time? Have I time?'

He began to run as fast as he could through the wind and the rain. 'Why didn't I think of it before? It those men are in the treasure caves, I can bolt the door on them, just as they did to us – and make them prisoners! Why didn't I think of it before? It may be too late now.'

He ran and ran, gasping and panting, hot as fire in spite of the wind and the rain.

'It won't be any good. The men will be out of the caves by now,' he thought. 'I may see them at any minute. Oh, why didn't I think of this before? I could have gone and bolted them in before I left Dinah and Lucy-Ann!'

It certainly was a most wonderful idea. The men would be absolute prisoners. They did not know the way out behind the picture, and would never think of looking for it there. Certainly the old people would not tell them. Oh, if only they were still in the caves!

The rain poured down. The wind blew like a gale. Fortunately it was behind Jack now and it helped him on. He was soaked through, but he didn't care.

There was no sign of the men. Jack slowed down when he came near the waterfall. He didn't want to run right into them. He began to think more calmly.

'Maybe they won't come out till the rain stops and the storm dies down. Rain would spoil the old books and papers and pictures. Yes, they'll be sure to wait. I may be in time yet. The men may even decide to stay the night there if the storm doesn't clear.'

Jack was right. The men, having looked out of the entrance hole of the caves, had seen the rain storm sweeping over the mountainside and had decided not to venture out with their treasures. They would be ruined.

'Better spend the night here,' said one of the men. 'In that room with the rugs. We'll turn the old people and children out.'

Only the old people were there. They made vague gestures when the men asked where the children were, pointing towards the passage that led to the sunny ledge. The men settled down on the rugs, and one of them got out a pack of cards. He set the lamp so that they could all see, and then began to deal the cards. The old people went into their 'sitting room,' sad and afraid. How they hoped that the men would not look behind the picture in the next room!

When Jack arrived at the treasure caves he could hardly walk through the passages. He stumbled along, past the cave of stalactites, past the cave of stars and into the first treasure cave, through the open door at the bottom of the curving stairway. He could see no men at all. His heart sank. Had they gone, then? Had he missed them?

He went cautiously on. When he came to the 'sitting room' he peeped in and saw the old couple there, with Martha the hen.

Then he heard the noise of the men in the next room. He beckoned to the old couple. They rose silently and followed him in surprise. Jack did not speak till he was well out of earshot of the men.

'Come,' he said, leading them out of the cave of statues and out of the stout door. 'I am going to bolt the men in. But I don't want to lock you in too.'

He shot all the bolts triumphantly. Crash! Crash! Crash! He'd done it! He'd done it!

# 28

# The day after the storm

As soon as he had shot the bolts safely home, Jack collapsed. His tussle with Pepi, his long run through the wind and the rain, and the terrific excitement of making the men prisoners had been too much for him. He sank down on the steps outside the bolted door, and lay there quite still.

It was dark there. The old couple felt about for Jack in alarm. What was happening to the poor boy?

They found his torch in his pocket and took it out. They switched it on and looked anxiously at Jack's pale face and closed eyes. They tried to drag him up the steps.

'His clothes are wet,' said the old woman, feeling Jack's soaked jersey and shorts. 'He will get a chill, a terrible chill. Maybe he will die of it. What shall we do, old man?'

The old man answered her in her own language. 'We will drag him up these steps. We will make him comfortable in the cave of stars. You shall wrap him in your shawl and he shall have my coat.'

Together the old couple managed to drag Jack up the steps. How they panted and groaned. They could not get him any further than the top. The old man stripped off Jack's wet things and put his coat round him. The old woman wrapped him all round in her thick shawl. They squeezed out his wet things and hung them on the rocky wall to dry.

They were frightened. What were they going to do now? Those men were bolted in the caves with what was left of their precious treasure. How angry they would be when they discovered what had happened!

Jack soon came to himself again. He sat up, wondering where he was. He had been in a kind of half faint, half

178

asleep. He clutched at his clothes. What on earth had he got on? A shawl? Gracious, was he dressed up as a statue again?

The old people heard him moving and switched on the torch again. They looked anxiously at him and were relieved to see that he was no longer so white.

'You are better now?' asked the old man gently.

'Yes, thanks. I'm all right,' said Jack, pulling at the shawl. 'Whatever's this?'

'Your clothes were so wet,' said the old man. 'We had to take them off to dry them or you would have got a terrible chill. You have my coat and my wife's shawl.'

'Oh – well, thank you,' said Jack, feeling rather foolish in the coat and shawl. 'Sorry I gave you a fright. But I just conked out – that run up the mountainside, I suppose. I say – wasn't it a good idea bolting those men in?'

'Ah – but what will they do to us when they know?' said the old man sadly.

'Nothing! How can they?' said Jack. 'They are on the wrong side of the bolted door, aren't they? Don't you worry, we're all right!'

He got up. His legs were not very steady, but he could walk all right. 'I'm just going to the entrance of the caves to see if by any chance that awful wind storm has died down,' he said. 'If it has, I'll make my way to the fern cave, where the two girls are. They'll be scared by themselves.'

Somehow he stumbled along to the entrance. The clouds were so low and black that it was like night outside. Rain still swept over the hillside in great torrents. It was quite impossible to go out.

'I should get completely lost,' thought Jack. 'Golly, the girls will be so worried about me! I hope they won't be frightened all by themselves. Well, it's no use – I'll have to spend the night here with the old people – but it won't be very comfortable.'

It wasn't comfortable. They found a place in the cave of

stars, a rounded, hollowed-out basin of rock, with only a few sharp edges. For the sake of warmth they all huddled together. Jack tried to make the old people take back their coat and shawl, saying that his clothes were almost dry.

But the old woman grew very angry when he suggested this, and scolded her husband hard in words that Jack could not understand, but whose meaning he could guess.

'My old one says that you are a bad bad boy to talk of putting on wet clothes,' said the old fellow. 'We will press close together. It is not cold in this cave.'

It wasn't very cold, it was true. Jack lay between the old man and his wife, looking up at the roof of the strange cave. He watched the curious greenish-blue stars shine and fade, flicker and glow. There were hundreds of them, most enchanting to watch. Jack wondered about them for a long time and then fell asleep.

In the morning the old people awoke first and felt stiff and uncomfortable. But they did not move for fear of disturbing Jack. He awoke at last and sat up. He saw the glowing stars above and around, and knew where he was at once.

'I wonder what the time is,' he said, looking at his watch. 'Half past seven! Gracious, I wonder what those men are doing! Are my clothes dry?'

Luckily they were. Jack put them on quickly, and gave back the coat and shawl with warm thanks. 'Now, you stay here a bit,' he said to the old couple. 'I'm just going to the bolted door to see if I can hear anything.'

He went off, feeling quite himself again now. As soon as he came to the top of the curving stairway that led down to the oaken door, he heard bangs and crashes. Ah – the men had discovered that they were bolted in!

Crash! Bang! Thud! Smash!

They were hammering at the stout door for all they were worth. How they shouted and yelled, how they kicked at that door and tried to smash it down!

Jack stood at the top of the steps and grinned in delight. Serve them right! They were getting a taste of their own medicine. They had locked the children in — and now they themselves were prisoners.

Suddenly there was a loud bang that made Jack jump. It was a revolver shot. The men were shooting at the door, hoping to smash the bolts.

Bang! Bang! Bang!

Jack went back a little way, afraid that a bullet might glance off somehow and hit him, though this was impossible. BANG! BANG!

The bolts could not be smashed. The men gave the door a few more blows with something then stopped. Jack ran back to tell the old couple all about it.

But they were frightened, so it wasn't much fun telling them. 'I think I'll take you to the fern cave, where the girls are,' he told the old man. 'We have food and rugs in that cave. Come with me.'

The old couple wouldn't stir out of the place they knew so well. They were terrified of the open air, of the hillside and the outer world. They shrank back and nothing that Jack could say would make them change their minds.

'Well, I shall just have to go to the girls myself, then,' said Jack at last. 'I'll bring them back here with food and rugs. We might as well all be together. Those men are no longer a danger to us. They can't possibly get out. Even if they find the hole behind that picture, I'm sure they won't get any further than the cave of echoes.'

He said good-bye to the frightened old people and went out into the sunshine. It was warm on his head and back — delicious. The sky was blue again, and the wind had gone.

He made his way to the waterfall, arriving there without any mistake, for he could follow the 'signposts' easily now. He was hailed by the girls as soon as they saw him. They were peeping out through the fern fronds.

'Jack! You didn't come back last night! Oh, Jack, I hardly slept at all, wondering what had happened to you,' cried Lucy-Ann.

'What happened?' asked Dinah, who was looking rather pale. She too had been very anxious, especially when the storm had come.

'Heaps!' said Jack. 'Marvellous news! Best in the world!'

'Gracious! Is Philip back, then? – and Bill here?' cried Lucy-Ann at once.

'No – that's not my news,' said Jack. 'Do you know what I've done? Bolted those men into the caves. What do you think of that?'

'What a *wonderful* idea!' said the girls together. 'But what about the old people?' asked Dinah.

'Oh, I got them out first,' said Jack. 'And I found Pepi back by the cowshed place, and tied him up properly. He's bound to that big tree where we once hid.'

'JACK! How marvellous you are!' cried Lucy-Ann. 'Did you fight him?'

'Well – not exactly,' said Jack. 'He caught me, and I kicked him hard. And just then the wind blew hard and a couple of our suitcases fell out of the tree and knocked him out. It was as much of a surprise to me as to him.'

'Oh – of course – we left our suitcases up there!' said Dinah. 'Oh, *Jack* – what a good thing we did!'

'Pepi must have had a most uncomfortable night,' said Jack. 'The rain and wind were his only companions.'

He told them how he had left the old couple in the cave of stars, and related the tale of the angry men trying to smash down the door.

'I can't get the old people to leave the caves,' he said. 'So we'd better take rugs and food and go back there to keep them company. They lent me their coat and shawl last night when my things were soaked. We can't leave them alone there without food or bedding.'

'Oh dear – I do like this cave so much better than any-where else,' sighed Lucy-Ann. 'Still – those old people have been very good to us. Is Martha there too, Jack?'

'Golly! – no, I'd forgotten all about her,' said Jack, remembering. 'I hope those men don't kill and eat her.'

This was a dreadful thought, and made poor Lucy-Ann quite dumb for a minute or two. Poor Martha. Surely the men would leave her alone?

Kiki, of course, was as delighted to see Jack as the girls had been. She nestled on his shoulder, making crooning noises all the time he was talking, pulling at his ear and ruffling up his hair. Jack scratched her poll, delighted to have her again.

The girls collected a few tins, and Jack piled rugs over his shoulder. Then, with Kiki flying ahead, they set off to follow the familiar 'signposts' to the treasure caves. The sun beat down hotly. It was a really lovely day.

'I wish I could draw a plan of how that hole behind the picture leads to our fern cave,' said Dinah. 'The mountain is riddled with holes and caves. I say, isn't the waterfall loud this morning? – and it seems bigger than ever. I suppose it's all the rain last night.'

They arrived at the entrance to the caves at last and went in. They made their way to the cave of stars and the old couple greeted them warmly and joyfully. The old woman was full of delight to see Lucy-Ann again, and greeted her lovingly.

'I'm hungry,' said Lucy-Ann, trying to wriggle out of Elsa's arms. 'Very hungry.'

They all were. It was a strange place to have a meal in – the cave of stars. The children watched the flickering, shin-ing lights, quite entranced by them. If only Lucy-Ann could take some home for her bedroom ceiling! She wished this once again as she watched the shining stars.

'Well, now, all we've got to do is to wait,' said Jack,

arranging the pile of rugs for everyone to sit on as comfortably as possible. 'Everything rests with Philip now. Those men evidently don't know he hid in a plane or they would have said something. He must have escaped all right. What is he doing, I wonder?'

# 29

## A very strange journey

What *had* happened to Philip? He was certainly having a most adventurous time.

He slept under the pile of coats and rugs in the plane until dawn. Then the planes landed, and bumped along the ground on their huge wheels. Philip awoke at once.

He made a peephole through the rugs and watched to see what the two men in his plane were doing. They were getting out. What a bit of luck that they hadn't even looked round the plane, or taken a coat from the pile!

Other men outside were greeting the new arrivals. Philip sat up and tried to hear what was said. But half of the speech was in a foreign language, and there was such a babel that it was impossible to make out anything.

He glanced round the plane. One of the crates was now in it, and a tarpaulin was tied loosely round it. Philip tried to see what was in it. Packed in straw was one of the statues, evidently one that was very valuable.

Philip peeped cautiously out of the window of the plane, for now the men's voices had ceased. Where were the men? Could he slip out now and escape to get help?

He stared in surprise. The planes, and others too, were on a vast grassy plain – and in front and all round was the blue sea. All round! Well, then, they must be on some island somewhere.

He sat and thought for a moment. These men were rogues. They were doing a deal in valuable treasures hidden and perhaps forgotten during the last war; they had planes of their own – and a secret landing ground. What could be better than a lonely island, say, off the coast of Scotland?

'Then I suppose they'll have motor boats or launches of their own to get the stuff away,' thought Philip. 'A proper gang of them! I'll never get away from here without being seen – never. If it's an island – and it seems as if it must be – I'm as much a prisoner here as I was in the treasure caves. Blow!'

Then Dinah's idea came into his mind. What about hiding in the crate? That figure would be sure to be put on board a boat and shipped off somewhere to be sold. Well, couldn't he go with it?

He peeped out again to see where the men were. They were evidently having food and drink in a hut some distance off. Philip reckoned that he would have at least half an hour to get to work.

He loosened the tarpaulin a little more. He found that the crate was fastened by a hasp. He pulled it undone, and the whole side of the crate opened, like a sideways lid. Straw began to tumble out.

The figure was inside, packed loosely round with straw. Philip thought it must be the statue of some old-time saint. He looked at it closely. Could it be made of gold? It looked like it. Anyway, it didn't matter. It was going to lie where Philip had just been lying – under the pile of rugs and coats. And Philip was going to take its place.

It was not really very difficult to get the figure out of the straw, but it was heavy once it was out. Philip almost fell under its weight, though it was only about as big as he was himself.

He dragged it to the pile of rugs. He put it right underneath, and piled the things over it so that not a scrap of it showed. Then he cleared up the fallen bits of straw and pushed them carefully back into the crate.

Then he had the task of creeping into the straw himself. The statue had made quite a hole, and Philip settled down in the same place. He pulled the straw carefully round him, and dragged the sideways lid shut. But he could not fasten the hasp, and had to leave it, hoping that if the men saw it open they would simply think it had come undone by accident.

It was terribly warm in the straw. Philip began to be alarmed in case he might not be able to breathe after a time, and burrowed a little tunnel from his mouth and nose to the outside of the straw. After that he felt better.

He had been in the crate about a quarter of an hour when two men drove up in a cart. They unloaded all the planes. They carefully slid the crate that Philip was in out of the plane, and when the side swung open, fastened the hasp carefully. They did not guess for one moment that a live boy was inside, instead of a silent statue.

Philip's crate was loaded into the cart with other things. Then the cart was driven off towards the sea, bumping over ruts as it went. Philip was terribly jolted. The straw tickled and pricked him everywhere. He could hardly breathe.

But he didn't mind. He would soon be on board ship, and taken to the mainland somewhere. Then he could escape and go to the police. So he lay there patiently, trying to avoid the sharp prickles of the straw by wriggling about every now and again.

He could see nothing in the crate. He could only guess when the cart arrived at a small jetty, beside which a big launch was moored. He was carried on board and dumped on a lower deck.

Bump! Philip gasped, for he was very much shaken. Other things were dumped beside him. Then there came the sound of shouts and orders. The motor of the launch started up and Philip felt the vessel moving smoothly over the water. They were off!

'These men don't lose much time,' thought Philip. 'They don't have these things on their hands very long. Wonder who buys them?'

The trip to the mainland, wherever it was, was a long one. Philip was now quite sure that the landing ground for the planes was on some lonely island. At last the launch eased into some kind of harbour and came to a stop. Men began to unload it at once.

The crate was rather roughly handled, and once poor Philip was put upside-down for half a minute. That was terrible. He thought he would have to call out. But just when he was certain he couldn't bear it any longer, he felt the crate being lifted again and put on a car or into a van, which drove off almost immediately.

After a while it stopped. Philip heard the sound of an engine whistling and his heart leapt for joy. They were probably at a railway station. Perhaps he would be put into the luggage van – or on a goods train. It would be easy enough to escape then. He had not dared to before, for he had felt certain that all the men handling the crate so far had been accomplices of the others.

He was not put on a train. He was left in a yard, along with other goods that were to go by a later train. He strained his ears, hoping to hear the van being driven off. Then, he thought, it would be safe for him to get out.

He waited for about twenty minutes. Then he began to try and wriggle out. But he could not undo the hasp. Blow!

He yelled. 'Hi! Hi! Help me!'

A porter not far off jumped in alarm. He looked all round. There was no one in sight except a solitary passenger waiting for the next train, and another porter on the opposite platform.

Philip yelled again, 'Hi! Hi! Let me out!'

The porter felt terribly scared. He looked at the waiting passenger. Had he heard the shouts too – or was it just the porter's own imagination? The passenger *had* heard them, and he was looking most alarmed.

'Somebody in trouble somewhere,' said the man, walking to the porter. 'Sounds as if he's in that little yard there.'

'There's nobody there,' said the porter, staring into the yard.

'Hi! Hurry up and let me out!' came Philip's urgent voice, and to the horror of the passenger and the porter, the big crate began to rock violently.

'There's someone in there!' cried the porter, and ran to the crate. He undid the hasp with trembling fingers and out came Philip, straw in his hair, straw down his neck, straw all over him, looking wild and terribly excited.

'I want the police station,' said Philip. 'Can't stop to explain anything to you now. Where's the police station?'

'Over there,' stuttered the porter, pointing to a small square building about a hundred yards away from the railway station. 'But— but— but . . .'

Philip left him 'but-ing' away, and sped off to the police station, thrilled at his escape. He had managed it wonderfully, he thought.

He shot into the police station and almost scared the policeman there out of his life.

'I want to report something important to somebody in authority,' said Philip. 'Who's the head man here?'

'I'm the constable here,' said the policeman. 'Who are you, and what do you want? You can report to me.'

'I want to use the telephone,' said Philip, thinking it would be a good thing to get into touch with Bill at once. 'Will you get a number for me, please?'

'Here here – you can't go using our police phones without good cause,' said the policeman, beginning to feel that this straw-strewn boy was mad. 'What's your name, and where do you live?'

'My name is Philip Mannering,' said Philip impatiently. 'Don't hold me up, please. I've very important things to report to somebody.'

The name caught the policeman's attention at once. 'Philip Mannering?' he said. 'Here – are you one of the missing children? There's four been missing for days. You one of them?'

He drew a leaflet from a drawer and looked at it. He passed it across to Philip. To the boy's surprise he saw a photograph of himself, Lucy-Ann, Jack and Dinah – and Kiki too, of course – at the head of the paper, and their names and descriptions underneath.

'Yes – I'm that boy,' he said, pointing to his photograph. 'Philip Mannering. And I went to get into touch with Bill Smugs – no, his real name's Cunningham, of course – at once. It's MOST IMPORTANT.'

The policeman suddenly got very busy. He took up the receiver of the phone. He barked a number into it, which he got at once. He evidently got on to somebody in high authority immediately.

'Sir, one of the missing children has just turned up here – Philip Mannering – wants to report something to Detective Inspector Cunningham. Yes, sir. I will, sir.' He turned to Philip.

'Are the other children with you?'

'No – but they're all right – so far,' said Philip. 'I've escaped and I want help to rescue them. Can I get on to Bill Cunningham, please?'

The policeman spoke into the telephone. 'The other children are all right, but not with him. Please notify Mrs Mannering. More news to follow. When will the Inspector be here?'

The policeman put the receiver down and gazed in a very

pleased manner at Philip. To think that this exciting case of Missing Children should be reported to *his* little station!

'Where am I?' asked Philip suddenly. 'What is this place called?'

'Don't you know?' said the policeman, surprised. 'It's Gairdon, on the north-east coast of Scotland.'

'I guessed that's about where I'd be,' said Philip. 'Sorry I can't tell you anything, constable – but I think I'd better wait for Bill.'

Bill came – in his aeroplane! He landed at the nearest aerodrome, took a fast police car, and arrived at Gairdon in two hours' time. Very good going. Philip heard the car roaring up and ran to meet it.

'Bill! I knew you'd come! Oh, Bill – I've got the most exciting news for you! I don't know where to begin.'

# 30

# Bill gets busy

Bill swung out of the car, took hold of Philip by the arm and had a good look at him. 'You're all right?' demanded. 'All of you? Your mother's been nearly off her head with worry.'

'I'm all right, Bill, so's everybody. But we've fallen right into the middle of a most extraordinary adventure,' said Philip. 'I must tell you quickly. We've got to get busy. You see . . .'

'Come into the police station,' said Bill. Philip followed the burly figure, full of relief to hear his determined voice, and to see his strong, clever face.

Soon the whole story was being poured out. Bill listened in amazement, occasionally rapping out a sharp question. When he heard how Philip had taken the statue out of the crate and put himself in its place, and was taken to the railway station, he burst out laughing.

'I never in my life knew children like you! Whatever will you do next? I can't cope with you. But, joking apart, this is a most extraordinary thing, Philip, most amazing. The men you got caught up with are the very men I'd been after for some time. We couldn't find out what they were up to – though we knew jolly well they were up to no good.'

'Really?' said Philip, astonished. 'By the way, Bill – that night we were to go with you in your plane – and got into the wrong one – we heard shots. Was that anything to do with you?'

'It was,' said Bill grimly. 'It so happened that two of the men were spotted there, and detained. They shot their way out – and that was what you heard. I nearly got a bullet in my leg. I can tell you, we shall be very glad to get our hands on them and have something to charge them with. Clever rogues! They are crooks from South America, in touch with the old Nazis, who have told them the whereabouts of many of the lost or hidden treasures in Europe. Many of them have never been found, you know.'

'Gosh – you wait till you see our treasure caves!' said Philip. 'Oh – by the way, here's a notebook I pinched from one of the men's coats.'

He handed it over. Bill squinted at it, and his eyes nearly fell out of his head.

'I say – my word! – look here – this is a code – the code the rascals use – and a list of all the people concerned in this racket – with their addresses in code! Philip, you deserve a medal. This is a first-class find. We can round up the whole gang.'

Philip was delighted at Bill's pleasure. Bill got up and went to the telephone. He made many calls, short, sharp and to the point. Philip listened but could not make much of them. He hoped Bill would soon set off to rescue the others.

They would be waiting most anxiously.

Bill put down the telephone receiver at last. 'We're taking my aeroplane and another, and twelve men counting myself,' he said. 'Starting at twelve.'

'I'm going too, aren't I?' said Philip anxiously.

'I think you'd better stay and see your mother,' said Bill. 'And also — there may be a bit of a dust-up, you know, when we get there.'

Philip stared at him in the greatest indignation. 'Bill! The others will be there — Jack and the rest — and you'd keep *me* out of it? Didn't I come here, didn't I . . . '

'All right, all right, old son,' said Bill. 'You shall come. Goodness knows what further adventure you'd get into if I left you behind.'

Philip cheered up at once. He took Lizzie out of his pocket and introduced her to Bill. 'Meet busy dizzy Lizzie,' he said, and Lizzie ran on to Bill's knee.

'Sounds like Kiki's make-up,' said Bill. 'Busy dizzy Lizzie! What a name for a lizard!'

'I suppose we can't get anything to eat here, can we?' asked Philip, wondering if there were ever any eatables at a police station. 'I've had chocolate to nibble at times, but that's all.'

'I was going to suggest that we should ask the good constable here to provide us with a really slap-up meal,' said Bill. 'We could go to the hotel, but you don't look very presentable at the moment — you seem to exude bits of straw from top to toe. We'll have a good meal and then give you a wash and brush-up.'

The wind got up as they ate their meal. Bill stared out of the window. 'Hope this wind dies down,' he said. 'Looks a bit stormy to me.'

Bill was right. Just before it was time for them to set off in the car to the aerodrome, the telephone rang. Bill answered it. He listened gravely and turned to Philip.

'There's a gale warning out,' he said. 'Afraid it's no good starting off yet, Philip. Very stormy weather where we want to go.'

'Blow!' said Philip, disappointed and anxious. 'The others will be so worried, waiting and waiting for us.'

'Yes, they will,' said Bill. 'But the aerodrome doesn't give out warnings like this without reason. They are apparently expecting one of those sudden gale-storms that mean a plane must fly absolutely blind. Not so funny. We'll have to wait a bit.'

Philip looked upset. It would be too awful if those men got back to the valley before they did and perhaps caught the others. And he did so badly want Bill to catch the men red-handed – wanted him to get there before them and wait for them to come again and take away the treasures.

'By the way, Bill – how do you know where to fly to?' he asked suddenly. '*I* didn't know what the valley was – or where – except that it is in Austria. Elsa and the old man told us that.'

'It's down in that interesting little notebook you gave me,' said Bill, 'together with other places where they may also find hidden treasures. Oh, that notebook told me quite a lot I wanted to know, Philip.'

Bill got out a map and showed Philip exactly where the valley was. 'It had a bad time in the war,' he said, 'and the only pass into it was bombed. It hasn't been unblocked again, as far as I know. Plans were afoot to work on it this year. A man called Julius Muller – the one you were told to get into touch with – has been trying to get permission to unblock the valley and enter it.'

'I wonder what happened to Otto,' said Philip. 'The poor prisoner, you know.'

'His address is in the book,' said Bill. 'I have already asked for information about him, I daresay I shall get some soon.'

He did. The telephone rang that afternoon and a voice

informed Bill that Otto Engler had been found outside a big hospital, unconscious. He had almost died of heart trouble, but was making slight progress now, though he could not speak a word.

'I bet those brutes ill-treated him and made him tell them the exact whereabouts of the treasure caves,' said Philp, 'and then took him and left him somewhere in the street, ill and terrified.'

'Quite likely,' agreed Bill. 'They wouldn't stop at much.' The telephone bell rang again, and Bill took up the receiver once more.

'Gale getting worse,' he told Philip. 'Have to put off our trip till tomorrow. Pity your mother's so far away or we could have dropped in to see her. I've been trying to get her on the phone.'

Philip did speak to his mother that afternoon, though it was only a three minute talk. Mrs Mannering was so relieved to hear his voice that she could hardly say a word herself. However, Philip found plenty to say, and had to stop halfway through because he was cut off.

Next day dawned fair and warm. The wind had almost gone — blown itself out in the night, which had been extremely stormy and wild. Philip had awakened once or twice and had felt glad they had not tried to fly through it, for certainly it was a very wild storm.

He had slept in a comfortable bed put up in the cell of the police station. This seemed very exciting to him. 'First time I've ever passed a night in prison,' he told Bill.

'Well, I hope it will be the last,' said Bill. 'Prison is not a pleasant place, my boy.'

Bill's car was brought to the door. It was large and bright and swift. He and Philip got in, Bill started up the engine and they roared away. Twenty, thirty, forty, fifty, sixty, seventy miles an hour and more! Philip was thrilled.

'She does go,' he said. 'Funny that a car seems faster than as aeroplane when you're in it. Much more of a rush, somehow.'

They reached the aerodrome at last. There was Bill's plane, its propellers whirring fast. Beside it was another, very like it. Eleven men stood about, waiting. They saluted Bill.

'Get into my plane,' Bill ordered Philip. 'I want a word with my men.'

He had his word and got in. Five of the men got in Bill's plane and six in the other. There was a terrific roar, and first Bill's plane took off and then the other one. They flew into the wind, circled round, rose higher and then made off for the east.

Philip gave a sigh of relief. Now things were on the move again. He would soon see the others. How glad they would be!

After some time Bill spoke to Philip. 'We're coming to that valley of yours, Philip, now – or should be. Have a look out and see if you recognise it.'

Philip looked down. 'Oh yes!' he cried. 'That's it! And look – there are four planes down there! That's where we land! You'd better look out in case the men are about and shoot!'

Bill's plane roared down lower. It swung into the wind and landed perfectly. The second plane followed suit.

The engines stopped. There was silence. Bill waited to see if anyone came running out. No, not a soul. He and the other men poured out. Philip followed.

There seemed to be no one about at all. Bill told his men to scatter and make a search before they went any further. Soon one of them gave a shout. 'Hey! There's one of them here! All tied up like a chicken!'

It was Pepi, half dead with cold and hunger. He was so

glad to be set free that he did not show much surprise at seeing so many strangers. In charge of one of the men he tottered over to Bill.

'Put him in the hut and lock him up,' ordered Bill. 'Who could have tied him up, Philip?'

'I can't imagine,' said Philip, puzzled. 'And look, Bill here are two of our suitcases – fallen out of the tree, I suppose. Funny.'

'There are still seven men to be accounted for,' said Bill. 'Right. Well, now – we'd better set off to these treasure caves. Look out, men, in case there's any ambush. We don't want to be shot up without warning.'

They set off, Philip telling Bill the way. Bill was filled with amazement to see the valley, the towering mountains, the burnt ruins . . . it seemed so extraordinary to think of the four children marooned here in the middle of such thrilling adventures.

'Can you hear the waterfall now?' asked Philip eagerly, after a time. 'I can! We're getting near.'

The men were amazed to hear the noise of the great waterfall, and even more astonished to see it. They did not say very much, for they were tough men, not easily surprised by anything. But they stood and stared for some time.

'Now – careful – because we're getting near to the cave entrance,' said Philip at last. 'Shall I go first? I think I'd better.'

# 31

## An exciting finish

Jack, Dinah, Lucy-Ann, Kiki and the old couple were still in the cave of stars. They had just finished their meal, and were wondering what to do. What a pity the old couple wouldn't come outside the mountain – it was such a lovely day!

'We could easily go and sun ourselves there,' said Lucy-Ann longingly. 'There's no danger from those men. They can't get out of that locked door.'

Just as she spoke, Jack clutched hold of her arm and made her jump. 'Sh! I can hear voices.'

They all listened fearfully. Yes – there *were* voices – coming down the tunnel that led from the cave of stalactites to the cave they were now in.

'More men! Quick, hide!' said Dinah urgently. In a panic the children began to run to the other end of the cave, stumbling and tripping, their feet echoing round the big vault.

'Halt!' cried a stern voice, and a big figure stood just inside the cave. 'Stand still! Put your hands up!'

Lucy-Ann knew that voice. Of course she did. 'Bill! BILL!' she squealed. 'Oh, Bill, we thought you were never coming!'

She ran across the cave and flung herself on the surprised Bill. Jack and Dinah followed, shouting in delight. Lucy-Ann caught sight of Philip and flung herself on him too.

'Philip! Dear Philip, you did escape and get Bill!'

Philip was astonished to see the children and the old couple there. He had left them in the treasure caves. How had they got out? And where were the men?

The old couple came slowly up, half frightened to see so

many people by the light of the powerful torches. Bill was gentle with them.

'Poor frightened moles,' he said to Philip. 'Well, they will be well looked after and rewarded. Now – where are these men?'

'I bolted them in,' said Jack proudly. 'They are prisoners in the treasure caves.'

This was news to Philip – and, of course, to Bill too. They questioned Jack eagerly, and he told them how the old woman had shown them the hole behind the picture, and how they had managed to escape through it to the cave of echoes and from there to their own fern cave. Then how Jack had gone to the men's hut, and had come up against Pepi and tied him up – finally how he had got his Great Idea, and slipped back to bolt the men in.

'Well – that seems pretty good work to me!' said Bill. 'But it won't be an easy job routing them out of those caves. I wonder if we could take them by surprise from the back – get in at the picture-hole and give them a shock.'

'Oh *yes*!' said Jack. 'Of course you could. You could leave one or two of your men at the bolted door here, attracting the attention of the seven men – and whilst they are shouting and yelling at one another, the rest of your men could go in the other way and surprise them.'

'That seems a very sound plan,' said Bill, and gave some orders. He turned to Philip. 'I'm leaving two men here. Take them to the bolted door in half an hour's time, and they will then attract the men's attention. Jack, you come with me and the others, and show me the way back to your fern-cave, and through the cave of echoes to the passage that leads to the hole at the back of that picture.'

The little procession set off. The two men left behind waited for half an hour and then went with Philip to the bolted door at the bottom of the curving steps. They rapped on it and shouted.

An answering shout came from inside. 'Who are you? Let us out! Open the door!'

The men inside banged at the door and the men outside did the same. It was a perfect babel of noise. All the seven men were there, arguing, banging, demanding to be set free, and generally losing their tempers.

Meantime Bill, Jack and the others had gone to the fern-cave. They had crawled in, and found to their dismay that they had to wriggle through the drain-pipe hole at the back. One of them almost got stuck.

'I must say you children manage to get into the most marvellous scrapes,' said Bill, emerging from the hole into the cave of echoes. 'My, I'm hot!'

'Hot, hot, HOT, HOT!' said the echoes at once. Bill jumped. 'What's that?'

'That, that, THAT, THAT!' shouted the echoes alarmingly. Jack laughed. 'It's only the echoes,' he said. Kiki began to squawk, and then whistled like an express engine. The noise was deafening.

'Kiki always does that here,' said Jack, leading the way. 'Shut up, Kiki! Bad bird!'

Soon they were in the passage that led to behind the waterfall – but before they got there they came to the hole in the roof.

'Have you got a rope on you, Bill!' said Jack. 'We've got to get up here. I used my rope to tie up Pepi. If you can get me on your shoulder, and shove me up, I can crawl into the hole, fix the rope and let it down.'

It was soon done. One after another the men crawled into the hole, thinking that never in their lives had they done so much climbing, creeping and crawling. They looked at Jack in admiration. What a boy!

Jack came to the hole behind the picture. He listened. Not a sound. The men were all at the bolted door, shouting, kicking and arguing.

Jack gave the picture a push and it fell. The room was empty. He jumped down and the others followed one by one.

'Hope there's no more of this, sir,' said one of the men to Bill. 'You want thinner men for this job.'

'Better go cautiously now,' said Jack. 'We are near the treasure caves. We go straight through three and then come to the cave of statues. That's where the bolted door is.'

'Quiet now,' ordered Bill, and, treading softly in their rubber-soled shoes, the men moved slowly forward, revolvers glinting in their hands.

Through the cave of gold – through the cave of books – through the cave of pictures. Jack laid his hand warningly on Bill's arm. He could hear something.

'It's the men,' he said. 'Hark! – they must have got rocks or something to hammer at the door like that. They really will break it down, I should think, by the noise.'

Bill stepped from the tunnel into the cave of statues. Although he had been prepared for them by Philip, he could not help jumping a little when he saw them in that dim greenish glow. His men stepped silently behind him.

At the far end were the seven men. They had found a big rock and were using it as a battering-ram. Crash! It struck the door violently. Crash!

'Now's our chance,' whispered Bill. 'They have their hands full – not a revolver to be seen among them. Come on!'

The men moved swiftly up behind Juan and the others. A sharp, stern voice barked out behind them:

'Hands up! We've got you cold!'

The men all had their backs to Bill. At his voice, they jumped in surprise, and put their hands above their heads at once. Then Juan swung round, his hands still high. His eyes swept the stern group of men in front of him.

'How did you get here?' he said, between his teeth. 'What

other way in is there? Who locked us in?'

'No questions answered now,' snapped Bill. He called loudly to the two men outside the door.

'Hey, Jim! Pete! Unbolt the door. We've got 'em.'

The door was unbolted. It swung open and Jim and Pete looked round it, grinning. 'Pretty little play we had,' said Pete. 'Quite enjoyed it, I did.'

Jack slipped down too. The girls had been told to keep away till the men had been captured. They were with the old couple in the cave of stars, waiting impatiently.

Bill counted the men. 'All seven here. Good. And we've got the eighth all right too. Pete, take these fellows back to the planes. Shoot at the first sign of trouble. I'll stay here and have a look-see. It looks mighty interesting.'

The men were marched off, handcuffed, swearing and stumbling. Jack watched them go, delighted to think that he had had the idea of bolting them in. Bill had clapped him on the back for that.

Once the men had passed through the cave of stars, the girls came running to join Jack, Philip and Bill. They showed the astonished Bill everything. He whistled when he saw so many treasures.

'Fortunes here,' he said. 'Well, it won't be an easy task finding out where all these things came from and sending them back. Perhaps Julius Muller can help.'

'And the old couple can too,' said Lucy-Ann eagerly. 'They know the histories of most of the statues, anyway.'

The old man and his wife were collected on the way out and taken with everyone else to the planes. They made no objection now to going into the open air. They evidently thought that Bill was some Great Man Who Must Be Obeyed. They bowed to him whenever he spoke to them.

'We'll have to take them with us for questioning,' said Bill. 'But we'll return them as soon as possible – to the village where this good man, Julius, lives. He may be good enough to look after these old people.'

Everyone got into one or other of the planes. There were six of them. In three of them were the eight prisoners with their guards. In two others were pilots and the old couple. Bill's plane carried the children.

Their plane rose up, and the children looked down at the strange valley for the last time.

'Yes, have a good look,' said Bill. It will be in all the papers presently – the Valley of Treasure.'

'No, Bill – the Valley of Adventure!' said Jack. 'That's what *we* shall always call it – the Valley of Adventure!'

'I'm glad we found Martha all right,' said Lucy-Ann suddenly. 'I did like her so much. She was sweet.'

'Good heavens! Who's Martha?' said Bill, startled. 'I thought the old woman was called Elsa. Don't tell me Martha is someone we've left behind!'

'Oh no, Bill – she's sitting on Elsa's knee now in one of the other planes – she might even lay an egg there,' said Lucy-Ann.

Bill looked even more astonished. 'She's a *hen*!' explained Lucy-Ann. 'She got left behind in the caves with the men and we were afraid she might have been killed by them. But she wasn't. She hid under the table and came clucking to join us when we went to find her. You were busy looking at the gold, I expect.'

'I must have missed her,' said Bill. 'To think I haven't yet made the acquaintance of one of the ladies in this thrilling adventure. What a pity!'

'What a pity, what a pity, what a pity!' said Kiki at once. 'Cluck-luck-luck! Pop goes Martha!'

# The Sea of
# Adventure

# Contents

1 No governess, thank you!     209
2 A glorious idea     215
3 Very mysterious     221
4 A visit from Bill – and a great idea     226
5 Exciting plans     232
6 Travelling far     238
7 On the sea at last     244
8 The island of birds     251
9 Hurrah for Puffin Island!     256
10 A little exploring     261
11 Huffin and Puffin     268
12 Bill goes off on his own     273
13 What happened in the night?     279
14 A few plans     285
15 A really terrible storm     290
16 Next day     296
17 A boat, a boat!     302
18 The enemy – and Kiki     307
19 Someone else comes to the island     313
20 Mr Horace Tipperlong gets a shock     318
21 Horace does not like Puffin Island     323
22 The enemy     330
23 The secret lagoon     335
24 An amazing discovery     341
25 Another surprise     347
26 Off to the enemy's island     352
27 Escape     358
28 A night of talking     364
29 Bill makes a grand find     371
30 Ahoy there! Show yourselves!     376
31 Over the sea of adventure     382

# 1

## No governess, thank you!

'Do you know, it's May the fifth already!' said Jack, in a very gloomy voice. 'All the fellows will be back at school today.'

'What a pity, what a pity!' said Kiki the parrot, in just as gloomy a voice as Jack's.

'This awful measles!' said Lucy-Ann. 'First Philip had it as soon as he came home for the hols, then Dinah, then she gave it to me, and then you had it!'

'Well, we're all out of quarantine now,' said Dinah, from her corner of the room. 'It's just *silly* of the doctor to say we ought to go away and have a change before we go back to school. Isn't it enough change to go back to school? I do so love the summer term too.'

'Yes – and I bet I'd have been in the first eleven' said Philip, pushing back the tuft of hair he had in front. 'Golly, I'll be glad to get my hair cut again! It feels tickly, now it's grown so long!'

The four children had all had a bad attack of measles in the holidays. Jack especially had had a very nasty time, and Dinah's eyes had given her a lot of trouble. This was partly her own fault, for she had been forbidden to read, and had disobeyed the doctor's orders. Now her eyes kept watering, and she blinked in any bright light.

'Certainly no school work for Dinah yet,' the doctor had said, sternly. 'I suppose you thought you knew better than I did, young lady, when you disobeyed orders. Think yourself lucky if you don't have to wear glasses a little later on!'

'I hope Mother won't send us away to some awful boarding-house by the sea,' said Dinah. 'She can't come with us herself, because she's taken on some kind of important job for the summer. I hope she doesn't get us a governess or something to take us away.'

'A *governess*!' said Philip in scorn. 'I jolly well wouldn't go. And anyway she wouldn't stay now that I'm training young rats.'

His sister Dinah looked at him in disgust. Philip always had some kind of creature about him, for he had a great love of animals. He could do anything he liked with them, and Lucy-Ann secretly thought that if he met a roaring tiger in a jungle, he would simply hold out his hand, and the tiger would lick it like a dog, and purr happily like a cat.

'I've told you, Philip, that if you so much as let me *see* one of your young rats I'll scream!' Dinah said.

'All right, then scream!' said Philip obligingly. 'Hey, Squeaker, where are you?'

Squeaker appeared above the neck of Philip's jersey collar, and true to his name squeaked loudly. Dinah screamed.

'You beast, Philip! How many of those things have you got down your neck? If we had a cat I'd give them all to her.'

'Well, we haven't,' said Philip, and poked Squeaker's head down his collar again.

'Three blind mice,' remarked Kiki the parrot, with great interest, cocking her head on one side and watching for Squeaker to appear again.

'Wrong, Kiki, old bird,' said Jack, lazily putting out a hand and pulling at his parrot's tail feathers. 'Far from being three blind mice, it's one very wide-awake rat. I say, Kiki, why didn't you catch measles from us?'

Kiki was quite prepared to have a conversation with Jack. She gave a loud cackle, and then put her head down to be scratched. 'How many times have I told you to shut the door?' she cried. 'How many times have I told you to wipe your feet? Wipe the door, shut your feet, wipe the . . .'

'Hey, you're getting muddled!' said Jack and the others

laughed. It was always comical when Kiki mixed up the things she loved to say. The parrot liked to make people laugh. She raised her head, put up her crest, and made a noise like a mowing-machine outside in the garden.

'That's enough,' said Jack, tapping her on the beak. 'Now stop it, Kiki!'

But Kiki, pleased with the noise, flew up to the top of the curtains, and went on being a mowing-machine, one that wanted oiling.

Mrs Mannering put her head in at the door. 'Children! *Don't* let Kiki make such a noise. I'm interviewing someone, and it's very annoying.'

'Who's come for an interview?' said Philip at once. 'Mother! You haven't gone and got a governess or something awful to take us away for a change, have you? Is she here?'

'Yes, she is,' said Mrs Mannering. All the children groaned. 'Well, dears, you know I can't spare the time to take you myself,' she went on. 'I've taken on this new job, though, of course, if I'd known you were going to be measly for so long, and then be so peaky afterwards . . . '

'We're *not* peaky!' said Philip indignantly. 'What an awful word!'

'Peaky Squeaky,' said Kiki at once, and cackled with laughter. She loved putting the same-sounding words together. 'Peaky Squeaky!'

'Shut up, Kiki!' called Jack, and threw a cushion at her. 'Aunt Allie – we can quite well go away by ourselves. We're old enough to look after ourselves perfectly.'

'Jack, as soon as I let you out of my sight in the holidays, you plunge into the middle of the most hair-raising adventures,' said Mrs Mannering. 'I shan't forget what happened in the last summer holidays – going off in the wrong aeroplane and being lost for ages in a strange valley.'

'Oh, that was a *marvellous* adventure!' cried Philip. 'I

wish we could have another. I'm fed up with being measly so long. Do, do let us go away by ourselves, Mother, there's a darling!'

'No,' said his mother. 'You're going to a perfectly safe seaside spot with a perfectly safe governess for a perfectly safe holiday.'

'Safe, safe, safe!' shrieked Kiki. 'Sound and safe, sound and safe!'

'Other way round, Kiki,' said Jack. Mrs Mannering put her fingers to her ears.

'That bird! I suppose I'm tired with nursing you all, but honestly Kiki gets dreadfully on my nerves just now. I shall be glad when she's gone with you.'

'I bet no governess will like Kiki,' said Jack. 'Aunt Allie, have you told her about Kiki?'

'Not yet,' admitted Mrs Mannering. 'But I suppose I'd better bring her in and introduce her to you all and to Kiki too.'

She went out. The children scowled at one another. 'I knew it would happen. Instead of having fun at school we shall mope about with somebody we can't bear,' said Dinah gloomily. 'Phil – can't you do something with those awful rats of yours when she comes in? If she knew you were the kind of boy that likes mice and rats and beetles and hedge-hogs living down his neck and in his pockets, she'd probably run for miles.'

'Jolly good idea, Dinah!' said everyone at once, and Philip beamed at her. 'It's not often you get a brainwave,' he said, 'but that's one all right. Hey, Squeaker! Come along out. Woffles, where are you? Nosey, come out of my pocket!'

Dinah retreated to the furthest corner of the room, watch-ing the young white rats in horror. However many had Philip got? She determined not to go near him if she could possibly help it.

'I think Kiki might perform also,' said Jack, grinning. 'Kiki – puff-puff-puff!'

That was the signal for the parrot to do her famous imitation of a railway engine screeching in a tunnel. She opened her beak and swelled out her throat in delight. It wasn't often that she was begged to make this fearful noise. Lucy-Ann put her hands to her ears.

The door opened and Mrs Mannering came in with a tall, rather stern-looking woman. It was quite plain that no adventure, nothing unusual, would ever be allowed to happen anywhere near Miss Lawson. 'Perfectly safe' was written all over her.

'Children, this is Miss Lawson,' began Mrs Mannering, and then her voice was drowned in Kiki's railway-engine screech. It was an even better imitation than usual, and longer drawn-out. Kiki was really letting herself go.

Miss Lawson gave a gasp and took a step backwards. At first she did not see Kiki, but looked at the children, thinking that one of them must be making the terrible noise.

'KIKI!' thundered Mrs Mannering, really angry. 'Children, how could you let her? I'm ashamed of you!'

Kiki stopped. She put her head on one side and looked cheekily at Miss Lawson. 'Wipe your feet!' she commanded. 'Shut the door! Where's your handkerchief? How many times have I told you to . . . '

'Take Kiki out, Jack,' said Mrs Mannering, red with annoyance. 'I'm so sorry, Miss Lawson. Kiki belongs to Jack, and she isn't usually so badly-behaved.'

'I see,' said Miss Lawson, looking very doubtful. 'I'm not very much used to parrots, Mrs Mannering. I suppose, of course, that this bird will not come away with us? I could not be responsible for pets of that kind – and I don't think that a boarding-house . . . '

'Well, we can discuss that later,' said Mrs Mannering hastily. 'Jack, did you hear what I said? Take Kiki out.'

'Polly, put the kettle on,' said Kiki to Miss Lawson, who took absolutely no notice at all. Kiki growled like a very fierce dog, and Miss Lawson looked startled. Jack caught the parrot, winked at the others and took Kiki out of the room.

'What a pity, what a pity!' mourned Kiki as the door shut behind them. Mrs Mannering gave a sigh of relief.

'Jack and Lucy-Ann Trent are not my own children,' she said to Miss Lawson. 'Lucy-Ann, shake hands with Miss Lawson. Lucy-Ann and her brother are great friends of my own children, and they live with us, and all go off to boarding-school together,' she explained.

Miss Lawson looked at the green-eyed, red-haired little girl and liked her. She was very like her brother, she thought. Then she looked at Philip and Dinah, each dark-eyed and dark-haired, with a queer tuft that stuck up in front. She would make them brush it down properly, thought Miss Lawson.

Dinah came forward politely and shook hands. She thought that Miss Lawson would be very proper, very strict and very dull – but oh, so safe!

Then Philip came forward, but before he could shake hands, he clutched at his neck. Then he clutched at one leg of his shorts. Then he clapped a hand over his middle. Miss Lawson stared at him in amazement.

'Excuse me – it's only my rats,' explained Philip, and to Miss Lawson's enormous horror she saw Squeaker running round his collar, Nosey making a lump here and there over his tummy, and Woffles coming out of his sleeve. Goodness, how many more had the awful boy got!

'I'm sorry,' said Miss Lawson faintly. 'I'm very sorry – but I can't take this post, Mrs Mannering. I really can't.'

# 2

## A glorious idea

After Miss Lawson had hurriedly said goodbye to Mrs Mannering, and the front door had shut after her, Mrs Mannering came back into the children's playroom looking very cross.

'That was too bad of you, really! I feel very annoyed and angry. How *could* you let Kiki behave like that, Jack! – and Philip, there was no need at all for you to make those rats all appear at once.'

'But, Mother,' argued Philip, 'I can't go away without my rats, so it was only fair to let Miss Lawson know what she was in for – I mean, I was really being very honest and . . . '

'You were being most obstructive,' said Mrs Mannering crossly. 'And you know you were. I consider you are all being really unhelpful. You know you can't go back to school yet – you all look thin and pale, and you really must pick up first – and I'm doing my best to give you a good holiday in the care of somebody responsible.'

'Sorry, Aunt Allie,' said Jack, seeing that Mrs Mannering really was upset. 'You see – it's the kind of holiday we'd hate. We're too big to be chivvied about by Miss Lawson. Now – if it was old Bill . . . '

Old Bill! Everyone brightened up at the thought of old Bill Smugs. His real name was Cunningham, but as he had introduced himself as Bill Smugs in their very first adventure, Bill Smugs he remained. What adventures they had had with him!

'Golly, yes! – if we could go away with Bill,' said Philip, rubbing Squeaker's nose affectionately.

'Yes – and dive into the middle of another dreadful adventure,' said Mrs Mannering. 'I know Bill!'

'Oh no, Aunt Allie – it's us children who have the adventures, and drag old Bill into them,' said Jack. 'Really it is. But we haven't heard from Bill for ages and ages.'

This was true. Bill seemed to have disappeared off the map. He hadn't answered the children's letters. Mrs Mannering hadn't heard a word. He was not at his home and hadn't been there for weeks.

But nobody worried much about him – Bill was always on secret and dangerous missions, and disappeared for weeks at a time. Still, this time he really had been gone for ages without a word to anyone. Never mind – he would suddenly turn up, ready for a holiday, grinning all over his cheerful ruddy face.

If only he would turn up now, this very afternoon! That would be grand. Nobody would mind missing the glorious summer term for a week or two if only they could go off with Bill.

But no Bill came – and something had to be decided about this holiday. Mrs Mannering looked at the mutinous children in despair.

'I suppose,' she said suddenly, 'I suppose you wouldn't like to go off to some place somewhere by the sea where you could study the wild sea-birds, and their nesting habits? I know Jack has always wanted to – but it has been impossible before, because you were all at school at the best time of year for it . . . and—'

'Aunt Allie!' yelled Jack, beside himself with joy. 'That's the most marvellous idea you've ever had in your life! Oh, I say . . . '

'Yes, Mother – it's gorgeous!' agreed Philip, rapping on the table to emphasise his feelings. Kiki at once rapped with her beak too.

'Come in,' she ordered solemnly, but no one took any notice. This new idea was too thrilling.

Lucy-Ann always loved to be where her brother Jack

was, so she beamed too, knowing how happy Jack would be among his beloved birds. Philip too, lover of animals and birds, could hardly believe that his mother had made such a wonderful suggestion.

Only Dinah looked blue. She was not fond of wild animals, and was really scared of most of them, though she was better than she had been. She liked birds but hadn't the same interest in and love for them that the boys had. Still – to be all by themselves in some wild, lonely place by the sea – wearing old clothes – doing what they liked, picnicking every day – what joy! So Dinah began to smile too, and joined in the cheerful hullabaloo.

'Can we really go? All by ourselves?'

'When? Do say when!'

'Tomorrow! Can't we go tomorrow? Golly, I feel better just at the thought of it!'

'Mother! Whatever made you think of it? Honestly, it's wizard!'

Kiki sat on Jack's shoulder, listening to the Babel of noise. The rats hidden about Philip's clothes burrowed deeply for safety, scared of such a sudden outburst of voices.

'Give me a chance to explain,' said Mrs Mannering. 'There's an expedition setting out in two days' time for some of the lonely coasts and islands off the north of Britain. Just a few naturalists, and one boy, the son of Dr Johns, the ornithologist.'

All the children knew what an ornithologist was – one who loved and studied birds and their ways. Philip's father had been a bird-lover. He was dead now, and the boy often wished he had known him, for he was very like him in his love for all wild creatures.

'Dr Johns!' said Philip. 'Why – that was one of Daddy's best friends.'

'Yes,' said his mother. 'I met him last week and he was telling me about this expedition. His boy is going, and he wondered if there was any chance of you and Dinah going, Philip. You weren't at all well then, and I said no at once. But now . . . '

'But now we can!' cried Philip, giving his mother a sudden hug. 'Fancy you thinking of somebody like Miss Lawson, when you knew about this! How could you?'

'Well – it seems a long way for you to go,' said Mrs Mannering. 'And it wasn't exactly the kind of holiday I had imagined for you. Still, if you think you'd like it, I'll ring up Dr Johns and arrange for him to add four more to his bird-expedition if he can manage it.'

'Of course he'll be able to manage it!' cried Lucy-Ann. 'We shall be company for his boy, too, Aunt Allie. I say – won't it be absolutely lovely to be up so far north, in this glorious early summer weather?'

The children felt happy and cheerful that teatime as they discussed the expedition. To go exploring among the northern islands, some of them only inhabited by birds! To swim and sail and walk, and watch hundreds, no, thousands of wild birds in their daily lives! . . .

'There'll be puffins up there,' said Jack happily. 'Thousands of them. They go there in nesting time. I've always wanted to study them, they're such comical-looking birds.'

'Puff-puff-puffin,' said Kiki at once, thinking it was an invitation to let off her railway-engine screech. But Jack stopped her sternly.

'No, Kiki. No more of that. Frighten the gulls and cormorants, the guillemots and the puffins all you like with that awful screech when we get to them – but you are not to let it off here. It gets on Aunt Allie's nerves.'

'What a pity, what a pity!' said Kiki mournfully. 'Puff-puff, ch-ch-ch!'

'Idiot,' said Jack, and ruffled the parrot's feathers. She sidled towards him on the tea-table, and rubbed her beak against his shoulder. Then she pecked a large strawberry out of the jar of jam.

'Oh, Jack!' began Mrs Mannering, 'you know I don't like Kiki on the table at mealtimes – and really, that's the third time she's helped herself to strawberries out of the jam.'

'Put it back, Kiki,' ordered Jack at once. But that didn't please Mrs Mannering either. Really, she thought, it would be very very nice and peaceful when the four children and the parrot were safely off on their holiday.

The children spent a very happy evening talking about the coming holiday. The next day Jack and Philip looked out their field-glasses and cleaned them up. Jack hunted for his camera, a very fine one indeed.

'I shall take some unique pictures of the puffins,' he told Lucy-Ann. 'I hope they'll be nesting when we get there, Lucy-Ann, though I think we might be a bit too early to find eggs.'

'Do they nest in trees?' asked Lucy-Ann. 'Can you take pictures of their nests too, and the puffins sitting on them?'

Jack smiled. 'Puffins don't nest in trees,' he explained. 'They nest in burrows underground.'

'Gracious!' said Lucy-Ann. 'Like rabbits!'

'Well, they even take rabbit burrows for nesting-places sometimes,' said Jack. 'It will be fun to see puffins scuttling underground to their nests. I bet they will be as tame as anything too, because on some of these bird-islands nobody has ever been known to set foot – so the birds don't know enough to fly off when people arrive.'

'You could have puffins for pets, easily, then,' said Lucy-Ann. 'I bet Philip will. I bet he'll only just have to whistle and all the puffins will come huffing and puffing to meet him.'

Everyone laughed at Lucy-Ann's comical way of putting things. 'Huffin and puffin,' said Kiki, scratching her head. 'Huffin and puffin, poor little piggy-wiggy-pig.'

'*Now* what's she talking about?' said Jack. 'Kiki, you do talk a lot of rubbish.'

'Poor little piggy-wiggy-pig,' repeated Kiki solemnly. 'Huffin and puffin, huffin and . . . '

Philip gave a shout of laughter. 'I know! She's remembered hearing the tale of the wolf and the three little pigs — don't you remember how the wolf came huffing and puffing to blow their house down? Oh, Kiki — you're a marvel!'

'She'll give the puffins something to think about,' said Dinah. 'Won't you, Kiki? They'll wonder what sort of a freak has come to visit them. Hallo — is that the telephone bell?'

'Yes,' said Jack, thrilled. 'Aunt Allie has put through a call to Dr Johns — to tell him we'll join his expedition — but he was out, so she asked for him to ring back when he got home. I bet that's his call.'

The children crowded out into the hall, where the telephone was. Mrs Mannering was already there. The children pressed close to her, eager to hear everything.

'Hallo!' said Mrs Mannering. 'Is that Dr Johns? — oh, it's Mrs Johns. Yes, Mrs Mannering here. What's that? Oh ... I'm so dreadfully sorry. How terrible for you! Oh, I do so hope it isn't anything serious. Yes, yes, of course, I quite understand. He will have to put the whole thing off — till next year perhaps. Well, I *do* hope you'll have good news soon. You'll be sure to let us know, won't you? Goodbye.'

She hung up the receiver and turned to the children with a solemn face. 'I'm so sorry, children — but Dr Johns has been in a car accident this morning — he's in hospital, so, of course, the whole expedition is off.'

Off! No bird-islands after all — no glorious carefree time in the wild seas of the north! What a terrible disappointment!

# 3

## Very mysterious

Everyone was upset. They were sorry for Mrs Johns, of course, and for her husband – but as they didn't know them at all, except as old friends of Mr Mannering long ago, the children felt far, far more miserable about their own disappointment.

'We'd talked about it such a lot – and made such plans – and got everything ready,' groaned Philip, looking sadly at the field-glasses hanging nearby in their brown leather cases. 'Now Mother will look for another Miss Lawson.'

'No, I won't,' said Mrs Mannering. 'I'll give up my new job, and take you away myself. I can't bear to see you so disappointed, poor things.'

'No, darling Aunt Allie, you shan't do that!' said Lucy-Ann, flinging herself on Mrs Mannering. 'We wouldn't let you. Oh dear – whatever can we do?'

Nobody knew. It seemed as if their sudden disappointment made everyone incapable of further planning. The bird-holiday or nothing, the bird-holiday or nothing – that was the thought in all the children's minds. They spent the rest of the day pottering about miserably, getting on each other's nerves. One of their sudden quarrels blew up between Philip and Dinah, and with yells and shouts they belaboured one another in a way they had not done for at least a year.

Lucy-Ann began to cry. Jack yelled angrily.

'Stop hitting Dinah, Philip. You'll hurt her!'

But Dinah could give as good as she got, and there was a loud crack as she slapped Philip full across his cheek. Philip caught her hands angrily, and she kicked him. He tripped her up, and down she went on the floor, with her brother rolling over and over too. Lucy-Ann got out of their way, still crying. Kiki flew up to the electric light, and cackled loudly. She thought Philip and Dinah were playing.

There was such a noise that nobody heard the telephone bell ringing again. Mrs Mannering, frowning at the yells and bumps from the playroom, went to answer it. Then she suddenly appeared at the door of the playroom, her face beaming.

It changed when she saw Dinah and Philip fighting on the floor. 'Dinah! Philip! Get up at once! You ought to be ashamed of yourselves, quarrelling like this now that you are so big. I've a good mind not to tell you who that was on the telephone.'

Philip sat up, rubbing his flaming cheek. Dinah wriggled away, holding her arm. Lucy-Ann mopped her tears, and Jack scowled down at the pair on the floor.

'What a collection of bad-tempered children!' said Mrs Mannering. Then she remembered that they all had had measles badly, and were probably feeling miserable and bad-tempered after their disappointment that day.

'Listen,' she said, more gently, 'guess who that was on the telephone.'

'Mrs Johns, to say that Dr Johns is all right after all,' suggested Lucy-Ann hopefully.

Mrs Mannering shook her head. 'No – it was old Bill.'

'Bill! Hurrah! So he's turned up again at last,' cried Jack. 'Is he coming to see us?'

'Well – he was very mysterious,' said Mrs Mannering. 'Wouldn't say who he was – just said he might pop in tonight, late – if nobody else was here. Of course I knew it was Bill. I'd know his voice anywhere.'

Quarrels and bad temper were immediately forgotten. The thought of seeing Bill again was like a tonic. 'Did you tell him we'd had measles and were all at home?' demanded Philip. 'Does he know he'll see us too?'

'No – I hadn't time to tell him anything,' said Mrs

Mannering. 'I tell you, he was most mysterious — hardly on the telephone for half a minute. Anyway, he'll be here tonight. I wonder why he didn't want to come if anyone else was here.'

'Because he doesn't want anyone to know where he is, I should think,' said Philip. 'He must be on one of his secret missions again. Mother, we can stay up to see him, can't we?'

'If he isn't later than half-past nine,' said Mrs Mannering.

She went out of the room. The four looked at one another. 'Good old Bill,' said Philip. 'We haven't seen him for ages. Hope he comes before half-past nine.'

'Well, I jolly well shan't go to sleep till I hear him come,' said Jack. 'Wonder why he was so mysterious.'

The children expected to see Bill all the evening, and were most disappointed when no car drove up, and nobody walked up to the front door. Half-past nine came, and no Bill.

'I'm afraid you must all go to bed,' said Mrs Mannering. 'I'm sorry — but really you all look so tired and pale. That horrid measles! I do feel so sorry that that expedition is off — it would have done you all the good in the world.'

The children went off to bed, grumbling. The girls had a bedroom at the back, and the boys at the front. Jack opened the window and looked out. It was a dark night. No car was to be heard, nor any footsteps.

'I shall listen for Bill,' he told Philip. 'I shall sit here by the window till he comes. You get into bed. I'll wake you if I hear him.'

'We'll take it in turns,' said Philip, getting into bed. 'You watch for an hour, then wake me up, and I'll watch.'

In the back bedroom the girls were already in bed. Lucy-Ann wished she could see Bill. She loved him very much — he was so safe and strong and wise. Lucy-Ann had no father or mother, and she often wished that Bill was her father. Aunt Allie was a lovely mother, and it was nice to share her with

223

Philip and Dinah. She couldn't share their father because he was dead.

'I hope I shall keep awake and hear Bill when he comes,' she thought. But soon she was fast asleep, and so was Dinah. The clock struck half-past ten, and then eleven.

Jack woke Philip. 'Nobody has come yet,' he said. 'Your turn to watch, Tufty. Funny that he's so late, isn't it?'

Philip sat down at the window. He yawned. He listened but he could hear nothing. And then he suddenly saw a streak of bright light as his mother, downstairs, pulled back a curtain, and the light flooded into the garden.

Philip knew what it was, of course – but he suddenly stiffened as the light struck on something pale, hidden in a bush by the front gate. The something was moved quickly back into the shadows, but Philip had guessed what it was.

'That was someone's face I saw! Somebody is hiding in the bushes by the gate. Why? It can't be Bill. He'd come right in. Then it must be somebody waiting in ambush for him. Golly!'

He slipped across to the bed and awoke Jack. He whispered to him what he had seen. Jack was out of bed and by the window at once. But he could see nothing, of course. Mrs Mannering had drawn the curtain back over the window, and no light shone out now. The garden was in darkness.

'We must do something quickly,' said Jack. 'If Bill comes, he'll be knocked out, if that's what that man there is waiting for. Can we warn Bill? It's plain he knows there's danger for himself, or he wouldn't have been so mysterious on the telephone – and insisted he couldn't come if anyone else was here. I wish Aunt Allie would go to bed. What's the time? The clock struck eleven some time ago, I know.'

There came the sound of somebody clicking off lights and a door closing. 'It's Mother,' said Philip. 'She's not going to wait any longer. She's coming up to bed. Good! Now the house will be in darkness, and maybe that fellow will go.'

'We'll have to see that he does,' said Jack. 'Do you suppose Bill will come now, Philip? – it's getting very late.'

'If he says he will, he will,' said Philip 'Sh – here's Mother.'

Both boys hopped into bed and pretended to be asleep. Mrs Mannering switched the light on, and then, seeing that both boys were apparently sound asleep, she switched it off again quickly. She did the same in the girls' room, and then went to her own room.

Philip was soon sitting by the window again, eyes and ears open for any sign of the hidden man in the bushes below. He thought he heard a faint cough.

'He's still there,' he said to Jack. 'He must have got wind of Bill coming here tonight.'

'Or more likely still, he knows that Bill is a great friend of ours, and whatever gang he belongs to has sent a man to watch in that bush every night,' said Jack. 'He's hoping that Bill will turn up sooner or later. Bill must have a lot of enemies. He's always tracking down crooks and criminals.'

'Listen,' said Philip, 'I'm going to creep out of the back door, and get through the hedge of the next-door garden, and out of their back gate, so as not to let that hidden man hear me. And I'm going up to watch for old Bill and warn him. He'll come up the road, not down, because that's the way he always comes.'

'Good idea!' said Jack. 'I'll come too.'

'No. One of us must watch to see what that man down there does,' said Philip. 'We'll have to know if he's there or not. I'll go. You stay at the window. If I find Bill coming along I'll warn him and turn him back.'

'All right,' said Jack, wishing he had the exciting job of creeping about the dark gardens to go and meet Bill. 'Give him our love – and tell him to phone us if he can, and we'll meet him somewhere safe.'

Philip slipped quietly out of the room. There was still a light in his mother's room, so he went very cautiously downstairs, anxious not to disturb her. She would be very scared if she knew about the hidden man.

He opened the back door quietly, shut it softly behind him, and went out into the dark garden. He had no torch, for he did not want to show any sign of himself at all.

He squeezed through a gap in the hedge, and came into the next-door garden. He knew it very well. He found the path, and then made his way quietly along the grass at the edge of it, afraid of making the gravel crunch a little, if he walked on it.

Then he thought he heard a sound. He stopped dead and listened. Surely there wasn't *another* man hiding somewhere? Could they be burglars, not men waiting for Bill, after all? Ought he to creep back and telephone to the police?

He listened again, straining his ears, and had a queer feeling that there was someone nearby, also listening. Listening for him, Philip, perhaps. It was not a nice thought, there in the darkness.

He took a step forward – and then suddenly someone fell on him savagely, pinned his arms behind him, and forced him on his face to the ground. Philip bit deep into the soft earth of a flower-bed, and choked. He could not even shout for help.

# 4

# A visit from Bill – and a great idea

Philip's captor was remarkably quiet in his movements. He had captured Philip with hardly a sound, and as the boy had not had time to utter a single cry, nobody had heard anything at all. Philip struggled frantically, for he was half choked with the soft earth that his face was buried in.

He was twisted over quickly, and a gag of some sort was put right across his mouth. His wrists, he found, were already tied together. Whatever could be happening? Did this fellow think he was Bill? But surely he knew that Bill was big and burly?

Trying to spit out the earth in his mouth behind the gag, Philip wriggled and struggled. But it was of no use, for his captor was strong and merciless.

He was picked up and carried to a summer-house, quite silently. 'And now,' hissed a voice, close to his ear, 'how many more of you are there here? Tell me that, or you'll be sorry. Grunt twice if there are more of you.'

Philip made no answer. He didn't know what to do, grunt or not grunt. Instead he groaned, for his mouth was still full of earth, and it did not taste at all nice.

His captor ran his hands over him. Then he got out a small pocket-torch, and flashed it once, very quickly, on Philip's gagged face. He saw the tuft of hair standing straight up on Philip's forehead and gave a gasp.

'Philip! You little ass! What are you doing out here, creeping about in the dark?'

With a shock of amazement and delight, Philip recognised Bill's voice. Gosh, so it was Bill! Well, he didn't mind his mouth being full of earth then. He pulled at the gag, making gurgling sounds.

'Shut up!' whispered Bill urgently, and he took off the gag. 'There may be others about. Don't make a sound. If you've anything to say whisper it right into my ear, like this.'

'Bill,' whispered Philip, his mouth finding Bill's ear, 'there's a man hidden in the bushes at our front gate. We spotted him there, and I slipped out to warn you if I could. Be careful.'

Bill undid Philip's wrists. The boy rubbed them tenderly, Bill knew how to tie people up, no doubt about that! Good thing he hadn't knocked him out.

'The back door's open,' he whispered into Bill's ear. 'As

227

far as I know there's nobody waiting about at the back. Let's try and get into the house. We can talk there.'

Very silently the two made their way back to the gap in the hedge that Philip knew so well. Neither of them trod on the gravel, in case the slight crunch might warn any hidden watcher.

They squeezed through the gap slowly and carefully. Now they were in Philip's own garden. Taking Bill by the arm he led him slowly over the dark lawn, under the trees, towards the house. There was no light in it anywhere now. Mrs Mannering had gone to bed.

The back door was still unlocked. Philip pushed it open, and the two of them went in. 'Don't put on the light,' whispered Bill. 'We don't want anyone to know that we're awake here. I'll lock this door.'

They went cautiously upstairs. One of the stairs creaked loudly, and Jack, who was waiting in the bedroom, shot to the door. Luckily he didn't switch the light on.

'It's all right – it's only me,' whispered Philip. 'And I've got old Bill.'

'Good egg!' said Jack in delight, and dragged them into his room. Bill gave his hand a hearty shake. He was very fond of the whole family.

'I must rinse my mouth out,' said Philip. 'It's full of earth still. I didn't dare to do any spitting out in the garden, because of the noise. Ugh! It's horrible!'

'Poor Philip!' said Bill remorsefully. 'I didn't know it was you, old fellow. I thought it was somebody lying in wait for me, and I meant to get him, before he got *me*!'

'You did it jolly well,' said Philip, rinsing his mouth out. 'Now where's my tooth-paste? I really must clean my teeth! Oh, blow!'

His hand, seeking for his tooth-paste in the dark, had knocked over a glass. It fell into the basin and smashed. It made a tremendous noise in the silent night.

'Go and warn the girls not to put their light on, if this has waked them ' said Bill urgently to Jack. 'Quick! And see if it has waked Aunt Allie. If it has, warn her too.'

Lucy-Ann was awake, and Jack just managed to stop her switching on the light. His mother did not stir. Her room was further away and she had not heard the sound of breaking glass. Lucy-Ann was astonished to hear Jack's urgent voice.

'What's up?' she asked. 'Anything gone wrong? Are you or Philip ill?'

'Of course not,' said Jack impatiently. 'Get your dressing-gown on, and wake Dinah. Bill's here! But we're not to put on any lights, see?'

Something fluttered by his head with a low squawk. 'Oh, Kiki! I wondered where you were,' said Jack. 'What made you sleep in the girls' room tonight? Come along and see Bill!'

Lucy-Ann awoke an astonished Dinah. The two girls put on their dressing-gowns and went to the boys' room. Kiki was already there, nibbling Bill's ear in delight, making soft noises in his ear.

'Hallo! hallo!' said Bill, when the girls crept softly into the room. 'Which is which? I can only feel you. Ah, this must be Lucy-Ann – I can smell your freckles!'

'You can't smell freckles,' said Lucy-Ann, giggling. 'But you're right, it is me, all the same. Oh, Bill, where have you been so long? You didn't answer any of our letters at all.'

'I know,' said Bill. 'You see – I was on a peculiar job – hunting down a gang of rogues – and then, before I knew what was happening, they got wind of what I was doing – and began to hunt *me* down! So I had to go into hiding, and keep dark.'

'Why – would they have kidnapped you or something, Bill?' asked Lucy-Ann, scared.

'Oh, there's no knowing what they would have done to me,' said Bill airily. 'I should certainly have disappeared for good. But here I am, as you see.'

'So that's what that man at the front gate was there for – hoping to get you,' said Philip. 'Why have you come to see us now, Bill? Do you want us to do anything?'

'Well,' said Bill, 'I've got to disappear for some time, and I wanted to see your mother particularly, to give her a few things to keep for me – just in case – well, just in case I didn't turn up again. I'm what is called a "marked man" now, as far as this particular gang is concerned. I know too much about them for their own comfort.'

'Oh, Bill – but where are you going to disappear to?' asked Lucy-Ann forlornly. 'I don't like you to disappear into the blue. Can't you tell us?'

'Oh – I'll probably lead the simple life somewhere in the wilds,' said Bill. 'Till these fellows have given up hunting for me, or get themselves caught. *I* don't want to disappear – don't think that! I'm not afraid of any of them, but my chiefs can't afford to let anyone get hold of me. So I've got to vanish completely for a time – and not even get into touch with you or my family.'

There was a silence. It wasn't nice to hear all this, told in a low voice in the darkness of midnight. Lucy-Ann groped for Bill's hand. He squeezed her fingers.

'Cheer up! You'll hear from me again some day – next year, or the year after. I shall take some kind of disguise – become a miner somewhere in the wilds of Alaska – or – or a lonely ornithologist on some desolate island – or . . . '

Jack gave a gasp. Something clicked in his mind as a really brilliant idea slid into place there.

'Bill! Oh, Bill! I've thought of something grand!'

'Sh! Not so loud!' said Bill. 'And just take Kiki on your shoulder now, will you, before she nibbles away the whole of my left ear.'

'Listen, Bill,' said Jack urgently. 'I've thought of something. We had a great disappointment today – I'll tell you about it first.'

'Go on, then,' said Bill, thankful that Kiki was no longer on his shoulder.

'I don't expect you know, but we've all had measles pretty badly,' said Jack. 'That's why we're not back at school. Well, the doctor said we ought to go away for a change, and Aunt Allie decided we could go on a bird-watching expedition, with Dr Johns and his party, to some lonely coasts and islands off the north of Britain – you know, places that only birds live on, and only bird-lovers visit.'

'I know,' said Bill, listening intently.

'Well, Dr Johns got hurt in an accident today,' said Jack. 'So we can't go because there is nobody to take us. But – why can't *you* take us – disguised as some bird-man or other? – then we'd have a perfectly glorious holiday, you'd be able to get off into the unknown without anyone knowing – and we could leave you behind there when we come back – quite safe!'

There was silence. All the children waited breathlessly for Bill's answer. Even Kiki seemed to be listening anxiously.

'I don't know,' said Bill at last. 'It's too much like using you as a smoke-screen – and if my enemies saw through the smoke – well, things wouldn't be too good for you or for me either. I don't think it's possible.'

The mere thought of Bill's turning the wonderful idea down made the children more enthusiastic and urgent about it. They each had a few words to contribute.

'We were *so* disappointed not to go – and now this does seem a way – and after all, it would only be for about two weeks, as far as we're concerned. We'd be going back to school then.'

'You're awfully good at disguises. You could *easily* look like an ornithologist – sort of earnest, and always peering into the distance for birds, and with field-glasses over your shoulder . . . '

'Nobody could possibly know. We'd all be absolutely safe

up in the northern seas, so wild and desolate, with you. Think of May up there -- the sea so blue, the birds all soaring and gliding, the sea-pinks out all over the place . . . '

'You'd be *safe*, Bill – no-one surely would ever dream of hunting for you in a place like that. And oh, we do want that kind of holiday. We've felt mouldy after measles.'

'Not so *loud*,' whispered Bill. 'I'll have to talk things over with your mother first – even if I think it's all right myself. It's a bold idea – and I don't think it would occur to anyone for one moment that I would go off openly like that. And I must say that a holiday with you four – and Kiki too, of course – is just what I'm needing at the moment.'

'Oh, Bill – I believe you'll do it!' said Lucy-Ann, hugging him with ecstasy. 'What a lovely ending to a horrid day!'

# 5

# Exciting plans

Bill spent the night, unknown to Mrs Mannering, in the little spare room. He said he would talk to her the next morning. He was relieved to find that a daily maid came in each morning, but that no-one except the family slept in the house at night.

'We children do all the beds and things upstairs, now that we have recovered,' said Dinah. 'So you can stay up here unseen, if you like. We'll bring breakfast up.'

But the next morning everything was upset again. Mrs Mannering knocked on the wall separating the girls' room from hers, and Dinah went running in to see what the matter was.

'Dinah! The most sickening thing has happened!' said Mrs Mannering in disgust. '*I've* got measles now – look at my spots. I thought I'd had it when I was your age – but it's measles right enough. Oh dear, I wish I had engaged that Miss Lawson and let her take you off to Bournemouth or somewhere yesterday. Now what are we to do?'

'Oh dear!' said Dinah. Then she decided to tell her mother about Bill being there. Perhaps that would help. 'I'll get you your dressing-jacket and tidy the room,' she said briskly, 'because there's someone who wants to see you. He may help quite a lot. It's Bill!'

'Bill!' said Mrs Mannering, amazed. 'When did he come? I waited up till eleven, but I felt so terribly tired I just had to go to bed. Well, now – I wonder if old Bill would take you off my hands for a bit and leave Hilda, the daily, to look after me!'

'I'm sure he would,' said Dinah, delighted. 'Poor Mother! You feel worst the first two or three days and after that it's not so bad. There – are your pillows comfy? I'll send Bill in now.'

The news was broken to the others. The children were sorry and dismayed. Did grown-ups actually get measles then? Poor Mother! Poor Aunt Allie! She would certainly want them out of the house now.

'She's ready to see you, Bill,' said Dinah. 'I say – I suppose you've had measles all right, haven't you?'

'Oh, dozens of times,' said Bill cheerfully, going to Mrs Mannering's room. 'Cheer up – we'll get things right in no time!'

'But you can only have measles once,' began Lucy-Ann. Then the door was shut, and the children could hear only a murmur of voices in the room.

They went down to breakfast. The boys had more or less got back their ordinary appetites, but the girls still only picked at their food. Dinah looked at Lucy-Ann.

'Your freckles hardly show,' she said. 'Nor do Jack's. A bit of sun will do us all good. I don't feel like this bacon, do you? Oh dear – I wish Bill would hurry up and come down. I do want to know what they've decided.'

Bill did not come down. The children heard the door above opening, and then a soft whistle. Bill was evidently afraid the daily was about. But she had gone out to do the shopping.

'It's all right,' called Dinah. 'Hilda's out. Come down if you want to. We've saved you some breakfast.'

Bill came down. 'Your mother doesn't want any breakfast except toast and tea,' he said. 'You make the toast, Dinah. I see the kettle's boiling – we can make tea as soon as the toast is ready. Then I'm going to ring up the doctor, and then ring up Miss Tremayne, your mother's friend, and ask her to come along for a week or two to be with the invalid. She says she'll like that.'

The children listened in silence. 'And what about *us*?' asked Jack at last. 'Didn't you decide?'

'Yes, I decided,' said Bill. 'Your aunt begged me to take you away for two weeks – and I told her I was due to disappear for a while, so I'd go off to the northern seas with you. I didn't scare her with my reasons for disappearing – she's really feeling bad this morning – and she's so thankful to think you'll get away for a change that she hardly asked me any questions at all.'

'So we're to go?' said Jack, unable to keep the joy out of his voice, even though he was very sorry about Aunt Allie. 'How absolutely super!'

The four faces glowed. Kiki picked a piece of rind out of the marmalade and, as nobody said anything, took a piece of lump sugar from the sugar-basin.

'Mother will be quite all right, won't she, with Miss Tremayne?' said Philip earnestly. 'She wouldn't like one of us to stay with her, would she? I'll stay, if so.'

'She would be much better with you all out of the house,' said Bill, helping himself to bacon. 'She's tired out and wants a really peaceful time. Measles is beastly, but at least it will make her rest in bed for a while!'

'Well, then, we can really look forward to going off with a

light heart,' said Jack cheerfully. 'Oh, Bill—you always turn up just exactly at the right moment!'

'Here's Hilda!' said Philip suddenly. 'You'd better hop upstairs, Bill. Take your plate. I'll bring you more toast and tea when we take Mother's up. Isn't that toast finished *yet*, Dinah?'

'Just,' said Dinah, and put the last piece in the toast-rack. 'No, Kiki, leave it alone. Oh, Jack, look at Kiki's beak—just *dripping* with marmalade. There won't be any left for us. Greedy bird!'

Bill disappeared upstairs. Hilda went into the kitchen and began to fill up the kitchen stove. Dinah went out to tell her about Mrs Mannering having the measles. Hilda was most sympathetic, but looked very worried.

'Well, I daresay I can manage,' she said, 'but what with all you children here too . . . '

'Oh, but we shan't be,' said Dinah. 'We're gcing off on a bird-expedition, as soon as we can—and Miss Tremayne is coming to see to Mother—so . . . '

'Hilda! Hill-da! Hilllll-da!' called a voice, and Hilda jumped.

'My, that's the missus calling!' she said. 'And you told me she was in bed! Coming, Madam!'

But it was only Kiki, of course, doing one of her imitations. She cackled with laughter when Hilda came running into the dining-room.

'Wipe your feet!' she ordered. 'Don't sniff! How many times have I told you to . . . '

Hilda went out and banged the door. 'I don't mind taking orders from them as has the right to give them,' she said to a giggling Dinah, 'but take orders from that ridiculous bird I will not. I hope, Miss, that you're taking that parrot with you. I don't want the minding of her whilst you're gone. Drive me crazy, she would.'

'Oh, of *course* we'll take her!' said Dinah. 'Jack would never dream of going without her.'

The doctor came. Miss Tremayne arrived. Hilda agreed to sleep in. Everything seemed to be going well. Bill, ensconced in the spare room, whose door he kept locked in case Hilda should come barging in, made a few quick plans.

'Pack up your things. Order a taxi for eight o'clock tomorrow night. We'll catch the night train to the north. I'll slip out tonight and make the rest of the plans for the journey and the holiday. I'll meet you at Euston, and it won't be as the Bill Smugs you know! I shall then be Dr Walker, the naturalist. I'll come over and introduce myself in a loud voice as soon as I see you arrive, in case there's anyone about that know you – or me either! Then off we l go.'

It all sounded very thrilling. What a mysterious way to begin a holiday! It sounded as if they were setting off for a first-class adventure, but of course they weren't. It would be fun if they were, but what could happen on lonely bird-islands? Nothing at all except birds, and more birds and y t more birds.

Bill slipped off that night. No one had known he was in the house, not even Miss Tremayne, who had been given the little dressing-room leading off Mrs Mannering's room. Mrs Mannering had promised not to say that Bill had been there, in case it meant danger to him. But she was so heavy and sleepy that day, that she really began to wonder if Bill *had* actually been there at all, or if she had dreamt it.

The children packed. No need to take best dresses or anything like that! Shorts and jerseys, rubber shoes, bathing-suits and mackintoshes were the things they would want. And a few cardigans, some towels – and what about some rugs? Were they going to sleep under a roof or not? Bill hadn't said. For all they knew they might be sleeping in tents. What fun! They decided not to take rugs. Bill would be sure to take things like that if they needed them.

'Field-glasses – note-books – pencils – my camera – and a

rope,' said Jack, trying to think of everything. Lucy-Ann looked astonished.

'A *rope*?' she said. 'Why a rope?'

'We might want to go cliff-climbing if we want to examine nesting-places there,' said Jack.

'Well, you can go cliff-climbing if you like. I shan't!' said Lucy-Ann, with a shiver. 'I'd hate to climb down steep cliffs with just a rope round me and hardly anything to put my feet on.'

'Kiki's taken your pencil,' said Dinah. 'Kiki, don't be such a nuisance. We shan't take you to see the puffins if you behave like this.'

'Huffin and puffin, puffin and huffin, muffin and puffin, muffins and crumpets,' pronounced Kiki, and cracked her beak in delight at having said something new. 'Huffin and puff—'

'Oh stop huffing and puffing,' called Dinah.

'God save the Queen,' said Kiki, and stood up very straight.

'Goodness knows what the birds up there will think of you,' said Lucy-Ann. 'Jack, shall we put her into a basket to take her with us on the train? You know how she will keep shouting "Guard, guard" and pretending to blow a whistle, and telling everyone to wipe their feet.'

'She can go on my shoulder,' said Jack. 'We shall be sleeping on the train, in beds or berths, and she'll be quite all right. Stop cracking your beak, Kiki. It's not clever to keep *on* making a nuisance of yourself.'

'Naughty Polly!' said Kiki. 'Sing Polly-wolly-oodle-all-the-day!'

Philip threw a cushion at her and she retired to the top of the curtains and sulked. The children went on discussing their coming holiday.

'Fancy having the luck to be with Bill after all!' said Jack. 'Much better than Dr Johns. I wonder if he'll have a boat and go exploring round. Golly, I'm going to enjoy the next week or two. We might even see a Great Auk!'

'You and your Great Auks!' said Philip. 'You know quite well they're extinct. Don't start all that again, Jack. We might find Little Auks up there, though – and razor-bills – and thousands of guillemots on the cliffs.'

The next day came at last and then dragged on till the evening. Mrs Mannering slept most of the time and Miss Tremayne would not let them go in and wake her to say goodbye.

'Better not,' she said. 'I'll say goodbye for you. Mind you write to her from wherever you're going. Is that the taxi I hear now? I'll come and see you off.'

'It *was* the taxi. They bundled in with all their luggage. Now to London – to meet Dr Walker – and to travel hundreds of miles to the north, to wild places where few people had ever been. No adventures this time, but just a glorious, carefree holiday with old Bill.

'All aboard!' said Kiki, in a deep voice that made the taxi-driver jump. 'One – two – three – OFF!'

# 6

# Travelling far

Bill had told the children exactly where to wait for him at Euston Station, so, each carrying a bag and a mackintosh, they went to the spot.

They stood there waiting. 'Suppose,' said Philip, in a mysterious voice, 'just suppose that one of the gang that Bill is after, knew Bill was going to meet us here – and came up and told us he was Bill – and took us all off with him, so that we were never heard of again!'

Poor Lucy-Ann stared at him in the greatest alarm. Her eyes nearly popped out of her head. 'Oh, Philip – do you think that might happen? Gracious, I hope to goodness we recognise Bill when we see him. I shall be scared stiff of going with him if we don't.'

A very fat man approached them, smiling. He was big all over, big head, big body, big feet – and big teeth that showed when he smiled. Lucy-Ann felt her heart sink. This couldn't be Bill! Nobody could make himself as big as that, if he wasn't fat to begin with. She clutched Philip's hand. Was it one of the gang?

'Little girl,' said the big man to Lucy-Ann, 'you've dropped your mackintosh behind you. You'll lose it if you don't pick it up.'

Lucy-Ann had gone pale when he first began to speak. Then she looked round and saw her mac on the ground. She picked it up. Then, scarlet in the face, she stammered out a few words of thanks.

The big man smiled again, showing all his fine teeth. 'Don't look so scared,' he said. 'I shan't eat you!'

'He looks just as if he might,' thought Lucy-Ann, retreating behind Jack.

'Pop goes the weasel,' said Kiki, in a polite conversational tone. 'Pop, pop, pop!'

'What a remarkably clever bird!' said the big man, and put out his hand to pat Kiki. She gave him a vicious nip with her beak, and then whistled like an engine.

The big man's smile vanished and he scowled. 'Dangerous bird, that,' he said, and disappeared into the crowd. The children were relieved. They didn't think, of course, that he was one of the gang – that had only been Philip's make-up – but they were worried in case he kept them talking, and prevented Bill from coming up and fetching them.

They stood there, under the clock, looking all round for Bill. They couldn't see anyone even remotely resembling him. Then a rather shambling, round-shouldered man came up, wearing thick glasses through which his eyes peered sharply.

He wore a thick long coat, had field-glasses slung across his back, and a curious black-checked cap. He also had a black beard. But he spoke in Bill's voice.

'Good evening, children. I am glad to see you are punctual. Now at last we start on our little expedition.'

Lucy-Ann beamed. That was Bill's nice warm voice all right, in spite of the beard and the strange get-up. She was just about to fling herself on him, crying, 'Oh, Bill, it's good to see you,' when Jack, feeling sure that Lucy-Ann was going to do something impulsive like that, pushed her away and held out his hand politely.

'Good evening, Dr Walker. How are you?'

The others took their cue from Jack, and anyone looking on would have thought that here were four children greeting a tutor or a guardian who was going to take them on a journey somewhere.

'Come this way,' said Dr Walker. 'I have a porter for your things. Hey, porter, put these bags on your barrow, will you, and find our reservations in the ten o'clock train. Thank you.'

It wasn't long before they were all safely on the night train. The children were thrilled with their little 'bedrooms.' Lucy-Ann liked the way everything could fold down or fold back, or be somehow pushed out of the way.

'Now, you must sleep all night,' said Bill, his eyes smiling at them from behind his thick glasses. 'Dr Walker will see that you are awake in time for breakfast.'

'How do we get to the place we're going to, and where exactly is it?' asked Jack.

'Well, we get there by this train and another, and then by motor-boat,' said Bill. The children looked thrilled. They loved travelling.

'I've got a map here,' said Bill, making sure that the door was shut. 'It's a map of all the many little islands dotted off the north-west coast of Scotland – hundreds of them. Some are too small to map. I don't expect anyone has ever visited all of them – only the birds live there. I thought we'd make

240

one of them our headquarters, and then cruise around a bit, taking photographs, and watching the birds in their daily life.'

The eyes of the two boys gleamed. What a glorious thing to do! They visualised days of sunshine on the water, chugging to and from tiny islands inhabited by half-tame birds, picnicking hungrily in the breeze, sitting on rocks with their feet dangling in the clear water. Their hearts lifted in happiness at the thought.

'What I should really like,' said Philip, 'would be a tame puffin or two. I've never seen a live puffin – only a stuffed one – but they look real characters.'

'I suppose you would teach them to sit up and beg,' said Bill, amused.

'Huffin and puffin,' announced Kiki. 'God save the Queen.'

Nobody took any notice. They were all too much absorbed in thinking of the unusual holiday.

'I shall remain behind there, once you have gone back,' said Bill. 'It'll be a bit lonely without you all, but no doubt you will leave me your tame puffins for company.'

'I shall hate leaving you,' said Lucy-Ann. 'Will you have to be there all alone for long, Bill?'

'A goodish time, I expect,' said Bill. 'Long enough for my enemies to forget about me, or to think I'm dead and gone.'

'Oh dear!' said Lucy-Ann. 'I wish you didn't have to lead such a dangerous life, Bill. Can't you do something else instead?'

'What? Be a gardener, or a tram conductor or something safe like that, do you mean?' asked Bill, grinning at Lucy-Ann's serious face. 'No, Lucy-Ann – this kind of life suits me. I'm on the side of law and order and right – and to my mind they're worth while running any risk for. Evil is strong and powerful, but I'm strong and powerful too, and it's good to try one's strength against bad men and their ways.'

'Well, I think you're marvellous,' said Lucy-Ann stoutly.

'And I'm sure you'll always win. Don't you hate having to hide now?'

'I'm furious about it,' said Bill, looking anything but furious, but with a note in his voice that made the others realize how desperate he felt, having to 'disappear' when there was work to be done. 'but – orders are orders. And anyway, my disappearance means a perfectly glorious holiday for all of us. Well, boys, have you finished studying that map?'

The two boys had been poring over the map of islands. Jack put his finger on one. 'Look – that sounds a good one – the Isle of Wings – it must be full of birds!'

'We'll try and go there,' said Bill. 'We shall probably get well and truly lost, but never mind. Who minds being lost on the blue-green sea in May-time, with all kinds of little enchanted islands ready to welcome you?'

'It sounds glorious,' said Dinah. 'Oh, look at Kiki. She's trying to pull the plug off its chain in that basin.'

Kiki had thoroughly explored the whole of the 'bedroom,' and had had a good drink out of one of the water decanters. Now she settled down on the little towel-rail and, with a remarkably human yawn, put her head under her wing. At the same moment there came a loud banging of doors all down the train. She took her head out again.

'Shut the door,' she remarked. 'Pop goes the door. Send for the doctor.'

The whistle blew, and to Kiki's alarm the whole 'bedroom' suddenly shook as the train pulled out of the station. She almost fell off the towel-rail.

'Poor Kiki, what a pity, what a pity!' she said, and flew to Jack's shoulder.

'Now it's time we all retired to bed and to sleep,' said Bill, getting up. He looked very queer in his black beard and thick glasses. Thank goodness he had taken off the awful black-checked cap.

'Do two of us sleep here, or four of us?' asked Lucy-Ann, looking doubtfully at the small beds, one on each side of the 'bedroom.'

'Two of us,' said Bill. 'I've got a single room on the right of you – and to the right again is another compartment, or room, for the two boys. I'm in the middle of you, you see – and you've only to bang hard on the wooden wall between us, if you want anything, and I'll come rushing in.'

'Oh, good!' said Lucy-Ann. 'I'm glad you're so near us. Bill, are you going to sleep in your beard?'

'Well, as it's rather painful to remove at the moment, being well and truly stuck on, I think I will,' said Bill. 'I'll take it off when we're safely among our little islands. No one will see us there. Don't you like me in my beautiful beard?'

'Not much,' said Lucy-Ann. 'I feel as if you're not you when I look at you, but when I hear your voice, it's all right.'

'Well, my child, look at me with your eyes shut, and you'll have no horrid feelings,' said Bill, with a grin. 'Now good night, and sleep well. Come on, boys, I'll take you to your compartment. I'll wake you in the morning, and we'll dress and go along to the restaurant car for breakfast.'

'I feel a bit hungry now,' said Philip, 'although we had a jolly good supper. But that's ages ago.'

'Well, I've got some sandwiches and some bananas,' said Bill. 'I'll get them. But don't be long turning in, because it's getting late.'

'Only just gone ten,' said Dinah, but she yawned loudly as she spoke. Kiki promptly imitated her, and that set everyone else yawning too.

Bill went into his own compartment and fetched sandwiches and ripe bananas. Then he said good night to the girls and took the boys to their own 'bedroom.' It really was very exciting to go to bed in a train. It was queer undressing with the train swaying about, rushing through the night at sixty miles an hour.

It was nice to be in bed, listening to the 'tutta-tut-*tah*! tutta-tut-*tah*!' of the train wheels turning rapidly over the rails.

'Travelling *far*, travelling *far*, travelling *far*,' said the wheels to Lucy-Ann, as her eyes closed, and her mind swung towards sleep. 'Travelling *far* . . . '

In spite of all the excitement the four children were soon fast asleep and dreaming. What were they dreaming of? That was easy to guess. Blue-green water, clear as crystal, enchanting little islands, big white clouds flying across an enormous blue sky, and birds, birds, birds . . . travelling *far*, travelling *far*, travelling *far*.

# 7

## On the sea at last

The journey was half over before the children awoke again. Bill banged on the walls, and they woke with a jump. They dressed and walked staggeringly along to the restaurant car, feeling very hungry. Lucy-Ann didn't much like walking across the bits that joined two carriages together. She clutched Bill's hand then.

'I'm always afraid the train might come in two, just when I'm walking through the bit where two carriages are joined,' she explained. Bill quite understood, though the others were very scornful of Lucy-Ann's extraordinary idea.

Kiki behaved very badly at breakfast, throwing the toast about, and squawking because she was not allowed any of the rather small helping of marmalade. She made rude noises at the sunflower seeds Jack offered her. The other passengers were amused at her and laughed – but that only made Kiki show off all the more.

'Stop it, Kiki,' said Bill, exasperated, and tapped her

smartly on the beak. Kiki screeched and made a pounce at his beard. A vicious tug and some of it came away. Kiki hadn't been able to understand why Bill had arrived with a strange mass of hair under his chin, and round his cheeks. Now, having got some of it, she retired under the table and began to peck it gently, separating the hairs one by one and murmuring to herself all the time.

'Let her be,' said Bill. 'She'll be happy pulling that bit of my beard to pieces.' He rubbed his chin. 'That hurt. I hope I don't look too peculiar now?'

'Oh no – it doesn't really show much,' Jack assured him. 'Kiki always gets excited on a journey like this. She's awful when I bring her back from school – whistles like the guard, and tells all the people in the carriage to blow their noses and wipe their feet, and screeches in the tunnels till we're almost deafened.'

'But she's a darling really,' said Lucy-Ann loyally, and didn't say a word about Kiki undoing her shoe-laces and pulling them out of her shoes at that very moment!

The journey was a long one. There was a change to be made at a very big and noisy station. The next train was not quite so long as the first one and did not go so fast. It took them to a place on the coast, and the children were delighted to see the blue sea shining like a thin bright line in the distance. Hurrah! They all loved the sea.

'Now I feel that our holiday has really begun,' said Lucy-Ann. 'Now that we've seen the sea, I mean. It gives me a proper holiday feeling.'

Everyone felt the same, even Kiki, who leapt about like a warrior doing a war-dance, on the luggage-rack above the children's heads. She flew down to Jack's shoulder when they got out of the train at a big seaside town.

The strong breeze blew in their faces, and the girls' hair streamed back. Bill's beard blew back too, and Kiki was careful to stand with her beak to the wind. She hated her feathers being ruffled the wrong way.

They had a very good meal in a hotel, and then Bill went down to the harbour to see if his motor-boat was there. It had just come in. The man who brought it knew Bill very well, and had been told in what disguise he was to be seen.

'Morning, Dr Walker, sir,' he said in loud tones. 'Fine weather for your expedition. Everything's ready, sir.'

'Plenty of provisions, Henty?' asked Dr Walker, blinking though his thick glasses.

'Enough to stand a siege, sir,' said Henty. 'I'm to pilot you out, sir – I've got a boat behind.'

Everyone went on board. It was a fine motor-boat, with a little cabin in front. Jack's eyes gleamed when he saw the stock of food – tins, tins, tins! The little refrigerator was full of stuff too. Good! There would be plenty to eat anyway, and that, in Jack's opinion, was one of the main things to be planned for, on a holiday. People always got so terribly hungry when they were holidaying.

Henty piloted them out of the harbour, his tiny boat bobbing about. When they were beyond the harbour Henty saluted and got into his boat.

'Well – good luck, sir,' he said. 'The wireless is O.K., sir – we'll be expecting a message regularly, to know you're all right. There are extra batteries, and a repair set as well. Good luck, sir. I'll be here in two weeks' time to pick up the kids.'

He rowed off, his oars making a soft plash-plash-plash in the water. He soon looked very small indeed, as Bill's motor-boat sped away.

'Well – we're off!' said Bill, with great satisfaction. 'And my beard can come off too – and my glasses, thank goodness. And my coat. Here, Philip, you know how to steer a motor-boat, don't you? Take the wheel whilst I make myself presentable again. No one is likely to see me now. Keep her going north-north-west.'

Proudly Philip took the wheel. The engine of the boat purred smoothly, and they sped fast over the blue water. It was a wonderful day, almost as hot as summer. The May sun shone down out of a sky flecked with tiny curly clouds, and little points of light danced on the waves.

'Gorgeous!' said Jack, sitting down with a grunt of joy near Philip. 'Simply absolutely perfectly gorgeous.'

'I've got such a lovely feeling,' said Lucy-Ann, looking the picture of happiness. 'You know – that feeling you get at the very beginning of a lovely holiday – when all the days spread out before you, sunny and lazy and sort of enchanted.'

'You'll end up by being a poet if you don't look out,' said Philip, from the wheel.

'Well, if a poet feels like I feel just exactly at this moment, I wouldn't mind being one for the rest of my life, even if it meant having to write poetry,' said Lucy-Ann.

'Three blind mice, see how they run,' remarked Kiki, and for one moment everyone thought that Kiki was joining in the talk about poetry, and giving what she thought was an example. But she was merely referring to the three tame rats that had suddenly appeared on Philip's shoulders. They stood there daintily, their pink noses raised, sniffing the salt sea air.

'Oh, blow you, Philip!' said Dinah, from her seat near Jack. 'I was hoping against hope you hadn't brought those detestable little creatures. I only hope the gulls eat them.'

But even Dinah couldn't feel annoyed for long as they glided over the green waves, leaving a white wake behind them, like a long feathery tail. When Bill appeared from the little cabin, they all hailed him in delight.

'Bill! Dear old Bill, you look like yourself again!'

'Oh, Bill – never wear a beard again. It does spoil your beauty.'

'Hurrah! We've lost Dr Walker for ever. Silly fellow, I never liked him.'

'Bill, you look nice again. I can see your mouth when you smile.'

'Pay the bill, pay the bill!'

'Shut up, Kiki, or the gulls will get you!'

'Ah, this is something like,' said Bill happily, taking the wheel from Philip. 'Golly, if we get this weather we'll all be quite sun-burnt in a day or two. Better keep your shirts on, boys, or you'll get blistered.'

Everyone had discarded coats and wraps at once. The breeze was cool, but the sun was really hot. The sea, in the distance, was unbelievevably blue, the colour of cornflowers, Lucy-Ann thought.

'Now, my friends,' said Bill, his white shirt billowing in the breeze, 'this is a holiday, not a hair-raising adventure. You've had enough of adventures. We've had three together, and this time I want a holiday.'

'Right,' said Jack. 'A holiday it shall be. Adventures keep out!'

'I don't want any adventures either,' said Lucy-Ann. 'I've had plenty. This is adventure enough for me. I like this kind best – not the kind where we have to hide, and creep through secret tunnels and live in caves. I just want a sunny, lazy, windy time with the people I like best. It would be nice if Aunt Allie was here too – but perhaps she wouldn't enjoy it very much.'

'I hope she's feeling better,' said Dinah. 'I say, where's the land? I can't see a bit – not even an island!'

'You'll see plenty tomorrow,' said Bill. 'You can choose one for your own.'

That was a wonderful afternoon and evening. They had a fine tea on board, prepared by the two girls, who found new bread, strawberry jam and a big chocolate cake in the cabin larder.

'Make the most of this,' said Bill. 'You won't get new bread often now. I doubt if we shall find any farmhouses at all, among the lonely islands we shall visit. But I've brought tins and tins of biscuits of all kinds. And as for this chocolate cake, eat it up and enjoy it – I don't think you'll get any more for two weeks.'

'I don't care,' said Dinah, munching away. 'When I'm

hungry I simply don't mind *what* I eat – and I can see I'm always going to be hungry on this holiday.'

The sun went down in a great golden blaze, and the tiny curly clouds turned a brilliant pink. Still the motor-boat went on and on and on, over a sea that blazed pink and gold too.

'The sun has drowned itself in the sea,' said Lucy-Ann at last, as it disappeared. 'I watched the very very last little bit go down into the water.'

'Where are we going to sleep tonight?' asked Jack. 'Not that I mind – but it would be fun to know.'

'There are two tents somewhere in the bow,' said Bill. 'I thought, when we came to an island we liked the look of, we'd land, put up the tents and sleep there for the night. What do you say?'

'Oh *yes*,' said everyone. 'Let's look for an island – a really nice wild one!'

But at the moment there was no land in sight, not even a small rocky island. Bill gave the wheel to Jack, and looked at the chart. He pointed with his finger. 'We've been running in this direction. We should come on these two islands presently. One has a few people on it, and, I believe, a tiny jetty. We'd better go there tonight, and then set off to the unknown tomorrow. It's getting too late to go hunting for islands further away. It would be dark before we got there.'

'It's still very light,' said Philip, looking at his watch. 'At home it would be getting dark.'

'The further north you go, the longer the evening light is,' said Bill. 'Don't ask me why at the moment. I don't feel capable of a lecture just now.'

'You don't *need* to tell us,' said Philip loftily. 'We learnt all about it last term. You see, owing to the sun being . . . '

'Spare me, spare me,' begged Bill, taking the wheel again. 'Look, one of your inquisitive little rats is sniffing at Kiki's tail. There will be murder done in a moment if you don't remove him.'

But Kiki knew better than to hurt any of Philip's pets. She contented herself with cracking her beak so loudly in Squeaker's ear that he ran back to Philip in alarm, scampering up his bare legs and into his shorts in a trice.

Gradually the sea lost its blue, and became grey-green. The breeze felt cold and everyone put on jerseys. Then far away in the distance a dark hump loomed up — land!

'That's it, that's one of the islands we want for tonight,' said Bill, pleased. 'I consider I've done pretty well to head so straight for it. We'll soon be there.'

It certainly was not long before they were nosing alongside a simple stone jetty. A fisherman was there, in a long blue jersey. He was astonished to see them.

Bill explained in a few words. 'Och, so it's bairds ye're after,' said the fisherman. 'Weel, there's plenty for you out yon,' and he nodded towards the sea. 'Where will you be sleeping the night? My bit cottage won't tak' sae mony.'

Lucy-Ann couldn't understand him, but the others gathered what he meant. 'Bring the tents,' ordered Bill. 'We'll soon have them up. We'll ask the fisherman's wife to give us a meal. It will save our own provisions. Maybe we can get some cream too, and good butter.'

By the time that darkness came at last they had all had a good meal, and were bedded down in the two tents, comfortable on ground-sheets and rugs. The fresh air had made them so sleepy that the girls fell asleep without even saying goodnight.

'They're a' daft,' said the fisherman to his wife. 'Wasting a fine boat like yon, looking for bairds. *Bairds*! When there's good fish to be got! Well, they'll soon see bairds in plenty. Och, they're a' dafties!'

# 8

## The island of birds

Next day, after a fine breakfast of porridge and cream, and grilled herrings, the tents were struck and the five went aboard their boat. It was called *Lucky Star*, which the children thought was a very nice name.

Kiki had not been popular with the old fisherman and his wife. They had never seen a parrot before, and they regarded Kiki with suspicion.

'God save the King,' said Kiki, having learnt by experience that most people thought this was a fine thing for her to say. But she spoilt it by adding. 'Pop goes the Queen, pop, pop, pop!'

Now she was aboard with the others, and once again the boat was skimming over the blue water. Once again the sky was blue and the sun was hot. True May weather, that made the sea a clear, translucent blue, and set thousands of little sparkles dancing over the water.

'I've still got that lovely feeling,' said Lucy-Ann happily, as she dangled her hand over the side of the boat and felt the cool, silky water catch hold of her fingers and trail them back. 'Now to find some bird-islands. We really are going to find some today, aren't we, Bill?'

'We certainly are,' said Bill, and gave the boat a little extra speed. Spray came up and fell lightly over everyone.

'Ooooh, lovely!' said Dinah. 'I was so hot. That cooled me beautifully. Let her out again, Bill! I could do with some more of that.'

For five hours they sped over the water, and then Jack gave a shout. 'The islands! Look, you can see little blobs here and there on the horizon! They must be the islands!'

And now the children began to see a great many different

birds on the water and in the air. Jack called out their names exitedly. 'There's a shearwater! Jolly good name for it. And look Philip, that's a razorbill! – and gosh, is that a Little Auk?'

The boys, well versed in the appearance of the wild sea-birds, almost fell overboard in their excitement. Many of the birds seemed to have no fear of the noisy boat at all, but went bobbing on their way, hardly bothering to swerve when it neared them.

'There's a shag diving,' shouted Jack. 'Look! you can see it swimming under water – it's caught a fish. Here it comes. It's clumsy getting out of the water to fly. Gosh, if only I'd got my camera ready!'

Kiki watched the many birds out of baleful eyes. She did not like the interest that Jack suddenly appeared to take in these other birds. When a great gull appeared, flying leisurely right over the boat, Kiki shot up underneath it, gave a fearful screech, and turned a somersault in the air. The gull, startled, rose vertically on its strong wings and let out an alarmed cry.

'EEE-oo-ee-ooooo!'

Kiki imitated it perfectly, and the gull, thinking that Kiki must be some strange kind of relation, circled round. Then it made a pounce at the parrot. But Kiki flipped round, and then dropped to Jack's shoulder.

'Eee-oo!' she called defiantly, and the gull, after a doubt-ful glance, went on its way, wondering, no doubt, what kind of a gull this was that behaved in such a peculiar manner.

'You're an idiot, Kiki,' said Jack. 'One of these days a gull will eat you for his dinner.'

'Poor old Kiki,' said the parrot, and gave a realistic groan. Bill laughed. 'I can't imagine what Kiki will do when we see the puffins, waddling about among the heather and sea-pinks,' he said. 'I'm afraid she will give them an awful time.'

As they came nearer to the first island, more and more birds were to be seen on and above the water. They glided gracefully on the wind, they dived down for fish, they bobbed along like toy ducks. There was a chorus of different cries, some shrill, some guttural, some mournful and for-lorn. They gave the children a wild, exultant kind of feeling.

As they came near to the island the children fell silent. A tall cliff towered in front of them, and it was covered from top to bottom with birds! The children stared in delight.

Birds, birds, birds! On every ledge they stood or squatted, thousands of white gannets, myriads of the browner guille-mots, and a mixture of other sea-birds that the boys could hardly make out, though they glued their field-glasses to their eyes for minutes on end.

'What a coming and going!' said Bill, staring with fasci-nated eyes, too. And it certainly was. Besides the birds that stood on the ledges, there were always others arriving and others leaving. That way and this went the busy birds, with a chorus of excited cries.

'They're not very careful with their eggs,' said Lucy-Ann, in distress, when she looked through Jack's glasses in her turn. The careless birds took off and knocked their precious eggs over the ledge and down the cliff, to be smashed on the rocks below.

'They can lay plenty more,' said Philip. 'Come on, Lucy-Ann — give me back my glasses! Golly, what a wonderful sight! I shall write this all up in my notes tonight.'

The motor-boat nosed carefully round the rocky cliffs. Bill stopped looking at the birds and kept a sharp look-out instead for rocks. Once round the steep cliffs the land sloped downwards, and Bill spotted a place that seemed suitable for the boat.

It was a little sheltered sandy cove. He ran the boat in and it grounded softly. He sprang out with the boys, and made it safe, by running the anchor well up the beach and digging it in.

'Is this going to be our headquarters?' asked Dinah, look-ing round.

'Oh, *no*,' said Jack at once. 'We want to cruise round a bit, don't we, Bill, and find a puffin island. I'd really like to be in the *midst* of the bird-islands, and be able to go from one to the other as we pleased. But we could stay here for tonight, couldn't we?'

That was a wonderful day for the four children, and for Bill too. With thousands of birds screaming round their heads, but apparently not in the least afraid of them, the children made their way to the steep cliffs they had seen from the other side of the island.

Birds were nesting on the ground, and it was difficult to tread sometimes, without disturbing sitting birds or squashing eggs. Some of the birds made vicious jabs at the children's legs, but nobody was touched. It was just a threatening gesture, nothing more.

Kiki was rather silent. She sat on Jack's shoulder, her head hunched into her neck. So many birds at once seemed to overwhelm her. But Jack knew that she would soon recover, and startle the surrounding birds by telling them to wipe their feet and shut the door.

They reached the top of the cliffs, and were almost deafened by the cries and calls around them. Birds rose and fell in the air, glided and soared, weaving endless patterns in the blue sky.

'It's funny they never bump into one another,' said Lucy-Ann, astonished. 'There's never a single collison. I've been watching.'

'Probably got a traffic policeman,' said Philip solemnly. 'For all you know some of them may have licences under their wings.'

'Don't be silly,' said Lucy-Ann. 'All the same, it *is* clever of them not to collide, when there's so many thousands. What a row! I can hardly hear myself speak.'

They came to the very edge of the cliff. Bill took Lucy-Ann's arm. 'Not too near,' he said. 'The cliffs are almost sheer here.'

They were. When the children lay down on their tummies and looked cautiously over, it gave them a queer feeling to see the sea so very very far below, moving slowly in and out, with only a far-off rumble to mark the breaking of the waves. Lucy-Ann found herself clutching the cushions of sea-pink beside her.

'I somehow feel I'm not safe on the ground,' she said with a laugh. 'I feel as if I've got to hold on. I feel sort of – well, sort of upside-down!'

Bill held on to her tightly after that speech. He knew that she felt giddy, and he wasn't going to risk anything with little Lucy-Ann! He liked all the children very much, but Lucy-Ann was his favourite.

The children watched the birds going and coming endlessly to and from the narrow cliff ledges. It was a marvellous sight. Jack looked through his glasses and chuckled at the squabbling and pushing that was going on, on some of the narrower shelves.

'Just like naughty children,' he said. 'Telling each other to move up and make room, or I'll push you off – and off somebody goes, sure enough. But it doesn't matter, because out go their wings and they have a lovely glide through the air. My word, I wouldn't mind being a sea-bird – able to stride along on the sea-shore, or bob on the sea, or dive for fish, or glide for miles on the strong breeze. I shouldn't mind be—'

'What's that?' said Philip suddenly, hearing a noise that wasn't made by sea-birds. 'Listen! An aeroplane, surely!'

They all listened, straining their eyes through the sun-washed air. And, far away, they saw a speck, steadily moving through the sky, and heard the *r-r-r-r* of an engine.

'A plane! Right off all the routes!' said Bill. 'Well – that's the last thing I expected to see here!'

# 9

# Hurrah for Puffin Island!

Bill seemed so astonished that the children stared at him. Surely it wasn't so surprising to see an aeroplane, even near these desolate bird-islands?

Bill took Jack's glasses and looked through them, but it was too late to make out anything.

'I wonder if it was a seaplane or an ordinary plane,' he said, half to himself. 'How strange.'

'Why is it strange?' asked Dinah. 'Aeroplanes go everywhere now.'

Bill said no more. He handed back the glasses to Jack. 'I think we'd better have a meal, and then put up our tents,' he said. 'What about putting them by that little stream we saw on our way here? About a quarter of a mile from the shore. It wouldn't be too far to carry everything if we all give a hand.'

The tents were set up. The ground-sheets were put down and the rugs tumbled over them. Then, sitting on a slight slope, looking out to the blue sea, the five of them had a glorious meal. 'I always think', began Lucy-Ann, munching a couple of biscuits with butter and cream cheese between them. 'I always think . . . '

'You needn't go on,' said Jack. 'We know what you're going to say and we quite agree with you.'

'You *don't* know what I'm going to say,' said Lucy-Ann indignantly.

'We do,' said Philip. 'You say it every holiday when we have a meal out of doors.'

'You're going to say, "I always think food tastes *much* nicer when it's eaten out of doors," ' said Dinah. 'Aren't you?'

'Well, I was,' said Lucy-Ann. 'Do I really always say it?

Anyway, it's quite true. I *do* think . . . '

'Yes, we know,' said Jack. 'You're an awful repeater, Lucy-Ann. You tell us the same things over and over again. Never mind. We think the same, even if we don't keep on saying it. Kiki, take your fat beak out of the cream cheese!'

'Kiki's awful,' said Dinah. 'She really is. She's pinched three biscuits already. I don't think you give her enough sunflower seeds, Jack.'

'Golly, I like *that*!' said Jack. 'She won't even *look* at sunflower seeds when there's a spread like this. Anyway, Philip, your rats can always eat them. I found Squeaker in my pocket a little while ago, nibbling one of them as fast as he could.'

'I hope it won't make him ill,' said Philip in alarm. 'I say, look! – here comes a gull – tame as anything. It wants a biscuit too, I should think.'

It did. It had watched Kiki pecking at a biscuit and enjoying it, and it didn't see why it shouldn't have a share. Kiki saw the gull out of the corner of her eye and sidled away. The gull made a pounce, got the biscuit and rose into the air, making a loud laughing noise. 'Ee-oo, ee-oo, ee-oo!'

Kiki flew up angrily, calling out all kinds of things to the gull. They were meant to be very rude, but unfortunatley the gull didn't understand. Kiki could not catch the strong-winged bird and flew disconsolately back to the children.

'You can't complain, Kiki,' said Jack. 'You shouldn't have pinched that biscuit out of the tin – and the gull shouldn't have pinched it from you. It's six of one and half a dozen of the other.'

'What a pity, what a pity!' said Kiki, and sidled near the biscuit-tin again.

'That bird is a real clown,' said Bill, shaking the crumbs off his jersey. 'Now, who's coming back to the boat with me to hear the news on the radio? Also I must send out a few messages – especially one for your mother, Philip, who will be sure to want to know if we've got here safely.'

They all wanted to stretch their legs, so they walked back over the soft cushions of the sea-pinks, whose bold little pink heads nodded everywhere in the wind.

They watched Bill as he put up his little radio mast and fiddled about with the set. It was a transmitter as well as a receiver.

'I suppose if you send messages home every night, we shan't need to post letters off to Aunt Allie,' said Lucy-Ann.

Everyone roared. 'And where would you post a letter, pray?' asked Jack. '*I* haven't seen a pillar-box anywhere about. Lucy-Ann, you're an idiot.'

'Yes, I am!' said Lucy-Ann, going red. 'Of course we can't post anything here! How useful that you can send messages, Bill! Then if any of us wanted help, you could get it.'

'Quite so,' said Bill. 'But I hope if you wanted help I could whizz you off in the motor-boat. Anyway I wouldn't have consented to bring you all away into the wilds like this, if I hadn't a transmitter with me, so that I could send messages every night. I send them to headquarters, and they telephone them to your aunt. So she'll follow our travels and adventures each night.'

They watched for a while, and then listened to part of a programme. Then Lucy-Ann yawned and Kiki imitated her. 'Blow! You make me feel sleepy,' said Dinah, rubbing her eyes. 'Look, it's getting dark!'

So back they went to their tents, and were soon cuddled into their rugs. The birds called incessantly from the cliffs and the sea. 'I believe they keep awake all night,' thought Dinah. But they didn't. They slept too when the darkness came at last.

The next day was very warm and close. 'Looks to me like a storm blowing up sooner or later,' said Bill, screwing up his eyes and looking into the bright sky. 'I almost think we'd better try and find our headquarters today, so that we have some shelter if a storm does blow up. This sort of holiday needs fine weather if it's going to be successful – a storm wouldn't be at all pleasant, with only tents to sleep in – we'd be blown to bits.'

'I just want to take a few photographs of these cliffs and the birds on them,' said Jack. 'I'll do that whilst you're getting down the tents, if you don't mind my not helping you.'

So off he went with Kiki towards the steep cliffs. Bill called after him that he was not to try any climbing down the cliffs, and he shouted back that he wouldn't.

Soon everything was packed away again on the motorboat, which was just being floated by the rising tide, and they waited paitently for Jack. He soon appeared, his glasses and his camera slung round his neck, and his face beaming.

'Got some beauties,' he said. 'Kiki was awfully useful to me. I got her to parade up and down, so that all the birds stayed still in amazement, watching her – and then, click! I got them beautifully. I ought to have some fine pictures.'

'Good!' said Bill, smiling at the enthusiastic boy. 'You'll have to have a book of bird photographs published. "*Masterpieces*, by Jack Trent, price thirty shillings." '

'I'd like that,' said Jack, his face shining. 'Not the thirty shillings I mean – but having a book about birds with my name on it.'

'Come on in,' said Philip impatiently, for Jack was still outside the boat. 'We want to be off. It's so warm I'm longing to get out to sea again, and feel the breeze on my face as the boat swings along.'

They soon felt it and were glad of it. It certainly was very hot for May. The boat went swiftly through the water, bobbing a little as it rode over the waves. Lucy-Ann let her fingers run through the water again – lovely and cool!

'What I should like is a bathe,' said Philip, little drops of perspiration appearing round his nose. 'Can we bathe from the boat, Bill?'

'Wait till we get to another island,' said Bill. 'I don't particularly want to stop out at sea, with a storm in the

259

offing. It's so jolly hot I feel there must be thunder about. I'm anxious to run for shelter before it comes. Now – here are more islands bobbing up out of the sea. Let's see if we can spot a puffin island. That's what you want, isn't it?'

Lucy-Ann, still dangling her hand in the water, suddenly felt something gently touching it. In surprise she looked down, withdrawing her hand at once, afraid of a jellyfish.

To her astonishment she saw that it was a piece of orange peel, bobbing away on the waves. She called to Bill.

'Bill, look – there's a bit of orange peel. Now whoever in the world eats oranges in these wild little islands? Do you suppose there are any other bird-lovers somewhere about?'

Everyone looked at the tiny bit of orange peel bobbing rapidly away. It did seem very much out of place there. Bill stared at it hard. He was puzzled. The fishermen, if there were any on the islands they were coming to, would not be at all likely to have oranges. And naturalists surely would not bother to load themselves up with them.

Then how did that bit of peel come to be there? No ships went anywhere near where they were. It was a wild and lonely part of the sea, where sudden storms blew up, and great gales made enormous waves.

'Beats me!' said Bill at last. 'I shall expect to see a pineapple or something next! Now look! – here is an island – fairly flattish – probably has puffins on it all right. Shall we make for it?'

'No – cruise round a bit,' begged Jack. 'Let's have a look at a few of the islands here. There is quite a colony of them round about.'

They cruised round, looking at first this island and then that. They came to one that had steep cliffs at the east side, then ran down into a kind of valley, then up again into cliffs.

Jack put his glasses to his eyes and yelled out excitedly. 'Puffins! Plenty of them! Can you see them, Philip? I bet the island is full of their burrows. Let's land here, Bill. There'll be masses of birds on the cliffs, and hundreds of puffins inland. It's quite a big island. We could probably find good shelter here and water too. The cliffs would protect us from both the east and west. What ho, for Puffin Island!'

'Right,' said Bill. He looked all round and about, and guided the boat towards the island. There were many other islands not far off, but as far as he could see they were inhabited only by birds. The sea chopped about between the islands, making little rippling waves.

Round Puffin Island went the boat, and Philip gave a shout. 'Here's a fine place to put the boat in, Bill — see, where that channel of water goes into a cleft of the cliff! It'll be deep there, and we can just tie the boat up to a rock. We'll put out the fenders, so that she doesn't bump against the rock sides.'

The boat nosed into the channel. As Philip said, the water was deep there — it was a natural little harbour. There was a ledge of rock on which they could land. Could anything be better? Hurrah for Puffin Island!

# 10

## A little exploring

'Isn't this a gorgeous place?' said Jack, as the boat glided gently into the little channel. There was just room for it. 'It might be a boat-house made specially for the *Lucky Star*.'

Bill leapt out on to the rocky ledge, which did very well for a landing-stage. Sheer above them on each side rose rocky cliffs. Rows and rows of birds sat on the ledges, and there was a continual dropping of eggs, knocked off by the careless birds. One broke near Bill, and splashed its yellow yolk over his foot.

'Good shot!' he yelled up to the circling birds, and the children roared.

They made the boat fast by tying the mooring-rope round a convenient rock. The boat bobbed up and down gently as waves ran up the little channel and back.

'Tide's up now,' said Bill. 'When it goes down there will still be plenty of water in this channel. The boat will look much lower down then. Now – is there a way up the cliff from here? We don't want to have to walk down the ledge and clamber round the cliffs over hundreds of rocks before we get on to the island proper.'

They looked round. Jack ran up the rocky ledge, and then turned and gave a shout. 'Hi! We can get up here, I think. There are rocky shelves, like rough steps, going up the cliff – and there's a break in it a bit above. We could probably clamber out all right, and find ourselves right on the island.'

'Well, you four go and explore,' said Bill. 'I'd better stay with the boat and see that she doesn't get her sides smashed in against these rocks. You look round the island and see if you can spot a sheltered cove somewhere, that I can take the boat round to.'

The children left the boat and followed Jack. Kiki flew on ahead, calling like a gull. Up the rocky ledges went Jack. They were almost like giant steps, roughly hewn by the great wintry seas for century after century.

As Jack said, the cliff had a deep cleft in it just there, and the children found that they could make their way through it, and come out on to the cushions of sea-pinks beyond. It needed a bit of clambering, and they were out of breath when they reached the top – but it was worth it.

The sea spread bright blue all round the island. The sky looked enormous. Other islands, blue in the distance, loomed up everywhere. A real colony of them, it seemed – and their island was in the centre.

Then Jack gave such a yell that everyone jumped. 'Puffins! Look! Hundreds and hundreds of them!'

The children looked to where Jack pointed, and there, among the sea-pinks and the old heather tufts, were the most curious-looking birds they had ever seen.

They were dressed in black and white. Their legs were orange – but it was their extraordinary bills that held the children's attention.

'Look at their beaks!' cried Dinah, laughing. 'Blue at the base – and then striped red and yellow!'

'But what *enormous* beaks!' cried Lucy-Ann. 'They remind me a bit of Kiki's.'

'Puffins are called sea parrots,' remarked Jack, amused to see the crowd of solemn-looking puffins.

'Their eyes are so comical,' said Philip. 'They stare at us with such a fixed expression! And look at the way they walk – so upright!'

The colony of puffins was as good as a pantomine to watch. There were hundreds, thousands of birds there. Some stood about, watching, their crimson-ringed eyes fixed seriously on their neighbours. Others walked about, rolling from side to side like a sailor. Some took off like small aeroplanes, eager to get to the sea.

'Look! – what's that one doing?' asked Lucy-Ann, as a puffin began to scrape vigorously at the soil, sending a shower of it backwards.

'It's digging a burrow, I should think,' said Dinah. 'They nest underground, don't they, Jack?'

'Rather! I bet this island is almost undermined with their holes and burrows,' said Jack, walking forward towards the colony of busy birds. 'Come on – do let's get near to them. Kiki, keep on my shoulder. I won't have you screaming like a railway engine at them, and scaring them all away.'

Kiki was most interested in the comical puffins. She imitated their call exactly. 'Arrrrr!' they said, in deep guttural voices. 'Arrrrrrrr!'

'Arrrrrr!' answered Kiki at once, and various birds looked up at her enquiringly.

To the children's huge delight the puffins were not in the least afraid of them. They did not even walk away when the children went near. They allowed them to walk among them, and although one aimed a peck at Philip's leg when he stumbled and almost fell on top of it, not one of the others attempted to jab with their great beaks.

'This is lovely!' said Lucy-Ann, standing and gazing at the extraordinary birds. 'Simply lovely! I never thought birds could be so tame.'

'They're not exactly tame,' said Jack. 'They're wild, but they are so little used to human beings that they have no fear of us at all.'

The puffins were all among the cushions of bright sea-pinks. As the children walked along, their feet sometimes sank right down through the soil. The burrows were just below, and their weight caused the earth to give way.

'It's absolutely mined with their burrows,' said Philip. 'And I say – it's not a very nice smell just about here is it?'

It certainly wasn't. They soon got used to it, but they didn't like it. 'Pooh!' said Lucy-Ann, wrinkling up her nose. 'It's getting worse and worse. I vote we don't put our tents up too near this colony of puffins – it's as bad as being near a pig-sty.'

'I don't mind it,' said Jack. 'Hey, come here, Kiki!'

But Kiki had flown down to make friends. The puffins gazed at her fixedly and solemnly.

'Arrrrr!' said Kiki politely. ARRRRRRR! God save the Queen!'

'Arrrrr!' replied a puffin, and walked up to Kiki, rolling from side to side like a small sailor. The two looked at one another.

'I shall expect Kiki to say how-do-you-do in a minute,' said Dinah, with a little squeal of laughter. 'They both look so polite.'

'Polly put the kettle on,' said Kiki.

'Arrrrr!' said the puffin, and waddled off to its hole. Kiki followed – but apparently there was another puffin down the hole, who did not want Kiki's company, for there was soon an agonised squeal from the parrot, who shot out of the hole much more rapidly than she had gone in.

She flew up to Jack's shoulder. 'Poor Kiki, what a pity, what a pity, what a pity!'

'Well, you shouldn't poke your nose in everywhere,' said Jack, and took a step forward. He trod on a tuft of sea-pinks, which immediately gave way, and he found his leg going down into quite a deep burrow. Whoever lived in it didn't like his leg at all, and gave a vicious nip.

'Ooooch!' said Jack, sitting down suddenly and rubbing his leg. 'Look at that—nearly had a bit right out of my calf!'

They went on through the amazing puffin colony. There were puffins on the ground, in the air – and on the sea too! 'Arrrrr! Arrrrr! Arrrrr!' their deep calls sounded every-where.

'I'll be able to take some magnificent photographs,' said Jack happily. 'It's a pity it's too early for young ones to be about. I don't expect there are many puffin eggs yet either.'

The puffins were living mainly in the green valley between the two high cliffs. Philip looked about to see if there was any good place to pitch their tents.

'I suppose we all want to make Puffin Island our head-quarters?' he said. 'I imagine that nothing will drag Jack away from here now. He's got cliffs where guillemots and gannets nest, and a valley where the puffins live – so I suppose he's happy.'

'Oh *yes*,' said Jack. 'We'll stay here. This shall be *our* island – we'll share it with the puffins.'

'Well, we'll find a good place for our tents,' said Philip. 'Then we'll bring our goods and chattels here and camp. We'd better find a place where there's a stream, though . . . if there *is* one on this island. We shall want water to drink. And let's look for a cover where we can put the boat. We can't very well leave it in that narrow channel.'

'Look – there's a dear little cove down there!' said Dinah suddenly, pointing to the sea. 'We could bathe there – and the boat would be quite all right there too. Let's go and tell Bill.'

'I'll go,' said Philip. 'Jack wants to stare at the puffins a bit more, I can see. I'll take the boat round to the cove with Bill, and you two girls can find a good place for our tents. Then we'll all help to bring the things there from the boat.'

He ran off quickly to find Bill and tell him where to put the boat. Jack sat down with Kiki to watch the puffins. The girls went to look for a good place to put up their tents for the night.

They wandered over the island. Beyond the puffin colony, just at the end of it, before they came to the high cliffs at the other side of the island, was a little dell. A few stunted birch-trees grew there, and banks of heather.

'This is just the place,' said Dinah, pleased. 'We can put up our tents here, be sheltered from the worst of the wind, watch the puffins, go down to bathe when we want to, and when we're tired of that, go cruising round the other islands.'

'A very nice life,' said Lucy-Ann, with a laugh. 'Now – is there any water about?'

There was no stream at all on the island – but Dinah found something that would do equally well. At least, she hoped it would.

'Look here!' she called to Lucy-Ann. 'Here's an enormous rock with a hollow in its middle, filled with water. I've tasted it and it isn't salt.'

Lucy-Ann came up, followed by Jack. Dinah dipped in her hand, scooped up a palmful of water and drank. It was as sweet and as pure as could be.

'Rain-water,' said Dinah pleased. 'Now we'll be all right – so long as it doesn't dry up in this hot weather. Come on – let's go back to the boat and collect all the things we want. We'll have to do a bit of hard work now.'

'We'll wait here a bit,' said Jack, coming up with Kiki. 'I expect Bill and Philip will be bringing the boat round to the

266

cove over there – then we'll go and tell them we've found a good place, and help to bring the things here.'

It was not long before Bill and Philip ran into the cove with the boat. Bill leapt out, took the anchor well up the beach and dug it in. He saw Jack and the girls and waved to them.

'Just coming!' he cried. 'Have you found a good place for the tents?'

He and Philip soon joined the others, and were pleased with the little dell. 'Just right!' said Bill. 'Well, we'll bring all the things we want from the boat straight away now.'

So they spent quite a time going to and from the cove, laden with goods. It did not take quite as long as they feared because there were five of them to do it, and even Kiki gave a hand – or rather a beak – and carried a tent-peg. She did it really to impress the watching puffins, who stared at her seriously as she flew by, the peg in her big curved beak.

'Arrrrrr!' she called, in a puffin voice.

'You're showing off, Kiki,' said Jack severely. 'You're a conceited bird.'

'Arrrrr!' said Kiki, and dropped the tent-peg on Jack's head.

It was fun arranging their new home. The boys and Bill were to have one tent. The girls were to have the other. Behind the tents Lucy-Ann found a ledge of rock and below it was a very large dry space.

'Just the spot for storing everything in,' said Lucy-Ann proudly. 'Jack, bring the tins here – and the extra clothes – there's room for heaps of things. Oh, we *are* going to have a lovely time here!'

# 11

## Huffin and Puffin

'Isn't it time we had a meal?' complained Jack, staggering over with a great pile of things in his arms. 'It makes my mouth water to read "Spam" and "Best Tinned Peaches" and see that milk chocolate.'

Bill looked at his watch and then at the sun. 'My word – it certainly is time! The sun is setting already! How the time has flown!'

It wasn't long before they were all sitting peacefully on tufts of sea-pink and heather, munching biscuits and potted meat, and looking forward to a plate of tinned peaches each. Bill had brought bottles of ginger-beer from the boat, and these were voted better than boiling a kettle to make tea or cocoa. It was very warm indeed.

'I feel so happy,' said Lucy-Ann, looking over the island to the deep-blue sea beyond. 'I feel so very very far away from everywhere – honestly I hardly believe there is such a thing as school, just at this very minute. And this potted meat tastes heavenly.'

Philip's white rats also thought it did. They came out from his clothes at once when they smelt the food. One sat daintily upright on his knee, nibbling. Another took his tit-bit into a dark pocket. The third perched on Philip's shoulder.

'You tickle the lobe of my ear,' said Philip. Dinah moved as far from him as she could, but, like Lucy-Ann, she was too happy to find fault with anything just then.

They all ate hungrily, Bill too, their eyes fixed on the setting sun and the gold-splashed sea, which was now losing its blue, and taking on sunset colours. Lucy-Ann glanced at Bill.

'Do you like disappearing, Bill?' she asked. 'Don't you think it's fun?'

'Well – for a fortnight, yes,' said Bill, 'but I'm not looking forward to living in these wild islands all alone, once you've gone. It's not my idea of fun. I'd rather live dangerously than like one of these puffins here.'

'Poor Bill,' said Dinah, thinking of him left by himself, with only books to read, and the radio, and nobody to talk to.

'I'll leave you my rats, if you like,' offered Philip generously.

'No, thanks,' said Bill promptly. 'I know your rats! They'd have umpteen babies, and by the time I left this would be Rat Island, not Puffin Island. Besides, I'm not so much in love with the rat-and-mouse tribe as you are.'

'Oh, look, do look!' suddenly said Dinah. Everyone looked. A puffin had left its nearby burrow and was walking solemnly towards them, rolling a little from side to side, as all the puffins did when they walked. 'It's come for its supper!'

'Then sing, puffin, sing!' commanded Jack. 'Sing for your supper!'

'Arrrrrrrr!' said the puffin deeply. Everyone laughed. The puffin advanced right up to Philip. It stood close against the boy's knee and looked at him fixedly.

'Philip's spell is working again,' said Lucy-Ann enviously. 'Philip, what makes all animals and birds want you to be friends with them? Just look at that puffin – it's going all goofy over you.'

'Don't know,' said Philip, pleased with his odd new friend. He stroked the bird's head softly, and the puffin gave a little *arrrrr* of pleasure. Then Philip gave it a bit of potted-meat sandwich and the bird tossed it off at once and turned for more.

'Now I suppose you'll be followed round by a devoted puffin,' said Dinah. 'Well, a puffin is better than three rats, any day – or mice – or that awful hedgehog with fleas that you had – or that pair of stag-beetles – or . . . '

'Spare us, Dinah, spare us,' begged Bill. 'We all know that Philip is a walking zoo. Personally, if he likes a goofy puffin, he can have it. I don't mind a bit. It's a pity we haven't brought a collar and lead.'

The puffin said 'Arrrr' again, a little more loudly, and then walked off, perfectly upright, its brilliant beak gleaming in the setting sun.

'Well, you didn't pay us a very long visit, old thing,' said Philip, quite disappointed. The puffin disappeared into its burrow – but reappeared again almost immediately with another puffin, a little smaller, but with an even more brilliant beak.

'Darby and Joan!' said Jack. The two birds waddled side by side to Philip. The children looked at them in delighted amusement.

'What shall we call them?' said Dinah. 'If they are going to join our little company, they'll have to have names. Funny little puffins!'

'Huffin and puffin, huffin and puffin,' remarked Kiki, remembering the words suddenly. 'Huffin and . . . '

'Yes, of course – Huffin and Puffin!' cried Lucy-Ann in delight. 'Clever old bird, Kiki! You've been talking about Huffin and Puffin ever since we started out on our holiday – and here they are, Huffin and Puffin, as large as life!'

Everyone laughed. Huffin and Puffin did seem to be perfectly lovely names for the two birds. They came close to Philip, and, to the boy's amusement, squatted down by him contentedly.

Kiki was not too pleased. She eyed them with her head on one side. They stared back at her with their crimson-ringed eyes. Kiki looked away and yawned.

'They've out-stared Kiki!' said Jack. 'It takes a lot to do that!'

The three rats had prudently decided that it was best to keep as far away from Huffin and Puffin as possible. They sat round Philip's neck, gazing down at the two birds. Then, at a movement from Huffin, they shot down the boy's shirt.

Bill stretched himself. 'Well, I don't know about you kids – but I'm tired,' he said. 'The sun is already dipping itself into the west. Let's clear up, and turn in. We'll have a lovely day tomorrow, bathing and sunning ourselves, and watching the birds. I'm getting used to their eternal chorus of cries now. At first I was almost deafened.'

The girls cleared up. Lucy-Ann dipped a bowl into the clear pool of water and handed it round for washing in. 'We oughtn't to wash in that pool, ought we, Bill?' she said seriously.

'Good gracious, no!' said Bill. 'It would be absolutely black after the boys had gone in! We'll keep it for drinking-water only, or just take our water from it when we want it for boiling or washing.'

'I think I'll go and have a dip now,' said Jack, getting up. 'No, not in the rock-pool, Lucy-Ann, so don't look so upset – I'll go down to the little cove where the boat is. Coming, Philip?'

'Right,' said Philip, and pushed Huffin and Puffin away from his knees. 'Move up, you! I'm not growing here!'

'I'll come too,' said Bill, and knocked out the pipe he had been smoking. 'I feel dirty. You girls want to come?'

'No,' said Lucy-Ann. 'I'll get the rugs and things ready for you in the tents.'

Dinah didn't want to go either, for she felt very tired. Measles had certainly taken some of the energy out of the two girls. They stayed behind whilst the others set off to the cove to bathe. The valley sloped right down to the sea just there, and the small sandy cove was just right for bathing. The boys and Bill threw off their things and plunged into the sea. It felt lovely and warm, and rippled over their limbs like silk.

'Lovely!' said Bill, and began to chase the boys. With howls and yells and splashings they eluded him, making such a terrific noise that Huffin and Puffin, who had solemnly accompanied Philip all the way, half walking and half flying, retreated a little way up the beach. They stared at the boys fixedly and thoughtfully. Philip saw them and was pleased. Surely nobody had ever had two puffins for pets before! .

The girls were setting out ground-sheets and rugs neatly in the two tents when Dinah suddenly stopped and listened. Lucy-Ann listened too.

'What is it?' she whispered – and then she heard the noise herself. An aeroplane again, surely!

The girls went out of the tent and looked all over the sky, trying to locate the sound. 'There! – there, look!' cried Lucy-Ann excitedly, and she pointed westwards. 'Can't you see it? Oh, Dinah – what's it doing?'

Dinah couldn't spot the plane. She tried and tried but she could not see the point in the sky where the aeroplane flew.

'Something's falling out of it,' said Lucy-Ann, straining her eyes. 'Oh, where are the boys' field-glasses? Quick, get them, Dinah!'

Dinah couldn't find them. Lucy-Ann stood watching the sky, her eyes screwed up.

'Something dropped slowly from it,' she said. 'Something white. I saw it. Whatever could it have been? I hope the aeroplane wasn't in any trouble.'

'Bill will know,' said Dinah. 'I expect he and the boys saw it all right. Maybe they took the glasses with them. I couldn't find them anywhere.'

Soon there was no more to be seen or heard of the plane, and the girls went on with their work. The tents looked very comfortable with the piles of rugs. It was such a hot night that Dinah fastened the tent-flaps right back, in order to get some air.

'That storm doesn't seem to have come,' she said, looking at the western sky to see if any big clouds were sweeping up. 'But it feels very thundery.'

'Here are the others,' said Lucy-Ann, as she saw Jack, Philip and Bill coming up from the shore. 'And Huffin and Puffin are still with them! Oh, Di – won't it be fun if we have two pet puffins!'

'I wouldn't mind *puffins*,' said Dinah. 'But I can't bear those rats. Hallo, Bill! Did you hear the aeroplane?'

'Good gracious, no! Was there one?' demanded Bill, with great interest. 'Where? How was it we didn't hear it?'

'We were making such a row,' said Jack, grinning. 'We shouldn't have heard a hundred aeroplanes.'

'It was funny,' said Lucy-Ann to Bill. 'I was watching the aeroplane when I saw something falling out of it. Something white.'

Bill stared, frowning intently. 'A parachute?' he said. 'Could you see?'

'No. It was too far away,' said Lucy-Ann. 'It might have been a parachute – or a puff of smoke – I don't know. But it did look as if something was falling slowly from the plane. Why do you look so serious, Bill?'

'Because – I've a feeling there's something – well, just a bit strange about these planes,' said Bill. 'I think I'll pop down to the motor-boat and send a message through on the radio. Maybe it's nothing at all – but it just *might* be important!'

# 12

# Bill goes off on his own

Bill went off down the valley to the cove where the motor-boat was moored. His feet sank deeply into the soft earth. The children stared after him.

Lucy looked solemn – as solemn as Huffin and Puffin, who were leaning against Philip, standing upright, their big beaks looking heavy and clumsy.

'Oh dear – what does Bill mean? Surely we're not going to tumble into an adventure again! Up here, where there's nothing but the sea, the wind and the birds! What *could* happen, I wonder?'

'Well, Bill isn't likely to tell us much,' said Philip. 'So don't bother him with questions. I'm going to turn in. Brrrrr! It's getting a bit cold now. Me for that big pile of rugs! Huffin and Puffin, you'd better keep outside for the night. There'll be little enough room in this tent for you, as well as us three, Kiki and the rats.'

Huffin and Puffin looked at one another. Then, with one accord, they began to scrape the earth just outside the tent, sending the soil up behind them. Lucy-Ann giggled.

'They're going to make a burrow as near you as possible, Philip. Oh, aren't they funny?'

Kiki walked round to examine what the two puffins were doing. She got a shower of earth all over her and was very indignant.

'Arrrrrr!' she growled, and the two puffins agreed politely. 'Arrrrrrr!'

Bill came back in about half an hour. All the children were cuddled up in their rugs, and Lucy-Ann was asleep. Dinah called out to him.

'Everything all right, Bill?'

'Yes. I got a message from London, to tell me that your mother is getting on as well as can be expected,' said Bill. 'But she's got measles pretty badly, apparently. Good thing you're all off her hands!'

'What about your own message, Bill — about the aeroplane?' said Dinah, who was very curious over Bill's great interest in it. 'Did that get through?'

'Yes,' said Bill shortly. 'It did. It's nothing to worry your head about. Good night, Dinah.'

In two minutes' time everyone was asleep. Squeaker and his relations were only to be seen as bumps about Philip's person. Kiki was sitting on Jack's tummy, though he had already pushed her off several times. Huffin and Puffin were squatting in their new-made tunnel, their big coloured beaks touching. Everything was very peaceful as the moon slid across the sky, making a silvery path on the restless waters.

The morning dawned bright and beautiful, and it seemed

as if the storm was not coming, for there was no longer any closeness in the air. Instead it was fresh and invigorating. The children ran down to the shore to bathe as soon as they got up. They ran so fast that Huffin and Puffin could not keep up, but had to fly. They went into the water with the children, and bobbed up and down, looking quite ridiculous.

Then they dived for fish, swimming with their wings under the water. They were very quick indeed, and soon came up with fish in their enormous beaks.

'What about giving us one for breakfast, Huffin?' called Philip, and tried to take a fish from the nearest puffin's beak. But it held on to it – and then swallowed it whole.

'You ought to teach them to catch fish for us,' said Jack, giggling. 'We could have grilled fish for breakfast then! Hey, get away, Puffin – that's my foot, not a fish!'

At breakfast they discussed their plans for the day. 'What shall we do? Let's explore the whole island, and give bits of it proper names. This glen, where we are now, is Sleepy Hollow, because it's where we sleep,' said Lucy-Ann.

'And the shore where we bathe is Splash Cove,' said Dinah. 'And where we first moored our motor-boat is Hidden Harbour.'

Bill had been rather silent at breakfast. Jack turned to him. 'Bill! What do *you* want to do? Will you come and explore the island with us?'

'Well,' said Bill, very surprisingly, 'if you don't mind, as you'll be very busy and happy on your own, I'll take the motor-boat and go cruising about a bit – round all these islands, you know.'

'What! Without *us*?' said Dinah in astonishment. 'We'll come with you, then, if you want to do that.'

'I'm going alone, this first time,' said Bill. 'Take you another time, old thing. But today I'll go alone.'

'Is there – is there anything up?' asked Jack, feeling that something wasn't quite right. 'Has something happened, Bill?'

'Not that I know of,' said Bill cheerfully. 'I just want to go off on my own a bit, that's all. And if I do a bit of exploring round on my own account, I shall know the best places to take you to, shan't I?'

'All right, Bill,' said Jack, still puzzled. 'You do what you want. It's your holiday too, even if it *is* a disappearing one!'

So Bill went off on his own that day, and the children heard the purr of the motor-boat as it went out to sea, and then set off apparently to explore all the islands round about.

'Bill's up to something,' said Philip. 'And I bet it's to do with those aeroplanes. I wish he'd tell us. But he never will talk.'

'I hope he comes back safely,' said Lucy-Ann anxiously. 'It would be awful to be stranded here on a bird-island, and nobody knowing where we were.'

'Gosh, so it would,' said Jack. 'I never thought of that. Cheer up, Lucy-Ann — Bill isn't likely to run into danger. He's got his head screwed on all right.'

The day passed happily. The children went to the cliffs and watched the great companies of sea-birds there. They sat down in the midst of the puffin colony and watched the colourful, big-beaked birds going about their daily business. Lucy-Ann wore a hanky tied round her nose. She couldn't bear the smell of the colony, but the others soon got used to the heavy sourness of the air, and anyway, the wind blew strongly.

Huffin and Puffin did not leave them. They walked or ran with the children. They flew round them, and they went to bathe with them. Kiki was half jealous, but having had one hard jab from Huffin's multi-coloured beak, she kept at a safe distance, and contented herself with making rude remarks.

'Blow your nose! How many times have I told you to wipe your feet? You bad boy! Huffin and puffin all the time. Pop goes huffin!'

The children sat in Sleepy Hollow after their tea and

watched for Bill to come back. The sun began to set. Lucy-Ann looked pale and worried. Where was Bill?

'He'll be along soon, don't worry,' said Philip. 'We'll hear his boat presently.'

But the sun went right down into the sea, and still there was no Bill. The darkness closed down on the island, and there was no longer any point in sitting up and waiting. It was four anxious children who went into their tents and lay down to sleep. But none of them could sleep a wink.

In the end the girls went into the boys' tent and sat there, talking. Then suddenly they heard a welcome sound — rr-rr-rr-rr-rr! They all leapt up at once and rushed from the tent.

'That's Bill! It must be! Where's a torch? Come on down to the cove.'

They stumbled through the puffin colony, waking up many a furious bird. They got to the beach just as Bill came walking up. They flung themselves on him in delight.

'Bill! Dear Bill! What happened to you? We honestly thought you'd got lost!'

'Oh, Bill — we shan't let you go off alone again!'

'Sorry to have worried you so,' said Bill. 'But I didn't want to return in the daylight in case I was spotted by an aeroplane. I had to wait till it was dark, though I knew you'd be worried. Still — here I am.'

'But, Bill — aren't you going to tell us anything?' cried Dinah. 'Why didn't you want to come back in daylight? Who would see you? And why would it matter?'

'Well,' said Bill slowly, 'there's something peculiar going on up here in these lonely waters. I don't know quite what. I'd like to find out. I didn't see a soul today, anywhere, though I nosed round umpteen islands. Not that I really expected to, because nobody would be fool enough to come up here for something secret, and let anything of it be seen. Still, I thought I might find some sign.'

'I suppose that bit of orange peel was a sign that someone's here besides ourselves, on some other island?' said Lucy-Ann, remembering the piece that had bobbed against her fingers. 'But what are they doing? Surely they can't do much in this desolate stretch of waters — with nothing but islands of birds around.'

'That's what I'm puzzled about,' said Bill. 'Can't be smuggling, because the coasts of the mainland are very well patrolled at the moment, and nothing could get through. Then what is it?'

'Bill, you're sure nobody saw you?' asked Dinah, anxiously. 'There might be hidden watchers on one of the islands, you know — and one might see you, without you seeing him.'

'That's true,' said Bill, 'but I had to risk that. It's not very likely, though. The risk of anyone coming to these islands and disturbing whatever secret game is going on, is very remote, and I don't think there would be sentinels posted anywhere.'

'Still — you *might* have been seen — or heard,' persisted Dinah. 'Oh, Bill — and you were supposed to be disappearing completely! Now perhaps your enemies have spotted you!'

'They would hardly be the same enemies that I've disappeared from,' said Bill with a laugh. 'I don't think anyone else would recognize me here, seen at a distance in a motor-boat. In any case they would just think I was a bird-man or a naturalist of some kind, who likes the solitude of these seas.'

They were soon back in their tents again, happy to have Bill with them in safety. The stars shone down from a clear sky. Huffin and Puffin shuffled down their burrow, glad that their new family had gone to rest. They did not approve of these night walks.

Lucy-Ann lay and worried. 'I can *feel* an adventure coming. It's on the way. Oh dear — and I did think this would be the very very last place for one.'

Lucy-Ann was quite right. An adventure *was* on the way — and had very nearly arrived.

# 13

## What happened in the night?

The next morning everything seemed all right. The children had forgotten their fears of the night before, and Bill joked and laughed as merrily as the others.

But all the same he was worried – and when an aeroplane appeared and flew two or three times over the islands, he made the children lie down flat, in the middle of the puffin colony, where they happened to be at that moment.

'I don't think our tents can be seen,' he said. 'I hope not, anyway.'

'Don't want anyone to know we're here, Bill?' asked Jack.

'No,' said Bill shortly. 'Not at present, anyway. If you hear a plane, bob down. And we won't light a fire to boil a kettle. We'll have ginger-beer or lemonade instead.'

The day passed happily enough. It was very hot again and the children went to bathe half a dozen times, lying in the sun to dry afterwards. Kiki was jealous of Huffin and Puffin because they could go into the water with the children. She stood on the sandy beach, her toes sinking in, shouting loudly.

'Polly's got a cold, send for the doctor! A-tish-*ooooo!*'

'Isn't she an idiot?' said Jack, and splashed her. She was most annoyed and walked a bit farther back. 'Poor Kiki! What a pity! Poor pity, what a Kiki!'

'Yes, what a Kiki!' shouted Jack, and dived under the water to catch Bill's legs.

They took a good many photographs, and Huffin and Puffin posed beautifully, staring straight at the camera in a most solemn manner.

'I almost feel they'll suddenly put their arms round one another,' said Jack, as he clicked the camera. 'Thank you,'

Huffin and Puffin. Very nice indeed! But I wish you'd smile next time. Kiki, get out of the way – and leave that tent peg alone. You've already pulled up three.'

That night the sky was full of clouds and the sun could not be seen. 'Looks as if that storm might be coming soon,' said Bill. 'I wonder if our tents will be all right.'

'Well, there's nowhere else to go,' said Jack. 'Sleepy Hollow is about the most sheltered place on this island. And, as far as I've seen, there are no caves or anything of that sort.'

'Perhaps the storm will blow over,' said Philip. 'Phew, it's hot! I really think I must have one last bathe.'

'You've had eight already today,' said Dinah. 'I counted.'

Darkness came earlier that night, because of the clouds. The children got into their rugs, yawning.

'I think,' said Bill, looking at the luminous face of his wrist-watch. 'I think I'll slip along to the boat and send a message or two on my transmitter. I might get some news too, for myself. You go to sleep. I shan't be long.'

'Right,' said the boys, sleepily. Bill slipped out of the tent. The girls were already asleep and did not hear him go. Philip fell asleep almost before Bill was out of the tent. Jack lay awake a few minutes longer, and pushed Kiki off his middle for the fifth time.

She went and stood on Philip's middle, and waited for a lump to come near her feet, which she knew would be one of the tame rats. When one did venture near, raising a little mound under the rug, Kiki gave a sharp jab at it. Philip awoke with a yell.

'You beast, Kiki! Jack, take her away! She's given me an awful peck in my middle. If I could see her I'd smack her on the beak.'

Kiki retired outside the tent till the boys were asleep again. She flew to the top of it, and perched there, wide awake.

Meanwhile Bill was in the cabin of the boat tuning in on

the radio. But because of the coming storm it was difficult to hear anything but atmospherics.

'Blow!' said Bill at last. 'I shan't get my messages through at this rate. I've a good mind to take the boat to the little channel – what is it the children call it? – Hidden Harbour. Maybe I could get the radio going better there – it's so sheltered.'

It was very important to Bill to be able to use the radio that night. He set the engine of the boat going, and was soon on his way to Hidden Harbour. He nosed in carefully and moored the boat.

Then he set to work on his radio again. After a while he thought he heard some noise out to sea – a noise getting nearer and nearer. Bill turned off his radio and listened, but the wind was getting up, and he heard nothing but that.

He tuned the knobs again, listening intently for any message. He had got one through, and now he had been told to stand by and wait for an important announcement from headquarters.

The radio fizzed and groaned and whistled. Bill waited patiently. Then, suddenly hearing a sound, he looked up, startled, half expecting to see one of the boys coming down into the cabin.

But it wasn't. It was a hard-faced man with a curious crooked nose who was staring down at him. As Bill turned and showed his face, the man uttered a cry of the utmost astonishment.

'*You*! What are *you* doing here? What do you know of . . . '

Bill leapt up – but at the same moment the man lunged out at him with a thick, fat, knobbly stick he held in his hand – and poor Bill went down like a ninepin. He struck his head against the edge of the radio, and slid to the floor, his eyes closed.

The man with the crooked nose whistled loudly. Another man came to the small cabin and looked in.

'See that?' said the first man, pointing to Bill. 'Bit of a surprise, eh, to find *him* up here? Do you suppose he guessed anything?'

'Must have, if he's here,' said the second man, who had a short thick beard hiding a very cruel mouth. 'Tie him up. He'll be useful. We'll make him talk.'

Bill was tied up like a trussed chicken. He did not open his eyes. The men carried him out, and took him into a small boat, moored beside the *Lucky Star*. It was a rowing-boat. Into it went poor Bill, and the men undid their rope, ready to row back to their own motor-boat, which lay, perfectly silent, a little way beyond the island.

'Do you suppose there's anyone else with him?' asked the man with the crooked nose. 'There was no-one on board but him.'

'No. When his boat was sighted yesterday, we only saw one man aboard – and it was him all right,' said the man with the beard. 'If there'd been anyone else we'd have seen them. He's all alone. Ho! He didn't know he was being watched all the way back here last night.'

'I suppose there really *isn't* anyone else here,' said the first man, who seemed very reluctant to go. 'Hadn't we better smash up the boat – just in case?'

'All right – and the radio too,' said the man with the beard. He found a hammer and soon there were crashing sounds as the engine of the motor-boat was damaged and the beautiful little radio was smashed to bits.

Then the men set off in their rowing boat with the unconscious Bill. They reached their motor-boat, and soon the purring of its engine getting fainter and fainter, sounded in the night. But nobody on Puffin Island heard it except Kiki and the sea-birds.

The children had no idea at all that Bill had not returned that night. They slept peacefully, hour after hour, dreaming of huffins and puffins, big waves and golden sands.

Jack awoke first. Kiki was nibbling at his ear. 'Blow you,

Kiki!' said Jack, pushing the parrot away. 'Oh, goodness, here's Huffin and Puffin too!'

So they were. They waddled over to Philip and stood patiently by his sleeping face. 'Arrrrrr!' said Huffin lovingly.

Philip awoke. He saw Huffin and Puffin and grinned. He sat up and yawned. 'Hallo, Jack!' he said. 'Bill up already?'

'Looks like it,' said Jack. 'Probably gone to bathe. He might have waked us up though! Come on. Let's wake the girls and go and bathe too.'

Soon all four were speeding to the sea, expecting to see Bill in the water. But he wasn't.

'Where is he, then?' said Lucy-Ann, puzzled. 'And good gracious – where's the boat?'

Yes – where was the boat? There was no sign of it, of course. The children stared at the cove, puzzled and dismayed.

'He must have taken it round to Hidden Harbour,' said Jack. 'Perhaps the radio wouldn't work or something. It still feels stormy, and that might have upset it.'

'Well, let's go to Hidden Harbour then,' said Philip. 'Perhaps Bill got sleepy down there in the boat and thought he'd snuggle up in the cabin.'

'He's probably there,' said Dinah. 'Fast asleep too! Let's go and give him a shock. We'll halloo down into the cabin and make him jump. The sleepy-head!'

'Oh, I do hope he's there,' said Lucy-Ann, shivering as much with worry as with cold.

They dressed quickly, shivering a little, for the sun was hidden behind angry-looking clouds. 'I do hope the weather isn't going to break up, just as we've begun such a lovely holiday,' said Dinah. 'Oh, Huffin, I'm sorry – but you got right under my feet. Did I knock you over?'

The puffin didn't seem to mind having Dinah tread on it. It shook out its wings, said, 'Arrrrr!' and hurried on after Puffin, who was trying to keep pace with Philip.

They went across the puffin colony, and came to the cleft

in the cliffs. There, below them, lay the motor-boat, swaying very gently as waves ran up under her, and then ran back again.

'There she is!' said Dinah in delight, 'Bill *did* take her round to the harbour!'

'He's not on deck,' said Jack. 'He must be in the cabin. Come on.'

'Let's call him,' said Lucy-Ann suddenly. 'Do let's. I want to know if he's there.'

And before the others could stop her she shouted at the top of her voice. 'BILL! OH, BILL, ARE YOU THERE?'

No Bill came out from the cabin, and for the first time a little uneasiness crept into the children's minds.

'*BILL!*' yelled Jack, making everyone jump violently. '*BILL!* Come on out!'

No sound from the boat. Suddenly panic stricken, all four children stumbled down the rocky ledge to the boat. They jumped on board and peered down into the little cabin.

'He's not there,' said Dinah, scared. 'Well, where is he, then?'

'He must be somewhere about, as the boat is still here,' said Jack sensibly. 'He'll come along soon. Maybe he's exploring somewhere on the island.'

They were just turning away when Philip caught sight of something. He stopped and clutched Jack, turning very pale.

'What?' said Jack, frightened. 'What's up?'

Silently Philip pointed to the radio. 'Smashed!' he said, in a whisper. 'Smashed to bits! Who did it?'

Lucy-Ann began to cry. Jack went up on deck and had a look round, feeling sick and upset. Then Philip gave an anguished howl from the cabin that sent the others running to his side.

'Look! The engine of the boat is smashed up too! Absolutely destroyed. My goodness — what's been happening here?'

'And where is Bill?' said Dinah, in a husky whisper.

284

'Gone. Kidnapped,' said Philip slowly. 'Someone came for him in the night. They don't know we're here, I suppose – they just thought Bill was alone. They've got him – and now we're prisoners on Puffin Island and we can't get away!'

# 14

# A few plans

Everyone felt suddenly sick. Lucy-Ann sat down in a heap. Dinah joined her. The boys stood staring at the smashed engine as if they couldn't believe their eyes.

'It must be a nightmare,' said Dinah at last. 'It can't be true. Why – why, everything was right as rain last night – and now . . .'

'Now the boat's smashed up so that we can't get away, the radio is smashed so that we can't get a message through – and Bill's gone,' said Philip. 'And it isn't a dream. It's real.'

'Let's sit down in the cabin, all together,' said Lucy-Ann, wiping her eyes. 'Let's sit close and talk. Let's not leave each other at all.'

'Poor Lucy-Ann!' said Philip, putting his arm round her, as she sat down unsteadily. 'Don't worry. We've been in worse fixes than this.'

'We haven't!' said Dinah. 'This is the worst fix we've *ever* been in!'

Kiki felt the tenseness of all the children. She sat quietly on Jack's shoulder, making little comforting noises. Huffin and Puffin sat solemnly on the deck, staring fixedly in front of them. Even they seemed to feel that something awful had happened.

In the cabin, sitting close together, the children felt a little better. Jack rummaged in a tiny cupboard beside him and brought out some bars of chocolate. The children had had no breakfast, and although the shock they had had seemed to have taken their appetites away, they thankfully took the chocolate to nibble.

'Let's try and think out carefully exactly what must have happened,' said Jack, giving a bit of his chocolate to Kiki.

'Well – we know that Bill was worried about something,' said Philip. 'Those planes, for instance. He felt certain something peculiar was going on up here. And that's why he went out by himself in the boat. He must have been seen.'

'Yes – and maybe in some way his enemies got to know he was here,' said Dinah. 'They could have followed him a long way back, using field-glasses to keep him in sight. Anyway – it's quite clear that they came looking for him here.'

'And found him,' said Jack. 'What a pity he went off to tinker with the radio last night!'

'Well, if he hadn't, the enemy, whoever they are, would probably have searched the island and found us too,' said Dinah. 'As it is – they probably don't know we're here.'

'It wouldn't matter if they did know,' said Lucy-Ann. 'They'd be quite sure we couldn't do any harm, living on an island we can't get off!'

'They got here – in a motor-boat probably,' went on Jack. 'Left the motor-boat out beyond, somewhere – and slipped inshore quietly in a rowing-boat. They must know this little channel – or maybe they saw a light from the boat. Bill would be sure to have the cabin light on, and it's a pretty bright one.'

'Yes. And they surprised him and knocked him out, I suppose,' said Philip gloomily. 'They've taken him away – goodness knows what'll happen to him!'

'They won't – they won't hurt him, will they?' said Lucy-Ann in rather a trembly voice. Nobody answered.

'Cheer up, Lucy-Ann,' said Philip. 'We've been in worse scrapes before, whatever Dinah says. We'll get out of this one all right.'

'How?' asked Lucy-Ann. 'I don't see *how* we can! You don't either.'

Philip didn't. He scratched his head and looked at Jack.

'Well – we've got to make *some* kind of plan,' said Jack. 'I mean – we must make up our minds what we are going to do to try and escape – and what we are going to do *till* we escape.'

'Won't Bill's friends come and look for us when they don't get Bill's messages through?' asked Dinah suddenly.

'Pooh! What would be the good of *that*?' said Philip at once. 'There are hundreds of these little bird-islands here. It might take years visiting and exploring every single one to find us!'

'We could light a fire on the cliff and keep it burning so that any searcher could see the smoke in the daytime and the flames at night,' said Dinah excitedly. 'You know – like ship-wrecked sailors do.'

'Yes, we could,' said Jack. 'Only – the enemy might see it too – and come along and find us before anyone else does.'

There was a silence. Nobody knew who the enemy were. They seemed mysterious and powerful and frightening.

'Well, I can't help it – I think we ought to follow Dinah's plan and light a fire,' said Philip at last. 'We've got to run the risk of the enemy seeing it and coming to find us. But we simply *must* do something to help anyone searching for us. We can keep a look-out for the enemy, and hide if they come.'

'*Hide! Where* can we hide?' asked Dinah scornfully. 'There isn't a single place on this island for *anyone* to hide!'

'No, that's true,' said Jack. 'No caves, no trees, except for those few little birches – and the cliffs too steep to explore. We really *are* in a fix!'

'Can't we do anything to help Bill?' asked Lucy-Ann dolefully. 'I keep on and on thinking of him.'

'So do I,' said Jack. 'But I don't see that we can do much to help ourselves, let alone Bill. Now – if we could escape from here – or radio for help and get some of Bill's friends along – it would be *some*thing. But there doesn't seem anything at all to do except stay here and wait.'

'There's plenty of food, anyway,' said Dinah. 'Stacks of tinned stuff, and biscuits and potted meat, and Nestlés milk and sardines . . . '

'I think we'd better strip the boat of them,' said Jack. 'I'm surprised the enemy didn't take what they could with them. Maybe they'll come back for them – so we'll take them first. We can hide them down some of the puffin burrows.'

'Let's have a bit of breakfast now,' said Philip, feeling better now that they had all talked the matter over and made a few plans. 'Open some tins and get some ginger-beer. Come on.'

They all felt better still when they had had something to eat and drink. They had put a cover over the poor smashed radio. They couldn't bear to look at it.

Jack went up on deck when they had finished their meal. It was very close again, and even the wind seemed warm. The sun shone through a thin veiling of cloud, and had a reddish hue. 'That storm is still about,' said Jack. 'Come on, everyone. Let's get to work before it comes.'

It was decided that Philip and Dinah should hunt for driftwood to make a fire up on the cliff. 'We don't *know* that those aeroplanes we sometimes see belong to the enemy,' said Philip. 'If they don't, they may see our signal and come to circle round. Then they will send help. One might come today, even. So we'll get a fire alight. We'll bank it with dry seaweed. That will smoulder well and send up plenty of smoke.'

Jack and Lucy-Ann were to carry things from the boat to the tents in Sleepy Hollow. 'Take all the tins and food you can,' said Philip. 'If the enemy happened to come back at night and take it we'd be done. We should starve! As it is, we've got heaps to last us for weeks.'

The four children worked very hard indeed. Jack and

Lucy carried sacks of tins from the boat to Sleepy Hollow. For the time being they bundled them in a heap by the tents. Kiki examined them with interest, and pecked at one or two.

'It's a good thing your beak isn't a tin-opener, Kiki,' said Jack, making the first little joke that day, to try and make Lucy-Ann smile. 'We shouldn't have much food left if it was.'

Philip and Dinah were also very busy. They took a sack each from the boat and wandered along the shore to pick up bits of wood. They found plenty at the tide-line and filled their sacks. Then they dragged them to the top of the cliff. Huffin and Puffin went with them, solemn as ever, sometimes walking, sometimes flying.

Philip emptied his sack of wood on a good spot. He began to build a fire. Dinah went off to fill her sack with dry seaweed. There was plenty.

Soon Jack and Lucy-Ann, emptying their own sacks in Sleepy Hollow, saw a spiral of smoke rising up from the cliff-top. 'Look!' said Jack. 'They've got it going already! Good work!'

The wind bent the smoke over towards the east. It was good thick smoke, and the children felt sure that it could be seen from quite a distance.

'One of us had always better be up here, feeding the fire, and keeping watch for enemies or friends,' said Philip.

'How shall we know which they are?' asked Dinah, throwing a stick on the fire.

'Well – I suppose we shan't know,' said Philip. 'What we'd better do if we see any boat coming is to hide – that is, if we can *find* anywhere to hide – and then try and discover if the searchers are enemies or friends. We are sure to hear them talking. We'd better get lots more wood, Di – this fire will simply *eat* it up!'

Lucy-Ann and Jack helped them when they had finished their own job. 'We've taken every single tin and every scrap of food out of the boat,' said Lucy-Ann. 'We really have got plenty to eat—and that rock-pool to drink from when we've finished the ginger-beer. There aren't an awful lot of bottles left now. Wouldn't you like to have dinner soon?'

'Yes. I'm jolly hungry,' said Philip. 'Let's have it up here, shall we? Or is it too much bother to fetch a meal here, Lucy-Ann? You see, one of us must keep the fire going all the time.'

'Well, it won't go out for a while, anyhow,' said Lucy-Ann. 'Bank it up with some more seaweed. Honestly, we feel fagged out, carrying all that stuff. Let's go to Sleepy Hollow and have a good rest and a jolly good meal.'

So they all returned to Sleepy Hollow, where the two tents flapped in the little breeze. They sat down and Lucy-Ann opened tins, and ladled the contents on to plates.

'You've got tinned salmon, biscuits and butter, tinned tomatoes and tinned pears,' she said.

Even Huffin and Puffin came closer than usual, to share such a nice meal. They would have eaten every scrap of the salmon if they could. Kiki preferred the tinned pears, but the children would only allow her one.

'Well, things would be a lot worse if we hadn't got all this nice food,' said Jack, leaning back in the warm sun, after a big meal. 'An adventure without good food would be awful! Kiki, take your head out of that tin. You've had more than any of us, you greedy glutton of a parrot!'

# 15

# A really terrible storm

The wind got up about five o'clock. It whipped the waves round the island until they towered into big white horses that raced up the beaches and broke with a sound of thunder. The sea-birds deserted the coves, and flew into the air, crying loudly. The wind took them and they soared for miles without beating a wing, enjoying themselves throughly.

Kiki didn't like so much wind. She could not glide or soar like the gulls and guillemots. It offended her dignity to be blown about too much. So she stayed close to the tents, which flapped like live things in the wind, and strained at the tent-pegs violently.

'Look here, we can't possibly watch the fire all night!' said Philip. 'We'll have to bank it up and hope for the best. Maybe it will send out a glow, anyway. Doesn't that sea-weed keep it in nicely? My goodness, the wind tears the smoke to rags now!'

The sun went down in a bank of angry purple clouds that gathered themselves together in the west. Jack and Philip stared at them.

'That's the storm coming up all right,' said Jack. 'Well, we've felt one coming for days – this hot weather was bound to end up like that. I hope the wind won't blow our tents away in the night.'

'So do I,' said Philip anxiously. 'Honestly, there's a perfect gale blowing up now! Look at those awful clouds! They look really wicked!'

The boys watched the clouds covering the sky, making the evening dark much sooner than usual. Philip put his hand into one of his pockets. 'My rats know there is a storm coming,' he said. 'They're all huddled up in a heap together right at the very bottom of my pocket. Funny how animals know things like that.'

'Jack!' called Lucy-Ann anxiously. 'Do you think the tents are safe? The wind is blowing them like anything!'

The boys went to examine them. They were as well pegged as they could be, but in this gale who knew what might happen?

'We just can't do anything about it but hope for the best,' said Jack rather gloomily. 'Philip, have you got your torch?

We'd better be prepared to be disturbed in the night, if this gale goes on – we might have to re-peg one of the tents.'

Both boys had torches with new batteries, so that was all right. They put them down beside their beds when they cuddled up into their rugs that night. They all went early because for one thing it was getting very dark, for another thing it had begun to rain heavily, and for a third thing they were all very tired with the day's work. Kiki retired with the boys as usual, and Huffin and Puffin scuttled into their burrows nearby.

'Wonder what poor old Bill is doing,' said Jack to Philip, as they lay listening to the wind howling round them. 'I bet he's worried stiff about us.'

'It's a shame, just as we were all set for a glorious holiday,' said Philip. 'And now the weather's broken too! What on earth shall we do with ourselves if it goes on like this for days? It will be frightful.'

'Oh, it may clear up again when the storm is over,' said Jack. 'Golly, hark at the waves on the beaches round the island – and how they must be dashing against those steep cliffs! I bet the gannets and guillemots aren't getting much sleep tonight!'

'The wind's pretty deafening too,' said Philip. 'Blow it! I feel so tired, and yet I can't possibly sleep  ˙ h all this din going on. And gosh – what's that?'

'Thunder,' said Jack, sitting up. 'The storm is on us now all right. Let's go into the girls' tent, Philip. Lucy-Ann will be pleased to see us if she's awake. A storm over this exposed little island won't be very funny.'

They crept into the other tent. The girls were wide awake and very glad to have them beside them. Dinah squeezed up into Lucy-Ann's rugs, and the boys got into Dinah's warm place. Jack flashed on his torch.

He saw that Lucy-Ann was very white. 'There's nothing to be frightened of, old thing,' he said gently. 'It's only a storm, and you're never frightened of those. Lucy-Ann, you know you aren't.'

'I know,' gulped Lucy-Ann. 'It's only that — well, the storm seems so wild and — and *spite*ful, somehow. It *tears* at our tent, and bellows at us. It seems alive.'

Jack laughed. The thunder came again and crashed more loudly than the waves on the shore. Kiki crept close to Jack.

'Pop, pop, pop!' she said, and put her head under her wing.

'Thunder doesn't pop, Kiki,' said Jack, trying to joke. But nobody smiled. The wind blew more wildly than ever and the children wished they had more rugs. It was very very draughty!

Then the lightning flashed. It made them all jump, for it was so vivid. For an instant the steep cliffs and the raging sea showed vividly. Then the picture was gone.

Crash! The thunder came again, this time sounding overhead. Then the lightning split the sky open again and once more the children saw the cliffs and the sea. They didn't seem quite real, somehow.

'Sort of unearthly,' said Philip. 'Gosh, hark at the rain! I'm getting spattered all over with it, though goodness knows how it's getting in here.

'The wind's getting worse,' said Lucy-Ann fearfully. 'Our tents will blow away. They will, they will!'

'No, they won't,' said Jack stoutly, taking Lucy-Ann's cold hand in his. 'They can't. They . . . '

But at that very moment there came a rending sound, a great flap-flap-flap, something hit Jack across the face — and their tent was gone.

The four children were struck dumb for a moment. The wind howled round them, the rain soaked them. They had nothing over them to protect them — their tent had vanished. Vanished with the wild wind in the darkness of the night.

Lucy-Ann screamed and clutched Jack. He put his torch on quickly.

'Gosh — it's gone! The gale has taken it away. Come into our tent, quickly!'

But before the children could even get up from their rugs,

the gale had taken the other tent too. It rushed by Philip, as he stood trying to help the girls up, and when he turned his torch to where his tent should be, there was nothing.

'Ours has gone too,' he cried, trying to out-shout the wind. 'Whatever are we to do?'

'We'd better get down to the boat – if we possibly can,' yelled Jack. 'Or do you think we shall be blown over? Had we better roll ourselves up in the ground-sheets and rugs and wait till the storm has blown itself out?'

'No. We'll be soaked. Better try for the boat,' said Philip. He dragged the girls up. Each of the children wrapped a rug round their shoulders to try and ward off the rain and the cold.

'Take hands and keep together!' yelled Philip. 'I'll go first.'

They took hands. Philip set off, staggering in the gale that was blowing in his face. Through the puffin colony he went, trying to keep on his feet.

Suddenly Dinah, who had hold of Philip's hand, felt him drag it away. Then she heard a cry. She called in fright.

'Philip! Philip! What's happened?'

There was no answer. Jack and Lucy-Ann came close to Dinah. 'What's up? Where's Philip?'

Jack's torch shone out in front of them. There was no Philip there. He had vanished completely. The children, their hearts beating painfully, stayed absolutely still in dismay and astonishment. Surely the gale hadn't blown him away!

'PHILIP! PHILIP!' yelled Jack. But only the wind answered him. Then all three yelled at the tops of their voices.

Jack thought he heard a faint answering cry. But where? It sounded at his feet! He swung his torch downwards, and to his immense surprise and fright he saw Philip's head – but only his head, on a level with the ground.

Dinah shrieked in fright. Jack knelt down, too dumbfounded to say a word. Just Philip's head – just Philip's . . .

Then he saw in a flash what had happened. Philip had trodden on soil so undermined by the puffins that it had given way – and he had fallen right through to a hole below. Jack could have cried with relief.

'Are you all right, Philip?' he yelled.

'Yes. Give me your torch. I've dropped mine. I've fallen through into a whopping big hole. There might be room for us all to shelter here for a bit,' shouted back Philip, the words being whipped away by the wind almost before Jack could hear them.

Jack gave Philip his torch. The boy's head disappeared. Then it came back again, looking very odd sticking up between some heather and a sea-pink cushion.

'Yes. It's an enormous hole. Can you all get down? We'd keep safe and dry here till the storm is over. Come on. It's a bit smelly, but otherwise not bad.'

Dinah slid through the opening of the hole and found herself beside Philip. Then came Lucy-Ann and then Jack. Jack had found Philip's torch and the two torches were now shone around the hole.

'I suppose the rabbits and the puffins together managed to burrow so much that they have made an enormous hole,' said Jack. 'Look, there's a puffin burrow leading out of it over there – and one of the puffins staring in astonishment at us! Hallo, old son. Sorry to burst in on you like this.'

The relief of finding that Philip was safe, and of being out of the wild noise of the storm, made Jack feel quite light-headed. Lucy-Ann's shivers stopped, and they all looked round them with interest.

'*I* should think this was a natural cavity of some sort,' said Philip, 'with a layer of good soil, held together by roots and things, making a surface above – but all that burrowing by the puffins made it give way when I trod on it – and down I fell. Well, it's just what we wanted, for the moment.'

Above them, deadened by tangled heather and sea-pinks, the storm raged on. No rain came into the cavity. The thunder sounded very far away. The lightning could not be seen.

'I don't see why we shouldn't sleep here for the night,' said Jack, spreading out the rug he had taken from his shoulders. 'The soil is dry and soft – and the air must be good enough, because that puffin is still there, gazing at us. I say – I hope Huffin and Puffin are all right.'

They all spread out their rugs and lay down, cuddled up together. 'Congratulations on finding us such a fine home for tonight, Philip,' said Jack sleepily. 'Very clever of you indeed! Good night, everybody!'

# 16

## Next day

They all slept soundly in their unexpected shelter. They did not awake until late in the morning, because for one thing it was dark in the hole, and for another they had all been tired out.

Jack awoke first, feeling Kiki stirring against his neck. He could not think where he was. A little daylight filtered through the entrance of the hole, but not much. It was very warm.

'Arrrrrr!' said a guttural voice, and made Jack jump. 'Arrrrrr!'

It was the puffin which had come down its burrow to see them the night before. Jack switched on his torch and grinned at it.

'Good morning – if it is morning. Sorry to have disturbed you! I'll get Huffin and Puffin to explain to you, when we see them again.'

Philip woke and sat up. Then the girls stirred. Soon they were all wide awake, looking round the curious cavity, and remembering the events of the night before.

'What a night!' said Dinah, shuddering. 'Oh – when our tents blew away – I really did feel awful!'

'And when Philip disappeared, I felt worse,' said Lucy-Ann. 'What time is it, Jack?'

Jack looked at his watch and whistled. 'My word – it's almost ten o'clock. How we've slept! Come on, let's see if the storm is still going strong.'

He stood up and pulled away the overhanging heather that blocked up the narrow entrance to the hole. At once a shaft of blinding sunlight entered, and the children blinked. Jack put his head out of the hole in delight.

'Golly! It's a *perfect* day! The sky is blue again, and there's sunshine everywhere. Not a sign of the storm left. Come on, let's go up into the sunlight and have a look around.'

Up they went, giving each other a hand. Once they were out of the hole, and the heather fell back into place again, there was no sign of where they had spent the night.

'Wouldn't it make an absolutely marvellous hiding-place?' said Jack. The others looked at hi~ ~~ same thought occurring to everyone at once.

'Yes. And if the enemy come – *that's* where we'll go,' said Dinah. 'Unless they actually walk over the place they can't possibly find it. Why – I don't know myself where it is now – though I've just come out of it!'

'Gosh, don't say we've lost it as soon as we've found it,' said Jack, and they looked about for the entrance. Jack found it in just the same way as Philip had the night before – by falling down it. He set an upright stick beside it, so that they would know the entrance easily next time. 'We might have to sleep down there each night now, as our tents have gone,' said Jack. 'It's a pity we've brought our rugs up. Still, they can do with a sunning. We'll spread them out on the heather.'

'Thank goodness that awful wind's gone,' said Dinah. 'There's hardly even a breeze today. It's going to be frightfully hot. We'll bathe.'

They had a dip in the quiet sea, which looked quite

different from the boiling, raging sea of the day before. Now it was calm and blue, and ran up the sand in frilly little waves edged with white. After their bathe the children had an enormous breakfast in the spot where their tents had been.

Huffin and Puffin appeared as soon as the children arrived and greeted them joyfully.

'Arrrrrr! Arrrrrrr!'

'They're saying that they hope we've got a good breakfast for them,' said Dinah. 'Huffin and Puffin, I wish you'd eat rats. You'd be very useful then.'

Philip's rats had appeared again, now that the storm was over, much to Dinah's disgust. They seemed very lively, and one went into Jack's pockets to find a sunflower seed. It brought one out, sat on Jack's knee and began to nibble it. But Kiki pounced at once, and snatched the seed away, whilst Squeaker scurried back to Philip in a hurry.

'You're a dog in the manger, Kiki,' said Jack. 'You don't really want that sunflower seed yourself, and you won't let Squeaker have it either. Fie!'

'Fie fo fum,' said Kiki promptly, and went off into a screech of laughter, right in Jack's ear. He pushed her off his shoulder.

'I shall be deaf for the rest of the day! Lucy-Ann, look out for that potted meat. Huffin is much too interested in it.'

'Really – what with Kiki pinching fruit out of the tin, and Huffin and Puffin wanting the potted meat, and Philip's rats sniffing round, it's a wonder we've got anything ourselves!' said Lucy-Ann. But all the same, it was fun to have the creatures joining in and being one with them. Huffin and Puffin were especially comical that morning, for now that they were really friendly, they wanted to look into everything. Huffin suddenly took an interest in Dinah's fork and picked it up with his beak.

'Oh, don't swallow that, silly!' cried Dinah, and tried to get her fork away. But Huffin had a very strong beak, and he won the tug of war. He waddled away to examine the fork in peace.

'He won't swallow it, don't worry,' said Philip, tossing Dinah his own fork. 'It'll keep him quiet a bit if he plays with it for a while.'

The children's fire was, of course, completely out. It had to be pulled to pieces and lighted all over again. This was not so easy as before, because everything had been soaked during the night. Still, the sun was so very hot that it wouldn't be long before the wood and the seaweed were bone-dry again.

The children missed out dinner completely that day, because it had been twelve o'clock before they had cleared up their breakfast things. 'We'll have a kind of high tea about five,' said Jack. 'We've plenty to do – look for our tents – light the fire – find some more wood – and go and see if the motor-boat is all right.'

Their tents were nowhere to be seen. One or two pegs were found but that was all. 'The tents are probably lying on some island miles and miles away,' said Jack. 'Scaring the sea-birds there. Well – shall we sleep in that hole to-night?'

'Oh no, please don't let's,' begged Lucy-Ann. 'It's smelly. And it's so very hot again now that surely we could put our rugs on cushions of heather and sleep out in the open. I should like that.'

Philip looked up at the clear blue sky. Not a cloud was to be seen. 'Well,' he said, 'if it's like this tonight, it would be quite comfortable to sleep in the open. We'll plan to do that unless the weather changes. Let's find a nice cushiony place, and put our rugs there, and our other clothes, with the ground-sheets over them. Good thing the ground-sheets only blew up against those birch-trees and got stuck there!'

They found a nice heathery place, not too far from where Lucy-Ann kept the stores beneath the big ledge of stone, and piled their extra jerseys, their mackintoshes, their rugs and their ground-sheets there. Lucy-Ann had stored their spare clothes with the food under the ledge, but the rain had driven in, and had made them damp. So it was decided that it would be better to use them as extra bedclothes at night, and keep them under the ground-sheets during the daytime.

After they had done all this they went to see their fire, which was burning well now. They sat on the top of the cliff, with the birds crying all round them, and looked out on the calm, brilliantly blue sea.

'What's that?' said Lucy-Ann suddenly, pointing to something floating not far off.

'Looks like a heap of wood, or something,' said Philip. 'Wreckage of some sort. Hope it comes inshore. We can use it for our fire.'

It came slowly in with the tide. Philip put his glasses to his eyes. Then he lowered them again, looking so taken-aback that the others were scared.

'Do you know,' he said, 'that wreckage looks awfully like bits of the *Lucky Star*. And there's more bits over there, look – and I dare-say we should find some down on the rocks.'

There was a shocked silence. Nobody had even *thought* that the motor-boat might have been taken by the storm and battered. Jack swallowed hard. That *would* be a blow! He got up.

'Come on. We'd better go and see. Of course I suppose it was bound to be smashed up, but anyhow we couldn't have moved it. Gosh – what bad luck if the boat's gone! Even if the engine was smashed, it was still a boat. We might have rigged up a sail – or something . . . '

In silence the children left the fire on the cliff and made their way through the cleft, and down the rocky ledges to the little harbour.

There was no boat there. Only a bit of the mooring-rope was left, still tied round the rock nearby, its ragged ends fluttering in the tiny breeze.

'Look!' said Jack, pointing. 'She must have been battered up and down by great waves rushing in and out of the channel – see the paint on the rocks – and look at the bits of wood about. When the rope broke she must have been taken right out of the channel, and then beaten to bits against the cliffs. What a frightful shame!'

The girls had tears in their eyes, and Philip had to turn away too. Such a lovely boat! Now she was nothing but masses of wreckage which they could burn on their fire. Poor *Lucky Star*. *Unlucky Star* should have been her name.

'Well, nothing we could have done would have helped,' said Jack at last. 'The storm would have wrecked her anyway — though if Bill had been here, and the boat was all right, he would have taken her round to Splash Cove and we could have dragged her right up the beach, out of reach of the waves. It wasn't our fault.'

They all felt sad and downcast as they left the little harbour and went back. The sun was going down now, and the evening was very peaceful and beautiful. There was hardly any wind at all.

'I can hear an aeroplane again!' said Lucy-Ann, her sharp ears picking up the distant throbbing before the others. 'Listen!'

Far away a small speck showed low down in the blue sky. The boys clapped their glasses to their eyes. Jack gave an exclamation.

'It's dropping something, look! Philip, what is it? Is it a parachute?'

'It looks like a small parachute — with something underneath it, swinging to and fro,' said Philip, his eyes glued to his glasses. 'Is it a man? No, it doesn't look like a man. Then what in the world is it? And why is the plane dropping things here? Gosh, I wish Bill was here to see this. There is something peculiar going on. Something the enemy are doing. I shouldn't be surprised if they get the wind up when they see our smoke and come along to search the island. Tomorrow one of us must always be on the lookout, from the cliff.'

Puzzled and anxious, the children went back to Sleepy Hollow. It was time for high tea, and Lucy-Ann and Dinah prepared it in silence. They were in the middle of an adventure again — and they couldn't possibly get out of it.

# 17

# A boat, a boat!

'Do you think it's worth while keeping the fire going, if the aeroplanes belong to the enemy?' asked Lucy-Ann at last.

'Well, if we're *ever* to be rescued, we shall have to show some kind of signal,' said Jack. 'We'll have to risk the aeroplanes seeing it. Perhaps, when no messages come through from Bill, motor-boats will come looking for us. Then they will see our signal, and come to the island.'

'I hope they do,' said Dinah. 'I don't want to be here for months. And it would be awful in the winter.'

'Good gracious! Don't talk about being here for the *winter*!' said Lucy-Ann, in alarm. 'Why, it's only May!'

'Dinah's looking on the black side of things as usual,' said Philip.

Dinah flared up. 'I'm not! I'm being sensible. You always call being sensible "looking on the black side of things." '

'Oh, don't quarrel just now, when we all ought to stick by each other,' begged Lucy-Ann. 'And *don't* put those rats near Dinah, Philip – don't be mean just now!'

Philip snapped his fingers and the rats scurried back to his pockets. Kiki snorted.

'Three blind mice, see how they run, pop goes Kiki!'

'Arrrrr!' said Huffin, agreeing politely. It was really very comical the way he and Puffin seemed to talk to Kiki. They never said anything but 'Arrrr,' but they said it in many different tones, and sounded quite conversational at times.

That night the children slept out in the open. It was a beautiful calm night, and the stars hung in the sky, big and bright. Lucy-Ann tried to keep awake to watch for shooting stars, which she loved, but she didn't see any.

Her bed was very comfortable. The children had chosen

thick heather to put their groundsheets and rugs on, and had used their extra clothes for pillows. A tiny breeze blew against their cheeks and hair. It was lovely lying there with the stars shining peacefully above, and the sound of the sea in the distance.

'It's like the wind in the trees,' thought Lucy-Ann sleepily. 'And the wind in trees is like the sound of the sea. Oh dear, I'm getting muddled – muddled – mudd—'

The weather was still lovely the next day, and the spiral of smoke from the signal fire went almost straight up in the air, there was so little wind. Jack and Philip took a good many bird-photographs, and Jack looked longingly over the steep bird-cliff, wishing he could climb down a little way and take some photographs of the birds there.

'Bill said not,' said Philip. 'And I think we oughtn't to. Suppose anything happened to us, what would the girls do? We've got heaps of fine photographs without bothering to take the eggs and birds on those ledges.'

'I wish the puffins had laid eggs,' said Jack. 'I haven't found a single puffin egg yet. It's a bit too early, I suppose. How sweet baby puffins must look! I wish I could see some.'

'Well, you're likely to, as things have turned out,' said Philip, with a half-comical groan. 'We may be here for quite a long time.'

It was arranged that one or other of the children should always be on the look-out somewhere on the bird-cliff. From there it was possible to see nearly all round the island, and no enemy could approach without being seen when still far off. That would give plenty of time for the others to be warned, and for all of them to go into hiding.

'We'd really better hide all the tins and things that are under our ledge, down in that hole, hadn't we?' said Lucy-Ann, when the plans were made. 'They might easily be found.'

'We'll stuff heather round them,' said Jack. 'It would be an awful bore to have to keep going down into the hole to fetch all the food each time we wanted something to eat.'

So clumps of heather were most realistically tucked under the rocky ledge where Lucy-Ann kept the tins. Nobody would guess it wasn't growing, it looked so natural there.

'We'd have plenty of time to chuck our clothes and things down into the hidey-hole, if we saw anyone coming,' said Jack. 'I'll take first watch. I shan't be a bit bored, because there are so many birds up there – and Kiki is such a clown with them, it's as good as a pantomine to watch her.'

Two days went by without anything exciting happening at all. Once they heard another aeroplane, but didn't see it. More wreckage was thrown up on the beach from the unfortunate *Lucky Star*. The children bathed and ate and slept, and took it in turns to keep watch, but they saw nothing to worry them at all.

Kiki always kept watch with Jack. Huffin and Puffin kept watch with Philip. Once another puffin came too near Philip for Huffin's liking, and the bird ran at it with his head down, growling *arrrrrrr* like an infuriated dog. Their big beaks locked together, and Philip almost cried with laughter as he watched the curious battle.

'The battle of beaks,' he called it, when he described it to the others afterwards. 'Talk about stags locking their antlers together and fighting – those two puffins were every bit as fierce with their huge beaks.'

'Who won?' asked Lucy-Ann, with great interest. 'Huffin, I suppose?'

'Of course,' said Philip. 'He not only won, he chased the other one right into its burrow, and they both came out again at another entrance, with Huffin winning the race. I'm surprised the other poor bird had any feathers left by the time Huffin had finished with him.'

On the afternoon of the third day, Jack was sitting up on the top of the bird-cliff. It was his turn to look out. He gazed lazily out to sea. There was just a little more breeze that day, and the waves had frills of white as they came in to shore.

Jack was thinking about Bill. Where was he? What had happened to him? Had he been able to escape, and if so, would he come quickly to rescue the four children? And what was Aunt Allie thinking? Had she heard that there was no word from Bill, and was she worried?

Jack thought deeply about all these things, listening to the different cries of the sea-birds about him, and watching their graceful fight over the sea. Then his eyes suddenly picked out something far off on the water.

He stiffened like a dog that suddenly sees something unusual. He reached down for his field-glasses and put them to his eyes. He had soon got the something out there into focus – and he saw that it was a small motor-boat.

'Enemies,' he thought, and was about to leap to his feet when he remembered that whoever was in the boat might also have glasses, and might see him. So he wriggled away on his tummy, and not until he was well down into the little valley did he jump up and run to the others.

'Hi!' he called breathlessly, as he tore down to Sleepy Hollow, where the others were having a laze. 'There's a boat coming!'

They all sat up at once. Lucy-Ann's green eyes were wide with excitement and fright. 'Where? How far away?'

'Quite a way off. It will take them about ten minutes to come in and tie up. We'd better chuck everything down into the hole at once.'

'What about the fire?' said Dinah, grabbing her pile of jerseys and coats.

'Have to leave that. They've already seen the smoke anyway,' said Jack. 'Come on, quick! Get a move on, Lucy-Ann!'

It didn't take long to part the heather over the narrow entrance to the hole and hurl everything down. Jack removed the stick he had put there to mark the place.

'No good leaving a signpost for them,' he said, trying to make Lucy-Ann smile. She gave him a watery grin.

'Now – everything cleared up?' said Philip, looking round. He pulled at the clumps of heather they had been lying on, which had got rather flattened, but the springy plants were already getting back into position themselves. Philip picked up a spoon that someone had left lying there and popped it into his pocket. There really did seem to be nothing left now that would show that the children had been there a few minutes before.

'Come on, Tufty! Don't wait about!' said Jack, in a fever of impatience to get below ground. The girls were already safely in the hole. Jack slid down himself and Philip followed almost at once.

Jack pulled the heather neatly over the hole. 'There! Now unless anybody actually treads in the hole, as Philip did the other night, we're safe. Nobody would ever know there was a big cavity underground.'

'I feel like a puffin,' said Philip. 'I feel I'd like to burrow. What about digging a nice little burrow for each of us to lie in?'

'Oh, don't make jokes now,' begged Lucy-Ann. 'I don't feel like jokes. I feel – I feel all sort of tight and breathless. And my heart simply *couldn't* beat any louder. Can you hear it?'

Nobody could. But then, their own hearts were beating so fast and so loudly that it was no wonder they could not hear anybody else's.

'Can we whisper?' asked Dinah, in a loud whisper that made everyone jump.

'I should think so. But don't talk out loud,' said Jack. 'And if we hear anyone coming, listen with all your might, so that we shall know if it's friends or enemies. It would be *too* awful if it was friends and we let them go away without finding us.'

That was indeed an awful thought – almost worse than the thought of being found by an enemy. Everyone sat quietly, holding their breaths, listening with all their might.

'Friend or enemy, friend or enemy, friend or enemy,' said a voice in Lucy-Ann's mind, and she couldn't stop it saying the words over and over again. 'Friend or . . . '

'Sh,' came Jack's whisper, suddenly. 'I can hear something.'

But it was only Huffin and Puffin arriving in the hole. They pushed the heather aside and flopped in, giving the children a terrible shock. The heather swung·back, and the puffins stared in the darkness, trying to find Philip.

'You wretched birds!' scolded Philip. 'You might have shown them our hiding-place. Don't you dare to say a word!'

'Arrrrrr!' said Huffin deeply. Philip gave him an angry push, and the bird walked away in astonishment. It was the first time he had ever had an angry word or gesture from his ·beloved Philip. He hopped up to the beginning of a nearby burrow, followed by Puffin, and began to walk up it, very much offended. The children were glad to hear them go.

'Sh!' came Jack's whisper again, and the others clutched one another. 'They're really coming now! Shhhhhhhh!'

# 18

## The enemy – and Kiki

The thud of footsteps could be felt in the dark hole below ground. Then came the sound of voices. 'We'll search the whole place. *Somebody* must be keeping that fire going!'

'There's nowhere much to hide on this small island,' said another voice. 'Nobody could get down those sheer cliffs, so that rules them out. And there's obviously nobody in this valley – except these ridiculous birds.'

There came the sound of a match being struck. One of the men was evidently lighting a cigarette. He tossed the match away – and it came trickling through the heather into the hole where the trembling children crouched. It fell on to Dinah's knee and she almost squealed.

'They're dreadfully near,' everyone was thinking. 'Dreadfully, dreadfully near!'

'Look here,' said one of the men's voices, suddenly. 'What's this? A bit of chocolate wrapping-paper! I bet the hiding-place isn't far off.'

The children's hearts almost stopped beating. Philip remembered that a bit of his chocolate-paper had blown away on the wind and he hadn't bothered to go and pick it up. Blow! Blow! Blow!

Jack felt about for Kiki. Where was she? She had slid off his shoulder, but he couldn't feel her anywhere near. He did hope she wouldn't suddenly make one of her loud remarks, just under the very feet of the men.

Kiki had gone up the burrow, after Huffin and Puffin. The two puffins were now staring at the men who had come to hunt. They stood at the entrance of a burrow, looking fixedly with their crimson-circled eyes.

'Look at those silly chaps,' said one man. 'Whatever are these ridiculous birds, with beaks like fireworks about to go off?'

'Don't know. Puffins or sea parrots, or something,' said the other man.

'Huffin and Puffin,' said Kiki, in a loud, conversational sort of voice. The men jumped violently and looked all round. Kiki was in the burrow behind Huffin and Puffin and could not be seen. She didn't want to push past them in case they nipped her.

'Did you hear that?' said the first man.

'Well – I thought I heard something,' said the other. 'But these birds all round make such a racket.'

'Yes – a frightful din,' said the first man.

'Din-din-dinner,' announced Kiki and went off into one of her cackles of laughter. The men stared in alarm at the two solemn puffins. 'I say – surely those birds can't *talk*?'

'It's a bit odd, isn't it?' said the first man, rubbing his chin and staring at Huffin and Puffin. It seemed as if it really must be the two puffins who were talking and coughing. Kiki could not be seen.

Huffin opened his beak. 'Arrrrrr!' he said solemnly.

'There!' said the man. 'I saw him that time. They *are* talking birds. Sea parrots perhaps – and parrots talk, don't they?'

'Yes, but they have to be taught,' said the other. 'And who taught these two?'

'Oh, come on – don't let's waste any time on the ridiculous creatures, said the first man, turning to go. 'We'll go down to the shore and walk along it to make sure there's no one there. Pity the boat's been smashed up in the gale. We could have taken off some of the food in it.'

Kiki gave an imitation of a motor-bike in the distance, and the men stopped suddenly in astonishment.

'I could have sworn that was a motor-bike!' said one, with a half-ashamed laugh. 'Come on – we're hearing things. Wait till I get hold of whoever is on this island – making us waste time hunting like this!'

To the children's enormous relief the men's voices got fainter and fainter and at last could not be heard at all. Kiki came back into the cave.

'What a pity, what a pity!' she said in a whisper, cracking her beak.

'Kiki, you awful idiot, you nearly gave the game away!' whispered Jack. 'Get on my shoulder – and I warn you, if you say just one more word, I'll tie your beak up with my hanky.'

'Arrrrrrr!' said Kiki, and settled down with her head under her wing. She was offended.

For what seemed like hours the children sat silently in the hole underground. They heard no more voices, and no more footsteps shook the ground nearby.

'How long have we got to stay here like this?' whispered Dinah at last. She was always the first to get impatient. 'I'm cramped.'

'I don't know,' said Jack, in a whisper that seemed to fill the underground cavity. 'It would be dangerous to pop my head out and take a look-see.'

'I'm hungry,' said Lucy-Ann. 'I wish we'd brought something to eat down with us. And I'm thirsty too.'

Jack wondered whether or not to risk sticking his head out. Just as he was making up his mind that he would, everyone in the hole heard a far-off, very welcome noise.

'It's the engine of their motor-boat being started up,' said Jack in relief. 'They must have given up the hunt, thank goodness. We'll give them a few minutes, then I'll hop out.'

They waited for five minutes. The motor-boat's engine sounded for a little while, then grew fainter and finally could not be heard at all.

Jack cautiously put his head out. He could see and hear nothing but puffins. Huffin and Puffin were squatting nearby and got up politely when they saw his head.

'Arrrrrrr!' they said.

Jack got right out of the hole. He lay down flat, put his field-glasses to his eyes and swept the sea around. At last he spotted what he was looking for – the motor-boat going away at top speed, getting smaller and smaller in the distance.

'It's all right!' he called down to the others. 'They're almost out of sight. Come on out.'

Soon they were all sitting in Sleepy Hollow, with the girls getting a meal ready, for by this time they were once again ravenous. The ginger-beer had now all been drunk, so they drank the water from the rock-pool, which was rather warm from the sun, but tasted very sweet. The rain from the storm had swelled it considerably.

'Well, that was a jolly narrow escape,' said Philip, his spirits rising as he tucked into slices of 'Spam.' 'I really did think one of them would tumble in on top of us.'

'Well, what do you suppose *I* felt like when the match one of them used fell through the hole and bounced on my knee?' said Dinah. 'I nearly let out a yell.'

'Kiki almost gave the game away too,' said Jack, putting potted meat on a biscuit. 'Calling out "din-din-dinner" like that. I'm ashamed of you, Kiki.'

'She's sulking,' said Dinah, laughing. 'Look at her — standing with her back to you, pretending not to take any notice. That's because you were cross with her.'

Jack grinned. He called to Huffin and Puffin, who were, as usual, standing patiently beside Philip. 'Hey, Huff and Puff — come and have a tit-bit. Nice birds, good birds, dear Huff and Puff.'

Huffin and Puffin walked over to Jack, doing their sailor-roll from side to side. They solemnly took a bit of biscuit from Jack's fingers. But that was more than Kiki could stand. She whisked round and screeched at the top of her voice.

'Naughty boy, naughty boy, naughty boy! Poor Polly, poor Polly! Polly's got a cold, put the kettle on, naughty boy, naughty boy!'

She rushed at the startled puffins and gave them a sharp jab with her curved beak. Huffin retaliated at once, and Kiki stepped back. She began to screech like a railway-train, and the two puffins hurriedly returned to Philip's knees, where they stood and stared in alarm at Kiki, ready to dart down a burrow at a moment's notice.

The children roared with laughter at this little panto-mime. Kiki went to Jack, sidling along in a comical manner. 'Poor Kiki, poor Kiki, naughty boy, naughty boy!'

Jack gave her a tit-bit and she sat on his shoulder to eat it, looking triumphantly at Huffin and Puffin. 'Arrrrrr!' she said to them, sounding like a snarling dog. 'Arrrrrr!'

'All right, Kiki. Don't *arrrrr* any more just by my ear,' said Jack. 'And I should advise you not to go too near Huffin for a bit. He won't forget that jab of yours.'

'Do you think it'll be safe to sleep out of doors again tonight?' asked Dinah, clearing up the meal. 'I don't fancy sleeping down that hole again, somehow.'

'Oh, I should think it would be all right,' said Jack. 'I don't somehow think those fellows, whoever they were, will come along in the dark of night. Pity we didn't catch a glimpse of them.'

'I didn't like their voices,' said Lucy-Ann. 'They sounded hard and horrid.'

'What a good thing that storm blew our tents away the other night!' said Dinah suddenly. 'If it hadn't, we wouldn't have stumbled on that hole, and been able to use it as a hiding-place. We wouldn't have known *where* to go, but for that.'

'That's true,' said Philip. 'I wonder if those men will come back again. We'll go on keeping watch anyway, and keep the fire going. It's our only hope of rescue – and Bill's only hope too, I should think – because if nobody comes to rescue us, certainly nobody will rescue Bill!'

'Poor Bill!' said Lucy-Ann. 'He wanted to disappear – and he has.'

'Those men must have put our fire out,' said Jack, suddenly noticing that there was no smoke. 'The wretches! I suppose they thought they'd put it out, and then, if it was lighted again, and the smoke rose up, they'd know for certain that somebody was here.'

'We'll jolly well go and light it again,' said Philip at once. 'We'll show them we're going to have our fire going if we want to. I guess they don't want it going, in case somebody does happen to come along and see it. They won't want people exploring this part of the world at the moment.'

So they all went up to the cliff-top, and set to work to light the fire again. The men had kicked it out, and the ashes and half-burnt sticks were scattered everywhere.

It didn't take long to get it going again. The children built it up carefully, and then Philip lighted it. It caught at once and flames sprang up. When it was going well, the children banked it with seaweed, and at once a thick spiral of smoke ascended in the air.

'Ha! You men! I hope you have caught sight of our signal again!' cried Jack, facing out to sea. 'You can't beat us! We'll get the better of you yet, you'll see!'

# 19

## Someone else comes to the island

The children were now very brown with the sun. 'If Mother could see us now, she wouldn't call us "peaky",' said Philip. 'And you've got back all your freckles, Jack and Lucy-Ann, and a few hundreds more!'

'Oh dear!' said Lucy-Ann, rubbing her brown freckled face. 'What a pity! I did think I looked so nice when my freckles faded away during measles.'

'I seem to be losing count of the days,' said Jack. 'I can't for the life of me make out whether today is Tuesday or Wednesday.'

'It's Friday,' said Philip promptly. 'I was counting up only this morning. We've been here quite a time now.'

'Well – is it a week since we left home?' wondered Dinah. 'It seems about six months. I wonder how Mother is getting on.'

'She must be feeling a bit worried about us,' said Philip. 'Except that she knows we're with Bill and she'll think we're quite all right, even if she doesn't get messages.'

'And we're not with Bill, and we're not all right,' said Lucy-Ann. 'I wish I knew where Bill was and what was happening to him. If only we had a boat, we could go off in it and try to find where he was. He must have been taken to the west of us somewhere – because that's where the planes seem to be.'

'Well – we're not likely to get a boat,' said Philip. 'Come on – let's go up on the cliff-top and see to the fire. The smoke doesn't seem very thick this morning. Huffin and Puffin, are you coming?'

'Arrrrrr!' said both Huffin and Puffin, and walked along beside Philip. Huffin had taken to bringing fish as a little present for Philip, and this amused the children immensely. The first time that Huffin had waddled up with the fish in his big beak, the children hadn't been able to make out what he was carrying. But when he came nearer they roared with laughter.

'Philip! He's got six or seven fish in his beak for you – and do look how he's arranged them!' cried Jack. 'Heads and tails alternately in a row all down his beak! Huffin, how did you do it?'

'Thanks awfully, old chap,' said Philip, as Huffin deposited the fish beside the boy. 'Very generous of you.'

Now Huffin brought fish two or three times a day, much to the children's amusement. Philip knew how to prepare it for cooking over the fire, and the children ate the bigger fish with biscuits and tinned butter. Huffin solemnly accepted a piece cooked, and seemed to enjoy it just as much as raw. But Puffin would not touch it.

'Well, as long as we've got Huffin to provide us with fish, we shan't starve,' said Jack. 'Kiki, don't be so jealous. If Huffin wants to be generous, let him.'

Kiki tried to head off Huffin when he arrived with fish. She could not catch fish herself, and did not like the way Huffin brought presents to the little company.

'Naughty, naughty, naughty boy!' she screeched, but Huffin took no notice at all.

The children were sitting by the fire, idly throwing sticks on it, and stirring it now and again to make it flare up a little. A spiral of smoke rose up, bent northwards. Jack took up his field-glasses and swept the lonely sea with them. You never know when friends – or enemies – might turn up.

'Hallo! There's a boat again!' cried Jack suddenly, his glasses focused on something small far away. 'Philip, get your glasses.'

The boys gazed through them, whilst the girls waited impatiently. They could see nothing with their bare eyes – not even a speck on the sea.

'Is it the same boat as before?' said Philip. 'It's getting nearer – we shall soon be able to find out.'

'It looks a different one to me,' said Jack. 'Smaller. And it's coming from a different direction. That might just be a trick though – to make us think it was a friend.'

'How shall we know?' said Lucy-Ann. 'Have we got to go and hide again'?'

Jack gave his glasses to her to look through. He turned to Philip, a gleam in his eye. 'Philip – there's only *one* man this time – he'll have to leave his boat moored somewhere, if he's come to look for us. What about capturing it?'

'Golly! If only we could!' said Philip, his face glowing. 'It's a motor-boat – a small one – but big enough to take us all easily.'

'Capture it! But how?' demanded Dinah, her eyes glued on the approaching boat. 'The man would see us easily, come running up, and capture *us*!'

'Here, let me have my glasses back,' said Philip, tugging them away from Dinah. 'That's the worst of you, Di – you will always make your turn so long!'

'Now let's think a bit,' said Jack, his eyes bright. 'That fellow can't be coming to *rescue* us, because anyone knowing we were all alone here would send a bigger boat, and probably more men, in case they had to tackle our enemy. If Bill had managed to get word to anyone, that's what they would do. Therefore, it seems to me that this boat is not one sent to rescue . . . '

'So it's probably a trick of the enemy's,' continued Philip.

'They may or may not know there are only children here – it depends on how much Bill has told them – but they might quite easily send someone who would pretend *not* to be an enemy, so as to take us in – and then we would be persuaded to get into his boat to go to safety – and he'd take us off somewhere to join Bill as prisoners.'

'Oh!' said Lucy-Ann, who didn't like the sound of this at all. 'Well, I certainly shan't get into his boat. Jack, what are we going to do?'

'Now listen,' said Jack. 'I really have got a good idea – but it needs all of us to carry it out, you girls too.'

'Well, what have we got to do?' said Dinah impatiently.

'We'll find out where he's going to moor his boat,' said Jack. 'He'll either go into that little channel where the *Lucky Star* was – or pull her up on a sandy beach. We shall soon know, because we shall watch.'

'Yes, what then?' asked Lucy-Ann, beginning to feel excited.

'Well, Dinah and I will hide nearby,' said Jack. 'The man will walk up on to the island, to look for us – and you and Lucy-Ann, Philip, must go and meet him.'

'Oh, I *couldn't*,' said Lucy-Ann, in alarm.

'All right then – you stay put somewhere,' said Jack, 'and Philip can meet him. And Philip, somehow or other you've got to get this fellow into that underground hole. We can easily keep him prisoner there – and if we can block him in somehow, with plenty of food, we can take the boat and go.'

There was a silence whilst everyone digested this remarkable plan. 'But how am I to get him into the hole?' asked Philip at last. 'It sounds a bit like " 'Won't you come into my parlour?' said the spider to the fly" – and somehow I don't think that the fly will oblige this time!'

'Can't you just take him through the puffin colony, and walk him near the hole – and then trip him up?' asked Jack impatiently. 'I'm sure *I* could do it all right.'

'Well, you do it then,' said Philip, 'and I'll hide near the boat to capture it. But suppose you don't trip the man up and make him fall into the hole and be a prisoner? What about the boat? What shall I do with it?'

'Well, silly, you'll hop into it, if you find that I haven't been able to manage the man, and you'll get out to sea,' said Jack. 'And there you'll stay till it begins to get dark, when you can creep in and see if you can find us and take us off. But you needn't worry – I shall get that fellow all right. I shall tackle him just like I tackle chaps at rugger, at school.'

Lucy-Ann gazed at Jack in admiration. She thought her brother was very clever!

'Well, I'll help too,' she said. 'I'll go and meet him with you.'

'We shall have to pretend to believe all he says,' said Jack. 'Every word! It'll be funny – him trying to take *us* in with a cock-and-bull story, and us doing the same!'

'I hope he won't be very fierce,' said Lucy-Ann.

'He'll pretend to be quite harmless, I expect,' said Jack. 'Probably say he's a naturalist, or something – and look very simple and friendly. Well – so shall I!'

'The boat's getting quite near,' said Philip. 'There *is* only one man. He's wearing dark glasses because of the sun.'

'To hide his fierce eyes, I expect,' said Lucy-Ann fearfully. 'Not because of the sun. Do we show ourselves?'

'Only two of us,' said Jack. 'You and I will get up, Lucy-Ann, and wave like mad, standing beside the fire. And mind, whatever story I tell, you've got to back me up. Philip, you and Dinah mustn't show yourselves.'

'Where's he going to park his boat?' wondered Dinah. 'Oh, he's making straight for the channel! He knows it then!'

'There you are, you see!' said Jack. 'Nobody would make straight for that hidden channel unless he had been here before. He's quite probably one of the men who came in that bigger boat.'

This did seem very likely indeed, for the boatman made

straight for the little channel as if he had been there before. Just as he came near the cliffs Jack and Lucy-Ann stood up and waved. The man waved back.

'Now, Dinah – you and Philip get down among the rocks that lead to the little harbour,' said Jack. 'There are some big ones there you can crouch behind till he's moored his boat, and comes up to find us here. Then down you must go and hop into the boat ready to go out to sea if we fail in *our* part. If we *don't* fail, things will be fine – we shall have a prisoner we can hold as hostage – and a boat to escape in!'

'Hurray!' said Philip, feeling suddenly excited.

'Hip-hip-hip-!' said Kiki, flying down to Jack's shoulder. She had been on an expedition of her own somewhere – probably chivvying the gulls around, Jack thought.

'You can join in the fun, Kiki,' said Jack. 'And mind you say all the right things!'

'Send for the doctor,' answered Kiki, solemnly. 'Pop goes the doctor!'

'He's going into the channel,' said Philip. 'Come on, Dinah – time we hid! Good luck, Jack and Lucy-Ann!'

# 20

## Mr Horace Tipperlong gets a shock

The man guided the motor-boat expertly into the narrow channel of water, where the *Lucky Star* had been battered to pieces. He saw the bit of broken rope still round one of the rocks, and looked at it, puzzled.

Dinah and Philip were crouching behind two or three large rocks further up the cliff. They could not see what the man was doing, for they were afraid of being spotted if they peeped out.

Jack and Lucy-Ann were waiting on the cliff-top. Lucy-

Ann was nervous. 'My knees feel funny,' she complained to Jack. He laughed.'

'Don't worry. Buck up, knees! Now – here he comes. You needn't say a word if you don't want to.'

The man came up the rocky steps that led to the top of the cleft in the cliff. He was a thin fellow, rather weedy, with skinny legs. He wore shorts and a pullover. He had been burnt by the sun, and his skin was blistered.

He had a thin little moustache, and a high forehead on which the hair grew far back. He wore very dark glasses indeed, so that it was quite impossible to see his eyes. He did not look anybody to be very much feared, Jack thought.

'Hallo, hallo, hallo,' said the man, as he and the children met. 'I was astonished to know there were people on this island.'

'Who told you?' asked Jack at once.

'Oh, nobody,' said the man. 'I saw your spire of smoke. Whatever are you doing here? Is there a camp of you, or something?'

'There might be,' said Jack, airily. 'Why have you come here?'

'I'm an ornithologist,' said the man, very earnestly. 'You won't know what that means, of course.'

Jack grinned to himself. Considering that he and Philip thought themselves very fine ornithologists, this amused him. But he wasn't going to let this man know that.

'Orni-orni-ornibologist?' he said innocently. 'What's that?'

'Well, my lad, it's a student of bird life,' said the man. 'A bird-lover, one who wants to know all he can about birds and their ways.'

'Is that why you've come here, then – to study birds?' asked Lucy-Ann, thinking she ought to say something. Her knees had stopped shaking and feeling funny, now that she saw the man was not at all fearsome.

'Yes. I've been to this island before, years and years ago,

319

when I was a lad,' said the man. 'And I wanted to come again, though I had a job finding it. I *was* surprised to see your smoke going up. What's it for? Playing at shipwrecked sailors, or something? I know what children are.'

It was plain that the man knew very little about children, and thought the two to be much younger than they were. 'He'll be reciting "Humpty Dumpty" to us in a moment,' thought Jack, with a secret grin.

'Do you know a lot about birds?' said Jack, not answering the man's question.

'Well, I don't know a *great* deal about sea-birds,' said the man. 'That's why I've come to these islands again. I know more about ordinary birds.'

'Aha!' thought Jack, 'he says that because he is afraid I'll ask him a few questions about the birds here.'

'We've got two tame puffins,' said Lucy-Ann suddenly. 'Would you like to see them?'

'Oh, very much, my dear, very much,' said the man, beaming at her. 'By the way, my name is Tipperlong – Horace Tipperlong.'

'Tripalong?' said Lucy-Ann, with a giggle, thinking it was a very good name for this man, who walked with curious mincing steps. Jack wanted to laugh.

'No, no – Tipperlong,' said Horace, and smiled all over his face at Lucy-Ann. 'What is your name?'

'My name's Lucy-Ann,' she said. 'And my brother's name is Jack. Are you coming to see the puffins? It's this way.'

'I should also like to meet whoever is in charge of you,' said Mr Horace Tipperlong. 'And – er – where is your boat?'

'It was smashed up in a storm,' said Jack solemnly. Mr Tipperlong tut-tutted with sympathy.

'How dreadful! Then how were you going to get back home?'

'Look out,' said Jack, just saving Horace as he was about to plunge down a puffin's burrow. 'This place is undermined by the puffins. Mind where you go!'

'My word – what a lot of birds!' said Horace Tipperlong, standing still. He had been so engrossed in polite talk that he did not seem to have noticed the amazing colony of puffins. Another black mark against him! Jack could not believe that a real ornithologist would walk half-way through the puffins without exclaiming at them.

'Extraordinary! Most astonishing! I don't remember ever seeing so many birds together before,' said Horace. 'And all those thousands on the cliffs to. Well, well, well! And do you mean to say you really have got two tame puffins ? I can hardly believe it.'

'They're Philip's,' said Lucy-Ann, and she could have bitten out her tongue.

'I thought you said your brother's name was Jack,' said Horace enquiringly.

'She must have made a mistake,' said Jack, saying the first thing he could think of. They were getting very near the entrance of the underground hole now. Look out, Mr Horace Tipperlong!

Lucy-Ann began to feel nervous. Suppose this man Trip-along, or whatever his name was, didn't fall into the hole when Jack tripped him – suppose instead he went for Jack? Suppose – well, suppose he had a revolver? He didn't *look* a desperate sort of a man, but you never knew. Lucy-Ann looked at the pockets of his shorts to see if she could spy anything like a lump in the shape of a revolver there.

But his pockets were so bulged out with dozens of things that it was impossible to tell. Jack nudged her. 'Keep out of the way now,' he said in a very low voice. Lucy-Ann obediently slipped behind, her heart beating fast.

Jack came to the entrance of the hole. A stick marked it as usual, for it really was almost impossible to find without some sort of signpost. Horace tripped along, looking short-sightedly through his dark glasses – and then, to his enormous astonishment, Jack put out a leg, pushed him, and tripped him right over. He fell at the side of the hole – but before he could get up, Jack had given him a shove – and right into the hole he went, crash!

Jack had a stout stick in his hand, which he had picked from the pile beside the bonfire. He parted the heather and looked into the hole. In the dim light he could see Horace Tipperlong sitting up, and he heard him groaning.

Tipperlong looked up and saw Jack. 'You wicked boy!' he said angrily. 'What do you mean by this?'

His glasses had fallen off in his headlong dive. His eyes certainly did not look very fierce. They looked rather weak and watery. He held his head as if he had hurt it.

'Sorry,' said Jack, 'but it had to be done. Either you caught us – or we caught you. We needn't go on pretending any more. We know quite well what gang you belong to.'

'What are you talking about?' cried the man, and he stood up. His head popped out of the hole. Jack raised his stick at once.

'Get back!' he said fiercely. 'You're our prisoner. You took Bill, didn't you? – well, now we've taken *you*. If you attempt to clamber out, I shall hit you on the head with this. You just try it.'

Horace hastily retreated. Lucy-Ann looked white and scared. 'Oh, Jack – is he hurt? Jack, you won't really hit him, will you?'

'I jolly well will,' said Jack. 'Think of Bill, Lucy-Ann – and our poor *Lucky Star* – and us stranded here because of this fellow and his precious friends. Don't you realise that if he gets out and back to his boat, they'll send heaps more, and won't rest till they've got us? Don't be feeble!'

'Well – I don't want to see you hit him,' said Lucy-Ann. 'Dinah wouldn't mind a bit, but I'm not like Dinah.'

'Look here – will you kindly tell me what all this nonsense is about?' shouted Horace. 'I never heard of such a thing! Here I come to a bird-island, which, as far as I know, certainly isn't a crime – and you two kids lead me here, trip me up, and shove me down this hole. I've hurt my head badly. And now you say if I try to get out, you'll brain me. You nasty little creatures!'

'I'm really very sorry about it,' said Jack again, 'but there wasn't anything else to be done. You realize that with our boat gone — and Bill disappeared — we had to get a boat somehow. We can't stay here for the rest of our lives.'

Horace was so amazed and upset at this speech that he stood up again. He sat down hurriedly when he saw Jack's stick. 'But look here — do you really mean to say you're now going to take my boat? I never heard such brazen cheek. You wait till I get hold of the people in charge of you, my boy — you'll get the worst hiding you've ever had in your life.'

# 21
## Horace does not like Puffin Island

'Lucy-Ann — see if you can spot either Philip or Dinah,' ordered Jack. 'Philip will probably be in the boat, ready to start her up, if he has to — but Dinah will possibly be looking out to see if there is any sign from us.'

Lucy-Ann stood up. She saw Dinah standing a good way off, waiting anxiously at the top of the cleft in the cliff. Philip was not to be seen. Presumably he was down in the boat.

Lucy-Ann waved violently. 'It's all right. We've got him in the hole!' she yelled.

Dinah waved back, then disappeared. She had gone to tell Philip. Soon the two appeared again, and came through the puffin colony at top speed to hear what had happened.

'We got him,' said Jack proudly. 'Easy as pie. Down he went, plonk!'

'Who's there?' enquired Horace plaintively. 'Is that somebody else? Look here — you've just *got* to tell me what's going on here. I'm all at sea.'

'That's where we'll be soon, I hope,' grinned Jack. 'And in your boat! Philip, meet Mr Horace Tripalong.'

'Gosh – is that really his name?' said Philip.

The incensed Mr Tipperlong roared up the hole. 'My name is TIPPERLONG and I'll thank you to remember it. Ill-mannered children! You wait till I make a complaint about you, and get you punished. I never heard of such behaviour in all my life.'

'You can't blame him for being wild,' said Jack. 'He says he's a-a-I say, Mr Tripalong, what did you say you were?'

'An ornithologist, ignorant boy!' yelled Mr Tipperlong.

'Golly, what's that?' said Philip innocently, and the others giggled.

'You let me out of this,' commanded Mr Tipperlong, and his head appeared cautiously near the entrance of the hole, ready to bob back if necessary.

It *was* necessary. 'Look here,' said Jack, exasperated, 'do you want me to give you a good old conk on the head before you know I mean what I say? Because I will! I don't *want* to; but I will! I bet you gave old Bill a few blows before you captured him. What's sauce for the goose is sauce for the gander.'

'You're talking double-Dutch,' said Horace, in a disgusted voice. 'I think you must be mad. Do you mean to tell me you kids are all alone on this island? I don't believe a word you say. You tell whoever is in charge of you to come and have a word with me. If you think I'm going to stay here much longer, you're mistaken. I've never met such unpleasant children in my life. I suppose you're all playing at being Just Williams. *Pah!*'

This was a lovely noise. Kiki, who had been listening with surprise and enjoyment to the animated conversation, now joined in.

'Pah! Pooh! Pah! Pop!'

She flew to the edge of the hole and looked in. 'Pah!' she

said again, and went off into a cackle of laughter.

Horace looked up in fresh alarm. Was that really a parrot at the hole entrance – saying 'pah' and 'pooh' to him in that rude way?

'Is that – is that one of the tame puffins you told me about?' he asked doubtfully.

'I thought you were an ornithologist,' said Jack in scorn. 'Kiki is a parrot. I should have thought anyone would have known that!'

'But – how can a parrot live here?' said Horace. 'It's not a sea-bird. Oh, this is all a dream. But what a very silly dream!'

At that moment a puffin came down the end of the burrow that led into the back of the hole.

'Arrrrrrr!' it announced in a deep and guttural voice. Mr Tipperlong jumped violently. All he could see in the dimness of the hole was a baleful eye and a big and many-coloured beak.

'Go away,' he said weakly. 'Shoo!'

'Shoo!' said Kiki from the hole entrance in great delight. 'Pah! Pooh! Shoo! Arrrrrrrrr!'

'You're all mad,' said poor Horace. 'I'm mad too, I suppose. Shoo, I tell you!'

The puffin said *arrr* again and then went back up its burrow. Judging by the flow of *arrrrs* that came down the hole, it was telling its wife all about the peculiar puffin-man it had just seen in the hole.

'What are we going to do now we've got him?' said Philip in a low voice. 'I suppose he *is* an enemy? I mean, – he does sound rather a goof, doesn't he?'

'All part of a clever plan,' said Jack. 'He's no ornithologist. He's been told to dress up like a goofy one and act the part. Some bird-men *are* awful goofs, you know. We've met them. Well, this one is just about too goofy for words – he's over-acting, if you know what I mean. I'm glad he hasn't got a revolver. I've been afraid of that all the time.'

'Yes. So was I,' admitted Philip. 'There may be one in the boat. I hope there is. It might come in useful. Well, what are we going to do?'

'Do you think he can hear what we're saying?' said Lucy-Ann, looking frightened.

'No, not if we talk as low as this,' said Philip. 'Jack, the boat is a nice little bit of work. Smaller than the *Lucky Star*, but it has a little cabin and will easily take us all, and some food.'

'Are there oars in it, in case we want to cut out the engine and go in quietly to shore anywhere?' asked Jack.

'Yes,' said Philip. 'I noticed those. Have you got a good plan, Jack? I keep on and on thinking, but all I can make up my mind about is to sail off in the boat—but where to I don't know. We want to escape – but we want to escape *to* somewhere. And not out of the frying-pan into the fire, either. We'd better do it soon, too, because if dear old Tripalong doesn't get back to the gang with news pretty soon they'll send others here.'

'Yes, I'd thought of all that too,' said Jack, and the girls nodded. 'The thing is – shall we try to make for the outer islands and find one where a few fishermen live, and try to get help? Or shall we try for the mainland? Or shall we hunt for Bill?'

There was a silence. Everyone was thinking hard. Lucy-Ann spoke first.

'I vote for hunting for Bill,' she said. 'We could try that first, anyway – and then make for safety afterwards if we're not successful. But I do think we ought to try to find Bill first.'

'Good for you, Lucy-Ann,' said Jack. 'That's what *I* think. Now for some more planning.'

Horace Tipperlong suddenly demanded their attention again. 'Stop all that talk, talk, talk,' he cried fretfully. 'I'm ravenous – and thirsty too. If you're going to try and starve me to death, say so. But at least let me know.'

'We're not going to starve you. Don't be an ass,' said Jack. 'Lucy-Ann, open some tins and give them to him. And chuck him down some biscuits too. Dinah, fill a pan with water from the pool.'

'Right, chief,' grinned Dinah, and went off to the pool in the rocks. Horace was handed down the full pan of water, and some tins and biscuits. He began to eat hungrily. The sight of the food made the others feel hungry too.

'We'll have a feed as well,' said Philip. 'Shall I take a turn at holding the stick and sitting by the hole, Jack?'

'Yes,' said Jack. 'But mind – give him a good old conk if he so much as shows a hair!'

This was said in a very loud voice, so that Horace was sure to hear. But Horace said nothing. Apparently he was willing to bide his time now.

The children were soon devouring a tinned chicken, tinned peas which they ate without heating, and a tinned fruit salad with tinned cream, washed down with water from the pool.

'Jolly good,' said Jack, with a comfortable sigh. 'I feel better. Wonderful what food does to you!'

'It would make me sick if I ate as much as you've just eaten,' said Dinah. 'You're a greedy pig. You ate twice as much as anyone else.'

'Can't help it,' said Jack. 'I was twice as hungry. Now then – lower your voices, please – we'll make our plans.'

'Shall we set out at night?' said Philip in a low voice.

'No,' said Jack at once. 'We'd never see our way, even in the moonlight. We'd better set off first thing tomorrow morning, about dawn. We'll hope old Tripalong is asleep then, so that we can get a good start without his interrupting us.'

'Yes – because we'll have to leave the hole unguarded when we all go to the boat,' said Lucy-Ann.

'I'd thought of that,' said Jack. 'You three can go to the boat, take food with you, and our clothes and rugs – get everything absolutely ready – and then, when you're ready to start, give me a yell and I'll come tearing along to join you. You can send Dinah up to the top of the cleft to wave.'

'And by the time Horace has realized nobody is on guard to conk him on the head, we'll be out to sea in his boat!' said Dinah, enjoying the thought. 'Poor old Horace! I feel quite sorry for him.'

'I don't,' said Jack unfeelingly. 'If he's Bill's enemy, he's jolly well mine. He deserves all he's got – honestly, except for being tripped into the hole, he's got nothing much to complain about. I shan't block him in, when we leave, and put food there, as I thought we would at first. It won't matter if he gets out once we're gone. And I shouldn't think it will be long before some others of the gang come along to see why he hasn't turned up at home – wherever that is!'

'It seems a bit of a wild-goose chase to try and find Bill, with all these scores of islands to choose from,' said Philip. 'But I shouldn't feel comfortable if we didn't have a shot, anyway.'

'Nor should I,' said Jack. 'Bill's often come to *our* rescue, in other adventures. It's time we went to his – if only we can find him. I suppose there's no doubt but that the enemy have taken him to their headquarters on some island or other here.'

'Don't you think it would be a good idea if we got everything ready this evening?' said Dinah suddenly. 'You know – all the food in the boat – and rugs and clothes and things – so as not to have to waste a single minute getting ready tomorrow morning. You said you wanted to set off at dawn.'

'Yes – that's a good idea,' said Jack. 'I'll take a turn at the hole with the stick now if you like, Philip – and you help the girls carry things down to the boat. What a bit of luck capturing one like that! I must say I think we've been pretty clever.'

'Pah!' said Kiki. 'Pooh! Pah!'

'Sorry you don't agree, old thing,' said Jack. 'Very sorry. But I still think we *have* been very clever!'

'We'd better leave some food for Tripalong, hadn't we?' asked Dinah. 'I mean – I know the gang will be along in a day or two to see what has happened to him – but he'll have to have things to eat till they come.'

'Yes. Leave him some tins and a tin-opener,' said Jack. 'And, Philip, were there any rugs in the boat, belonging to him?'

'Yes,' said Philip. 'I'll bring them back here, after I've taken some food to the boat. We'll chuck them down to him. I think we're being awfully kind to our enemy.'

Horace didn't think so. He got all upset again after a bit, and began to shout wildly down in the hole.

'This has gone on long enough. You let me out, you little villains! Wait till I get my hands on you! What is the meaning of this, I'd like to know!'

'Oh, don't keep up the pretence any more, Mr Horace Tripalong,' said Jack, bored. 'We're enemies, both of us, and you know it. You open up a bit and tell me where Bill is and a few things more. You might get off more lightly in the end, if you do.'

'Who's this Bill you keep talking about?' said Horace in an exasperated tone. 'Look here, are you playing at pirates or bandits or what? I never heard of anyone being kept prisoner down a hole like this, by a pack of villainous children!'

'No – I never heard of it either, now I come to think of it,' said Jack. 'Well, dear Horace, if you won't admit what we all know, keep quiet.'

'Pah!' said Horace, aggravated beyond words.

'Pah!' said Kiki at once, and went to the hole entrance. She looked down.

'Pah! Naughty boy! Pop goes the weasel! How many times have I told you to shut that door? God save the Queen! Pah!'

Mr Tipperlong listened in amazed horror. Was he really and truly mad? *Could* that be a parrot talking to him so rudely?

'I'll wring that bird's neck,' he said fiercely, and got up.

'Ring the bell, please!' said Kiki, and went off into one of her cackles. Then she poked her head in again and screeched like a railway engine in a tunnel. It was absolutely deafening in the hole below, and Horace fell back on the ground defeated.

'Mad! Quite mad! All mad!' he muttered, and, putting his head in his hands, he said no more.

# 22

# The enemy

The three children, accompanied by Huffin and Puffin, made various journeys to and from Sleepy Hollow with food, rugs and clothes. Philip brought back a pile of rugs from the boat and thrust them down the hole entrance. They descended on poor Horace and enveloped him. He was very much startled, but glad to find in a moment or two that his captors were actually offering him something warm and soft to lie on.

He arranged them underneath himself. Ah, that was more comfortable. He began to think longingly of all the things he would do to those children, once he got free.

At last everything was in the motor-boat, ready for the early start. It was now getting dusk. Philip, Lucy-Ann and Dinah came and sat beside Jack.

'I suppose one or other of must keep watch over the hole all night, in case Horace escapes?' whispered Philip. Jack nodded.

'Yes. We can't risk his getting out, just as we've got

everything set. You take first watch, Philip. We won't ask the girls to watch, because I'm pretty sure they wouldn't enjoy hitting Horace good and hard if he popped his head out.'

'I would!' said Dinah indignantly. 'Lucy-Ann is kind, but I'm not.'

Lucy-Ann said nothing. She felt sure she wouldn't like to hit Horace hard. Anyway the boys decided that only they should keep watch, so that was all right.

The sun had gone down into the sea. The sky was pricked with the first few stars. The children lay about comfortably on the heather, talking in low voices. There was no sound from Horace. Perhaps he was alseep.

Philip's three rats, which had suddenly begun to look very grown-up, came out to sniff the evening air. Dinah removed herself at once. Huffin and Puffin regarded the rats with fixed eyes. Kiki yawned and then sneezed. Then she coughed in a very hollow manner.

'Shut up, Kiki,' said Jack. 'If you want to practise your awful noises, go up on the cliff and make the seagulls and guillemots listen.'

'Arrrr!' said Huffin solemnly.

'Huffin agrees with me,' said Jack.

'Pah!' said Kiki.

'And pah to you,' said Jack. 'Now shut up, Kiki, do. It's a lovely evening. Don't spoil it with your pahing and poohing.'

Just as he finished speaking, there came a noise from far out to sea – a very small noise at first, hardly heard above the sound of the sea and the wind – but becoming quite unmistakable after a while.

'A motor-boat!' said Jack, sitting upright. 'Now what in the world . . .'

'Have they come to look for Horace already?' said Philip, in a low voice. 'Blow! This upsets our plans like anything!'

Nothing could be seen on the darkening sea, but the noise

came nearer and nearer. Jack clutched Philip and spoke in his ear.

'There's only one thing to do. We must all go and get into our boat now, this very minute — and get out to sea. We mustn't let the enemy see the boat in the channel there, or they'll take it, and our only chance will be gone. Come on, quickly!'

Silently the four children rose to their feet. Kiki flew to Jack's shoulder, not uttering a sound. Huffin and Puffin, who had retired to their burrow, came out again. They flew beside the hurrying children, not even remarking *arrrr* to one another.

Across the puffin colony they went, stumbling and staggering between the hundreds of burrows. Up the little slope of the cliff and over to the cleft in the rock. Down the rocky ledges, be careful, be careful! And into the rocking boat, their breath coming fast and their hearts beating like hammers.

'Start her up,' ordered Philip, and Jack started the engine. Philip threw off the mooring-rope and it skittered into the boat by the girls' feet. In a moment more they were backing gently out of the little channel.

Soon they were right out of it. Philip went to the east a little. It was almost dark now.

'We'll stop the engine,' said Philip. 'And wait here till the other boat goes into the channel, because I expect she'll make for it. I don't want to bump into her. And the men on board her might hear our engine.'

So the engine was stopped, and the motor-boat swung up and down gently as waves ran beneath her to the rocky cliffs some way off.

The sound of the other boat's engine was now very loud. Philip wished he had gone a bit further off after all. But the bigger boat swung by without stopping and then nosed its way into the hidden harbour. The children, crouching in their boat, straining their eyes, had just been able to make

332

out a dark shape and that was all.

The other boat's engine stopped and peace came back into the night. Some of the sea-birds, disturbed, uttered a few wild cries and then flew back to their roosting-places on the ledges.

'Horace will be glad to be rescued,' said Dinah at last.

'Yes, he'll probably be out of the hole already,' said Jack. 'He'd soon know when we were gone. I've no doubt there'll be a lot of bad language going on when they find out how we imprisoned poor Horace — and gosh, when they find out we've taken his boat . . . '

'Arrrrrr!' said a deep voice from the rail round the deck.

The children jumped in the darkness. 'Oh — it must be Huffin or Puffin,' said Philip, pleased. 'Fancy them coming with us. I do think that's friendly of them.'

'They're sweet,' said Lucy-Ann, and put out her hand to Huffin. Both the puffins were there, sitting side by side in the darkness. Kiki flew to join them.

'What are we going to do now?' said Dinah. 'Dare we go off in the dark? We might bump into rocks and wreck the boat.'

'We'll have to stay here till the first light of day,' said Philip. 'Then we'll set off, and hope the men on the island won't hear our engine, and come after us!'

'We shall have got a good start,' said Jack. 'Well, what about having a snooze, if we're going to stay here? Where's the anchor? Shall we let it down? I don't fancy drifting about at the mercy of the waves all night long.'

Whilst the boys were busy, the girls laid out rugs, mackintoshes and jerseys to lie on. It was a lovely warm night, and nobody minded.

'It's so nice to have the stars above us instead of a ceiling or a tent roof,' said Lucy-Ann, snuggling down. 'I don't feel a bit sleepy, somehow. I suppose it's all the excitement. I've got used to this adventure now. Oh dear, how glad I am that I didn't have to hit Horace on the head! I should have dreamt about that for ages.'

They lay for some time, talking. They all felt very wide awake indeed. Huffin and Puffin appeared to be awake too, because they occasionally remarked *arrr* to one another. Kiki was on Jack's feet.

She was also wide awake, and began to recite the nursery rhymes she knew: 'Humpty Dumpty, puddingy pie, ding dong bell, ring his neck!'

'Shut up!' said Jack. 'We're trying to go to sleep, you tiresome bird!'

'I hope Huffin and Puffin stay with us,' said Lucy-Ann. 'Wouldn't it be lovely if we could take them home with us?'

'Shut up!' said Kiki, and cackled.

'Parrots are not allowed to say that,' said Jack severely, and sat up to tap her on her beak. But she had promptly put her head under her wing, so he couldn't.

'Artful creature,' said Jack, and heard a faint 'Pah!' from under Kiki's wing.

Just as Lucy-Ann was falling off to sleep, the others sat up so suddenly that she was jerked awake. 'What's the matter?' she began. And then she knew.

The engine of the other motor-boat was going again. Lucy-Ann sat up with the others, her eyes straining through the darkness.

'They must have found Horace, heard his report, and all have gone back on board,' said Jack. 'They are evidently not going to spend the night here. Look – here they come – gosh, they've got their lights on this time.'

'Jack – Jack! They'll be going back to their headquarters,' said Philip urgently. 'Let's follow them. Get the anchor up, quick. They won't hear our engine because theirs makes such a row. Come on, let's follow them! They'll take us to where Bill is!'

The men's motor-boat had swung round when it had come from the channel, and was now headed out to sea. It was not long before the children's boat set off in its wake.

They could not hear the other boat's engine because of their own, and they knew that theirs would not be heard by the men for the same reason.

Huffin and Puffin were still on the deck-rail. Clearly they meant to go wherever the children went. Lucy-Ann thought it was nice to have such staunch, loyal friends, even if they were only puffins. Kiki was on Jack's shoulder again, her beak to the breeze.

'All aboard,' she kept saying. 'All aboard. Pah!'

The first boat sped along quickly. It was easy to follow because of its light. The children stood with their noses to the wind in silence. Lucy-Ann spoke first.

'This adventure is getting more adventurous,' she said. 'Oh dear – it really is!'

# 23

## The secret lagoon

For a long time the two boats sped across the sea. 'It's the Sea of Adventure!' Lucy-Ann thought. 'Anything might happen here. Oh, I do hope we find Bill. Things always seem right when he's with us.'

'You girls had better have a nap,' said Jack at last. 'You'll be tired out. Philip and I will keep awake and take turns at the wheel. You snuggle down and go to sleep.'

So they did, and it wasn't long before both girls were asleep and dreaming of swings and hammocks, because of the swinging, swaying motion of the boat they were in.

After a good long time, Jack spoke to Philip. 'Tufty – do you see the light flashing over there? It must be a signal of some sort, I should think. The boat in front is heading towards it. I hope we're soon coming to our journey's end, because the moon will be up soon, and we might be seen.'

'That light must be a guide to the boat – or perhaps to an aeroplane,' said Philip. 'Blow, here comes the moon! – out of that bank of clouds. Well, she's not very bright, that's one good thing.'

By the light of the moon the boys could see an island looming up in front of the boats. To the left was another island, two or three miles away from the first, or so it seemed to the boys.

'Look here, Jack – we don't want to drive right into the jaws of danger,' said Philip, 'which is what we shall do if we follow the first boat right up to that island it's heading for. I think it would be better to go to that other one, over there, look – we could probably see enough in the moonlight to make out a cove to land in. We could pull this boat into safety between us.'

'Right,' said Jack, swinging the wheel round. Now they were no longer following the first boat. It was soon out of sight, and was probably by now safely in some little harbour. Their own boat headed for the further island. By the time they got there their eyes were used to the moonlight, and they could see everything fairly clearly.

'Doesn't seem very rocky,' said Jack, nosing in gently. 'No – all sand and fine shingle. I'll run her straight up this beach, Philip. Be ready to jump out as soon as she stops.'

The girls awoke and scrambled out of their wraps. Jack ran the boat straight up the shingly beach. It drove into the fine shingle and stopped. Philip sprang out.

'Can't shift her at all,' he panted, when he and the others had tried to pull the boat further up. 'Let's chuck out the anchor and let her be. It's nearly low tide now, so we'll just paddle out and drop the anchor, and give the boat a push – it will be quite all right then, if the sea keeps calm.'

The boys did this and then lay on the shingle to get their breath. They were both very tired. They almost fell asleep as they lay there.

'Come on, boys,' said Dinah, at last. 'Bring some rugs and

find a sheltered place somewhere. You're half asleep.'

'Well, we're safe till the morning anyway,' said Jack, as he stumbled up the beach with the others, almost asleep as he walked. 'Nobody knows we're here. Another bird-island, I suppose.'

They came to a low cliff. Lucy-Ann saw a dark cave at the foot. 'Put your torch on,' she called to Philip. 'We might be able to sleep here.'

It proved to be a small cave, with a soft, dry sandy floor. It smelt a little of seaweed, but nobody minded that. They dragged their rugs in, and flung themselves down. Huffin and Puffin squatted at the opening of the cave, as if they had put themsleves on guard.

Almost before their heads touched the rugs the boys were alseep. The girls followed suit, and soon there was nothing to be heard but tiny snores from Jack, who was flat on his back. Kiki examined his face in the darkness to find out why her beloved Jack was making such queer little noises, then decided they weren't worth bothering about. She sat herself down in the middle of his tummy and went to sleep too.

The next morning Huffin and Puffin walked over to Philip and stood heavily on him. 'Arrrr!' they said, meaning 'Come on, wake up!'

Philip awoke. 'Get off,' he said. 'Don't copy Kiki's bad ways, Huffin and Puffin. Oh, I say – thanks for the fish – but don't put them all over my chest, Huffin!'

Huffin had been diving for fish. He now deposited them carefully on Philip, opened and shut his mouth a few times, and made his one and only remark, in a deep and satisfied voice. 'Arrrrrrrrrrr!'

The children laughed when they heard about Huffin's morning offering. They rubbed their eyes and decided to have a dip in the sea, for they all felt dirty.

'Then we'll have breakfast,' said Jack. 'Gosh, I wish I wasn't always so frightfully hungry. I say, this is rather a nice island, isn't it? Look, you can see the enemy's island on the horizon over there. Wonder if Bill is there.'

'Well go up to the highest point on this island after breakfast, and have a good look round at all the others,' said Philip. 'Let's go and get some food from the boat.'

The boat was afloat on the high tide. The children had to swim out to her. They rifled her for food – and whilst she was looking for a tin of salmon she knew she had put in, Lucy-Ann found something that made her shout.

'I say, look! – a radio! Do you suppose it is a transmitter as well as a receiver? Can we send a message on it?'

'Don't know,' said Jack, examining it. 'It's not a bit like Bill's. If only we knew! Anyway, even if we *could* send out messages on it, I wouldn't know how to. I expect it's just some sort of portable radio. Come on, let's have breakfast. Phew, this sun's hot.'

With Huffin, Puffin, Kiki and the three rats all sharing their breakfast, the four children made a very good meal on the boat. 'Now, what next?' said Jack. 'Shall we go up to the topmost height in this island and see what's all round us?'

'Yes,' said the others, so, leaving the boat by itself, they made their way up the low cliff and on to the grass-grown land behind. It was not so heathery as Puffin Island had been, nor were there many birds on it.

'It's funny. You'd think there would be plenty on a nice little island like this,' said Jack. 'Look, there's a hill at the other end of the island! – let's climb it.'

They climbed to the very top – and then they stood still in astonishment. Beyond them, sparkling blue, was a lagoon, flat and still as a mirror. It lay between two islands, but the islands were joined by broad strips of rocks that enclosed the whole lagoon, so that it was impossible to say which island it really belonged to. The rocks ran out from each one, in some places as high as cliffs – and there between them lay this unbelievably lovely sea-lake.

'Look at that!' said Jack in awe. 'We've seen some wonderful sights – but never one as beautiful as that blue

338

lagoon. It can't be real.'

But it was. It stretched out below them for about a mile and a half, so sheltered and protected that not a ripple broke its calm blue surface.

And then something happened that gave the children a shock of amazement. They heard the low hum of an aeroplane. They saw it coming towards them. Jack pulled them down flat in case they were seen. It flew right over the lagoon, and as it flew, something dropped from it – something that opened out, billowed white, and had something else fixed below it.

The children watched in amazement. All sorts of ridiculous things flashed through their minds – was it a scientific experiment – bombs – atom bombs – what was it?

A little parachute had opened, and was swinging down to the lagoon. The package underneath it was wrapped in glistening stuff – some kind of waterproof material, Jack thought. It reached the water and disappeared. The parachute spread itself out on the calm surface and lay still. But as the children watched, it seemed to dissolve and finally it too disappeared into the water.

'Look – the plane is circling the lagoon again. It's going to drop another,' said Philip. They all watched as the plane once more dropped a parachute, and the same thing happened.

Down to the water it floated with its unknown package, and in a few minutes all trace of it had disappeared. A third one was sent down and then the aeroplane circled round once and headed away. Soon it was lost in the distance.

'Well, whatever in the world was it doing, dropping things into this lagoon?' said Jack in astonishment. 'What a strange thing to do! What's in those enormous packages the parachutes carry?'

'And why drop them into the lagoon?' wondered Dinah. 'It seems so silly. Do they want to get rid of something? What a strange way to do it!'

'Let's take the boat and go and sail over the lagoon to see if we can see down into the depths,' said Lucy-Ann.

'And how do you think we are going to get *in*to the lagoon, idiot?' said Jack. 'No boat can get into that water – unless it's dragged over that barrier or rocks surrounding it.'

'Yes – of course – how silly of me!' said Lucy-Ann. 'I do wish we could see down into that water though – and find out what secrets it is holding, down in the blue depths.'

'Arrrrr!' said Huffin and Puffin, and, their wings vibrating quickly, they sailed down to the lagoon as if to say 'You want to go there? Well, it's easy.'

They bobbed there on the lagoon, very small specks indeed, diving under the water for fish. The children watched them.

'I don't see why we can't go and have a bathe there,' said Jack at last. 'We could swim a good way out and then dive down to see if we could find out anything. You never know!'

'Well, let's go now then,' said Dinah eagerly. 'I feel as if I simply *must* find out what all this is about. It's the most peculiar secret, I must say!'

They began to scramble down the hill. It grew rocky as they got lower down, but there were plenty of sea-pink cushions to soften the way for their feet. At last they reached the edge of the calm blue water.

They undressed and went in. The water was very warm indeed, and rippled like soft silk over their arms. They swam out slowly, enjoying the warmth of the lake and of the sun on their shoulders.

'Now I'm going to dive down and see if I can make out anything,' said Jack, and turning himself up like a duck, down he went, down and down and down. What would he find at the bottom?

# 24

# An amazing discovery

The lagoon was quite deep. Jack could not swim to the bottom, because he couldn't possibly hold his breath long enough. He came up, gasping.

'All I could see was a pile of silvery stuff lying on the bottom,' he gasped to the others. 'Nothing else at all. I couldn't go right down to it, because I hadn't enough breath.'

'Well, that's not much use,' said Dinah. 'We want to see what's *inside* the waterproof wrapping – tear it off, so that we can see what it holds.'

'We wouldn't be able to do that very easily,' said Philip. 'I bet it's sewn up pretty tightly – or sealed in some clever way. I'll go down, Jack – perhaps I can get near enough to *feel* what's inside.'

'Oh dear – do be careful,' said Lucy-Ann. 'You don't know *what* might be inside!'

'Well – it's hardly likely to be anything that will eat us,' grinned Jack. 'Kiki, why don't *you* do a little diving, like Huffin and Puffin do – you could be a bit of help then!'

But Kiki did not approve of all this love of bathing. She flew about above the children in the water and tried occasionally to perch on a bare shoulder. Huffin and Puffin loved having the children in the water, and swam and dived beside them, uttering deep *arrrrrs* of satisfaction.

Philip dived under, and swam rapidly downwards, his eyes wide open in the salt water. Far below him he saw the silvery mass, gleaming dimly on the lagoon bed. He swam right down to it, and put out his hand to touch it. Beneath the wrapping he felt something very hard indeed.

Then, his breath giving out, he rose up to the surface,

almost bursting. He took in great gulps of air.

'I felt something hard,' he said at last. 'But it was impossible to tell what it was. Blow! Isn't it sickening to be right on top of a mystery like this, and not be able to solve it?'

'We shall have to give it up,' said Jack. 'I know perfectly well I haven't enough breath to go down and probe the wrappings. I should burst for want of breath.'

'I do hate giving things up,' said Dinah.

'Well, swim under the water yourself and see if *you* can find out anything,' said Philip.

'You know I can't hold my breath even as long as you can,' said Dinah. 'So what's the good of that?'

'I'm going to swim back to shore,' said Lucy-Ann. 'There's a nice sunny rock over there, covered with seaweed. I shall have a sunbathe there.'

She swam slowly over to it. Huffin and Puffin dived under, just beside her. 'I wonder what they look like when they swim under water,' thought Lucy-Ann. 'I'd love to see them chasing a fish.'

She turned herself up, and duck-dived under the water. Ah, there was Huffin, using his wings to swim swiftly through the water after a big fish. Quick, Huffin, or you'll lose it!

Just as she was going to swim upwards again Lucy-Ann noticed something below her. The lagoon was not nearly so deep just there, for a shelf of rocks ran out into the water, making it fairly shallow, although it was much too deep still for Lucy-Ann's feet to touch the bottom.

The little girl took a quick glance to see what it was on the rocks below the water, but then her breath gave out, and, half choking, she rose up to the surface, gasping and spluttering.

When she had got her breath again, down she went – and then she realized what it was she saw. One of the parachuted packages, instead of falling into the deeper waters of the lagoon, had fallen on to the shallow rocky bed just below her. The package had split open – and all its contents were spread and scattered on the rocky bottom below.

But whatever were they? Lucy-Ann could not make them out at all. They looked such peculiar shapes. She rose up to the surface again and yelled to Jack.

'Hi, Jack! One of those secret packages has split open on the rocky bottom just here – but I can't make out what was in it!'

The boys and Dinah swam up in great excitement. They all duck-dived and down they went, down, down, down. They came to where the silvery wrapping was split open, moving gently up and down with the flow of the water. All around it were the split contents.

The boys, almost bursting for breath, examined them quickly, then shot up to the surface, gasping.

They looked at one another, and then both shouted the same words.

'Guns! Guns! Scores of them!'

The children swam to the sunny rock that Lucy-Ann was now sitting on, and clambered up.

'Fancy that! Guns! What in the wide world do they want to drop guns down in this lagoon for? Are they getting rid of them? And why?'

'No. They wouldn't wrap them up so carefully in water-proof stuff if they were just dumping them,' said Philip soberly. 'They're hiding them.'

'*Hiding* them! But what a very peculiar place to hide guns in!' said Dinah. 'What are they going to do with them?'

'They're probably gun-running,' said Jack, 'bringing hundreds of guns here from somewhere, and hiding them till they're ready for them – ready for some revolution somewhere – South America, perhaps.'

'Something like that, I bet,' said Philip. 'There are always people stirring up trouble *some*where, and wanting weapons to fight with. Those who can supply them with guns would make a lot of money. Yes, that's what it is – gun-running!'

'*Well*!' said Lucy-Ann, 'to think we've dropped right into an awful thing like that! I expect Bill guessed it – and they saw him snooping round – and captured him so that he couldn't give the game away.'

'However do they get the guns away from here?' wondered Jack. 'I mean – they can't be got away by boat, because this lagoon is absolutely enclosed by rocks. Yet the guns must be taken out of the water, to be sent to wherever they are wanted. It's jolly strange.'

'Well, now we *do* know what that aeroplane was dropping,' said Philip. 'My word – this lagoon must be full of armaments! What an absolutely wonderful hiding-place – nobody to see what happens, nobody to discover the guns at the bottom . . . '

'Except us,' said Lucy-Ann promptly. '*I* discovered that split package. I suppose it hit the rocks just below the surface and split open at once.'

They lay basking in the sun, talking over the curious discovery. Then Kiki suddenly uttered an astonished cry, and the children sat up to see why.

'Goodness – there's a boat coming,' said Jack in dismay. 'Coming towards this very place, too, from the seaward side of the rocky barrier.'

'What shall we do?' said Lucy-Ann, frightened. 'There's nowhere to hide, and we haven't time to make our way back without being seen.'

The boys gazed round in desperation. What could be done? Then Philip suddenly grabbed up a great armful of seaweed and flung it over the surprised Lucy-Ann.

'We'll cover ourselves up with this!' he said. 'There's stacks of it! Quick! Pull it up and cover yourselves with it. It's the only way we can hide.'

Their hearts thumping loudly again, the four children piled the thickly growing seaweed, with its great ribbon-like fronds, all over themselves. Jack peered through his and spoke urgently to Dinah.

'One of your feet is showing, Di. Put some seaweed over it, quick!'

Huffin and Puffin were amazed at this sudden seaweed game. They decided which lump was Philip and went to perch solemnly on him. He felt their weight, and almost laughed.

'Nobody could possibly guess there was a boy under these two puffins and all the seaweed,' he thought. 'I only hope the others are really well covered.'

The boat grounded not far off. The voices of two or three men could be heard, coming nearer and nearer. The children held their breath. 'Don't tread on us, oh, don't tread on us!' prayed Lucy-Ann, feeling quite sick, especially as there was a great flabby piece of seaweed across her mouth.

The men did not tread on them. They came and stood quite nearby, however, and all of them lighted cigarettes as they stood there.

'The last lot of stuff came today,' said one man, in a husky, deep voice. 'This lagoon must be almost full now.'

'Yes. Time we got some of it away,' said another voice, a sharp, commanding kind of voice. 'We don't know how much information that fellow we've got has passed on to his headquarters. He won't talk. Better send a message through to the chief, to tell him to collect as much as he wants, in case anyone else is sent along to snoop.'

'What about the second fellow? He won't talk either,' said the first voice. 'What are we going to do with them?'

'They can't remain up here,' said the commanding voice. 'Put them on the boat tonight, and we'll dump them somewhere where they won't be heard of again. I'm not going to waste my time on that first fellow any more – what's his name? — Cunningham. He's been enough trouble to us, poking his noise into all we do for the last year. Time he disappeared.'

The four hidden children, feeling very damp and cold under their seaweed, shivered to hear all this. They knew perfectly well what was meant. They, these men, were Bill's bitter enemies, because he had been successful in keeping on their track — now they had got him, and they were afraid he knew too much, though actually it was likely that Bill didn't know as much as they, the children, did.

'And so they are going to remove all these guns and then dump poor Bill somewhere so that he never *will* be heard of again, because he will be drowned,' thought Jack desperately. 'We shall *have* to rescue him. And as quickly as possible too. I wonder who the other fellow is they are talking about. Surely it can't be Horace. I thought he was one of the enemy.'

The men wandered away over the rocks. Evidently they had come to survey their extraordinary hiding-place though they could see very little of its contents. The children lay perfectly still, not daring to move, in case they should be noticed. They got very tired indeed of lying there, and Lucy-Ann was shivering.

Then they heard the sound of the motor-boat's engine starting up again. Thank goodness! They waited a while, and then Jack sat cautiously up. He looked round. There was no-one to be seen. The men had gone back to the boat by a different way, and it was now some distance out to sea.

'Phew!' said Jack. 'I didn't like that at all. Another inch or two nearer, and one of the men would have trodden on my foot!'

# 25

## Another surprise

They all sat up and removed the slippery seaweed from themselves. Huffin and Puffin walked down Philip's body, where they had perched the whole time. Kiki, to her fright and dismay, had been covered with seaweed by Jack, and forced to stay beside him, for he was afraid she might give them away by talking. She talked angrily now.

'Poor, poor Polly! Send for the doctor! What a pity, what a pity, ding dong bell, Polly's in the well!'

The children looked at one another solemnly when they had finished uncovering themselves. Bill was in great danger, there was no doubt of that at all.

'What are we going to do?' said Lucy-Ann, with tears in her eyes. Nobody quite knew. There seemed to be danger wherever they turned.

'Well,' said Jack at last, 'we've got a boat of our own, that's one thing – and I think when it's dark tonight we'd better set out for the other island, the one the men are on, and see if we can't find where they keep their motor-boat. We know that Bill will be there.'

'And rescue him!' said Dinah, thrilled, 'But how shall we get close in to shore without being seen or heard?'

'We'll go when it's dark, as I said,' said Jack, 'and when we get near to the shore, we'll stop our engine and get the oars. Then we can row in without being heard.'

'Oh, yes. I'd forgotten there were oars in our boat,' said Dinah. 'Thank goodness!'

'Can't we get back to our little cave, on the shore at the other side of the island?' asked Lucy-Ann. 'I don't feel safe here, somehow. And I'd be glad to know our boat was all right.'

'Also, we can't have anything to eat till we get back there,' said Philip, getting up. 'Come on, I'm frozen. We shall get warm climbing up the rocks, on to the height over there, and then over the island to the boat.'

So they went back over the rocks, and found their clothes where they had left them. They stripped off their wet suits and dressed quickly. Philip's rats, which he had left in his pockets, were extremely pleased to see him again, and ran all over him with little squeals of delight.

Huffin and Puffin accompanied the children as usual. All of them were secretly relieved to find their boat was safe on the shingly beach. They went to her and chose some tins of food.

'Better have something with lots of juice to drink,' said Jack. 'There's no fresh water here as far as I can see, and I'm awfully thirsty. Let's open a tin of pineapple. There's always lots of juice in that.'

'Better open *two* tins if Kiki's going to have any,' said Dinah. 'You know what a pig she is over pineapple.'

They all tried to be jolly and cheerful, but somehow, what with their strange discovery of the guns in the lagoon, and the news that Bill was in real danger, none of them could talk for long. One by one they fell silent, and hardly knew what they were eating.

'I suppose,' said Dinah at last, after a long silence in which the only noise was the sound of Kiki's beak scraping against the bottom of one of the pineapple tins, 'I suppose we had better set out as soon as it's dark — but I do feel quaky about it!'

'Well, look here,' said Jack, 'I've been thinking hard — and I'm sure it would be best if Philip and I went alone to get Bill. It's very risky, and we don't know a bit what we shall be up against, and I don't like the idea of you girls coming.'

'Oh, we *must* come!' cried Lucy-Ann, who couldn't bear the thought of Jack going off without her. 'Supposing something happened to you — we'd be here on this island all alone, and nobody would know about us! Anyway, I'm going with you, Jack. You can't stop me!'

'All right,' said Jack. 'Perhaps it would be better if we stuck together. I say – I suppose that other fellow they spoke about couldn't be Horace? We couldn't have made a mistake about him, could we?'

'Well, I did think he was too idiotic for words,' said Dinah. 'I mean – he *looked* it, not only acted it. I believe we did make a mistake. I think perhaps he really was a bird-lover.'

'Gosh! He must have thought we were frightful!' said Jack, horrified. 'And we took his boat too – and left him to be taken prisoner by the enemy!'

'And they must have thought he was Bill's friend, and have been wild with him when he said he didn't know Bill or anything about him,' said Philip.

Everyone thought solemnly about poor Horace. 'I'm jolly glad none of us hit him on the head, after all,' said Jack. 'Poor old Horace Tripalong!'

'We'll have to rescue him, too,' said Lucy-Ann. 'That'll make up a bit for taking his boat. But won't he be *furious* with us for all we've done!'

Huffin appeared at this moment with his familiar gift of half a dozen fish, neatly arranged head and tail alternately in his large beak. He deposited them at Philip's feet.

'Thanks, old man,' said Philip. 'But won't you eat them yourself? We daren't make a fire here to cook anything on.'

'Arrrrr!' said Huffin, and walked over to have a look in the empty tins. Puffin took the opportunity of gobbling up the fish, and Kiki watched her in disgust. Kiki had no use for fish fresh from the sea.

'Pah!' she said, in Horace's voice, and the children smiled.

'Kiki, you'll have to be jolly quiet tonight,' said Jack, scratching her head. 'No pahing or poohing to warn the enemy we're near!'

When the sun began to sink the children took the motor-boat a little way out to sea, to make sure that there were no rocks about that they must avoid when setting out at night. Far away on the horizon line they saw the island of the enemy. Somewhere there was Bill – and perhaps Horace too.

'I hope to goodness we see some kind of light to show us where to go inshore,' said Jack. 'We can't go all round the island, looking for the right place. We'd be heard. And we couldn't possibly row round.'

'Well, we saw that light that was signalling to the other boat last night,' said Philip. 'Maybe it will be signalling again. Let's go back now. There doesn't seem to be any rock to avoid tonight. We'll set out as soon as it is dark.'

They went back – and no sooner had they got to their little beach than they heard the humming of an aeroplane.

'Surely they're not going to drop any more packages!' said Jack. 'Lie down flat, all of you. We don't want to be spotted. Get near those rocks.'

They crouched down near a mass of rocks. The aeroplane made an enormous noise as it came nearer and nearer.

Jack gave a cry. 'It's a seaplane! Look, it's got floats underneath!'

'What an enormous one!' said Dinah. 'It's coming down!'

So it was. It circled the island once and then came lower as it circled it again. It seemed almost to brush the hill that towered at the other end of the island, the hill that over-looked the lagoon.

Then the engines were cut out, and there was a silence.

'She's landed,' said Jack. 'She's on the lagoon! I bet you anything you like that's where she is!'

'Oh, do let's go and see, as soon as dusk comes,' begged Dinah. 'Do you think she's going to get up the hidden guns?'

'However could she do that?' said Jack, rather scornfully.

'Well, she's pretty big and hefty,' said Philip. 'It's possible she's got some sort of apparatus on her for dragging up the hidden armaments. If the men think there's a danger of our Government sending patrols up here to look into the matter, always supposing that Bill has sent a message through to his headquarters, then our enemy will certainly try to remove the guns as soon as possible. It rather looks, seeing that this is a seaplane, as if the guns are going to be flown to South America – or somewhere far across the sea.'

As soon as it was dusk the children could not resist the temptation to go across the island and climb up the heights to peep over and see the lagoon. Even in the twilight they might be able to see something interesting.

They were soon on the cliff overlooking the lagoon. They could just make out the great shape of the giant seaplane in the middle of the sea-lake. Then suddenly lights shone out from it, and a noise began – a grating, dragging noise, as if some kind of machinery was being set to do some heavy work.

'I bet they're dragging up the packages of guns,' whispered Jack. 'We can't very well see – but we can hear enough to know something is at work, something needing winches, I should think.'

Lucy-Ann couldn't see any winches, but she could quite well imagine the kind of machinery that would send hooked cables overboard to drag up the heavy bundles of guns. Then the seaplane, when loaded up, would fly off again. And another would come, and another! Or maybe the same one would come back again and again.

The lights showed the children the vast shape of the seaplane. It looked weird lying quietly there in the middle of the dark lagoon. Lucy-Ann shivered.

'It's awful to be up against enemies who have boats and aeroplanes and seaplanes and guns,' she thought. 'We haven't anything except poor Horace's little motor-boat, and our own wits.'

They went back soberly to their boat. The tide had taken

it out a little way, but as they had tied a rope to a convenient rock, they pulled it in without difficulty. They all got on board.

'Now this is the greatest adventure of all,' said Jack, rather solemnly. 'Hiding is an adventure. Escaping is an adventure. But rescuing somebody else from the very jaws of the enemy is the greatest adventure of all.'

'If only we don't get captured ourselves!' said Lucy-Ann.

Jack started up the engine. The little boat nosed out to sea, leaving the lagoon island behind. Huffin and Puffin settled themselves on the deck-rail as usual, and Kiki sat on Jack's shoulder. Philip's rats, frightened at the sudden noise of the engine, twined themselves together in a large bump in the hollow of Philip's back. 'You tickle me!' he said, but the rats took no notice.

'Well, good luck to us all!' said Dinah. 'May we rescue Bill – and Horace too – defeat the enemy – and get back home in safety!'

'God save the Queen!' said Kiki devoutly, in exactly the same tone of voice, and everyone laughed. Funny old Kiki!

# 26

## Off to the enemy's island

The little boat sped along in the darkness. Philip was at the wheel. He took a large star as guide, and kept the boat well on its course.

After a while Jack touched his arm. 'See that light? It must come from the enemy's island. It's not the bright signalling light we saw before, but it certainly comes from the island.'

'I'll set course for it,' said Philip. 'You'll make certain Kiki doesn't go off into one of her cackles or screeches, won't you, Jack? Any noise out here on the water would be easily heard on land. Sound over water carries such a distance. I'll have to shut off the engine soon, or that will be heard.'

'Kiki won't make a sound,' said Jack.

'Shhhhhhh!' said Kiki at once.

'Yes. Good bird! Shhhhhhh!' said Jack. Philip shut off the engine and the boat gradually lost way until it was just drifting on. Then it came to a gentle stop on the restless sea.

Jack looked through his glasses at the light he could see on the island. 'I think it must be some sort of harbour light,' he said. 'Perhaps they have a small harbour there – they may have quite a fleet of motor-boats, you know, continually patrolling to make sure no-one visits islands near here. It's quite a steady light.'

Philip fumbled for the oars. 'Now for a spot of hard rowing!' he said. 'What's the time, Jack? Can you see by your wrist-watch? It's got a luminous face, hasn't it?'

'It's almost eleven o'clock,' said Jack. 'Just about right. We shall be nearing land about midnight, when we can hope that the enemy won't be wide awake.'

The boys took an oar each. Splish-splash! the oars went in and out of the water as the boys pulled with a will, and the boat glided smoothly along.

'We'll take turns when you're tired,' said Dinah. 'Philip, where are your rats? Something brushed against my leg just now. I shan't be able to help squealing if you let them run about.'

'They're in my pocket,' said Philip. 'You're imagining things as usual. And if you dare to squeal, I'll jolly well tip you overboard!'

'She won't, she won't,' said Lucy-Ann. 'It's only Huffin and Puffin walking about the deck, Dinah. One of them perched on my leg just now.'

'Arrr!' said a guttural voice from the deck-rail.

'Shhhhhhh!' said Kiki at once.

'She doesn't understand that it doesn't in the least matter Huffin and Puffin *arrr*ing all they like,' said Jack. 'They make a natural bird-noise that wouldn't put anyone on guard.'

'Shhhhh!' said Kiki reprovingly.

The light from the shore gleamed steadily. 'Must be from a lantern,' said Jack, in a low voice, pulling hard at his oar. 'Probably a guide to any motor-boat going in or out. Philip, let's have a rest. I'm getting puffed.'

'Right,' said Philip. The girls wanted to take a turn, but Jack wouldn't let them. 'No, we're just having a rest. There's no hurry. The later we are the better, in a way.'

They soon took the oars again, and their boat moved steadily over the water towards the light.

'No more talking now,' whispered Jack. 'Only tiny whispers.'

Lucy-Ann's knees went queer again. Her tummy felt peculiar too. Dinah was strung up and her breath came fast, although she was not rowing. The two boys were tense with excitement. Would they find the enemy's motor-boat there, with Bill already in it, ready to be 'dumped,' as the man had said that day? And would there be many men on guard?

'Whatever's that noise?' whispered Dinah at last, as their boat drew nearer to land. 'It does sound queer.'

The boys paused in their rowing, and leaned on their oars to listen.

'Sounds like a band playing,' said Jack. 'Of course – it's a radio!'

'Good!' said Philip. 'Then the enemy won't be so likely to hear us creeping in. Jack, look! – I think that's a little jetty there – you can just make it out by the light of that lantern. Can we possibly creep in without being seen or heard? And look! – is that a boat lying under the lantern?'

'I'll get the glasses,' said Philip, and felt about for them. He put them to his eyes. 'Yes – it *is* a boat – quite a big one. I should think it's the one the enemy came to our island in. I bet Bill is on it, battened down in the cabin!'

The band continued playing on the radio. 'Somebody on

board has got it on,' said Jack. 'The guard, I should think. Will he be on deck, then – the guard, I mean? There's no light there.'

'If you ask me, he's having a nice lazy time, snoozing on deck with his radio playing him nice tunes,' whispered back Philip. 'Look! – can you see that little glow, Jack? I bet that's the end of a cigarette the guard is smoking.'

'Yes, it probably is,' said Jack.

'I don't think we dare go in any closer,' said Philip. 'We don't want to be seen. If the guard gives the alarm, we're done for. I wonder how many there are on the deck. I can only see one glowing cigarette-end.'

'What are you going to do?' whispered Lucy-Ann. 'Do do something. I feel awful! I shall burst in a minute.'

Philip put out his hand and took hers. 'Don't worry,' he whispered. 'We shall have to do something soon! It looks to be rather a good time. If only that guard would fall asleep!'

'I say, Tufty – do you know what I think would be much the best thing to do?' said Jack suddenly. 'If you and I swam to the harbour, climbed up, got on the boat and surprised the guard, we could probably tip him into the water, and before he could raise the alarm, we'd open up the hatch and get Bill out. Why, we could probably drive the motor-boat off too – then we'd have two!'

'Sounds a good plan,' said Philip. 'But we don't know yet if Bill is there – and it's quite likely we couldn't tip the guard overboard – especially if there are more than one. We'd better do a little exploring first. Your idea of slipping overboard and swimming to the harbour is jolly good though. We'll certainly do that. We can clamber up a part where there are shadows, away from that light.'

'Oh dear – must you go swimming in the dark?' said Lucy-Ann, looking at the black water with a shiver. 'I should hate it. Do, do be careful, Jack!'

'I'll be all right,' said Jack. 'Come on, Philip. Strip off your clothes. We'll swim in our pants.'

It wasn't long before the boys silently slid overboard and entered the water. It was cold and they drew their breaths in sharply. But they soon felt warm as they swam rapidly towards the harbour. They could hear the radio more plainly as they came near. 'Good thing,' thought Jack. 'They won't be able to hear us coming at all.'

They avoided the light, and clambered up the part of the jetty where there were black shadows. It was not easy. 'The boat's just there,' whispered Jack in Philip's ear. 'Not right under the light, thank goodness!'

A sound made them stop suddenly. A loud and prolonged yawn came from the deck of the boat. Then the radio was snapped off and silence came back to the night.

'He may be going to sleep,' hissed Jack. 'Let's wait.'

They waited in complete silence for about ten minutes. The man tossed a glowing cigarette-end overboard but did not light another. The boys heard him give several grunts as if he was settling down comfortably. Then he gave a loud yawn again.

Still the boys waited, shivering in the darkness of the jetty, keeping close to one another in order to get a little bit of warmth from each other's bodies.

Then, on the night air, came very very welcome sounds. 'He's snoring,' whispered Jack, pressing Philip's arm in joy. 'He's asleep. I'm sure there's only one guard, because otherwise they would have been talking together. Now's our chance. Come on – but quietly, so as not to wake him!'

The two boys, shivering now with excitement as much as with cold, crept along the jetty to the boat. They climbed cautiously on board, their bare feet making no sound at all. On the deck lay the sleeping guard – if he was a guard!

Then another sound stopped them. This time it came from beneath their feet. Philip clutched Jack's bare arm and made him jump violently. They stood and listened.

It was somebody talking, down below in the cabin. Who was it? Could it be Bill? And who was he with? Horace perhaps. But maybe after all it wasn't Bill down there, maybe it was the enemy, playing cards, and perhaps the sleeping man wasn't a guard. It would be very foolish to toss him overboard and open the cabin hatch to find the enemy down in the cabin.

'We'd better listen and find out if it's Bill,' said Jack, right in Philip's ear. The boys could see thin streaks of light where the hatch was fitted down into the deck, covering in the little cabin; so they knew exactly where it was. They crept forward and then knelt down by the closed hatch. They put their ears to the cracks and strained to listen to the voices talking.

They could not hear what was being said – but, when one of the talkers suddenly cleared his throat and gave a little cough, the boys knew who it was all right! It was one of Bill's little ways. Bill was down there. It was Bill who was talking. Both boys felt a surge of tremendous relief. If only they could get Bill out, and let him take charge of things!

'If we throw this fellow overboard, we may find he raised the alarm so quickly that we shan't be able to get Bill out and explain things to him fast enough,' said Jack, in Philip's ear. 'As he's so fast asleep, what about unbolting the hatch and letting Bill see we're here? Then he could help us with the guard, and take charge of the boat.'

'You undo the hatch, and I'll stand by the guard, so that if he wakes I can knock him overboard,' said Philip. 'Go on. Quick!'

Jack felt for the bolt. His fingers were trembling and he could hardly pull it. He was afraid it might make a grating noise, but it didn't. It slid back easily and smoothly. Jack felt for the iron handle that raised the hatch, and then lifted up the hatch itself, so that a bright mass of light came up from the cabin below.

The men in the cabin heard the slight noise and looked up. One was Bill – and the other was Horace. When Bill saw Jack's face peering down out of the darkness he leapt to his feet in amazement. Jack put his finger to his lips, and Bill bit back the exclamation on his tongue.

'Come on out,' whispered Jack. 'Quick! We've got to deal with the guard here.'

But Horace spoilt everything. As soon as he saw Jack, the hated boy who had shut him into the hole on Puffin Island, he sprang up furiously. 'There's that villainous boy! Wait till I get him!' he shouted.

# 27

## Escape

'Sh!' said Jack fiercely, and pointed over his shoulder towards the guard. But it was too late. The man awoke with a jump, as the shouting penetrated into his dreams. He sat up blinking, and then, seeing the brilliant light streaming up from the open hatch, he leapt to his feet.

Bill had the sense to switch off the light. Now all was darkness. Bill began to climb up the hatchway, and the guard began to shout.

'What's all this? Hi, what are you doing? Who's there?'

Philip sprang at him and tried to push him overboard, but the man was strong and began to struggle. In the end it was poor Philip who was thrown overobard, with a most terrifc splash. Then Bill came up and, guided by the sound of the panting of the guard, hit out with his right fist. The surprised guard felt the sudden blow and reeled over. Bill put out a foot, hoping to trip him, and down he went to the deck. In a trice Bill was on top of him, and Jack came to help. 'Who was that going overboard?' panted Bill.

'Philip,' answered Jack, sitting firmly on the guard's legs. 'He's all right. He can swim to the other boat.'

'Get the guard down into the cabin,' ordered Bill.

'Where's the other fellow – Tipperlong? The idiot spoilt the whole show.'

Horace was standing well out of the way, wondering what was happening. He could hear pants and groans and strugglings, and he was scared. Then there came another yell from the guard, and down the man went into the cabin, slithering sideways down the steps.

Bang! The hatch shut down on him and Bill slid the bolt across.

'He's safe for the moment,' said Bill grimly. 'Now let's get the boat going, quick! We'll be off before the enemy know what we're up to!'

'That's what I planned we'd do!' panted Jack, thrilled that his wildest hopes seemed to be coming true. 'How do we start up the engine? Blow this darkness! I haven't a torch on me.'

The guard below was kicking up a terrific row. He was yelling and banging for all he was worth. Bill made his way in the darkness to the wheel of the boat.

And then things began to happen. Lights sprang up on shore, and voices began to shout. There came the sound of running feet.

'We shan't have time to get her free from her moorings and start her up before they're on us,' groaned Bill. 'Did you say you've got another boat here, Jack? Where is it? And what about Philip? Quick, answer me!'

'Yes – there's a boat off the end of the jetty there – with the girls in it – and Philip will probably be there by now, too,' said Jack, his words falling over one another in his excitement. 'We'd better swim for it!'

'Overboard then!' said Bill. 'Tipperlong, where are you? You'd better come too.'

'I c-c-c-can't swim,' stammered poor Horace.

'Well, jump overboard and I'll help you,' commanded Bill. But the thought of leaping into the dark cold water in the middle of the night, with enemies all round, was too much for Horace. He crawled into a corner and refused to move.

'Well, stay where you are, then,' said Bill scornfully. 'I'll have to go with these kids – can't let them down now!'

Overboard went Bill and Jack. Horace heard the splashes and shivered. Nothing would have induced him to do the same. He trembled in his corner, waiting for the enemy to come pounding down the jetty.

And come they did, with torches flashing, and voices that urgently demanded from the guard what all the noise was about. They swarmed on board the motor-boat, and found Horace at once, shivering in the corner. They dragged him out.

The guard was still hammering down in the cabin, getting hoarse with fury. The enemy, not really certain of what had happened, flung questions at poor Horace.

Bill and Jack, swimming swiftly through the dark water, heard the excited voices, and prayed that Horace would not give them away. The guard would soon tell them all they wanted to know, but perhaps the few minutes' start they had would be all they needed.

Philip was already on board the boat, reassuring the two frightened girls. When he heard the splash of Bill and Jack jumping overboard from the other boat, he strained his eyes to watch for them. As he caught the sound of their swift armstrokes through the water, he cautiously held his torch down over the sea, and flicked it on once or twice, to mark their way for them.

They saw the slight flashes of light and thankfully swam towards them. Jack had been afraid of missing the boat altogether in his excitement. Soon they were clambering up, and Lucy-Ann and Dinah caught hold of Bill's wet, hairy arms, so strong and firm and comforting.

'Come on – we must get going,' said Bill, giving each girl a quick pat. 'My, what a row there is on that boat! They've let the guard out now. Come on, before they know where we are.'

'The engine will tell them, when we start it up,' said Jack. 'We've got oars. Shall we row?'

'No,' said Bill. 'We must get away as quickly as possible. They'll chase us, and we *must* get a good start. You girls lie flat on your tummies, and you boys lie on top of them There'll be bullets flying after me in a tick!'

Bill started up the engine. Lucy-Ann and Dinah lay down flat. The boys lay on top of them, almost squeezing the breath out of the girls. It was most uncomfortable.

Oddly enough not one of the children felt frightened They all felt a terrific excitement, and Lucy-Ann had a mad feeling that she would like to yell and dance about. It was hard to have to keep flat on the deck, with Jack squashing her breath out of her.

As soon as the engine of the motor-boat started up, there came an astonished silence on board the other boat. Plainly the guard had not gathered that there was a second boat not far off, and had not told his friends about it. The enemy had thought that Bill and his rescuers were swimming some-where about, and they were still quite in the dark about what had happened.

But when the engine of Bill's (or rather Horace's) boat purred out in the night, the enemy knew that they must stop it somehow. That boat could not be allowed to get away!

Crack! Somebody's revolver went off, and a bullet sped over the sea, towards the boat.

Crack! Crack! Crack! Bill crouched as low as he could by the wheel, as he heard a bullet whizz much too near the boat for his liking.

'Keep down, you kids!' he ordered anxiously. 'We'll soon be out of reach.'

Crack! Another bullet went pinging by, and struck the water beyond the boat. Bill said several things under his breath, and wished the motor-boat would go a little faster.

*R-r-r-r-r-r* went the engine steadily, and the boat swung over the waves out to sea.

Crack! Crack!

There came a sudden squeal from Kiki, who was sitting on top of Jack, puzzled by all the noise and excitement. Then she screeched wildly.

'Oh! Kiki's hit!' shouted Jack, and sat up in anxiety, feeling for his beloved parrot.

Kiki didn't say a single word, but continued to screech as if she was in the most terrible pain. Jack was beside himself with grief.

'Keep down, you idiot!' roared Bill, sensing that Jack was not lying flat. 'Do you hear what I say?'

'But Kiki,' began Jack, only to be drowned by an even more furious roar from Bill.

'Kiki's all right! She couldn't screech like that if she was really hurt. Lie down flat, and do as you're told!'

Jack obeyed orders. He lay down again, and listened with anxiety to Kiki's screeching. The others, quite certain that the bird was wounded, were very anxious too.

Lucy-Ann wondered what had happened to Huffin and Puffin. She had not heard them say *arrrrr* for a long time. Perhaps they were shot too! Oh dear, when would they be out of reach of the enemy, and safe?

The shooting stopped – but another noise came, sounding faintly over the chugging of their own boat. Bill's sharp ears heard it.

'They're after us!' he called. 'They've started up their own boat. Thank goodness it's a dark night. We must just go on and on till our petrol gives out, and hope for the best.'

The motor-boat chasing them switched on a powerful searchlight. It swept the sea all round.

'We're just out of reach,' said Bill thankfully. 'This little boat can certainly get a move on. Kiki, shut up screeching! You're NOT hurt!'

'Bill, we might have enough petrol to get to the island we came from, over to the east there,' said Jack suddenly. 'The men would probably think we'd try and make for safety miles away, and if we do, we shall certainly be overtaken. Their boat is more powerful than ours, and as soon as we get within the range of their searchlight, we'll be seen. Let's swing off to the left.'

'What island did you come from?' demanded Bill. 'And what's been happening to you all since I was fool enough to let myself get captured? I've been worrying my head off about you!'

'We were worried about you, too,' said Jack. 'Swing her to port, Bill – we'll make for the lagoon-island, and hope that the men won't guess we're there.'

The boat set course for the other island, across the dark, heaving sea. Far behind them the searchlight was still sweeping the waters, but it was plain that the enemy's motor-boat was now going off in the other direction. Another few minutes and they would be out of sight and hearing.

'Arrrrrrr!' said a guttural voice from just beyond Bill. He jumped. Then he laughed.

'My goodness – have you still got Huffin and Puffin? Now don't start screeching again, Kiki. I'm absolutley certain you're not hurt.'

'Can I sit up now and just *feel* if Kiki is hurt?' begged Jack anxiously. 'They're not doing any more shooting.'

But before Bill could answer, the engine of the motor-boat gave a series of coughs and wheezes, and then, with a curious sound like a tired sigh, stopped altogether.

'Petrol's run out,' said Bill bitterly. 'It would, of course! Now we'll have to row, and it won't be long before the enemy catch us up!'

# 28

## A night of talking

The children all sat up at once, and the girls thankfully stretched their arms and legs. 'You are heavy, Philip,' grumbled Dinah. 'Oh Bill – what awful bad luck to have no petrol just as we must be so near shore!'

Jack reached out for Kiki. His hands felt over her body anxiously, and down her legs, and over her beak. Where was she hurt?

Kiki nestled close to him, murmuring funny little words that had no sense. 'You're not hurt, silly bird,' said Jack thankfully. 'You made a fuss for nothing. I'm ashamed of you.'

'Poor Kiki, poor Kiki, send for the doctor,' murmured Kiki, and put her head under her wing.

'She's not hurt, as far as I can make out,' said Jack to the others, 'but she must have had an awful scare. Perhaps a bullet zipped very near her.'

'Oh, forget Kiki for a moment and let's talk about ourselves,' said Dinah. 'Bill, what are we going to do?'

Bill sat lost in thought. What was the best thing to do? It was no joke to be in charge of four children, with such dangerous enemies so near. Would it be best to make for this lagoon-island, whatever it was? It should at least be within rowing distance. Or would it be best to row further on?

'We'll make for your lagoon-island,' he said at last. 'It's the best idea.'

'It can't be far away,' said Jack, straining his eyes in the darkness. 'I think I can make out a dark shape over there. Can you, Philip?'

'Yes,' said Philip. 'Look, over there, Bill! Can you see?'

'Not a thing,' said Bill. 'But I'll take your word for it. You youngsters have got such sharp eyes and ears. Now, where are the oars?'

They were soon found, and the slow splish-splash of rowing came to the ears of the girls, as they sat huddled together for warmth.

'Yes – it *is* land of some sort,' said Bill, after a while, with satisfaction. 'We'll be ashore soon. I only hope there are no rocks to run aground on.'

'Oh no,' said Jack. 'We'll be all right. There aren't any rocks near the lagoon-island. At least, not the part where we should be coming to now.'

But hardly were the words out of his mouth before there came a horrid grinding noise, and the boat shivered from end to end. Everyone got a terrible shock. Whatever was happening now?

'On the rocks!' said Bill grimly. 'And I don't somehow think we'll get her off! She means to stay here all right!'

The boat could not be moved. Jack anxiously switched on a torch, and tried to see what had happened. It was only too plain!

'There are rocks all round,' he said dolefully. 'We haven't come to the right part of the island at all. Goodness knows where we are.'

'Let's see if we're holed,' said Bill, and took Jack's torch. He examined the boat thoroughly, and gave a sigh of relief. 'No. It looks as if we're safe so far. She must have run right on to a shallow ledge of rock. It's no use doing anything about it now. We'll have to wait till it's light and then see if we can shift her. If we mess about now and do get her off, we shall only get on to other rocks at once.'

'Well, let's snuggle down in rugs and have something to eat, and talk then,' said Lucy-Ann. 'I should never, never be able to go to sleep.'

'None of us could tonight,' said Jack. 'I've never felt so wide awake in my life. I'm going to get some clothes on first. I haven't had time to put any on. Wasn't I glad to get some rugs round me, though!'

'I'm pretty wet through myself,' said Bill. 'I'll have a few rugs too, I think.'

'There's some clothes of Horace's in that locker,' said Dinah. 'The one behind you. We gave him all of his, as we thought, but I found some more yesterday, tucked away there. They won't fit you, Bill, but at least they'll keep you warm.'

'Good,' said Bill, and opened the locker. 'I'll put them on now, if I can feel what they are in the dark. You girls get some food, if you've got any. Pity we can't boil a kettle and get something hot into us!'

Soon Bill and the boys had dry clothes on. Then all five of them sat close together for warmth, and ate biscuits and chocolate hungrily.

'Now suppose we tell each other what's happened since I so hurriedly departed from Puffin Island,' said Bill.

'You tell your tale first,' said Lucy-Ann, pressing close to him. 'Oh, Bill, it's good to have you back! I was so scared when we found you were gone, and the engine of the motor-boat smashed up, and the radio too.'

'Yes. They told me they'd done that,' said Bill. 'Apparently they didn't know you kids were on the island at all — so I didn't say a word, of course. Well — to make a long story short, when I was fiddling about with the radio that night, on our boat, trying to get a message through — and not succeeding, unfortunately . . . '

'Oh, Bill — then we shan't be rescued!' said Lucy-Ann at once. 'Oh, we did hope you would have sent a message for help or something! . . . '

'Well, headquarters knew that I was on to something up here, but no more than that,' said Bill. 'Anyway, as I say, I was fiddling with the radio — when I suddenly got a blow on the head, and down I went. Then I knew nothing more at all until I woke up on some other island, a prisoner in a shack!'

'The enemy didn't hurt you, did they?' asked Lucy-Ann anxiously.

Bill didn't answer that. He went on with his tale. 'They questioned me, of course, and got nothing out of me at all. The queer part was that the very men I'd been told to disappear from, because they were after me, were the very men we bumped into up here! *This* was where they were carrying on their activities! I had thought it was somewhere in Wales – but they made me think that by laying false clues.'

'Oh, Bill – and to think this wild desolate sea, with all its little islands, was the very place they had chosen, and *we*, too, chose to come to!' said Jack. 'They must have thought you'd found out their hiding-place, and had come to track them down.'

'Just what they did think,' said Bill. 'And what's more they imagined that one or other of their men must have given their secret away, and they wanted to find out from me who it was. That was why they held me for questioning, I imagine – instead of bumping me off at once.'

'Humpy-dumpy-bumpy,' said Kiki, taking her head out from under her wing. But nobody paid the slightest attention. Bill's story was too absorbing.

'They wanted to know *how* much I knew, and *who* had told me,' said Bill. 'Well, I didn't actually know very much, and what I did know nobody had told me, so they didn't get a great deal out of me – and they were not pleased.'

'Didn't you *really* know very much then?' said Philip, astonished.

'I knew this gang were up to something illegal – I knew they were getting a lot of money from somewhere – I guessed it was something to do with guns,' said Bill. 'I tried to put several spokes in their wheel, and they got wise to the fact that I was after them. I'd cleaned up a nasty little business of theirs once before – though we didn't get the chief ones then – so I wasn't popular.'

'And they decided to track *you* down and bump you off!' said Jack. 'So you were told to disappear – and lo and behold! you came here to disappear . . . '

'And walked right into the hornets nest,' agreed Bill. 'And took you with me too! How is it you kids always attract adventures? As soon as I go near you, an adventure leaps up, and we all get caught in it.'

'It *is* very peculiar,' said Jack. 'Go on, Bill.'

'Well, then my guards suddenly brought Mr Horace Tipperlong to my shack,' said Bill. 'They appeared to think that he was a pal of mine, and was up here among these islands to help me in my snooping. He was just as bewildered as I was. I couldn't make him out at all. But when we were alone, he began to tell me about you kids, and I guessed what had happened. You were absolute little demons to him, according to his story.'

'Yes, we were,' said Jack remorsefully, remembering their treatment of the puzzled and angry Horace. 'You see, we honestly thought he was one of the enemy, got up to look like a rather goofy ornithologist, sent to capture us and make us get into his boat – so . . . '

'We captured him instead, and pushed him down a hole we found, and kept him there,' said Dinah.

'And conked him on the head every time he popped up, it appears,' said Bill. 'I shouldn't have thought you were so bloodthirsty. He said even the girls took turns at hitting him.'

'*Well*!' said everyone, in shocked astonishment at such colossal untruths. 'Bill! We never hit him once!'

'I wouldn't have been surprised at the boys giving him one or two knocks, if they really thought he was one of the enemy sent to capture them,' said Bill, 'but I simply could not *imagine* the girls hitting him. He said Lucy-Ann was the worst.'

'*Oh!* And I was the only one that said I couldn't possibly,' said Lucy-Ann, really shocked at such wicked statements.

'Anyway, apparently you gave him an awful time, and then made off with his boat, leaving him to be captured by the enemy,' said Bill. 'You know, I couldn't help grinning when I heard it all. There's plenty of pluck in you kids! The enemy took him off in their boat and didn't believe a word of his story about your taking him prisoner. They really thought he was a pal of mine. Of course, I pretended not to believe his tale about there being children on the island either, because I didn't want you captured as well. But I did wonder what was happening to you when I heard you'd taken his boat. Horace said it was no longer in the little harbour when he was yanked on board the enemy's boat.'

'I don't like Horace,' said Lucy-Ann. 'I hope the enemy give him an *awful* time! He's silly and he's untruthful and he's a coward.'

'And if he hadn't yelled out when he did tonight, just after I'd opened the hatch of the cabin to let you out, Bill, we'd have been able to capture that big fast motor-boat, and get right back to the mainland,' said Jack gloomily. 'Silly idiot – yelling like that!'

'Yes, that was a great pity,' said Bill. 'Now you tell me *your* story.'

So the children told it, and Bill listened with interest and amazement. When they came to the bit about the lagoon, and what was hidden there, he held his breath in astonishment.

'So *that's* where they put the guns – dropped them by parachute into a secret lagoon – and then meant to get them up again as soon as the time was ripe – and take them away by seaplane. Gun-running on the grand scale!'

'We were jolly astonished when we watched it all happening,' said Jack.

'I should think so!' said Bill. 'It's beyond belief! And to think you children stumbled on the whole secret. My word, if only I could get a message through to headquarters, we'd catch the whole gang red-handed!'

'It's been pretty thrilling,' said Philip. 'We had some scares, I can tell you, Bill.'

'You're good kids,' said Bill. 'Good and plucky kids. I'm proud of you. But there's one thing I don't understand. Why didn't you make for safety, when you captured Horace's boat? Why did you mess about here?'

'Well . . . ' said Jack, 'you see – we had the choice of making for safety – or trying to find you. And we chose to try and find you, Bill. Even Lucy-Ann voted for that.'

There was a silence. Then Bill put his big arms all round the huddled-up four and gave them such a hug that Lucy-Ann gasped.

'I don't know what to say,' said Bill, in a queer sort of voice. 'You're only kids – but you're the finest company of friends anyone could have. You know the meaning of loyalty already, and even if you're scared you don't give up. I'm proud to have you for my friends.'

'Oh, *Bill*!' said Lucy-Ann, tremendously thrilled to hear such a speech from her hero. 'You *are* nice. You're our very very best friend, and you always will be.'

'Always,' said Dinah.

The boys said nothing, but they glowed inwardly at Bill's praise. Friendship – loyalty – staunchness in face of danger – they and Bill both knew these things and recognised them for the fine things they were. They felt very close to Bill indeed.

'Look!' said Lucy-Ann suddenly. 'The dawn! Over there, in the east. Oh, Bill – I wonder what's going to happen today?'

# 29

# Bill makes a grand find

The sky grew silvery in the east. Then a golden glow spread slowly upwards, and the sea became a milky colour that gradually turned to gold.

Almost at once there came a crying of seabirds as guillemots, gannets, cormorants, puffins and gulls came from their roosting-places to greet the new day. Soon the sea around the children was dotted thickly with hundreds of birds eagerly seeking fish for food. Huffin and Puffin joined them.

Jack gave an exclamation as he looked all round him. 'This isn't the lagoon-island. There were no rocky cliffs to it like this, facing the sea. This is another island we've come to!'

'Yes, it is,' said Philip. 'One I don't remember to have seen before. Blow! Where are we?'

'I should think it must be the island we once noticed on the chart,' said Lucy-Ann, remembering. 'The Isle of Wings. Just *look* at the mass of birds on the waters round us! It's more than we've ever seen before!'

'Extraordinary!' said Bill, amazed. 'There must be millions of birds. Some of them are so close that they bob against each other.'

Not only the sea was full of birds, but the air too, and the screaming and calling was deafening. Soon one bird after another flew up from the water with fish in its beak. Huffin flew to the boat and presented Philip with his usual beakful of neatly arranged fish.

'Kiki's very quiet,' said Philip, looking at her. 'What's the matter with her? Kiki, put up your crest, you ridiculous bird!'

'Send for the doctor,' said Kiki mournfully. Jack looked at her closely. Then he gave an exclamation.

'She's lost some of her crest! She's hardly got any! Oh, Bill – that's what she screeched for last night! A bullet must have zipped through her crest – right through her top-knot – and taken some of the feathers off with it.'

'Poor Polly, poor Polly, what a pity, what a pity!' said Kiki, glad to be the centre of attention.

'Yes, poor old Kiki!' said Jack, and he stroked her. 'What a shock you must have got! No wonder you screeched. Never mind, old thing – the crest will grow again. You'll look a bit mangy for a while, but *we* shan't mind.'

Bill had been looking to see exactly what had happened to the boat. It had run on to a shelf of rock, and had settled there so firmly that until high tide came there was no hope of getting off. They were not on the mainland of the island, but on an outcrop of tall rocks, hung with thick seaweed, and inhabited by about two hundred or more birds. They did not seem to mind the boat and its load of people in the least. In fact, seeing Huffin and Puffin perched there, some of the birds came on deck too. Jack was thrilled.

'I don't think the boat's damaged at all,' said Bill. 'Once she gets afloat again with the tide, she'll be all right. But the thing is – what in the world are we going to do if she does get afloat?'

'Row to safety,' said Lucy-Ann promptly.

'Sounds easy,' said Jack regretfully. 'But you don't realize what a wild and desolate sea this is, Lucy-Ann, or how few people ever come to these little bird-islands. We couldn't possibly row to the mainland, for instance, could we, Bill?'

'No. I don't think so,' said Bill. 'I'm glad to see we've got a good store of food. That's something. But what about drinking-water?'

'We'll have to drink pineapple juice or something like that,' said Dinah. 'And if it rains we'll catch rainwater.'

'What *is* the best thing to do?' said Bill, talking to himself, with a frown. 'They'll be looking for us, I expect. They'll know we couldn't get far. They'll send out patrols — probably even an aeroplane. They can't afford to let me get away now.'

The children knew that 'they' meant the enemy. Dinah looked all round them. 'If the enemy do come round this island, they can't help seeing us. We'd be spotted at once in our boat.'

'Well — we'll make up our minds what to do when the boat's afloat again,' said Bill at last. 'What about a spot of sleep? Lucy-Ann is looking as white as a sheet. She's had no sleep at all.'

'I do feel awfully sleepy,' admitted Lucy-Ann, trying not to yawn. 'But I feel dirty and sticky too.'

'Let's have a quick dip in the sea, and then have a snooze,' said Jack. 'We can take it in turn to keep watch for the enemy.'

'I don't want a dip,' said Dinah. 'I'm too sleepy. You three and Bill have a dip, and I'll make up our beds again and get the rugs and things set out comfortably.'

'I'll help you,' said Lucy-Ann. 'I'm too tired to bathe.'

Bill and the boys soon slipped into the water. The girls watched them. 'You know,' said Lucy-Ann, after a while, 'it's almost impossible to see the boys and Bill among all those birds bobbing about. Once I lose sight of them I can't spot them again.

It was quite true. There were so many birds bobbing about on the water that the boys' wet dark heads, and Bill's, could hardly be picked out from the crowd.

'Let's tell Bill when they come back,' said Dinah, a sudden idea sliding into her head. 'I bet if we all slid into the water if the enemy came, nobody would ever spot us among the birds there.'

'No, they wouldn't,' agreed Lucy-Ann. 'It would be a marvellous idea, Dinah!'

They told the others when they came back, glowing from

their bathe. Bill nodded, pleased. 'Yes – a fine idea. If the enemy comes in sight, that's what we'll do. Our heads would be completely lost among the bodies of the swimming birds.'

'What about the boat though?' said Jack.

'We could do what we did for ourselves, when we were on the rocks beside the lagoon,' said Philip. 'Drape it with seaweed so that it looks like a rock!'

'You're full of bright ideas, you kids,' said Bill. 'Whilst you're all having a snooze I'll do a little boat-draping. If the enemy come, they'll come soon. They won't waste many hours before they try to find us. I'll wake you if I see or hear any sign of them, and you must all be prepared to drop over the side of the boat. Better sleep in your undies, so that you don't wet all your clothes. Your bathing-suits are wet.'

'Ours aren't,' said Lucy-Ann. 'Oh dear – I'm so awfully sleepy. I do hope the enemy don't come yet. I'm not at all sure I shall wake if they do!'

Bill tucked them all up in rugs. They were asleep in a moment or two, tired out. Bill began to do a little boat-draping. He pulled great fronds of seaweed off the nearby rocks and hung them over the boat-sides, till the little vessel looked like a boat-shaped rock.

Having finished his task, Bill sat down in the cabin. He idly removed a cover from something there – and then stared in surprise.

A radio! Was it a transmitter too? Surely Horace going off all alone into the wilds, would have had the sense to take a transmitter with him; in case he got hurt, or became ill? With trembling hands Bill began to examine the radio.

He gave a loud exclamation that woke up Jack. The boy sat up in alarm. 'Is it the enemy, Bill?'

'No. But look here – why on earth didn't you tell me there was a radio in this boat? I can get a message through, with luck.'

'Golly, I forgot all about it!' said Jack. 'But is it a transmitter, Bill?'

'Yes. Not a very good one – but I'll do my best to try and work it so that I can send a message to headquarters,' said Bill. 'There's always someone standing by there, hoping to hear from me. I haven't reported for days.'

Bill began to hunt about and Jack wondered why. 'What are you looking for, Bill?' he asked.

'The aerial,' said Bill. 'There must be an aerial somewhere, for the transmitter. Where on earth can it be?'

'I remember seeing something on a shelf at the back of the cabin,' said Jack sleepily. 'It was about six feet long.'

'That would be it!' said Bill, and went to look. He pulled out something long and slender. 'Good! Here it is. I can soon fix it up.'

Jack watched Bill for a few minutes, then he felt his eyes closing and he slumped down in his rugs again. It was very, very exciting to watch Bill putting up the aerial and trying to make the transmitter work – but not even that excitement could make Jack's eyes keep open. In half a second he was fast asleep again.

Bill worked and worked, groaning occasionally with disappointment as first one thing failed and then another. Curious sounds came from the radio, and little lights glowed here and there within it. There was something the matter with it, and Bill didn't know what. If only he knew! Oh, if only he could get the thing to work, just for a minute or two!

At last he thought he had got it fixed. Now to send a message through. Now to send out his code number and wait for a reply.

He sent out his code time and again. There was no reply. The radio seemed to be quite dead at his end. There was nothing for it but to send a message and hope it would be received – but Bill had grave doubts about it.

He rapidly sent a message through in code, asking for

immediate help. He repeated the message time and time again, but got no reply at all. He gave the lagoon-island as a guide to their whereabouts, knowing that they must be somewhere near it. Surely it must be on some map, and could be located?

He was so busy trying to send his message and listening for a reply which never came, that he almost didn't hear the distant purr of a powerful motor-boat. But the sound did at last penetrate his mind and he looked up with a start.

He shouted to the children. 'Wake up! Quick! Into the water with you – the enemy are here! WAKE UP!'

They all woke up with a jump. The enemy! Splash! Into the water they slid, all five of them, the two girls hardly awake. The enemy! Yes, there was the motor-boat heading straight for them all!

# 30

# Ahoy there! Show yourselves!

There was a sudden flash of sunlight on the lenses of a pair of field-glasses. They were being levelled at the island, on whose rocks the children's boat had been grounded. The glasses swept the rocks and the island, and then came back to the rocks again.

The boat was there, draped end to end with seaweed. The glasses rested on it for a few moments. Then they swept the sea, but among the bobbing birds it was impossible to pick out the five wet heads.

The children kept as close to swimming birds as possible. Philip was all right because Huffin and Puffin perched on his head, and hid him beautifully. Lucy-Ann was near a big cormorant, who eyed her with interest but did not swim away from her. Dinah and Jack were among a crowd of bobbing, diving puffins, and Bill, fearful of his big, somewhat bald head being spotted, kept bobbing under the water, and holding his breath there as long as he could.

After what seemed an age the enemy's motor-boat swung round and went away, going right round the island – or so Bill thought. They heard the sound of its engine growing fainter and fainter.

Not until it had completely died away did Bill let the children get back into the boat. Then, when he thought it was quite safe, they all clambered back, wet and hungry, but no longer sleepy.

'How slippery the boat is, with all this seaweed!' said Jack. 'Dinah, your idea worked well. I don't think the enemy even *guessed* there was anyone here – and there were five people and a boat within easy sight of their glasses.'

'Yes, a very fine idea, Dinah,' said Bill. 'Now – what about breakfast? I'm starving!'

They sat down and opened a few tins. Kiki screeched with delight when she saw the chunks of pineapple in one of them. She tried to raise her crest, but as she had only one or two feathers left in it, it was not a very successful effort.

Jack suddenly thought of something. 'Bill! Do I remember something – something about you and Horace's radio – or did I dream it? Yes, perhaps I dreamt it.'

'You certainly didn't, said Bill. 'I found Horace's radio – most unexpectedly, I must say – and discovered to my joy that it was a transmitter as well as a receiver – so that I ought to be able to send messages as well as receive them.'

'Oh, *Bill*! So you've radioed for help – and we shall be saved!' said Lucy-Ann joyfully.

'Unfortunately there's something wrong with the thing,' said Bill. 'Couldn't get a chirp out of it – and whether or not my messages have gone through I can't tell. But probably not. It's not a very good set, this one of Horace's.'

'Oh – so it's not very likely it was of much use,' said Dinah, disappointed.

'Not very,' said Bill. 'By the way, did anyone feel a slight upward lift then? I have an idea the boat is coming off the rocks.'

He was right. It was soon afloat, and Bill took the oars. He rowed for some distance away from the island, and then a thought struck him.

'Look here – Horace couldn't possibly have come all the way up here – and hoped to get back again – without a store of petrol. Have you examined this boat thoroughly?'

'No, not really thoroughly,' said Jack. 'It isn't much of a boat.'

'I grant you that – but there really *should* be some petrol somewhere,' said Bill. 'Philip, pull up those piles of rope and stuff. There would be room under the board there for tins of petrol.'

Philip and Jack did as they were told. They hauled up three loose boards – and there, neatly arranged below, was Horace's store of petrol!

'Gosh!' said Jack. 'What a find! *Now* we'll be all right. We'll be on the mainland in no time. Good old Horace!'

They handed Bill a tin. He emptied it into the petrol tank of the engine and then took another tin. That was emptied in too. Hurrah! Now they could really make headway.

Soon the engine was purring happily away and the little boat was speeding over the waves. No more rowing! Bill set his course for the south-east.

'Hark! There's an aeroplane about somewhere!' said Lucy-Ann suddenly. 'I can hear it.'

They all looked up into the sky. Soon they saw the plane, coming from the north-east. It was flying low.

'Looks as if it's trying to spot us,' said Bill uneasily.

'It belongs to the enemy then!' said Jack. They all looked intently at the approaching plane. It seemed suddenly to see them, and veered in their direction. It flew down very low, circled round them, and then made off.

'Blow!' said Bill. 'Now we're for it! They'll send out their most powerful motor-boat – or maybe one of the seaplanes they seem to use – and that'll be that!'

'Well, we've got plenty of petrol,' said Jack, 'so we can keep on quickly for miles. We'll be well away from here before long.'

The boat sped on, Bill giving her her top speed. When he reckoned that her petrol would soon be running out he called to Jack, 'Get out the other tins, Jack. I'll put some more in before she's empty.'

But what a shock for the boys! All the other tins were empty! Bill stared in dismay.

'Gosh! Somebody has swindled Horace properly! He probably gave orders for all the tins to be filled – and somebody took the money for the lot, and only filled half. What a dirty trick!'

'But just the sort that *would* be played on poor silly Horace!' said Philip. 'Oh, Bill – we're out on the open sea now, miles away from any island. What will we do if the petrol gives out before we've reached anywhere?'

Bill wiped his forehead. 'I don't like this,' he said. 'There's not much left in the tank now. Once we run out, we can't get far with oars, and we shall be at the mercy of any fast motor-boat sent out to catch us. I think perhaps one of the bullets must have glanced off the petrol tank and made it leak a bit.'

Nobody said anything. 'Oh dear,' thought Lucy-Ann, 'just as we think things are all right, they turn out all wrong again.'

After a while the engine stopped with a series of coughs and splutters. 'No more petrol,' said Jack gloomily.

'Send for the doctor,' said Kiki.

'Wish we could,' said Philip.

'Arrrrr!' said Huffin from the deck-rail. Both Huffin and Puffin were still with the little company. Lucy-Ann had begun to hope that they would travel right home with them. What excitement they would cause!

'This is really disgusting,' said Bill. 'So near and yet so far!'

There was a dead silence, and only the plish-plash of the sea against the sides of the boat could be heard. Philip's rats, surprised at the quiet, ran out of the various hiding-places in his clothes, and sniffed the air. Bill hadn't seen them since he had been captured from Puffin Island, and he stared in surprise.

'My word – how they've grown! Well, well, who knows, we may have to eat them in the end!'

He meant this as a joke, but both Lucy-Ann and Dinah squealed in horror.

'Ugh! Bill! How could you say such a horrible thing! Eat a *rat*! I'd rather die!'

'Shall we row, just for something to do?' said Jack. 'Or have a meal? Or what?'

'Oh, have a meal,' said Philip. Then a thought struck him. 'I say, Bill – I suppose we oughtn't to start rationing ourselves, ought we? I mean – do you think we may be marooned out here on this lonely sea for days on end?'

'No,' said Bill, who privately thought that before the day was up they would all be back on the island in the hands of the enemy, now that their plane had spotted them. 'No. We really don't need to think of things like that at the moment. All the same – I wouldn't have headed out for the open sea as we have done, if I'd thought the petrol was going to give out – I'd have kept near the islands.'

It was a boring and anxious day. The four children were still very tired, but refused to try and sleep. No motor-boat appeared in chase of them. The sun began to sink in the west, and it looked as if the little company was going to spend a night out on the open sea.

'Well, thank goodness it isn't cold, anyway,' said Dinah. 'Even the wind is warm tonight. Don't we seem a long long way from home – and from school – and from all the ordinary things we know?'

Lucy-Ann gazed round her at the vast open sea, green

near the boat, but a deep blue beyond. 'Yes,' she said, 'we're far away from everywhere – lost on the Sea of Adventure.'

The sun slid down further still. Then, on the evening air, came a familiar sound – the throb-throb-throb of a powerful engine.

Everyone sat up straight at once. Motor-boat? Aeroplane? Seaplane? What was it?

'There it is!' cried Jack, making everyone jump. 'Look, over there!' Golly, what a big one! It's a seaplane.'

'It must be the one we saw on the lagoon the other day,' said Dinah. 'They've sent it after us. Oh, Bill – what can we do?'

'All lie down flat,' said Bill at once. 'You've got to remember that if it's the enemy they don't know I've got children with me – they probably think there are three or four men in the boat – and they may shoot, as they did before. So lie down flat and don't move. Don't show your heads at all.'

Lucy-Ann's knees began their familiar wobbly feeling. She lay down flat at once, glad that Bill had not suggested that the boys should squash on top of them again. Bill put his arm over her.

'Don't you worry, Lucy-Ann,' he said. 'You'll be all right. They won't hurt children.'

But Lucy-Ann didn't want 'them' to hurt Bill either, and she was very much afraid they would. With her pale face pressed into the rugs, she lay as still as a mouse.

The roar of the seaplane came much nearer. It circled just overhead. Then its engine cut out and it landed not far off. Waves from it rippled under the boat and sent it up and down.

Nobody dared to look overboard and see the great seaplane. Bill was afraid of a bullet if he did.

Then a colossal voice came booming over the sea, the voice of a giant: 'AHOY THERE! SHOW YOURSELVES!'

'Don't move,' said Bill urgently. 'Don't move. Don't be frightened, Lucy-Ann. They're using a megaphone, that's why the voice sounds so loud.'

The giant voice came again: 'WE'VE GOT OUR GUNS ON YOU. ANY FUNNY BUSINESS AND YOU'LL BE BLOWN TO SMITHEREENS. SHOW YOURSELVES!'

# 31

## Over the sea of adventure

'It's no good,' said Bill, in a low voice. 'I must stand up. I don't want them to machine-gun the boat.'

He stood up and waved, then put both hands up to show that he surrendered. A boat put off from the seaplane and came rapidly towards Bill's boat. In it were three men, one of them holding a revolver in his hand.

The children waited, panic-stricken, fearing to hear a shot at Bill. They had none of them raised their heads, but they could picture all too plainly what was happening.

The boat came near – and then there came a loud cry of amazement from it.

'BILL! By all that's wonderful, it's BILL! Why on earth didn't you welcome us, instead of making us think you were part of the gang!'

'Good heavens! It's you, Joe!' yelled Bill, and the relief in his voice brought all the children to their feet at once. 'Look here, kids – it's Joe – my colleague. Hey, Joe, you got my message then, all right?'

The boat came alongside with a gentle bump. Joe put away his revolver, grinning. 'Yes, I got your radio message all right – but I guess you didn't get ours. We kept asking you questions, and all you did was to go on repeating the same old thing. So this seaplane was sent out and we were just cruising along looking for the lagoon you told us about, when we spotted your boat here. So down we came to investigate.'

'Thank goodness,' said Bill. 'We'd run out of petrol. We were expecting the enemy to send a plane or a boat out after us at any moment!'

'Come along to the seaplane,' said Joe, who had bright-blue eyes and a very wide grin. 'Will the kids mind flying?'

'Oh no. We're used to it,' said Jack, and helped the girls into the boat where Joe stood.

'Are we rescued?' said Lucy-Ann, hardly believing it could be true, after all their alarms and fears.

'You are,' said Joe, and grinned at her. 'Sent one of our biggest seaplanes after you, to take you home! Have to do that for Bill here, you know. He's a V.I.P.'

'What's that?' asked Lucy-Ann, as they sped towards the seaplane.

'Very Important Person, of course,' said Joe. 'Didn't you know he was?'

'Yes,' said Lucy-Ann, beaming. 'Oh yes. I always knew he was.'

'We've left Huffin and Puffin behind,' suddenly wailed Dinah.

'Good heavens! Was there somebody else in your boat then?' said Joe in alarm. 'Never saw them!'

'Oh, they're only puffins,' said Jack. 'But awfully nice ones, quite tame. Oh, there they are, flying after the boat.'

'Can we take them with us?' begged Lucy-Ann. But Bill shook his head.

'No, Lucy-Ann. They'd be miserable away from their home here in the islands. Soon they will nest again and lay an egg. Then they will forget all about us.'

'I shall never, never forget them,' said Lucy-Ann. 'They kept with us all the time!'

'Here we are,' said Joe, as they came to the enormous seaplane. They were helped into it, and then the plane took off smoothly and sweetly, circling into the air like a broad-winged gull. Horace's boat was left bobbing alone, waiting for one of the police boats to collect it.

'What about that lagoon?' said Joe suddenly. 'I'd like to spot it, and plot it on our maps. I think we can find it. Will these kids know it if they see it?'

'Oh *yes*, said Jack. 'You can't mistake it. It's a most extraordinary sea-lake, and much bluer than the sea. I shouldn't be surprised if you can see some of the packages under the water, if you go down low. The water's so clear there.'

The seaplane roared through the sky. The children were thrilled. Down below was the blue sea, looking smooth and still. Then, as they looked, they saw little islands coming into view. What hosts of them there were!

Then Jack caught sight of the lagoon. 'There it is, there it is!' he shouted. 'Look down there! You can't mistake it, lying between those two islands, shut in by a reef of rocks all the way round.'

The seaplane circled round the surprising lagoon. It dropped lower. The children watched to see if they could make out any of the underwater packages – and sure enough, through the clear water glimmered the silvery-grey wrapping that covered the hidden guns.

'That's where the guns are,' said Philip. 'Look, Bill – you can see the waterproof wrappings! They had already begun to lift the packages from the water and load them on to seaplanes. We watched them loading one.'

Bill and Joe exchanged glances. 'We've got some pretty good witnesses then,' said Joe. 'Good bunch of kids, this, Bill. Are they the ones you've gone adventuring with before?'

'They are,' said Bill. 'You can't keep them out of adventures, you know. And they will drag me into them too!'

They left the lagoon with its sinister secret behind them and flew over the island where Bill had been a prisoner.

'There's the little jetty,' said Jack, as they flew low. 'And look, there are *two* motor-boats there now! I say, Bill – what about Horace?'

'Horace will be rescued when we clean up these scoundrels,' said Bill. 'They're the men who make fortunes when one country goes to war with another, or when civil war is fought – because they get the guns and sell them to each side. We try to stop it by all kinds of international treaties – but these men are against the law, and scorn it. That's where I come in – to stop them!'

'How will you stop them now?' asked Jack. 'Will you raid the island – and capture the men? And destroy all the hidden guns? Suppose they escape by motor-boat or plane?'

'Don't you worry about that,' said Joe, with his wide grin stretching across his brown face. 'We've got messages through already. There'll be a fleet of our seaplanes up here in a few hours – and armed boats patrolling all round. There's no hope for any of the gang now.'

Except for the little jetty, which would hardly have been noticed if the children and Bill hadn't known it was there, there was nothing to see on the enemy's island at all.

'Everything well camouflaged,' said Bill. 'A clever lot, and I've been after them for a long time. They sent me off on all kinds of false trails and I'd almost given up hope of finding their lair. But there it is.'

'They *must* have been surprised to see you up here, Bill!' said Lucy-Ann, as the seaplane left the enemy's island behind.

'Oh, look – there's the island where we landed with Bill!' cried Dinah. 'Puffin Island! Do look! There's the bird-cliff – and you can just see the little narrow channel going into the cliff – only you have to look hard to see it. And there's where we had our signal fire.'

'And there's where we had our tents that blew away in the storm – by those few trees,' said Jack. 'And look, there's the puffin colony!'

The seaplane flew down as low as it dared. It flew low enough for the children to see a moving mass of birds, scared of the enormous noise made by the seaplane's powerful engines.

'I can see Huffin and Puffin!' cried Lucy-Ann. The others roared with laughter.

'You can't, you fibber!' said Dinah.

'No, I can't really. I'm pretending to,' said Lucy-Ann. 'I want them to be there always. I want them to have their own burrow, and a nest – and an egg! I want them to have a lovely baby puffin that would be tame too. Goodbye, dear Huffin and Puffin! We did so love having you for pets.'

'Arrrrrrrr!' suddenly said Kiki, for all the world as if she understood what Lucy-Ann was saying.

'Kiki's saying "goodbye" in puffin language,' said Lucy-Ann. 'Arrrrr, Huffin and Puffin! I'm saying goodbye too.'

And from the scared puffin colony rose a medley of deep guttural *arrrrrrrs* as the birds settled down once more. Those that had run down burrows popped up again and added their *arrrrr* to the chorus.

'What a lot we shall have to tell Mother,' said Philip. 'I wonder how she is?'

Joe smiled at him. 'Getting on fine, except for worrying about you four,' he said. 'She'll feel better still when she gets our radio message.'

'Oh, have you sent one already?' asked Dinah. 'Oh, good! Now she'll know we're all right. Goodness – won't it be strange to go back to school after all this?'

School! Sitting at a desk, learning French grammar, getting into rows for leaving tennis racquets about, playing silly tricks, having music lessons, going to bed at the proper time – how very, very strange it would all seem!

Only Lucy-Ann thought of it with real pleasure. 'It'll be so nice to wake up in the mornings and know there's only lessons and tennis and things to worry about,' she said to Bill. 'Instead of wondering if the enemy is coming, and seeing planes parachuting guns down into lagoons, and rushing about in motor-boats, and . . . '

'Conking poor Horace on the head,' said Bill, grinning.

'Well, we *didn't* do that, whatever he said to you,' said Lucy-Ann. 'And if ever I see him again I'm going to tell him I'm sorry we made such an awful mistake – but that honestly he deserves a good old – a good old . . . '

'Conk,' said Philip, chuckling.

'Well, conk if you like,' said Lucy-Ann. 'A good old conk for telling such awful stories.'

The seaplane was flying south now. It had left behind all the exciting little islands, and all the millions of noisy sea-birds. The sun was now almost gone and the sea was shadowed a deep blue. In a few minutes the first stars would prick through the evening sky, as bright as diamonds.

'We'll be over the mainland soon,' said Bill. 'Thank goodness it's all ended up well! I thought it was the finish of everything when this seaplane landed beside us and hailed us. Another adventure to talk over when we see each other in the holidays. What a lot we've had together!'

'I think I've liked this one the best,' said Jack thoughtfully, and he scratched what was left of Kiki's crest. 'All those islands – and this lonely sea, with its blues and greens and greys.'

'The Sea of Adventure,' said Lucy-Ann, looking down at its vast expanse of dark blue, touched here and there with the golden reflection of the sky. 'Goodbye, Sea of Adventure! You're a lovely place – but *much* too exciting for me!'

# The Island of Adventure

For Philip, Dinah, Lucy-Ann and Jack, the holiday
in Cornwall is everything they'd hoped for – until
they begin to realize that something sinister is taking
place on the mysterious Isle of Gloom.

But they're not prepared for the dangerous adventure that awaits them in the abandoned copper
mines and secret tunnels beneath the sea.

# The Castle of Adventure

What was the secret of the old castle on the hill, and why were the locals so afraid of it?

When flashing lights are seen in a distant tower, Philip, Dinah, Lucy-Ann and Jack decide to investigate – and discover a very sinister plot concealed within its hidden rooms and gloomy underground passages.

# The Ship of Adventure

All aboard for a quiet cruise among the Greek islands!

But when Kiki the parrot breaks a birthday present, Philip, Dinah, Lucy-Ann and Jack are plunged into another adventure: a desperate race against time – with the long-lost treasure of the Andra as the prize.

# The Circus of Adventure

Why on earth did Bill have to bring the wimpish
Gustavus with them on holiday? Neither Jack nor
Kiki the parrot liked the boy at all.

But when Gustavus is kidnapped along with Philip,
Dinah and Lucy-Ann, Jack must follow them to a
faraway country and unravel a plot to kill the King.

# The River of Adventure

A river cruise through ancient desert lands will be an adventure in itself, thought Philip, Dinah, Lucy-Ann and Jack.

An adventure it certainly is, especially when Bill disappears and the children, along with Kiki the parrot, are trapped beneath a forgotten temple where no one has set foot for 7,000 years.

# A selected list of titles available from Macmillan Children's Books

The prices shown below are correct at the time of going to press.
However, Macmillan Publishers reserves the right to show new retail prices
on covers, which may differ from those previously advertised.

---

**Enid Blyton**

| | | |
|---|---|---|
| THE ISLAND OF ADVENTURE | 978-0-330-44629-7 | £4.99 |
| THE CASTLE OF ADVENTURE | 978-0-330-44630-3 | £4.99 |
| THE VALLEY OF ADVENTURE | 978-0-330-44335-2 | £4.99 |
| THE SEA OF ADVENTURE | 978-0-330-44336-9 | £4.99 |
| THE MOUNTAIN OF ADVENTURE | 978-0-330-44837-6 | £4.99 |
| THE SHIP OF ADVENTURE | 978-0-330-44839-0 | £4.99 |
| THE CIRCUS OF ADVENTURE | 978-0-330-44834-5 | £4.99 |
| THE RIVER OF ADVENTURE | 978-0-330-44838-3 | £4.99 |

---

All Pan Macmillan titles can be ordered from our website,
www.panmacmillan.com, or from your local bookshop
and are also available by post from:

**Bookpost, PO Box 29, Douglas, Isle of Man IM99 1BQ**
Credit cards accepted. For details:
Telephone: 01624 677237
Fax: 01624 670923
Email: bookshop@enterprise.net
www.bookpost.co.uk

**Free postage and packing in the United Kingdom**